BOGOTÁ
39

BOGOTÁ 39

NEW VOICES FROM LATIN AMERICA

With an Introduction by Gaby Wood

Edited by Juliet Mabey

HAY FESTIVAL
BOGOTÁ 39

ONEWORLD

A Oneworld Book

First published by Oneworld Publications, 2018

This edition copyright © Hay Festival of Literature and the Arts Limited, 2018

The copyright of the pieces in this anthology remains with the individual authors and translators

The moral rights of the authors and translators have been asserted

ISBN 978-1-78607-333-4
eBook ISBN 978-1-78607-334-1

Typeset by Tetragon, London
Printed and bound in Great Britain by Clays Ltd, St Ives plc

This work has been published with the support of the Instituto Cervantes and English PEN.

Oneworld Publications
10 Bloomsbury Street
London WC1B 3SR
England

Stay up to date with the latest books,
special offers, and exclusive content from
Oneworld with our newsletter

Sign up on our website
oneworld-publications.com

MIX
Paper from
responsible sources
FSC
www.fsc.org
FSC® C018072

Contents

Preface by Cristina Fuentes La Roche ix

Map of Authors x

Introduction by Gaby Wood xiii

Second-hand News CARLOS MANUEL ÁLVAREZ
translated by Serafina Vick 1

Snow FRANK BÁEZ
translated by Anwen Roys 8

Perhaps an Animal NATALIA BORGES POLESSO
translated by Sophie Lewis 16

An Orphan World GIUSEPPE CAPUTO
translated by Sophie Hughes 24

A Time with No Bad News JUAN CÁRDENAS
translated by Megan McDowell 29

(Irrelevant) Mass Delusion in Cajas
MAURO JAVIER CÁRDENAS 38

Christmas Tree MARÍA JOSÉ CARO
translated by Isabelle Kaufeler 43

Soldiers, Bring Everything Back Home!
MARTÍN FELIPE CASTAGNET
translated by Daniel Hahn 50

Chaco LILIANA COLANZI
translated by Julia Sanches 57

Villa Torlonia JUAN ESTEBAN CONSTAÍN
translated by Simon Bruni 67

Physiologus   LOLITA COPACABANA
translated by Samantha Schnee   74

The Days Gone By   GONZALO ELTESCH
translated by Katherine Rucker   82

Dead Hares   DIEGO ERLAN
translated by Sam Gordon   87

The Year of the Black Sun   DANIEL FERREIRA
translated by Catherine Mansfield   94

The Southward March   CARLOS FONSECA
translated by Megan McDowell   103

Lid / 1981   DAMIÁN GONZÁLEZ BERTOLINO
translated by Lily Meyer   110

Scene in a Fast-food Restaurant
SERGIO GUTIÉRREZ NEGRÓN
translated by Nick Caistor   115

Recording 1   GABRIELA JAUREGUI
translated by Annie McDermott   121

Umami   LAIA JUFRESA
translated by Sophie Hughes   128

Work in Progress   MAURO LIBERTELLA
translated by Nick Caistor   136

How Do Stones Think?   BRENDA LOZANO
translated by Lucy Greaves   142

Fictio Legis   VALERIA LUISELLI
translated by Christina MacSweeney   149

Titans on the Beach   ALAN MILLS
translated by Delaina Haslam   162

Come to Raise   EMILIANO MONGE
translated by Frank Wynne   170

Papi's False Teeth   MÓNICA OJEDA
translated by Anna Milsom   178

Teresa   EDUARDO PLAZA
translated by Rahul Bery   191

Suffering Creature   EDUARDO RABASA
translated by Christina MacSweeney   198

The Art of Vanishing   FELIPE RESTREPO POMBO
translated by Daniel Hahn   206

Valentina in the Clouds   JUAN MANUEL ROBLES
translated by Sarah Moses   214

Family   CRISTIAN ROMERO
translated by Anne McLean   223

Children   JUAN PABŁO RONCONE
translated by Ellen Jones   230

The Summer of '94   DANIEL SALDAÑA PARÍS
translated by Christina MacSweeney   237

An Unlucky Man   SAMANTA SCHWEBLIN
translated by Megan McDowell   243

Naked Animals   JESÚS MIGUEL SOTO
translated by Emily Davis   253

56 (the Fall)   LUCIANA SOUSA
translated by Peter Bush   259

Roots   MARIANA TORRES
translated by Lisa Dillman   265

Forests Where There Was Nothing
VALENTÍN TRUJILLO
translated by Simon Bruni   271

Alarm   CLAUDIA ULLOA DONOSO
translated by Lily Meyer   278

Castaways   DIEGO ZÚÑIGA
translated by Megan McDowell   283

About the Authors   289
About the Translators   305
Acknowledgements   315

Preface

This selection by the Hay Festival of thirty-nine of the best Latin American fiction writers aged under forty aims to celebrate great literature and boost the quality and diversity of literary production on the continent.

This is the second selection of rising literary stars of Latin America, and celebrates the tenth anniversary of the first *Bogotá 39*, published as part of the 2007 Bogotá World Book Capital event. That publication created considerable interest and led to a greater dissemination of the work of the thirty-nine writers selected, raising their profile both within their countries of origin and around the world.

We asked the authors selected for the first *Bogotá 39* volume a decade ago to recommend authors for *Bogotá 39 2017*. In addition, after an open survey of more than eighty publishers, writers and literary critics in Latin America, a further 200 names were added to the list. The final selection for this volume was made by the judges Darío Jaramillo (Colombia), Leila Guerriero (Argentina) and Carmen Boullosa (Mexico), who read and discussed the work of the proposed authors before producing the definitive list you will find here. Our thanks go to all those who assisted us in the selection process.

CRISTINA FUENTES LA ROCHE
INTERNATIONAL DIRECTOR, HAY FESTIVAL

AUTHORS

CUBA

DOMINICAN
REPUBLIC

MEXICO

GUATEMALA

PUERTO
RICO

COSTA
RICA

VENEZUELA

COLOMBIA

GUATEMALA:
Alan Mills

ECUADOR

COSTA RICA:
Carlos Fonseca

PERU

BRAZIL

BOLIVIA

MEXICO:
Gabriela Jauregui
Laia Jufresa
Brenda Lozano
Valeria Luiselli
Emiliano Monge
Eduardo Rabasa
Daniel Saldaña París

ARGENTINA

URUGUAY

CHILE

CHILE:
Gonzalo Eltesch
Eduardo Plaza
Juan Pablo Roncone
Diego Zúñiga

ARGENTINA:
Martín Felipe Castagnet
Lolita Copacabana
Diego Erlan
Mauro Libertella
Samanta Schweblin
Luciana Sousa

CUBA:
Carlos Manuel Álvarez

DOMINICAN REPUBLIC:
Frank Báez

PUERTO RICO:
Sergio Gutiérrez Negrón

VENEZUELA:
Jesús Miguel Soto

COLOMBIA:
Giuseppe Caputo
Juan Cárdenas
Juan Esteban Constain
Daniel Ferreira
Felipe Restrepo Pombo
Cristian Romero

ECUADOR:
Mauro Javier Cárdenas
Mónica Ojeda

BRAZIL:
Natalia Borges Polesso
Mariana Torres

PERU:
María José Caro
Juan Manuel Robles
Claudia Ulloa Donoso

BOLIVIA:
Liliana Colanzi

URUGUAY:
Damián González Bertolino
Valentín Trujillo

Introduction

'The whole time, the jungle has done nothing but contradict their expectations', Carlos Fonseca writes in his story 'The Southward March', included in this volume. 'Where they supposed they'd find naked natives, instead there are men wearing rock band T-shirts.'

Something similar might be said of this collection of thirty-nine young Latin American writers. If, to the world at large, the equivalent of 'naked natives' is the magical realist tradition in literature, then the myriad styles and subjects – the sheer range of imagination – gathered here will show the confidence with which these writers have felt free to depart from it.

In the past couple of decades, many Latin American authors have felt that the generation that came to prominence in the sixties had a lot to answer for. The 'Boom', a movement that brought together such writers as Julio Cortázar, Gabriel García Márquez, Mario Vargas Llosa and Carlos Fuentes, was born in Paris. In a sense, it was a European story before it was a Latin American story, and that's how word came to be spread. Vargas Llosa, a Peruvian, later commented drily that he didn't realize he was Latin American until he moved to France: the continent in question being so vast, such a multi-national grouping made little sense until it was forged elsewhere, returning to its various roots fully-formed.

Those writers are still more widely read internationally than any of their younger compatriots – with the exception, perhaps, of Roberto Bolaño – but by the nineties, a backlash was under way. Playing on the word 'Boom', a group of Mexican novelists announced themselves as a new sound: the 'Crack' generation. Among them were Jorge Volpi and Ignacio Padilla, and their assertion was, broadly, this: magical realism has become a ghetto. Just because we're Latin American, they said, that doesn't mean we have to write about levitating priests and blood that travels with a mind of its own. What if we're interested in Adolf Eichmann, or chess, or Nazi mathematicians? Can't we help ourselves to those subjects?

The road they paved, long ago, is now so well-travelled the question need no longer be asked. In this book you'll find a middle-class Brazilian woman so down on her luck she finds herself eating food out of a rubbish bin (Natalia Borges Polesso's 'Perhaps an Animal'). You'll read about an encounter between G.K. Chesterton and Benito Mussolini (by Juan Esteban Constaín), and a pregnancy test taken in a Wendy's fast food restaurant in Puerto Rico (by Sergio Gutiérrez Negrón). Eduardo Rabasa's single-paragraph story 'Suffering Creature' delivers PTSD sex with strangers in a semi-stream of consciousness. Juan Manuel Robles imagines a near-future in which 'astronomers' – digital voyeurs somewhere between hackers and CCTV cameramen – can send you hundreds of aerial photographs taken of you on any given day.

There is a broad range of writing even within what one might loosely link with magic. In Marina Torres's story 'Roots', an emigrant girl grows plant shoots from her body. In Mónica Ojeda's 'Papi's False Teeth', a woman treasures her dead father's dentures like a trophy or a pet, triggering a strange disorder of remembrance. In Liliana Colanzi's 'Chaco', a young child murders a 'Mataco', or indigenous Bolivian, before going on to kill others. We meet a psychic in mourning for her father ('Recording 1'), and a couple of teenage boys witnessing a miracle in Ecuador ('Mass Delusion in Cajas'). In Giuseppe Caputo's novel *An Orphan World*, a father tells his son stories about life on another planet in order to encourage the boy to see magical qualities in himself.

The tone of these texts ranges from loose and chatty to poetic, fabular, funny or even feral. They are brought to you by some of the best translators of their time, who are deft and modest, often finding ingenious ways to solve word-play puzzles. They are excellent listeners as well as elegant stylists.

Many of these writers will be new discoveries to the English-speaking world. Yet it's worth knowing that they are, as a group, not rarefied 'finds': thirteen have already been translated into other languages. Though they are all under the age of forty, a few are very well-established. Valeria Luiselli, a Mexican writer whose virtuosically witty story 'Fictio Legis', translated by Christina MacSweeney, is published here, is already highly respected in the US and the UK for her succinct, sly prose. Laia Jufresa's exceptional debut novel *Umami*, translated by Sophie Hughes and extracted here, was published in the UK last year. Samanta Schweblin, an Argentinian, was shortlisted for the Man Booker International Prize in 2017 with her taut novel of dread, *Fever Dream*. Here, she contributes 'An Unlucky Man', translated by Megan McDowell, a perfectly paced story that is both creepy and companionable.

Altogether, this selection is not just a sampling but a collective pleasure, and if it doesn't tell a single story about the direction in which Latin American fiction is heading, its many destinations are to be celebrated all the more.

GABY WOOD
LITERARY DIRECTOR OF THE BOOKER PRIZE FOUNDATION

Second-hand News

CARLOS MANUEL ÁLVAREZ

Translated by Serafina Vick

I'm twenty-two, I've straight black hair and a thin nose. I'm over six feet tall. The child of divorced parents. My dad lives in Miami, he left a few months ago, and my mum's still hibernating with my little sister in some sickly town in central Cuba. I visit them for the weekend every six weeks or so, but we talk on the phone practically every day. I'm pretty much always hungry, though that's nothing special; most young Cubans are always hungry.

Young Cubans all have the same anaemic complexion you get from unsatisfied hunger, the same dry skin, the same sort of ashen expression, the same languid gestures and carefully cultivated *joie de vivre* – an insistent happiness that contradicts everything else. A young Cuban's life is spent swimming against their body's current.

Today is Tuesday the twentieth, the year's '16, and within the stone walls of the Moro-Cabaña, at the mouth of the polluted puddle that is the Bay of Havana – in which no moon dares be reflected – the publishing house Gobierno Arte y Literatura is about to release the novel *1984* by George Orwell. This is something that seems to have left everyone discombobulated, as dictatorships, so they say, don't publish ferocious denunciations of themselves.

I'm saying this here as I can't in the paper. But anyway, no need to go into all that. It's Book Week and Remy Alfonso, head of Current Affairs at *Granpa*, has taken me off National News and sent me to support the Culture team. I'm to cover the book launch.

Granpa is the party's official mouthpiece. That makes it sound petrifying, but as far as I'm concerned, I can safely say it's not. I graduated from university two weeks ago and started at the paper. I could have been assigned to a radio station, a TV channel or a young-communist comic. I was assigned *Granpa* pretty much randomly. It's not true that there are special requirements to get into these places. Like I said, my dad's living in Miami and I'm in regular contact with him, yet here I am, working for the longest-running propaganda machine in the Western world. No one thinks I'm dangerous or a potential pariah.

I can remember the day they announced our work placements at university. It's a memory I share with anyone who has studied journalism in Havana in the last forty years. It was nine in the morning and I felt that this was going to be a pivotal moment. Unlike most things in life, this was a point of no return – you don't get many moments like that, just enough to give the universe a sense of invincibility.

I knew there was no reason to be nervous, but we pretend, and even believe, that some things really are under our control. This isn't necessarily sad or contemptible. I mean, who really wants a responsibility as huge as control over your own existence, or your actions depending solely on yourself? Honestly, given the disaster most people make of their lives when left to their own devices, I don't think I'd want that kind of burden on myself.

But there I was the day they announced our placements, nervous as anything, as though there were any real difference between the places they could assign me. I sank into my corner and nobody took much notice. The faculty of journalism is full of carefree, happy, idiotic students. Around midday, after a long parade of classmates, my name was called. I cautiously stepped forward, my face deadpan. I opened the office door and saw a spotted vase, a tablecloth covered in filigree roses, files of stationery and three bureaucrats sitting gassing behind a desk. In front of the desk was a black chair: empty, almost thronelike.

I was asked to make myself comfortable. I immediately fixed on the one who seemed to be in charge of the placements. I looked deeply into his moustache, like a camera zooming in until everything else goes blurry. When his mouth opened to say where they'd decided to send me, his moustache moved like a giant eyebrow. On moustachioed faces it's always the moustache that steals the show.

'What will I be doing?' I asked.

'You'll be writing about national affairs,' he said.

'I'd like to write about sports.'

'You like sports?'

'Yes, I do.'

'Well, we'll bear that in mind' – he paused – 'but for the moment we can't accommodate your request. You'll write for the national page.'

I waited a moment, but it didn't look like he was going to say anything else.

'All right then,' I accepted in the end.

I stood up and held out my hand. I thought things. I was acting, obviously. Here you act from the head inwards. You are your own audience. I was glad they hadn't assigned me to some rural station. But then as soon as I stepped onto the street I was stabbed with hunger and that's all I could think about until I ate a while later. Maybe a bit of bread, or maybe a whole roll.

I won't waste any time recounting my first days at *Granpa*, as I suspect they were very similar to the weeks, months and years to come, and there's no point going over the same thing twice. It's three in the afternoon, my shirt's stuck to my back with sweat, and I'm wandering around the paved alleys of La Cabaña. There's still another half hour until the launch of *1984* in one of the main halls. I'll fill in the spare time with a description of this place, just to give you an idea.

La Cabaña is a colonial fortress on top of a steep hill at the mouth of the city's bay. Three centuries ago its damp, light-filled battlements housed soldiers from the motherland sworn to protect Havana from buccaneers and pirates; today they host Book Week.

Every day at 9 p.m. a group of poor teenage devils on military service dress up like colonial soldiers, all very Spanish and monarchical with sabres, wigs, elaborate silk and damask uniforms – you get the picture – and then fire a bit of cardboard into the bay from an old cannon.

It's a tradition that no one takes much interest in. At best, four bored cats watch every now and then, maybe a pair of newly-wed medics with no money to go anywhere else, a group of raucous freshers, or a Swedish backpacker with ten dollars in his pocket. The show's depressing and monotonous. Save the first few weeks of January and Book Week, La Cabaña fortress is a wasteland.

Today, however, it's full to bursting. There are tents and book stands covering every inch of grass, even though no one comes here to read. They've got the right idea. I don't read either; I can't stand it. After a few brief forays, I once had a serious crack at it but gave up, though that's irrelevant just now – maybe I'll save that story for later. If I find a hole to fill, I'll tell it. If not, I'll keep it to myself.

People only bother coming here to buy cheap food, to cover their hands in grease from some piece of microwaved chicken and then lick their fingers and surreptitiously wipe them on their top. At *Granpa* we publish photos of the attendees and claim that the public loves books, but if it weren't about books, if it were about pyrography, they'd come anyway, because there's nowhere else to go in this city and nothing else to do.

There's not much else to say about La Cabaña. If you like I could tell you how I ended up here. I'm not sure we should go into it, but let's try for a few paragraphs.

The press doesn't particularly interest me. I applied for journalism because I wanted to move to Havana. I got here when I was eighteen and couldn't stop thinking about that old axiom that there are only two kinds of story. One: a man who goes on a journey. Two: a man who arrives in a new city. I kind of miss who I was, who I was going to be. The city seemed full of promise and I quickly started to walk it, cautiously, certain I could be attacked at any moment.

I saw journalism as a stop-off, a motel to shelter myself in until the storm passed and the stars aligned, allowing me to live my life. But I never got round to living my life. What I got round to was *Granpa* and that's where I've stayed. To be honest, it makes absolutely no difference to me whether I'm here or not. I don't know why I'm telling you all this. If I get bored tomorrow, I'll leave it here.

The foreign press said it couldn't believe a book like *1984* was being published in Cuba. I'd never heard of this Orwell. I mean, he was English – what does an English guy know? Apparently people in Cuba's secret reading circles have read it. It's considered a kind of premonition. Four days ago Remy Alfonso gave me one of Arte y Literatura's copies, one they had sent especially to the paper, and told me to read it as I was set to cover the launch. Having read it, I think the stir it's caused unnecessary and pretty stupid.

Think about it – Orwell's book doesn't even get close to considering the possibility that the Ministry of Truth would review a work like his in its own paper. And that's exactly what's just happened. But I'll tell you something else. Orwell goes on about efficiency but he never mentions cack-handedness. Anyway, I'm getting bored.

I'm going to walk around a bit more. Today's heat is an old green guy kissing my skin.

Ministry of Love? The Ministry of Construction is in front of my apartment. That, I can tell you, is a ministry.

The launch of *1984* lasted fifteen minutes. It was presented with utter sangfroid, as though it were some literary novelty written only yesterday. End of story.

It took me an hour to cross the city. An irritable mob surged onto the 101 bus. I managed to get on through the middle door. Someone shouted that we shouldn't shove each other, that the powers that be wanted us to exterminate each other from within. We all laughed. That happens sometimes. People in Havana act like a family in a giant, seventy-square-kilometre apartment. All our lives are so intertwined that most strangers recognize each other at a glance.

The bus went through the tunnel under the bay and followed Puerto, then it passed the train station and headed up Reina. Within that time dozens of people got on and off. There are times on the bus you can hardly breathe. Times when people step on your foot and mess up your hair, when some guy subtly frees his elbow so he can shove you out of the way with it. Boyfriends guard their girl-friends' backsides from perverts, and women watch their handbags. There's a tangible unease; everyone's on high alert. The passengers know that their fellow passengers are The Enemy and the driver's The Enemy too.

Then there's the half-starved volunteer who sits in the seat about a metre away from the driver. They collect everyone's money and dictate where and how we should arrange ourselves. For twenty minutes or half an hour this poor sod has control over our lives and brings out our dark and savage sides. Theft, sweat, dirt, fights, suffocation, delays, the minor occurrences, the daily grind. The passengers don't seem to be to blame. The driver doesn't seem to be to blame.

In the early hours of the morning, however, Havana's buses are generally empty. There's always at least one journey a day that the driver makes alone, justified by the possibility of coming across a passenger. But there doesn't need to be anyone waiting either. After all the noise, all the chaos, what's the driver thinking? Do they want to go on like this forever? What do they think of the first person to get on the bus and invade their space? How do they see them? As an enemy? A soothing balm? A distant sun?

The journey a bus driver in Havana makes is really circular, without any stops; like carrying a rock up a mountain and then letting it roll down again. On route 101, every driver has been a passenger and every passenger has been a half-starved volunteer.

I was meditating on these sorts of things, lulled by the bus's accordion, until I got off at the stop for the paper. *Granpa* is on the corner of General Suarez and Territorial, a four-storey building flanked by climbing plants and bushes in rectangular cement pots. Each floor has brown windows that make the building look like an oily fish tank; each pane of glass has a scotch-tape cross stuck to it to stop it from smashing to pieces if a hurricane hits Havana. Something that luckily, or unluckily, hasn't happened.

I'm at *Granpa* standing waiting for Remy Alfonso's edit of my piece.

FROM THE NOVEL *SECOND-HAND NEWS*

Snow

FRANK BÁEZ

Translated by Anwen Roys

The night I arrived in Chicago it was minus twenty. I'd just left behind the sunny Dominican Republic to study survey design at the University of Illinois. At the time, I was working as a poll monitor and I went all over the island conducting research and surveys, but until they gave me the scholarship, I had no idea that what I did could be studied.

They also gave a scholarship to Diógenes Lamarche, a colleague who I'd worked with on various NGO projects. Neither of us had been to Chicago before. My ex had, though, and she kept telling me that there was a giant bean in the middle of the city. So when the pilot announced our descent, we pressed our faces to the window and tried to catch sight of it, but all we managed to see was sky-scrapers and a city which glittered like gold. Before we got off the plane, we looked out of the window again, and this time we saw workers wrapped up like Eskimos walking on the runway, and we asked ourselves if we'd landed at the North Pole.

At the luggage belt, we collected our suitcases, took out our coats, and waited for Nora Bonnin, an Argentinian who would be helping us settle in. When she caught sight of us, she gestured us over and before we could introduce ourselves, she asked us whether we'd brought our winter clothing.

'We're wearing it,' we told her.

She couldn't disguise her smile as she looked at the jackets and sweaters we'd bought from the mall in Santo Domingo.

'Guys, those won't help with the cold. It's not that I don't like them, but it's freezing here. I brought some of my husband's coats for you. You can borrow them until you manage to buy some of your own.'

As well as the jackets, we'd brought with us woolly socks, corduroy trousers, scarves, hats and those thermal tights that the gringos call *long johns*. We really believed that they'd be enough to help us survive winter in the Windy City.

'Wait at that bus stop while I go and look for the car.'

Before rushing out, Nora put on her gloves, pulled the zip of her coat up past her neck and adjusted her hood. We saw her sprint towards the car park. Following her example, we walked through the automatic doors and into the cold, which was so biting it almost floored us.

'Welcome to Chicago,' said Nora sarcastically once we'd closed the doors of the Audi.

The next day, she took us to see various apartments and we ended up renting a three-bedroom place in Little Italy. The landlord was Pete, a well-to-do middle-class guy, who showed us the terrace and the laundry room along with the apartment. We picked up some mattresses from a trader in Greektown, which we dragged back to the apartment, with difficulty, in Nora's Audi. We tidied up, we cleaned and we disinfected. Afterwards, we went up to the terrace and took in the view of the neighbourhood and of the skyscrapers in the Loop, which looked like they were smoking and coughing in the distance.

We had dinner in a Thai restaurant, looking at the pretty young things walking past in their coloured scarves and expensive coats.

When we got back to the apartment, it was like stepping into a butcher's freezer. Even with the ancient heater that Pete had pointed out to us, the place was freezing and we couldn't stop shivering. Halfway through the night, we decided to move the mattresses into the living room, next to the heater, which every half an hour turned itself on, as if by magic.

At dawn, we noticed that the cold was coming in through the broken windows. At midday, when we went to Pete's office to sign the contract, we took the opportunity to ask him to fix them. But he was irascible, and did nothing but talk about Sammy Sosa, specifically about the cork-bat incident. Even though it had happened years ago, the Chicago Cubs fanatic was still angry with the Dominican baseball player, especially after he'd announced he was leaving the team. Pete, demonstrating with the wooden bat he kept under his desk, showed us the difference between a cork bat and a regulation one. Afterwards, he went back to talking about the famous Cubs vs Tampa Bay game, where Sammy Sosa's bat got broke. Nobody had really paid much attention to the matter. In big-league games, bats got broken all the time. Nevertheless, after one of the umps verified that there were pieces of cork in the bat, he summoned the others and together they decided to disqualify him from the game. Later, a committee would sanction him and he would apologize and say it was just a mistake, because instead of using his regulation bat he'd picked up the one he used in practice.

But Pete did not believe him, and he'd brought all of this up because he didn't believe us either, because as well as being his new tenants we were Sammy Sosa's compatriots. Before we signed the contract we mentioned the subject of the windows and he assured us that he'd repair them that very night. However, that evening when we came back from classes, they still had no glass. We sealed them with plastic, but the wind got in, and we had no choice but to sleep next to the heater again.

We had to wait two weeks for the missing glass to be installed. One morning, a Nuyorican in his fifties came over. He stood on a chair and pulled out the broken panes, and later, with a screwdriver, installed the new ones. When he'd finished, I offered him some juice.

'What kind do you have?' he asked.

'*Arándano.*'

'Sorry?'

'Cranberry.'

'Oh, okay. Yeah, sure.'

He drank it down in one.

'Where's the *furnitura?*' he asked.

'*Furnitura?*'

'Yeah, you know. The table, the chairs, the couch.'

'Oh yeah. We still have to buy all that.'

We saw him again a week later.

'*Quisqueyanos!* Dominicans!' he shouted up from below.

'What's up?' I shouted, once I'd managed to open the window.

'I've got a table. Come down and get it.'

When we thanked him for his gesture, he explained that Pete had sent him and that we were not in any way to consider it a favour, because it was already included in the contract. With the table and some chairs that we'd picked up, the apartment started to look better. But we were still missing the couch the Nuyorican had mentioned. We went to thrift stores and we contacted students selling things on Craigslist, but it was all out of our budget. Until one morning, when I was printing something in Nora's office, Diógenes called to tell me he'd found one.

He'd been walking to class when he saw it in the street. It was love at first sight. Black, real leather and practically new. He asked a student who was hanging around whether he knew who it belonged to, and he told him that if it was there, it was because someone had thrown it out.

I forgot about what I was printing and ran to help Diógenes with the couch. To counteract the cold, I took huge strides. I crossed the streets, going past the student dormitories, the park full of squirrels and the statue of Columbus as fat as John Goodman. Crossing Loomis, I saw the alley and, further ahead, Diógenes reclining on the couch. It was enormous. I realized it would be like carrying a hippopotamus. And we were more than four blocks from our building.

'On the island this would cost more than twenty thousand pesos,' I said, before throwing myself onto it.

'You're crazy, much more than that!' replied Diógenes. 'Forty thousand!'

We geared ourselves up. Before each of us took one end, we stretched and flexed our muscles.

'One, two, three!' we shouted in unison.

We hadn't moved four metres before Diógenes started complaining.

'It's going to take us a week to get it back to the apartment.'

'Yep,' I replied, panting.

After several attempts, we got to the entrance of the street that led to our building. We were about ninety metres away. Exhausted, we gasped for breath and argued about where in the apartment we were going to put it. While this was going on, an elderly couple approached us, without a doubt descendants of the Italian immigrants who had founded the neighbourhood.

'It must be theirs,' murmured Diógenes.

The elderly woman kept her distance but the man hit the couch with his walking stick and asked, with mad greenish eyes:

'You guys aren't going to leave that there, are you?'

We started to explain that we were taking it to our apartment when the woman began to have a coughing fit. We took this as a signal to pick it back up. This time we moved it seven metres. We heard Mexican *ranchera* music blaring full volume, followed by a sharp break and the sound of a horn. When the horn blasted again, we put the sofa down and turned around.

'This has to be the owner,' I said to Diógenes.

The driver of the van turned off the radio, wound down the window and asked us in Spanish if we needed help.

'We're taking it to the building at the end of this street,' explained Diógenes.

'Go on then, get it in!'

He helped us put it in the back. In less than a minute, we'd offloaded it in front of our building.

'My name is Jesús,' said the driver.

We didn't recognize any religious undertones in his name or in the way in which he'd assisted us. What we noticed really was his similarity to Quico, the character in the sitcom *El Chavo del Ocho*. Instead of a winter hat he was wearing a White Sox cap. As soon as we told him we were Dominican, he started listing his favourite *bachatas*.

'Which floor do you live on?' he asked suddenly.

'The third floor,' Diógenes replied.

'Ah. I'd help you but I've got a delivery to do. I work in the Mexican restaurant.'

'In El Pancho Villa?' I asked.

'That's the one.'

'Well, we'll see you there later then,' said Diógenes.

We finally left the couch in our living room at around five. All in all, it had taken seven hours from the moment Diógenes stumbled upon the couch, to the moment we got it inside the apartment. We even had to take a break halfway through to eat, and as Diógenes had promised Jesús, we went to El Pancho Villa, where we ordered giant burritos washed down with Coca-Cola. When we asked the waitress about Jesús, she told us he did the deliveries and helped out in the kitchen.

'My name is María, at your service.'

'This really is a biblical day,' Diógenes said under his breath.

'Sorry?'

'Nothing,' I said. 'Incidentally, Jesús helped us to carry a couch to our apartment.'

'Ah, have you already taken it up?'

'Just as far as the second floor.'

Instead of bringing us the bill, María came back with some left-over burritos wrapped up in a package. When we asked her about it, she said it was better we saved our money to buy books.

'They're so expensive,' she added.

Before she cleared the table, she told us to get the couch in as quickly as possible, because Telemundo had just announced the first snow of the year was due that night. So we picked it up, and after several false starts, we got to the third floor. We thought it would be impossible to get it in through the kitchen door, but with determination and the help of our Hindu neighbours, we managed it.

That night, I sat on the sofa with a bottle of rum in my hand. It was the last one I had left. I'd brought loads to give away, but hadn't found anyone worthy of them, so I'd been drinking them myself. Diógenes was frying something in the kitchen. From there, he remarked that we were like cavemen who'd spent the day hunting, dragging our prey back to the lair. That's how I felt, like one of our far-gone ancestors, drinking rum bit by bit from the bottle, looking round at the living room, the kitchen, and the floor which had been recently swept and scrubbed with a sponge to get rid of the filth. Despite the lack of decoration and pictures on the walls, I felt for the first time that I had a home in Chicago. I went to my room and looked for the music I'd brought, but could only find a copied Raulín Rodríguez CD that my uncle had put in my suitcase, so that, as he explained, I wouldn't forget my origins.

know what to do. She had a home, and she used to have a dead-end kind of job until a few days earlier. But there was never anything left over. For some time nothing left over. She'd lost the dead-end job and now she spent her afternoons in and out of employment agencies, offices, shops, apartment blocks – whatever it took. That week she'd gone through all her drawers hunting for change in order to pay the rent on time. She paid it. She wasn't in debt. She shared a tiny basement apartment with Flávia. She wouldn't have her friend knowing that she hadn't a single damn real left. With the plastic bag lying open on her lap, she shoved her fingers into the yellow rice. Saffron? The fresh smell of rocket awoke her appetite and, using her fingers as a scoop, she shovelled a handful into her mouth, and another and one more and again. When she saw the morsel of steak, she closed her eyes and chewed for a while. Mouth full of food. She hadn't eaten anything this tasty in a long time. All she'd been eating was bread and the little seventy-five-centavo biscuits that she bought at the mini-market round the corner. You could still get biscuits for seventy-five centavos. She saw a man crossing the road towards her. She froze. The man went by, eyes glued to his phone. He hadn't seen her. She wiped her mouth with the back of her hand and let the open plastic bag fall to the ground. The food scattered. She felt sick. She had eaten out of a bin. That this might've been her best meal in days didn't matter: she had eaten out of a bin. Light-headed, she wondered how her life had reached this point. The explanation was simple: she'd been hungry. She looked at the rice all spread out on the pavement. Whoever it was had taken care to put it all in a bag. I didn't, she thought. No one would eat it off the ground, now. An animal, perhaps. She caught sight of her reflection in the frosted vitrine of the shop opposite: body bent double, herself practically an animal. Through the glass, beneath the vast sign announcing a brand-new property venture, uniformed office employees were watching the scene, torn between hilarity and horror. She grimaced. She had eaten out of a bin. Stepping on the rice, she headed into the street. As she went, she looked deep into everything, right into the foundations, as if she had to understand it all again, from first principles.

Staring into space, she walked down the stairs alongside the shared terrace. She didn't even notice that Fernando, who owned the building, was sitting there.

'Elvira, where are you off to?'

'Hi, Fernando. Just home.'

'Not even a hello.'

'Hi, Fernando,' she said again.

'You're short on the rent, you know.'

'Can't be. I added it up a hundred times.' She'd counted it so many times, all the small change she'd found to make up the total; she'd added up her own and the cash she got from Flávia, everything.

'But the rent went up – remember? Flávia's covered. You're missing thirty-five, but we'll say thirty. No need to pay cash, even, if you're running low.'

Fernando picked at his nails, eyes on the ground. Not once did he look up to meet Elvira's gaze. He exhaled slowly through pursed lips. Pressure. Still neither of them caught the other's eye. Elvira swallowed her fury and only went on down the flight of stairs.

'Think about it, okay? Nothing to worry about. A favour between friends.'

She went inside and slammed the door. Flávia started. She was on the sofa, a towel wrapped round her head. It had been a stifling afternoon. Through the room's only window, the sun was blazing right onto the TV screen, which was doing its best to show a soap that had Flávia engrossed. The musty smell had strengthened, and Elvira thought that if the terrace hadn't that odd slant to it, the sun wouldn't ever come in at that end-of-the-afternoon moment.

'Let's go to Igor's party,' said Flávia.

'What's the party?'

'Igor's birthday – let's.'

'No. I feel shit. I'm skint, I don't feel like a party.'

'But it's free to get in and I can pay for our taxi back. Or we can get the bus back in the morning.'

'No, I really don't feel like it. I owe thirty-five reais' rent to Fernando.'

Flávia squinted harder and made a face like she was just waiting for the next bad excuse.

'Can we just go to Igor's party, please? I really want to see the venue. This is our chance.'

'What's the venue?'

'The Loop.'

'The What?'

'That gay club on Visconde.'

'Oh, yeah. I know it.'

The next excuse Elvira thought of was that her stomach was playing up because her only decent meal that day had come out of the rubbish and perhaps this was a sign that life wasn't going so well. And the excuse after that, should one be required, could be the fact that the owner of the house where they lived had hinted a minute ago that she could pay her rent with sex.

In the end, staying home by herself seemed much worse.

'Well?'

'Okay, I'm coming.'

Flávia smiled. She got up from the sofa and went into her bed-room. Elvira frowned and, as the last of the sun vanished over the horizon, she felt the heat in her body drain away along with the light. This place she was in was no good. But she couldn't get the situation clear in her head. When she was little, she had imagined how her life would be at fifteen. How it would be when she could hold her exercise books without needing a satchel, as the older girls

19

did. When she could stop wearing uniform and choose her own clothes, like the older girls. When she turned fifteen, she'd decided to go on wearing the uniform. It was better than the clothes her mother used to buy at the supermarket or that came from charities. Once she had gone to school wearing a school-friend's old T-shirt. They started to call her 'Second-hand'. She used to think that things would be better at eighteen, because she'd be independent and would be able to go out and work. That all came even sooner. Her mother disappeared. Elvira had woken with the kettle whistling and no trace of her. No trace of her clothes. Not a toothbrush. Not even the smell of her. Independent at last, Elvira had gone out to find a payphone, and from the open booth had called her father. She'd tried to explain that Mum had cut loose, but he hadn't understood. No one understood, in fact. Her dad came to clear out the house and take Elvira home. Long separated from her mother, Dad lived in a box room at his older sister's place. He was a nurse and was looking after the sister, who had Alzheimer's. Elvira spent a year sleeping on a mattress beside her father's bed in that box room. Through that year she had listened to her father snore, weep and fart every night. Until the day she had saved enough money to get out of there. She had gone to live in another town, in a hostel for female students. She needed to complete the final year of school which she had missed. She only finished when she was twenty. The twilight years of public schooling. That year, more days were spent on strike than in class. She attended the union meetings and joined the student council, and thought that at twenty-five her life would surely begin. Now, almost thirty, she'd given up on expectations. Unemployed, she had just eaten rubbish and, should she wish, could pay her rent with a hand-job.

'Elvira, how long are you going to stand there like a statue? I'm practically ready.'

'Sorry.' Elvira came out of her reverie. 'Isn't it a bit early?'

'No. The party starts early for people on the guest list. There'll be some drinks.'

Elvira thought that a drink, or an ocean of alcohol, was an excellent idea.

'I'll just brush my teeth and we can go.'

At the party, she avoided Márcia. She avoided talking to almost everyone there. She said hi to Igor, wished him happy birthday, left Flávia to her own devices and danced until she could barely stand. In the blink of an eye that separated reality from her desire to reduce her existence to this single moment, she saw Douglas. She didn't pay much attention to the boy, merely accepted his company. He seemed to be inside her bubble.

She fucked Douglas that night. End of the party. Amid the endless shots of vodka they drank, he said that he wanted to be rich, he wanted to be somebody. She said that she felt like a nobody and that she had eaten rubbish. Douglas with his cap tipped back on his head, thin, his nails bitten right down, his beautiful, clean face. His rough voice backsliding into posh here and there, specially when his camp side showed through. He cleared his throat and went on. He told her his whole life-plan – plan A – and how it had all gone wrong. He'd run away to São Paulo and now, five years later, he was living in the city, working as a baker.

'You're a baker?'

'Yeah, I make pastries, sweets, cakes too.'

'Why'd you come to São Paulo in the first place?'

'To be a model. I had a contract and everything.'

'What happened?'

'I gave the agency girl the slip. Don't really know why I did it. I just left her behind at the airport. I wanted to vanish clean out of my stupid town.'

'And you washed up here?'

They laughed. He told her he wasn't taking his hormones but

wanted to go back on them and, soon as life got back on track again, which would be soon, everything would go according to plan – plan B this time.

They didn't know how it happened. They knew that, when they left the party, beneath the viaduct, they'd started to kiss. Elvira felt Douglas's cock against her thighs, then in her hand and then inside. She woke in a studio bedroom that stank of mothballs. Douglas was staring wide-eyed at her and chewing his lip. He said he had never had sex with a woman.

'These things happen.'

'They do.'

'And how are you doing on your plan to be Mr Rich?'

'Mrs.'

'Mrs Rich.'

'I don't know yet. But you see I have to be rich as a woman. I want to be a woman – I want a new life.'

'I also want to be a woman and get myself a new life.'

'What do you mean you want to be a woman?'

'I dunno.' Elvira closed her mouth and breathed out hard through her nose. 'What happened to me yesterday shouldn't happen to anyone. I've practically become an animal.'

'Because we had sex?'

'No! Well – because of that, too. I think. But that's not the main thing. You seem really cool. There's other stuff. My life is awful. You know when you get to the point where you're trying to understand what's going on but it just doesn't make sense?'

'I think so. But what actually happened to you?'

'I ate food out of the bin. And I think I'm going to have to have sex to pay some bills.'

'You mean become a prostitute?'

'No! I mean, I don't know. Is that all you have to do? You see how bad things have got?'

'If you're having sex for money it's prostitution. End of. I've got lots of friends who do it. Who am I to judge? It's not my scene. I don't know the score. Are you hungry now? There's food in the house, we can eat together.'

'I also don't know where I'd start – and I don't want to know, either. But I've got no choice. How much do you pay for this place?'

'Four hundred reais.'

'Not bad.'

'I pay the owner direct. But what happened? I don't get what makes you want to be a woman. Or – what makes you think you're not a woman.'

'I don't get it either. I just don't feel like a woman. I don't feel like a person at all. It feels like I've failed in life.'

'You feel like an animal?'

'Something like that.'

'There're times it's good to be an animal. I think we hang on to this idea that humans and humanity are always the best thing to be. What we're really talking about is kindness – except it's not always like that. Humanity is far from being a good thing. Look around. If everyone was an animal, at least no one would feel guilty. No one would be bearing grudges, no one would be judging.'

Douglas was chewing at the skin on his fingers as he talked. Elvira couldn't believe she was hearing this, couldn't believe this boy's precarious innocence, but she kept listening, and found herself thinking he could be right. Perhaps it really would be better to be an animal.

FROM THE NOVEL *BICHO TALVEZ* (*PERHAPS AN ANIMAL*)

An Orphan World

GIUSEPPE CAPUTO

Translated by Sophie Hughes

When, years ago, I would ask about the circumstances of my birth, my father would sit me down beside him, or on his knee, and tell me all about the stars and the sky, and one planet in particular, which, he said, existed on the outskirts of the universe. This planet had no name, or at least not for us on earth – it was so far away that nobody had thought to name it. And this, according to him, was what made it important: because although it existed and we knew of its existence, it had no name.

It was an orphan world with no sun, living in perpetual darkness. 'There are lots of planets like that,' he would say looking up at the sky and encouraging me to do the same, 'orphans of the mother star, from after the dawn of the solar systems.' To give me a sense of what life there was like, of the world that was that planet, he would recount a typical night, paying particular attention to the appearance of its inhabitants: 'Anyone there could mix with anyone else. Anyone or any*thing*, which meant that there were always new creatures being born, thousands by the hour, and all completely bizarre to our eyes. Just leaving your house each day was like step- ping into a new world.'

The landscapes in this strange order (or disorder, depending on your point of view) were constantly changing. If one night the streets were lined with trees – trees like ours, with roots, a trunk, branches and leaves, hundreds of leaves – it was highly likely that the following night there would be new variations: a winged tree with claws at the tips of its roots and black feathers, the spawn of a pine tree and a crow (and this poor tree, despite having wings, couldn't fly, for its hefty trunk prevented it from taking off). Another tree came to light – or rather to dark, since it was always night there – crowned with a giant shell, the product of the nocturnal coupling between a chestnut and a turtle (and you could see its branches poking out of the holes in its carapace, as if they were the turtle's feet). There were also occasions – and not all that infrequent – when those paths became bare. Of course, for every tree that was born and grew and stayed on, there was another that would gallop off ('Ah,' my father sighed, 'imagine the neigh on those horse-trees!'). Or, as in the case of the cypress and snake's offspring, they would slither away.

And that's how the pine and the crow were able to breed crow-trees, and the turtle and the chestnut tree bore carapaced chestnuts. They could also produce pine-crows and sapling-turtles respectively. And if the pine-crows grew tired mid-flight, they had to take extra care when landing, for they had shoots for feet and those tubers were capable of taking root in the ground and never letting go again (the pine-crows also had to prevent other animals from munching on their leaves, which grew right alongside their black feathers). As for the sapling-turtles, my father said that some were frustrated at having been born without a shell: they felt exposed (and their canopies did little to ease their mortification), although it was also true that some were born with their modesty already protected by a wooden trunk. These creatures were very long and from a distance they looked like sideways chestnut trees lumbering around with a reptile head and feet.

It was quite common for that planet's inhabitants to plod along as if counting their steps, whether they were turtle cross-breeds or not. They walked – all of them, so many of them – to catch the spectacle of the eternal night sky. There were the stars, very close and bright white, but also star creatures, hard to see with the naked eye. Sometimes, those down below might be able to pick out what looked like dances: a blinking, whirling light searching out another – also blinking and whirling – to come together and form something else: a bigger light, an explosion. The birth of a flame. At other times, though, they could see exactly what was going on up there, millions of years away: such was the size of some of those star creatures. 'What might they see?' I would ask my father, and occasionally, if he was impatient to finish story time, he would simply answer 'the vastness'. But more often he would reel off long descriptions of luminescent creatures: a comet man with a tail of gas and dust who tore through the sky as fast as light; or the monster stars, with their claws and jaws. 'Whenever they heard a rumbling in the sky or sensed more light coming from up there, the inhabitants would gaze up and become nostalgic.'

My father's tales of the planet almost always involved made-up inhabitants, and not all of them were born of two parents: three, four, even ten – as many as they liked – could join to become the ancestors of these newly engendered creatures. And so he would tell me about the burrowing reptile-cow, born of a cow, a lizard and a mole; a creature with black fur, a big body, stubby legs and a ferocious snout, much longer than it was wide. It lived underground, but that wouldn't stop it from catching those cosmic spectacles: in order to see them it would poke its small eyes out of a special hole and then moo and whip its scaly tail excitedly when it sensed the emergence of a new light overhead.

While it's true that my father was always coming up with weird and wonderful creatures, usually forgetting the ones he'd already invented, one remained immutable in all his versions: the rocket-man, who blasted through the universe at remarkable speeds, leaving behind pieces of himself in the void. 'Every so often, this rocket-man would shoot past earth. On one of his voyages, years ago, he accidentally came off course, or he decided to stay, who can say: the point is that a number of humans spotted him up there among the clouds and as he descended on his great arched course they shouted: "A man in the sky!" His landing on earth brought with it a sense of the infinite possibilities up there, at the edges of the universe.'

One night I said to him: 'But we don't get cross-breeds like that here,' and my father, with the gleeful look of someone who had waited a lifetime to hear that comment, replied: 'What do you mean we don't get cross-breeds here? Look,' and he led me to the mirror. 'Look.' And I looked and I looked and I asked: 'What? What am I meant to be looking at?' And he repeated: 'Look.' And I repeated: 'At what?' And so he began pointing out the differences between us: he mentioned my eyes, comparing them to his. He said: 'See how shiny yours are? What do they look like to you?' I said: 'I dunno, you tell me.' My father grew exasperated, and even a little annoyed. He repeated the question: 'What do they look like? Take a good look.' And I said reticently: 'I don't know. I really don't know.' Instead of giving me an answer, my father got down on his knees, where, still towering over me, he wrapped me in his arms and begged: 'I need you to tell me what they look like.' Worn down by his pleas, I finally answered: 'They're black.' And he said: 'Black like what?' And a memory came to me then: a butterfly. 'Black like the black butterfly.' And my father, visibly relieved, like someone who'd finally solved an equation, cried: 'Exactly! See the cross?' And I, captivated, said: 'Yes.' 'And what else do you see? Your arms, for example. What do you see?' 'They're skinny.' 'Skinny like what?' I didn't answer, so he jumped in to say: 'Skinny like the arms and antennae of the butterfly . . .' And so the conversation went on. And this is how, if only for a short while, I ended up being the son of a man – my father – and the butterfly from my memory.

FROM THE NOVEL *AN ORPHAN WORLD*

A Time with No Bad News

JUAN CÁRDENAS

Translated by Megan McDowell

We were on the bus home, almost at the Moncloa station, when the darkness caught us off guard. 'The electricity's out,' he said, after he'd been quiet during the whole bus ride. I was surprised when he spoke, because I'd already asked him several times if something was wrong and he'd said no, that he was just tired from so much swimming. I knew it wasn't true, or rather, it *was* true he was tired, because we'd spent the whole day out at a reservoir, but it wasn't true that nothing was wrong. We'd only been going out a few months and he'd already pulled that same little scene with me a few times, thick silences and his eyes staring out the window. I knew it was something else. And I also knew that if I complained, he would take his little show to the next level: he'd get furious, run away, leave me stranded right there and, lamest of all, he'd disappear for the next four or five days.

Moncloa was really weird in that gloom. The Air Ministry building, which always watched people pass by like a pedantic old man with his arms crossed, was now wrapped in some blue and grey shadows that altered its whole architecture. It didn't even seem human, or anthropomorphic, but rather something else, like the inside of a cave with irregular stalactites, shapes possessed of a will that had nothing to do with laughter or presumptuousness or melancholy or any human feeling. In any case, it was an image of the Air Ministry that we'd never seen before.

He grabbed my hand and I had the impression the building had startled him; he was looking at it as if he'd seen a flying saucer.

I proposed we go for a few beers. 'Everything's closed around here,' he said. 'It's Sunday, and there's no power.' I had to admit he was right, but I still suggested we could take the metro and hole up in one of our dive bars on Callao. 'You think there'll be electricity on Callao?' he asked, standing on tiptoe to see the horizon of Calle Princesa, which was dark as far as the eye could see.

'I mean, the power can't be out in all of Madrid,' I said. 'It must be a breaker that blew in the neighbourhood. It happens all the time in summer.'

In the end we decided to walk, and to go into the first place we found open.

And so we went along discovering that the damage was much more serious than we'd thought. We joked about the zombie apocalypse, because back then it wasn't such a popular idea; the TV series and movies hadn't come out yet, and it was still pretty funny to invoke the zombie apocalypse in Madrid. We riffed on the idea, like how the first victims would be Dominicans from the Dominican bars, because everybody knows zombies are Haitian, and if they're not Haitian, it's like they take on that nationality when they turn into zombies, even if they're Basque. We passed about three Dominican bars and they were all closed. 'See?' he said. 'They're the first ones to go. Haiti was only waiting for its moment.'

We laughed because we were both thinking the same thing. That afternoon we had been swimming in the reservoir with a gay French couple, and one of them insisted that Haiti was the country of the future, that it was only waiting for favourable winds to blow. 'Its moment will come, you'll see,' he said. And his boyfriend, who was black – not Haitian but Senegalese – nodded very seriously as he stood over the grill making sure the meat we were barbecuing didn't burn.

We walked a couple of streets in silence and everything was still hit by the blackout, profoundly affected, as if there really had been a catastrophe.

'What could have happened?' he asked, and he was like someone asking a question in the midst of a dream, with a giggling nervousness and deep metaphysical doubts.

I shrugged my shoulders, doing my best Sancho Panza. 'I don't know,' I said, 'nothing serious.' But deep down I was considering the possibility of a terrorist attack, a terrorist attack kept quiet by the media, which even then seemed pretty unlikely, because those were still the days of Zapatero. A time with no bad news, I remember.

He didn't seem so convinced. He looked at the buildings with that same fearful face he'd had on scrutinizing the alien forms of the Air Ministry, and every once in a while he squeezed my hand, and sure, suddenly I understood that he had something to tell me, that he was biting his tongue to hold back something that was tormenting him. I figured he wanted to break up, and that on the trip back he'd been searching for the right words. I also figured that the power outage in Madrid had completely thrown him off, and now he didn't know if this new context would be favourable to his words, whether his words would pass through me in the same way in the middle of all that darkness.

Past Alberto Aguilera, he proposed we walk along Juan Álvarez Mendizábal, three streets down, where we'd be more likely to find something open. But things were much worse there than on Princesa. It was a scary place to walk; the street was narrower and the buildings loomed over you like the trees in an enchanted forest.

It was a very strange moment. I felt absolutely foreign in a way I had not in all these years, a Bolivian adrift in Madrid, walking hand in hand with another wetback who had also become a total stranger to me. It was all so unsettling I felt like the events at the reservoir had taken place in another space–time dimension, or been lived by other people totally different from the two of us.

What had happened at the reservoir? We'd gone to spend the day there, along with a lot of other people, invited by some friends whose parents had a vacation house at the foot of the basin. We had eaten barbecue, we'd gone swimming, we'd gone out in a little motor boat, we'd visited some friends of our friends who lived on a cliff, far from all the other houses, and then we'd taken the boat back to the cabin; we'd drunk wine during each and every one of the day's activities. Okay. That was clear, but I felt like I was missing something, and so I asked him directly. And as I was formulating the question, I felt like I was unintentionally pulling a mask off the whole situation, the blackout and the reservoir, as if in the act of speaking I was making a discovery, uncovering something. But I still didn't know what it was I was discovering because – and I think this now – discovering can simply be the act of removing something that covers, and doesn't necessarily mean you access what lies underneath. One can also uncover with eyes blindfolded. For an audience, for example. Or for an audience whose eyes are also blindfolded. It's possible to discover something that no one wants to see.

'Did something happen at the reservoir?' was the way I asked it.

He looked at me and let out a sigh of relief, which surprised me again.

'You noticed it too?' he asked. 'I thought it was just me. I swear I thought I was going crazy, I was scared to tell you, I was afraid you'd think I was nuts.'

And when he told me this I started trembling in fear, because I did think that just then his face looked crazy, there surrounded by those buildings that were trying to lean over and listen to what we were whispering about in the shadows.

'Tell me what you saw, and then I'll tell you,' I proposed. And he, wild, riding the pure and savage need to tell, started to describe how at dusk, while we were all drinking wine on the terrace and watching the sunset, he had started to watch some birds that were pecking at the leftovers scattered on the table, and then, when everyone else was spellbound by the colours that the slow orange light was painting on the water in the reservoir, while he was distracted by the birds gulping bits of tuna and ham and bread, he felt a hand on his thigh, and it took him a few seconds to realize that the hand was going into the pocket of his shorts, and when he finally reacted he saw it was the hand of a woman who had been lurking around all day, a woman with dark glasses who seemed to be the girlfriend of another one of the guests, a guy we didn't know at all.

I, of course, hadn't noticed a thing, but I didn't tell him that.

'And of course,' he went on, talking fast, 'I didn't know what to do, I just stood there looking at her, disconcerted, and she gave me a little smile, and I smiled back but I must have looked hysterical. She turned around and disappeared inside the house. And then I put my hand in my pocket and found a little paper there, a little wad of paper. It was a napkin, and in the napkin was an olive pit. And there was something written on the napkin. I had to smooth it all out so I could read it: *Don't come back here*, it said. I can't even tell you the bad feeling it gave me. I threw the napkin and the olive pit on the table, and here's the weirdest part of all: the birds that were there all flew away, and they never came back to eat. They circled above us, but they didn't land on the table, and they didn't try to peck at anything.

'I didn't know whether to laugh, or what,' he said, after I was silent for a while, trying to process the story. Some harpy stuck her hand into my boyfriend's pocket and left him a note, a rejection or provocation or who knows what. It could even be a xenophobic message, I thought.

'You saw the whole thing?' he asked.

'Yes, everything,' I lied.

'What a relief,' he said. 'I swear I thought I was going crazy.'

Our conversation was interrupted then because we finally came to a bar that was open, a Chinese bar, of course, in the middle of nowhere. It was operating because they had an electrical generator that gave enough power to half-light the place and keep the refrigerators cold.

There weren't many customers. Just the four losers who probably spent their whole lives in the place.

We sat at the bar and ordered bottles of beer, which were at the perfect temperature for that hot July night. 'Ahhhh,' he sighed after the first sip, '*estupidamente gelada!*' He always said the same phrase in Portuguese whenever he took the first sip of a cold beer, I don't know why. He tended to repeat the most trivial behaviours, like those comics who make up routines specifically to form emotional ties with the audience. But I never really was much for performing, and it was hard for me to cheer him on in his nonsense.

'Cheers, chimp,' I said. And we clinked bottles.

'Does anyone know what happened?' he asked, raising his voice so the patrons around us would hear him and know that yes, he was talking to them.

There was a quick exchange of glances, as if deciding who would answer.

'The blackout, you mean?' coughed one man with greasy hair combed back from his face. 'What do I know, man, must be a sub-station that blew out. But no one really knows.'

We stayed in the bar for a long time, talking about nothing and laughing at people we didn't like. He was merciless as he related the antics of a co-worker at the bookstore, a Valencian guy who tried to hook up with practically every person of the female persuasion who came in to ask for a book. I told him intimate things about some of my girlfriends, really personal things like how Nancy, the Ecuadorian, had got HPV; his face showed clearly that he enjoyed hearing the gossip more than I enjoyed telling it. It was an enjoyment free of malice, in any case – he didn't delight in other people's misfortune. He wasn't a bad person. It was just that sometimes he acted like those little kids who like to pour gasoline into an anthill.

The Chinese owners ended up kicking us out, and they locked the door with the four regulars still inside.

We went home with all that beer in our bodies, walking the same dark streets that now didn't seem so threatening.

'Can you imagine if the electricity never came back?' he asked, drunk and lucid. 'Can you imagine if they'd passed a law and sent us back to the Palaeolithic? If the forces of tyranny or of freedom – doesn't matter, same thing – just decided it's time to turn back the clocks and live without the comforts of modern life, starting with electricity?'

At home we had to light candles, and I thought that was pleasant, after all.

It was hotter than hell so we went to bed naked, like two lizards, staring at the ceiling in that kind of partial trance that comes on a summer night after drinking.

He turned his back to me, and almost immediately fell asleep.

I didn't. I went on thinking, thinking, restless, as if there were things I'd forgotten at some point of the day or night. And my mind returned to the reservoir, the note, the olive pit, and of course the possibility existed that he had lied to me, who knows to what end. That's how he was, he liked to make up stories, maybe he wanted me to start fantasizing and imagining things so something inside me, like a spark plug or a motor, would start spinning around on its own axis. But on the other hand, that woman in the dark glasses was a real witch, right? Hadn't I seen her myself, flirting with the other guests while her boyfriend was distracted helping the Senegalese guy at the grill? Hadn't we seen her go underwater several times and then, after waiting for what seemed a desperately long time, watched her surface with some silly thing in her hand, a stone or a stick? And hadn't she been the one who'd brushed against my arm in the kitchen at noon, when I was mixing a salad? *Motherfucker!* I said out loud (my boyfriend didn't even move). I jumped up, went to find my trousers, and searched my pockets. Surely she'd left a note or something for me, too. But no, there was nothing there. I looked through my handbag, even dumping it out beside one of the candles. Nothing. She hadn't left me any notes. *That bitch,* I thought. *Only for him, the fucking shrew,* and suddenly I was splayed out on the floor, surrounded by the things my bag had just vomited out, and I realized I was totally wet and I wanted to touch myself – not be touched, but touch myself the way I know how to, while I thought about her. And I started to touch myself, slowly, *fucking bitch,* I thought with fake rage and a strange telepathic complicity, *you didn't give me anything, you left nothing for me,* and as my fingers started speeding up, as my image of her became clearer and clearer and more palpable and I was starting to discover, to finally understand what was behind the discovery, as the thing became almost visible even for those of us with our eyes blindfolded, I felt all through my body how the electricity of the whole city was restored in the body of the building, in the freezer, and at almost the same instant, the apartment's lights came on.

The blackout was over.

I saw myself totally exposed. Naked, over-illuminated, with my legs wide open in a pose that seemed ridiculous with all that light.

I couldn't keep touching myself.

After I blew out the candles and restored darkness in the whole apartment, I tried to get back into my fantasy about the girl with the dark glasses, but I couldn't.

From one instant to the next it was all part of another life, other people's lives. Lives of people who didn't have anything to do with me, or my desire. *Don't come back here*, I thought. And the phrase suddenly took on a full, round meaning, and at that moment it was clear that the goodbye was gestating everywhere, here inside me and out there, in the city. *Everything is saying goodbye to everything, all the time*, I thought.

My boyfriend was still sleeping like a log. I lay down beside him and embraced him. I pressed my body against his even though the heat was unbearable. I didn't care. I sighed with relief that he didn't want to leave me, relief that for once, I'd been wrong.

(Irrelevant)
Mass Delusion in Cajas

MAURO JAVIER CÁRDENAS

On the other hand if someone were to ask Leopoldo about his pilgrimage to Cajas, where according to everyone the Virgin Mary had been appearing to a sixteen-year-old girl from Cuenca, Leopoldo wouldn't assume a resigned facial expression or shake his head as if about to relay an unfortunate incident that happened to some other studious teenager from San Javier but instead he would claim, in his most matter-of-fact voice, or perhaps in a voice that conceded how ridiculously unbelievable what he was about to claim was but also underscored how commonly accepted phenomena like gravity or photosynthesis were kind of unbelievable too, that he didn't care if what he'd witnessed in Cajas had been real or not, didn't care if it had been mass delusion, as some had called it later, he'd been there and had seen the sun move, thousands of believers who had pilgrimaged from Guayaquil, Quito, Cuenca, Machala for what had been announced as the last apparition of La Virgen del Cajas had gathered in a cold altiplane in the cordillera and had seen the sun move (how many times does the Virgin Mary need to appear to remind us of what we already know? how many times do we need to induce ourselves into believing she has come to warn us again that we're on the wrong path? in how many places around the world does she need to appear for no one to disbelieve any more or are

her recurrent appearances what perpetuate disbelief?), and because
so much time has passed since Leopoldo and thousands of believers
saw the sun move, he has had plenty of time to think of ways to
describe it to those lucky enough not to have been there (because
their first question is likely to be what exactly do you mean the sun
moved?), searching for the most accurate descriptions by associating
the sun's movements with everything in the world, no, this isn't
true, he hasn't been able to associate it with anything, or perhaps
he has not associated it with anything because he doesn't want to
steer it away from the world of phenomena and into the world of
metaphors, or perhaps he doesn't need to associate it with anything
because tracing stochastic patterns in the air with his index finger
would probably be enough to describe to others how the sun moved,
and on the bus on his way to Julio's party he still doesn't feel the
need to associate it with anything, the sun moved and that was that,
the sun as agitated as a firefly, no not like firefly, he hasn't even seen
a firefly up close, as if the sun were angry, as if the sun had burned
itself on a stove, as if the sun wanted to remind everyone below that
the Lord was among them and that the Lord can manipulate his
creation whichever way he pleases for the benefit of those who'd
come to venerate the mother of His only son (whatever happened
to those thousands of people who'd arrived in Cajas after an interminable uphill procession on that cold mountain? to those thousands
of people who had been waiting for something celestial to happen
and who had seen the sun move and who had cried like he imagines
mothers must cry upon the irreversible death of their children?
whatever did those thousands of people do with their lives? did they
disseminate her message through good deeds or did they, like
Leopoldo, simply – simply what? what have you done with the
memory of what was given to you? – forgot her?), and yet since the
people who might ask him about his pilgrimage to Cajas are likely
to be or have been devoted Catholics, they aren't likely to disbelieve

him too much or probe him further about this concept of mass delusion, a concept he has, surprisingly, never researched, although perhaps it isn't surprising he hasn't researched it because what difference would it make to him to discover that indeed scientists have concluded that when thousands of believers gather in one place expecting the same unbelievable event to happen, that same unbelievable event is bound to happen, the same sun moving inside everyone's heads at the same time, the same process inside everyone's heads, unearthing devotional images from documentaries about the Virgin of Lourdes or Fatima or Guadalupe or Medjugorje or from those thousands of hours praying the rosary out loud, when you were sure you could sense her presence nearby, the same process so overwhelming that on that cold altiplane it triggered the same delusional process in one person, and in the next person, and then in Leopoldo, and then in Antonio, who had been there too, who was crying and had embraced Leopoldo after the sun moved and later was to say we must do something to change these situations of dramatic poverty, Leopoldo, everyone crying as the sun moved (why were they all crying? because God had finally appeared or because all those hours imagining a personal relationship with God had not been in vain?), no, he didn't know why and didn't care to know why he was also crying and embracing everyone nearby, searching for his father who'd insisted on this pilgrimage but instead finding Antonio and embracing him, thousands of people on a cold altiplane in the Andes crying at the same time, embracing at the same time, sure, he knew it was possible a few hysterics had cried first, leading everyone else to cry as well, and it was also possible a few Catholic lunatics had shrieked and said look the sun's moving, leading everyone to believe the sun was indeed moving, and although he doesn't remember too many particulars of his pilgrimage to Cajas, for instance how he arrived there or how he descended from there or what his father was thinking during the entirety of the trip or whether the sun moved before or after nothing happened during the specified hour in which the Virgin was supposed to appear for the last time to a young Patricia Talbot from Cuenca (that silent hour in which the Virgin was supposed to appear and him not seeing or feeling anything and yet seeing and hearing people around him convulsing as if Mary had touched them and him wondering if they were the typical Catholic lunatics for whom everything's a sign from God or if Mary just didn't love him), he does remember what followed the week after, when he returned to San Javier, the intensity with which Leopoldo and Antonio disseminated her message, for instance, a message he doesn't remember any more, and yet that he doesn't remember her message doesn't diminish the memory of the intensity with which Leopoldo and Antonio disseminated her message, organizing daily rosary prayers during recess, promulgating to their classmates that joining the apostolic group was imperative not only to their salvation but to the salvation of the world, how are we to be Christians in a world of destitution and injustice, teaching catechism in Mapasingue, debating with Antonio the specifics of their duty to her and God and the future of their country, and then one day it was over, one day like any other day that intensity, which had expanded inside of them as if making room for everything God wanted from them, went away, leaving behind so much empty space that even in dreams they couldn't escape what later Father Lucio told them was called desolation, which is a test from God, he said, omitting that this test might never end, as in fact it hasn't, a test they were too young to handle or perhaps no age is a good age to handle desolation, and yet it wasn't true that Leopoldo had forgotten her: one day you're building a pyramid of sand and pebbles inside a cave in Punta Barandua, one day you climb a mountain and see the sun move, one day you're on a jam-packed bus en route to Julio's party to meet up with your dear friend Antonio who will not ask you if you remember what happened to them because of Cajas, although if they were both women they would be allowed to bring it up and cry about the love they felt and the love they lost, and yet I haven't forgotten her, Leopoldo would say, I just didn't know what to do with her after I graduated from San Javier so I relegated her to the farthest possible space, where she's probably still shining her Llama de Amor, which is what the Catholic lunatics came to call the intensity they'd felt, although this isn't quite right, Leopoldo would say, I didn't relegate her anywhere, I didn't participate in her banishment or at least I wasn't aware of my participation, this is just how it happened and is still happening, and if I could talk to Antonio about it I'm sure he would understand why it makes no difference to know what scientists have discovered about mass delusion, you feel what you feel and that is that, Antonio would say, thousands of people witnessing the sun moving and then descending from that mountain and then rejoicing at the inexpungible mud on their soles and then a year later prostrating themselves in complete desolation, but don't exaggerate, Antonio would say, don't make it sound like we suddenly found ourselves inside a dark place wailing and despairing, it wasn't that bad, we didn't really spend weeks prostrate in bed, or we did but not any more, Antonio would say, we, having no alternative, went on, flattening what happened to us into the daily inflow of our lives, and yet what would be the point of asking Antonio about Cajas except to bring it all back so that once again they'll be forced to suppress what is likely to surface in their chest and face and eyes? (I know you aren't supposed to be able to look into the sun but that's just how it happened, Leopoldo would say, of course I wouldn't believe it either and would be actually glad to concede it was mass delusion but what good would that do me if I still have all these feelings I don't know what to do with or do know what to do with, which is nothing?).

FROM THE NOVEL *THE REVOLUTIONARIES TRY AGAIN*

Christmas Tree

MARÍA JOSÉ CARO

Translated by Isabelle Kaufeler

In my memories, the tree is always different. Sometimes it's a bushy rubber tree, attached to the car roof like a Christmas tree in a film; other times, it's a scrawny trunk with yellowy leaves that slips down the windscreen. What never changes is the car: a grey Nissan three-door which my father always said had been imported especially from Japan. The expression on my mother's face as she watches him get out of the car with his shirt half-buttoned, bulging eyes and dirty trousers doesn't change either. I remember her checking the roof and the bumper and kicking the passenger door while my father stumbled towards the house. I see myself following them, dressed in my Caspar the Friendly Ghost pyjamas, which had lost their shape from the top being pulled down so often.

'Did you buy any rockets?' asked Sergio, coming down the stairs.

My father didn't answer. He switched on the radio and turned up the volume. Mama went over to him asking for explanations; she was frowning and holding up the car keys with a small twig between her fingers. He didn't even look at her. He started singing the Camilo Sesto song that was emanating from the stereo. My mother threw the keys at his stomach and turned away. Then Sergio went over to my father and tugged on his shirt. He asked him again whether he had bought any rockets. Papa stared at him and took him by the arm.

'What more do you want from me? I have nothing left!' he shouted.

Sergio tried to wriggle free, but my father was holding his wrist as though he were applying a tourniquet. My brother's eyes filled with tears.

'I have nothing left!' my father shouted again.

My mother went over and bent his fingers back until he let go of my brother.

Sergio ran towards the stairs without looking at me. Papa shrugged his shoulders, changed the song on the radio and slumped into a chair. My mother took me by the hand and we went up to my bedroom. She closed the door, opened my clothes drawers, rummaged frantically. 'Put this on,' she said, handing me a purple matching outfit. Then she left my room. I put the clothes on over my pyjamas and waited motionless on the edge of my bed.

We went back downstairs, trying not to make a sound, sure that my father would say something if he saw us, but what we found was only the shell of him. He was like a model of himself with half-closed eyes and a crooked smile, swaying in time to Nino Bravo. 'You always ruin everything!' shouted Sergio, and he ran towards the garage. My father tried to get up, leaning on the back of his chair, but the wood creaked and it collapsed immediately. We left the house as his body hit the floor.

It was easy to recognize the hotel. Soap operas would often use its facade as a prop to show that Lima was gradually becoming more modern. They were brief aerial shots, focusing on the flow of traffic on Paseo de la República. When we reached the lobby, Mama asked for a room away from the celebrations. The lady at the desk gave us one on the tenth floor and handed Mama a key and a little bag that contained streamers and a wreath. In my memories of that night I stay silent. Sergio takes a leaflet from the desk. 'They have a swimming pool,' he says, his eyes wide. He immediately lost interest in any fireworks my father might set off. In the hallway we came across a woman wearing a mask and a yellow hat who was vomiting onto the marble floor. My mother hurried towards the lift. 'It's all right, sweetheart,' she murmured. In that moment I thought of my father. Whenever we were faced with a lift, he would go up the stairs with me. By day he was an athletic man who could climb up seven flights with no sign of fatigue. But by night he became somebody else, a slumped body, held up by the banister rail, counting each step until he reached the bedroom, where he would collapse onto the bed and become a doll that snored automatically. I closed my eyes as soon as we entered the lift, concentrating on the bell which chimed each time the doors opened. 'We're here,' my mother said when we arrived. My brother was the first to leave the lift. I had never stayed in a hotel like this. The carpeted corridors overlooked the ground-floor lobby. Sergio stood on tiptoe and leaned against the waist-high concrete wall that prevented him from falling to his death. My mother tugged him away brusquely and made him walk on the other side of the corridor. We didn't speak until we stopped in front of door number 1001. The room was large. It had a king-sized bed and cable TV, which my brother turned on immediately. It also had a large desk with a telephone directory and a pad of headed notepaper on it. Mama went over to the window and opened the curtains. Our room looked over the swimming pool which, from this high up, was a perfect rectangle, dark and unchanging. From time to time the sky was illuminated by the rockets that were going off in the city centre. They were lengthy explosions, twinkles that lit up the sky for several seconds. My father would let off set-piece fireworks that he bought from the street vendors on Avenida Aviación. He would explain the route of the fuse. He said that there had to be harmony, that it was a case of using the gunpowder to make the light dance. My brother and I would watch him from the covered patio that overlooked the garden. Papa would light the firework, mop his sweaty brow and wait near the flame until the last light died away. I picked up the blank notepaper and began to draw on it while Sergio flicked through the cable channels.

'Don't leave the room,' my mother warned us. 'I'll be back in ten minutes.'

'I bet you Uncle Mario's at our house,' Sergio said to me in a low voice.

I ignored his words and closed my eyes. Uncle Mario used to turn up at every family celebration, even though he was only a friend of my father's. He combed his hair forward to hide his baldness. Whenever there was a get-together he was always the last to go home, in spite of Mama's hints. The only time I saw my father cry was with Uncle Mario. I had gone down to the kitchen for a glass of water and I ended up watching them from the bottom of the stairs. My father's eyes were puffy and there were splashes of alcohol on his shirt. 'We're screwed, mate. What are we going to do?' he said, rubbing his temples. He looked up in my direction and then turned back to the ashtray in front of him without speaking. He lost control of the tears he had been holding back. Perhaps my presence had been a trigger. Perhaps he remembered the four of us together on a happy day and each of us became one of the component sobs of his crying. I ran up to my room and hid under the sheets until my tears became an inevitable extension of his.

Mama came back to the room with two bags hanging from her arm. One contained polo shirts she had bought in the hotel shop. I took off my jumper and the ghost made his appearance. Even so, my mother insisted that I use the printed T-shirt that she laid out on the bed as a nightie. I refused point-blank, wrapping my arms around myself and the ghost, with his open mouth and big eyes, depicted on my chest. Sergio put on a polo shirt that came down

46

to his knees. I lay back next to him while my mother took snacks and fizzy drinks out of the other bag. After giving us the food, she picked up the telephone and moved as far away as she could, pulling the wire of the receiver taut. I could tell she was calling home from the way she was clenching her teeth and touching her nose. She dialled several times. She gave up after the fifth attempt and went over to the window.

'Sergio, Macarena, come here. It's five minutes to midnight.'

I leaned my forehead against the glass until my reflection disappeared and concentrated my gaze on the silent and fleeting world outside the room. I pretended that my father was among that pack of tiny cars that sped along the avenue. I imagined him asking for his family when he arrived in the lobby, running up the stairs to the tenth floor, turning the handle of the room seconds before twelve o'clock. I imagined his apologies and my mother's shouting before returning home in that state of contradictory peace that follows once the tears stop. But we saw in midnight watching the show put on by the families on the other side of the glass. We hugged one another as if it were a duty. Sergio crashed out between the sheets in a matter of seconds. I made myself comfortable in the middle of the bed while Mama turned off the lights. When she lay down next to me, I started to play with her black hair. That ritual was our lullaby. I would wind my fingers into her hair and twist it into spirals that would gradually hypnotize me. 'I'll be back in a moment, sweetheart,' she whispered, getting up from the mattress. She looked in her handbag and took out a packet of Winstons which she hid immediately in her trouser pocket. She went into the bathroom, shuffling her feet. When she came back I was still awake. My mother lay down on the bed carefully. I snuggled into her body, put my arm around her waist and inhaled that mixture of tobacco and perfume that had become her personal fragrance. Then she was the one who began to play with my hair. I could feel her caresses become more irregular and her fingers gradually slipping out of my hair. Mama fell asleep first. I followed her, closing my eyes, losing myself in her deep breathing, while every so often a light from outside would flash briefly off our window.

We left the hotel in the morning, when there were still some drunk people stumbling along the pavements and a certain smell of gunpowder still hung in the air. Mama chose a route at random. She set off along Jirón Lampa and we made our way into the centre of Lima until we arrived at the Plaza de Armas. Sergio pointed out the remains of big *ratablanca* bangers and other smaller ones under blackened benches in the middle of the square.

'Before we go home . . . is there anywhere you want to stop off?' Mama asked in the rear-view mirror.

I shook my head. Sergio asked to go to our grandparents' house, so we made for their neighbourhood in Miraflores. When we reached their apartment building my mother was the only one who got out of the car. She went to the intercom and came back in a matter of minutes. I never asked her if she rang the bell. It was probably an act so Sergio wouldn't go on about it. My grandmother didn't know how to lie. She had hidden my parents' wedding photo behind a vase so she didn't have to look at it. Perhaps she felt complicit in the failed plan our family had become. After all, she was also one of the people smiling in the photo, a witness who failed to spot the warning signs. Mama started the car and turned on a news station. It was the best way to keep us quiet, although her own attention was elsewhere.

In my memories, I always find my father in a different place. Sometimes I tell myself that we found him stretched out on the sofa in the living room. Other times, sitting on the rug next to the remains of the broken chair. What is always the same is his face, his mouth open and his eyes completely shut. The untouched set-piece beside the Christmas tree. My brother says we'll set it off the following night. I try to imagine it: a single firework set-piece lighting up the entire street.

Soldiers, Bring Everything Back Home!

MARTÍN FELIPE CASTAGNET

Translated by Daniel Hahn

I always dream about the same room. The room is on the upper floor of a house, but there are no doors leading into it, and no staircase. The only visible way to get in is by climbing up to a hole at the top of the wall. In my dream, I climb by a route that only I know. It's the perfect refuge, and the mere idea of reaching it is enough to leave me shaken.

I thought: the internet is the perfect place to hide. I thought: the only way they won't find me is if I maintain a constant state of flight, at least until I reach my refuge. I thought: the best way for a woman like me to escape from everyone who's looking for her is to get those very same people, without their even realizing they're doing it, to commission her to go as far away as possible; and I don't know any place else so close that is so far away.

And so I signed up as an explorer, and went off to spend two years in the net.

*

On the internet there is no day and night, but it is possible to tap into the code so that every explorer can experience the interface they prefer. My partner Irina and I are like owls and larks. She's an early-morning type; I'm better suited to the night-time. I would rather wake up when it's getting dark and explore in the calm of the half-light. She likes to chat; I like to listen to her. In this place there's no need to eat, though we do it anyway just so as not to go crazy; every once in a while we put our equipment down on the floor and have lunch. Irina tells me what life used to be like when reality was complete, before the great reset: all the animals and plants and machines in a natural context, she says, and not in these junk zoos. I admire her bravery: a big woman like her in an environment she despises but where she forces herself to go. And yet, she is unable to see the brutal beauty of these storage landscapes; and the fact that at this point the internet itself is also a natural surrounding, and that above all it, too, is unpredictable.

Of course, Irina knows nothing of my flight; still less of the house with the room.

Today she said to me: I am here because everyone else is searching for comfortable things instead of true things. She was looking out at the horizon, at the volcanic peat into which the statues of unknown gods were gradually sinking. Our task was to put them into storage before they were lost for good. One statue had all but disappeared, except for its head: the god's eye sockets were empty. I put my finger into the left-hand hole and pulled out a gelatinous substance: probably the nest of some hybrid animal. Irina went off in tears, and I knew it must have been something she had projected.

What is it that we do, exactly? We search the archives of the internet for everything that has been lost in our world and we put it into storage so that it can be restored to reality. We are like metal prospectors, but our scope is infinitely greater. One of each extinct species, yes, but also historic objects, works of art, precious stones, ordinary stones, books that are sometimes distorted. Our detector has a handle with a gauge, a padded armrest and a long shaft that ends in a plate that is interchangeable depending on whether we are looking for objects that are alive, dead, inert or mechanical.

The biggest problem is that here on the internet emotions also materialize. Each visitor brings mental baggage that can contaminate the environment we are visiting. Hybrids, impossibilities, alien structures: the substratum of mythical creatures that inhabit the tales of our parents. We mustn't transport those things that do not exist in reality, so we have to be very careful about which objects we store in our devices so as not to contaminate our world when we finally return.

Careful with the wild animals, Irina said the first time we met, the pain is the same. Careful with unstable domains. And careful with the viruses from our emotional deposits. If you ever bring back one of those, I'll kill you. I imagined my corpse, abandoned on some data dune, still clinging to my device. Ever since then, I've done a health check on my equipment every night before bed.

The biggest difference between Irina and me: her concern is only for the side we have come from, the side from which I am escaping. She believes too fervently in the official line: Soldiers, bring everything back home! It's time to repopulate reality! Whereas for me, the internet itself is my country. This is where my home is, even if I won't ever find it, even if it's really only the idea of a home.

Cities on the internet operate like an archive: a way of ordering its information, the enforced attempt to endow meaning to a source of incoherent data. As if the networks had dreamed about their own downloads and out of this a digital environment had eventually formed. The topological solidification of information.

Amid all the cities there is one in particular I am looking for. I don't know what it's called, but in any case, most have no name. They have only levels: you need to pass through one to reach the next. What with their being nameless, our job must include describing them. For example: the aquatic city, the cloud city, the paper city . . . I'm already quite clear that to get to where I'm going it's necessary to pass through all the other levels to reach degree zero.

Sometimes I dream about the room, other times I dream about the house, but I always dream about the city where the room and the house are to be found. I could recognize it anytime: the walls protecting it, the contours of its terrain, the rolling shape of its harbour. Whenever the dream reappears, the city grows: a new cafe, a new pool hall, new nooks and crannies. The more complete it is, I think, the safer my refuge will be. Then I really will be able to take a rest, not least from the work the dreaming causes me.

I encountered Irina's anger for the first time. It happened after I had made a mistake. We were in a public library piled high with cars, one on top of another. I climbed from car to car till I had gained enough altitude: on one of the upper shelves there was a scorpions' nest. I checked to see whether the species was registered, and it was. But all the same the creatures frightened me, and I just stored the books as best I could: books are always much-appreciated loot for helping to recover what has been lost. This time they were mostly corrupted texts, meaningless characters, undoubtedly the result of a poorly executed conversion. It never occurred to me that this illegibility might be the result of an emotional contamination, but it was, and it was Irina who realized this. You've been checking over my files, I said, accusingly. What of it? she replied, the only thing that matters is that reality is kept stable, and you put that at risk. She made me return the books to their places. Why can't we just leave them somewhere else, I asked, if basically there's no order here? But Irina was inflexible, and we made our way across the dunes back to the library. My humiliation vanished when I looked down from on top of the cars and I could see tracks that hadn't been there before.

I think: there are other teams of explorers in the internet, but I don't know them and I've never come across one. Is the net really that big? Or is it we who create the cities with our own leavings, as we proceed on our way? The act of seeking changes the surroundings until we are transformed into prisoners of our own trash: the more we seek, the more we hide what it is we wanted to find.

Irina always stops to feed the cats. A useless task, since they don't need to eat, and we no longer need to store them. Our digital inventories are already full of every feline species, big and small. It's a method I use when I have trouble sleeping: going over inventories to check what we do have and what we're still missing; the canids, for example, are still incomplete and there's always some coyote or other that gets away. But she finds them, abandoned to the rain and the cold, and she can't help giving them shelter.

Today's cat had a torn nose and a tail that curled into a circle whenever Irina stroked it. Later I noticed she had scratches on her arms, new marks I couldn't identify as coming from any of the previous days' cats. After we had set off again, on our way to city level seven, I invented some excuse to go back to where the cat was. I saw it close-up: the pads of its paws were made of rubber. It was a hybrid, obviously. I grabbed a stone from the path and killed it with two blows. I covered it over with snow, and hurried to catch up with her. I don't know if she knew or guessed what I had done, but she did look extremely relieved. She laughed and patted me on the back. Come on, then, explorer, still a couple of years to go before we reach level zero, eh?

It was only later, as we were finally coming down the mountain, that I thought of all the creatures projected by my own emotions that Irina must have killed. The skeletons under the snow, under the sand, in the drawers of wardrobes, a dying trail of my fear, of my permanent escape. Perhaps the house I dream about is a projection, too, and when the other explorers find it they'll set fire to it because it doesn't belong to this world.

I think: Irina doesn't just check over my inventory, she also checks over my dreams, and most likely also my browser data. I've come from so far away only to have them follow me from so close by. But then I think: if she really is keeping an eye on my flight, why doesn't she arrest me? Or perhaps all these projections, this work, this constant flight are my prison and Irina my warder. My head's in chaos; it's my own city, filled with incoherent information.

I decide to tell her. We are in a sheet-metal shed on level two, during a download storm in the middle of the countryside. It's night-time, at least according to my interface; the downloads shine like meteorites just before crashing down onto the dark grass. She looks like her mind is far away, an expression I've been seeing more and more often. Irina, I know everything. She remains still for a few seconds longer, as though interrupted in the middle of a dream. Very well, she says, it was too much weight anyway and I'm carrying too much already.

The shed has no walls, a sheet-metal roof that only barely serves for shelter. But we see it approaching. It looks as much like a man as it's possible for an animal to look. It walks hunched slightly forward, arms tattooed like a dictionary with its pages jumbled. It follows me wherever I go, says Irina. I never got round to killing it when it was small and now it's too late. Will they let me bring it back?

We waited together till the storm ended, with the man curled like a dog at the entrance to the shed. When it stopped raining we resumed our endless walk towards the final level – never early enough, yet not definitely late: back and forth, like rocking.

Chaco

LILIANA COLANZI

Translated by Julia Sanches

My grandfather used to say that every word has its master and that a well-chosen word can make the earth quake. The word is a lightning bolt, a tiger, a high wind, the old man would say, fixing me with furious eyes as he served himself a glass of surgical spirit, but oh, I pity the fool who uses it lightly. Do you know what happens to liars? he'd ask. I'd try to ignore him and look out the window at the vultures circling in the village's filthy sky. Or I'd turn up the volume on the TV. The signal was weak, the screen an explosion of white dots. Sometimes that was all we could see on the TV: white dots. Do you know what happens to liars? my skeletal grandfather would ask again, threatening me with his walking stick: the word abandons them, and anyone can kill a person empty of words.

Grandfather would spend all day in his armchair, drinking and bickering with his own drunkenness. At night, Mama and I would pick him up and drag him off to his bedroom: he was so far gone by then he didn't even know who we were. As a young man, he'd been a violinist, in demand at parties all over Chaco, but I'd only ever known him as a surly shut-in, muttering nonsense to his bottle of booze. Quiet, quiet, quiet, he'd whisper nervously to the bottle, as if there were voices tempting him from inside the glass. Other times, he'd murmur in the language of the Indians. What's he saying? I'd ask Mama, as she set out rat poison in the many corners of the house. L-l-leave y-y-our g-g-grandpa alone, she'd say. C-c-curiosity is the d-d-d-devil's spit.

Once, though, Vargas, who was from the Altiplano, announced in front of everyone that as a young man my grandfather had col-laborated with the government to expel the Matacos from their lands. A javelina hunter had found oil there while digging a hole to bury his dog, which had died from a snakebite. Government men had driven out the Matacos, riddling them with bullets and setting fire to their houses. Then they'd built the Viborita refinery. Thanks to that oilfield, a road was put down along one side of the village. Some greedy bastards took advantage of the situation to rape Mataco women, Vargas said. Some of them were blonde with blue eyes, children of Swedish missionaries. They were prettier than our own women, those savages, he said. My grandfather didn't get the money he was promised for running the Matacos off their land, money he needed to pay off a debt. He lost everything. He turned mean, a drunk. So the story went.

Almost nothing ever happened in the village. Toxic clouds from the cement factory hung, bloated and heavy, above our heads, and at sunset gleamed in every colour. Those who didn't have a skin condition had sick lungs. Mama had asthma and was always carrying an inhaler around with her. Foxes howled on the other side of the road, which is why the village was called Aguarajasë. Every year, the river grew angry and rose up roaring with mosquitoes. The world was far, far away. Mama got pregnant by a salesman who'd passed through the village selling Tramontina pots and pans, and who was never seen or heard of again. Eighteen years later, folk were still talking about how the Stutterer had been so in love that, while the pots-and-pans salesman was passing through, she'd spoken without a single stammer.

Once, on my way back from school, I found a Mataco lying by the roadside. He was drunk and swarming with flies. He was big and tall, and his loincloth barely covered his balls. Filthy, dirty Indian, people said. Truckers drove round him and honked their horns, but no one could wake him. What was he dreaming? Why was he far from his own people? I envied him. I wanted him to notice me, but he didn't need me to be what he was. One day, I picked up a big rock and threw it as hard as I could from the other side of the road. Bam! Smack on the head. He didn't budge, but a red stream started snaking its way down the asphalt. The south wind blew fierce those days! Heavy with the hissing of chulupaca beetles. We would listen, anxiously, in the dark. I didn't tell anyone about what had happened. The next day, two policemen came and carted the Mataco off in a black bag. They didn't ask many questions, he was only an Indian after all. No one claimed him. I heard them cracking jokes as they threw the body bag in the back of the truck. I picked up the rock, stained with the Mataco's blood, took it home and hid it in the back of a drawer, next to my underpants.

Soon after, the Mataco's voice got inside my head. He mostly sang. He'd no idea what had happened to him and crooned in that mournful, almost swampy way that Indians do. Ay-ay-ay, he cried. I dreamed his dreams: herds of javelinas fleeing through the forest, the warm wound of a deer struck by an arrow, an earthy steam rising up to the sky. Ay-ay-ay ... The Mataco's heart was a red mist. Who are you? What do you want? Why have you come to live inside me? I asked. I am the Ayayay, the Avenger, he who Gives and Takes Away, the Killer, the Furious Rage, said the Mataco, and asked, in turn: Who are you? There's no you or me any more, I said. From now on, we are only one will.

I was euphoric, I couldn't believe my luck. I grew chatty. I'd start saying something almost by accident and then, suddenly, there was no going back: the Mataco's stories and mine became one. Doña María, Tevi says that his Papa was swallowed up by a whirlpool in the forest. Don Arsenio, your grandson says he skinned a jaguar and ate its heart raw, is that true? Mama cried, which was the only thing she knew how to do. My grandfather said I'd caught the lying disease and beat me so hard his stick broke in his hands. I had to go to school with welts on my arms and legs and put up with everyone staring at me. Stares that blinked back laughter. There goes the jaguar-slayer, thrashed by the old drunk, their eyes said. I saw red, I was aflame with anger. The Mataco read my heart: Wait, don't rush into anything; I'll tell you when your time has come.

Then the bikers passed through the village. Everyone went to watch since there was going to be a cockfight and Don Clemente had promised to bring out two of his best fighters. D-d-do you want to g-g-go? asked Mama. I didn't, my head ached from the heat. As soon as Mama left, the Mataco began raising the red mist. The chulupacas hissed inside me. The aching in my head clouded my sight. I went to the kitchen and grabbed a glass of water. Quiet, quiet, the old man whispered to the bottle. A urine stain spreading like a spider web down his trousers. He looked up and stared at me. You weakling, you poofter, you liar, get out of here, he hissed. I held his gaze, the glass of water in my hand. The old man, defiant in his drunkenness. You're like bamboo, hollow on the inside, whose seed must have spawned you, he said. And he spat on the floor in disgust. My blood rose, my veins crawled with fire ants. The Mataco started jumping about inside me. What are you waiting for to get your revenge, you son of a viper? Are you going to let that old drunk talk to you like that? Or is your blood as cold as a toad's? I went to grab the rock. I crept up behind my grandfather and hit him hard, just once, on the side of his head. He fell and lay there panting hoarsely, life passing from his lips. I stood watching, in wonder: so old, and yet he still clung to this world?

Mama arrived later to find him on the floor choking on his own vomit. He must have fallen over while he was drunk, the people in the village said. He took several days to die, then, on the seventh day, he finally kicked the bucket. I saw his soul detach itself from his body like a little white puff of smoke before vanishing into the air. We sold the house to pay the hospital bills, and moved into a room in Vargas's house, behind the warehouse. We couldn't afford anything else. Vargas's wife wasn't at all pleased and would scowl whenever she saw us. The Stutterer's kid is so strange, I heard her say to her husband. Why did you take them in? Or is something going on between you and that woman? She burst into tears. If Vargas's wife had seen Mama as I saw her every night, she wouldn't have been jealous: under her nightgown, Mama's tits hung down to her waist. We slept in the same bed. Every night, as soon as we lay down, Mama would turn her back to me and pray until she fell asleep. I'd lie there awake, playing with the throbbing rock in my hands and listening to the murmuring of the other who was also me: The cold came to the forest, and the river dried up. Ayayay. The frog jumped onto the branch, the snake ate it up. The girl went to fetch water, and turned up dead. Ayayay. The young man went hunting, and turned up dead. Ayayay. The old man went back home, and turned up dead. Ayayay. The girl who danced with another turned up dead. Ayayay. The boy who laughed like a monkey turned up dead. Ayayay. The girl with the long chin turned up dead. Ayayay. No one wanted to touch the dead. In the middle of the brush, they began to rot. The souls of the dear departed returned in tears. Ayayay. Will we be left to live alone among souls? she asked, and the next day she was gone. Ayayay. The winds are changing for you, son of a poisonous spider. A new cycle is beginning, the sky is splitting open, pay attention. Ayayay.

Sometimes, Mama would look at me hard, as if she were about to say something. One day, she announced that she was leaving to live with a widowed aunt on the other side of the river and that I was free to do as I wanted.

When? I asked.

A-a-any d-d-day now, she said. Her upper lip quivered. She took a breath from her inhaler, which was something she did when she was nervous. For the first time, I knew what it felt like to know someone was afraid of me. I liked it. Wh-what's that r-r-rock you've always g-g-got in your h-h-hand?

I picked it up on the road, I said.

Wh-what were you d-d-doing the d-d-day G-g-grandpa f-f-fell? I was watching TV, I said.

Y-y-you d-d-didn't h-hear anything? she asked.

The volume was up real loud, I said.

The Stutterer pressed her lips together and, with one look, disowned me as her son.

I c-c-can't s-s-stand it any more, she said and shut herself in the room, slamming the door.

I went for a walk. By the time I got back, the Stutterer had left with all her things. Now what do we do? Go out on the road. Don't hang around, don't say goodbye, don't look back. Someone will be waiting for you there. I put the rock in my backpack, along with a couple of changes of clothing, and left the village without a word to Vargas or his wife. The clouds were high and laden with poison. Five minutes later, a tanker taking fuel to Santa Cruz stopped to pick me up. The trucker was on his own and didn't hesitate to give me a lift. I didn't turn around and didn't take one last look at the village. We sat around chewing coca and now and then tuned into a Guaraní radio station. We saw miles and miles of scorched trees scraping at the sky. We saw a sloth, its back burnt, dragging itself along the highway. We saw a sign that said

Christ is coming and another further ahead that said We've got bread and gas.

The trucker was one of those men who's old enough to have a family somewhere, but not too old to want a good sucking off. Soon enough, he parked beneath some trees, pushed his seat back as far as it would go, and unzipped his fly.

Go on then, mate, he said.

It wasn't easy at first, what with the smell of old man and of piss. But I got hard, too, after a while. The slimy old geezer wheezed and jerked me off while I blew him. We came almost at the same time. He zipped his fly back up, took out a fag he kept behind his ear and smoked it, passing it to me now and then without looking my way.

Just so you know, you're only a queer if you give head, he said.

The trucker seemed light, happy, satisfied. Should I kill him? If you kill him now you'll never make it to the place where they're waiting for you. Or is the white man brother to the scorpion, eager to stab himself with his own stinger? Ayayay. You pig-headed Indian, why don't you shut up already. I'm sick of your ayayay. I fell asleep to the truck's rattling and the wind pummelling the window, and dreamed I'd died and that on the other side of death, a boy as beautiful as the sun was waiting for me. I cut out my tongue and handed it to him and in doing so I became mute, though my heart called him by name: My Saviour. I woke up to the shuddering of the engine as it turned off.

We're going to stop here for a bit, the trucker said. It was a house on the side of the road with busted-up windows covered in cardboard. A dark-skinned woman leaned against the doorway smoking a cigarette, carved into that position. She was older, about twenty-eight. Around her the wind dragged up coils of dust that dissolved in the air. The trucker handed her a bag of supplies, which she took without thanking him. On the kitchen floor, two kids played table football with bottle caps. Neither of them looked up at us when we walked in. The woman drank maté and the man sat in a plastic chair. They didn't speak and barely looked at one another, but kept sniffing at the other's movements.

I felt this in the air and went out for a walk along the trail behind the house. The forest grew thick with thorny cacti covered in those prickly pears that cowbirds will swoop down to peck at. In a clearing, a hot spring bubbled open like boiling soup. The sun was in my eyes and, at first, I was blinded by the rising steam and the reflection on the surface of the water. Then I saw it. Splayed on a rock, an octopus curled its tentacles – fat, pink boas with suckers the size of billiard balls. Its arms were wrapped around a quivering fox pup too terrified even to flee. The creature was like an enormous mound of jelly melting in the sun. The place reeked of fish, of woman. Sensing me come closer, the octopus crossed its arms like a fat lady gathering up her skirts to cross a river and, swift and leery, dragged itself to the water, leaving behind its prey. Its final tentacle vanished into the water with a lash: hot bubbles burst on the surface. The little fox leaped into the forest, free. Soon everything was quiet again and it was as if the creature had never existed. Translucent fish, the kind whose intestines show through their skin, nibbled at the water's edge. But the enormous creature must be sleeping, or waiting, below, at the bottom of the spring. The murmuring in my head grew loud again. The river was poison, the fish were dead. The hunger was great, the food all gone. Three men were sent hunting, none returned. Sucking on pig bones, they were found. Ayayay. They were brought back, their hands bound up. By every child, with a stick they were struck. The head of the youngest popped like a squash. To the dogs they went, their meat slurped up. We stabbed them with skewers, the fire burned them up. We ate our fill, our bellies swelled up. Ayayay. I listened to us and threw stones into the spring until I grew bored.

By the time we returned, the trucker and the woman had shut themselves up in the bedroom. The sounds of their panting cascaded out of the room. The kids kept playing on the floor, paying no mind to the noise. One of them, the smallest, was clumsy and his head was shaped like a balloon twice the size of a normal head. We were surprised we hadn't seen him earlier: the little boy was a mongoloid. He played with his mouth half-open, bottle caps slipping through his fingers. The mongoloid head beckoned to us in invitation. We took the rock out of our bag and felt its weight with both our hands. The rock throbbed with life. Ayayay. The wind galloped around the house making the trees creak. We slinked towards the kid like a jaguar, calculating the force needed to make his head burst. His brother looked up at us and our eyes met with a spark. He knew at once and gazed up at us with interest. We stayed like that, suspended, for a moment. Then, the bedroom door opened and the trucker came out, wiping off his sweat with the edge of his shirt.

Time to go, mate, he said.

We walked back to the truck. The setback had put us in a mood. Our blood had risen and refused to settle. We didn't want to talk. Luckily, emptied of his seed, the vile old dog had lost interest in us and kept his eyes on the road. But we weren't satisfied. Should I kill him? Didn't I say no? Aren't you the Avenger, the Killer? Oh, brainless white man of the restless race, what are you talking about? Your heart is like a blind ant that can only sting. I'm running out of patience. Where's my task? Once you have eyes for it, you will see.

We arrived in Santa Cruz at nightfall. The trucker let us out at a stop light and signalled that we'd reach the square if we kept on walking. And there we were, alone, standing in the middle of cars that came and went in every direction. We didn't have a dime, didn't know where we'd be sleeping that night. But we were the man of the house. We let ourselves be dragged along by crowds of hurried people, let ourselves be stunned by loud street noises, all the while carrying with us our rock and our voice. The buildings sprang up around us every which way, the city glowing as if just polished.

Then, we heard the screeching of brakes. Car tyres skidded on the asphalt and we shot up into the sky. We spat out all the air in our lungs, and the spirit split from the body. A woman's shrieking came bouncing towards us. Before we fell, our soul floated up above the cars. A pigeon eyed us in shock, and we saw people behind the glass windows of one of those tall buildings. As we fell, our eyes met the trucker's: he was the most beautiful boy we'd ever known in all our life. He watched us, his mouth ajar, a look of pure wonder dancing in his eyes. He is the Beautiful, the one of your dreams. My Saviour, we thought, recognizing him, here, take our tongue, yours is our voice. One last sound, and we embraced the darkness.

Villa Torlonia

JUAN ESTEBAN CONSTAÍN

Translated by Simon Bruni

Much has been written on Chesterton's interview with Mussolini in late October 1929. His detractors, of course, have chosen to view it as the best evidence of the great writer flirting with fascism: on several occasions, he celebrated what was happening in Italy at that sinister time, looking favourably upon the traditionalism and Catholicism of Il Duce and his followers. In addition to being considered a conservative, and a reactionary in the most profound sense of the word, which he was, Chesterton has also been accused many times of alleged (and not merely alleged) antisemitism, for failing to distance himself clearly from the powerful governments then rising up in Europe on the shoulders of the devil. Chesterton's defenders, as if he really needed any, almost always adopt the stupid tactic of denying or playing down the facts, seeking to justify why he said what he said or did what he did, as if, indeed, there was always a reason for everything in life. There isn't. And there is also the question of the way in which Chesterton became a fetish for the most cringeworthy, blinkered radicals, who appropriated his name and his thinking – took ownership of everything he represented, which was no small thing – in order to administer it all as if they were in a church where the real or invented merits of the great idol were recited through spirals of incense smoke. There is nothing worse, as someone once said, than the dogmatism of the acolyte; nothing more dangerous to the magnificent things of the world than the admiration that morons feel for them. Nobody is going to deny that Chesterton was an obstinate Catholic, and proud of it – proud of being Catholic and obstinate – and that much of the charm of his work as a polemicist resides in this, in the tenacious and brilliant way in which he defends his truths – *The Truth*, as he would call it – without giving a damn about his popularity or political correctness. Clinging to his beliefs, Chesterton allowed himself the luxury of disregarding reason as often as was necessary, with an argument that was not entirely false: that there was nothing in the world that inspired more fanaticism and irrationality than reason itself; that far from being an instrument for understanding the world, rationality was an ideology, or at least, it was to him. That was why he battled 'like Saint Gilbert': because he felt that it was his destiny and his duty as a Christian and a humorist. He championed the Pope, marriage, chastity, tradition, sanctity: the obstacles to the modern world. Yet Chesterton was much more than that, as much as it pains his most arbitrary exponents, as if idiocy really was a valid source of authority and interpretation; and it often is, sometimes the only one. Hence his generous and tolerant and compassionate attitude, his genuine and exceptional Christianity, his friendship with the great heretics of his time. Hence also his passion for debate, his respect for others. Only through dialogue may a person conquer an idea; only through listening may a person engage in dialogue.

So no: what sense is there in denying that Chesterton interviewed Mussolini and that he felt some sympathy for him, that there were things about Il Duce that he liked more than chaos and communism, even if Mussolini himself had been a communist almost his entire life and that many of his methods, and ultimately his whole ideology, aspired to the same thing as the Soviet State: the suppression of the individual, crushing the person under the overwhelming force of the system and the masses, the people united under their leader in a monstrous frenzy that would very soon show its awful defects, its claws? Of course, Chesterton did not like that, for there was nothing more important to him, except God, than the individual: every person, every one of us, every soul that populates the world and gives it meaning. That was why he was a Catholic, he would say. And nor did he like Hitler with his racial delusions, with his Germanophile ravings, because he was essentially sowing the seeds of a religion based on the superiority of Germany. A desecration, an abyss. But at heart Chesterton was a man of his time – and with this I do not mean to defend him; it seems to me misfortune enough for any man at any time – and also just a man: a fallible being subject to the life and time that befell him for good or bad, someone bound to make all manner of mistakes; who doesn't? Could he have done and thought and said many things differently, like several other contemporaries of his? Of course. But a man is what he is, and that's that. A confused, frightened, misguided creature. Always.

Chesterton arrived at the Villa Torlonia, Il Duce's residence, at dusk. It was a truly gigantic palazzo, even for him, for the enormous body that he so often made jokes about. A page received Chesterton and showed him to the study, where there were two chairs and a table for the coffee. Mussolini was there and, very energetically, he shot to his feet to greet him. They shook hands and, in French, Il Duce asked him if they could speak French, to which Chesterton answered yes, that his French was very bad but yes. Then they both sat down on their chairs, the two of them smiling. His account of the meeting appeared in a book the following year entitled *The Resurrection of Rome*, a sort of notebook of Chestertonian observations on Roman life and art and faith during his three-month visit to the hilltop Trinità dei Monti. To date, many critics and admirers consider it a failed book, and it is: disjointed, chaotic, unfocused and negligent. Chesterton was even bold enough to employ a little of his wit in an attempt to justify a text which was so inferior to all the others that had come from his pen: *I suddenly saw lie open before me a book that I cannot write. This book is the printed proof that I cannot write it*, he said in the prologue. He attributed the impossibility of dealing with it and understanding it and writing about it, about Rome and about eternity, to the enormousness of the subject and his own smallness. The fact is that the book is a reflection of his bewilderment at the mission that the Pope had entrusted him with. Even there, with Mussolini, it was all he could think about. Hence, the account of the meeting is much more vivid and sincere in his diary, with transcripts of the entire conversation between the two of them and not just the fragments that came out later in the book, most of them all but made up, with the exception of the part on the 'distributionism' that Chesterton had such a passion for.

'My good friend, it's a pleasure,' Il Duce said to him when they were sitting at the little table, while servants brought coffee and biscuits and a bottle of wine; he said it to him in a French that was far from perfect – in those days poor French was the universal language in which half the world communicated.

'The pleasure is all mine,' replied Chesterton, trying to wring what he could out of the memories of his trips to France, in particular the first he went on with his father in 1892: all the French he knew he had learned then, when he was eighteen years old.

'Tell me one thing, dear teacher: what is the Church of England?'

'Well . . .' Chesterton tried to reply to the question that had taken him by surprise and to which he really had no answer. 'Well, I'm sure you'll understand: that's not an easy question for an Englishman . . .'

'Of course it's not,' said Mussolini, now holding a glass of wine from which he took little sips, savouring it with his chin in the air, very gently clicking his tongue against his palate and teeth: a set of small, sharp teeth, thought Chesterton before writing it in his diary. Like a wolf's. 'Of course it's not: that's why I'm asking you.'

'Look, it may be a most complex matter, but if you're going to spring the question on me like this, I think it's actually very simple. For me, the Church of England is the same as our church, the Catholic Church, only without the Pope: or without pontifical authority, perhaps I should say. And I like authority; that's why I became a Catholic.'

'And what do you say about the controversy surrounding the Book of Common Prayer?' Mussolini asked, pouring himself more wine in a nervous, electric fashion. His question referred to the dispute between Anglican communities over the revision of the prayer book that Parliament had approved just a year earlier, in 1928.

'I don't know,' said Chesterton, shrugging; now he was having wine. 'As long as they don't revise our Church's prayer book, let the British parliament do as it wishes.'

Mussolini sat looking at him with curiosity and fascination, his glass still half full (from the last refill) and his head tilted to one side, leaning forward a little with his body. 'To the Church of England!' Il Duce cried in a fit of enthusiasm, and then he asked Chesterton to sit again, since both of them had stood up during their ecclesiastical conversation. Now they had to discuss literature, 'for I am a great reader,' said the dictator, who imposed his frantic pace on the interview, in which the poor English poet, according to his own diary, sweated and trembled and observed with horror that the grammatical and lexical resources of his meagre French were fast running out. What was incredible was that Mussolini had in fact read many of the best British writers of the last three centuries, and accounted for them and their works in a veritable torrent of names and titles with which he peppered Chesterton, while the Englishman merely stammered, smiled, shrugged again, drank wine, wiped the sweat from his face with a handkerchief and looked towards the window.

Only when the literary chapter had ended did Il Duce request that they 'speak' of politics, to which his interviewer could but respond with a modest view on imperialism; he would have expanded on this view, but it proved impossible. Then came another display of the florid and powerful Mediterranean rhetoric that only Mussolini was capable of, as he paced the room with great vehemence, fist in the air. At one point, he even began to march and sing: fascist songs with extravagant words among which Chesterton could now perceive a hint of the influence of wine. He told the Englishman not to be shy: *'Come on man, don't be shy . . .!' he told me in French, and I pretended, without much effort, not to understand him; but he began to urge me with his hands, saying: 'Come on, come on, don't just sit there, my good fellow, dance and march with me . . .!' to which I could only stand up and dance and march* . . . and he invited him to dance and march with him. The scene is not described in detail in the diary, needless to say, but just imagining it brings on a fit of laughter: the tyrant marching back and forth in his uniform, and poor Chesterton behind him, accustomed as he was to almost never being surprised by anything, to understanding the human condition and its frailties, and to experiencing everything as it really is: a farce, an operetta that, were it staged at a theatre, would be incredible in its absurdity. But that's life. And what's more, he enjoyed any opportunity to show off his talent as an actor and dramatist, so now that he was here, and now that the wine had permeated him too, he began to dance and march and sing on his own account, songs he improvised in English and in Italian, without caring that he did not even know Italian. Exhausted after their big performance, the two comedians returned to the little table where the bottle stood. They drank another glass. Then, Mussolini, slumped in his chair with the placid grin of a drunk, asked Chesterton to tell him about 'distributionism'. 'Please, tell me about this curious doctrine of yours,' he said. What came next Chesterton recounted both in his diary and in *The Resurrection of*

Rome, with very little variation between the two versions: *I was so excited at the possibility of talking to one of Europe's heads of state about distributionism, that the little French I still had fell to pieces. What began to issue from my mouth was now an incomprehensible gabble, I know not to what wild barbaric tongue, older than Babel, its gasps and nasal noises might be supposed to belong. Thinking it not improbable that Signor Mussolini might think I was mad, I rose as if to bow myself out. Smiling and lurching, he returned the bow to me, with a civility that flattered me even from beyond the wine: 'I will think about everything you have said...'* The Villa Torlonia's pages helped Chesterton down the steps, which felt to him like a descent into Vesuvius overflowing with lava. He put on his overcoat and walked out, bidding farewell to the two chamberlains.

Physiologus

LOLITA COPACABANA

Translated by Samantha Schnee

ON LATE DARWINISM

Yesterday we were speaking about a recent movement against racing greyhounds, thanks to which greyhound racing has now been banned throughout Argentina. We were speaking amongst ourselves, because although people widely favour the ban, it's a sensitive issue – particularly with greyhound breeders – and because we don't know much about the subject; people seem generally opposed to greyhound racing.

We're not opposed to this law, but we don't understand what the difference is between racing greyhounds and horses. We don't understand why a dead dolphin being held by a tourist from Santa Teresita matters more than the smoked salmon someone else is eating on a bagel, or why a dog being made to race is so different from a video of a calf being broken in on YouTube. We respect the vegan movement but are confused by an argument at a barbecue about signing a petition to protect 'non-human animals'.

The risk of extinction is a eugenic argument. Domestication is a psychopathic strategy for survival.

OTHER FORMS OF TORTURE

1. In the gym I asked the trainer to show me how to use the new machines. I'm putting it that way because it reveals a few things: that previously I used one machine, or maybe two; that the 'trainer' is just there, training other people, or that I greet him every day without making much eye contact and every once in a while I graciously let him correct my technique. I wanted to tell my husband about him, so I did, even though he was busy – I didn't bother to ask what he was typing. I told him everything in detail despite the fact I could see from the tiny changes in his body as I was speaking that he would have preferred me to keep it short. The same changes I love to watch when other people talk to him, which usually indicate that he'd prefer to be with me. So I tried to cut it short, as short as possible, but I was so excited. I had learned to use three new machines.

2. On my father's birthday I asked him to take a photo of me drinking champagne straight from the bottle. It's my good fortune that the benefits of alcohol are exaggerated in me: the vast majority of my close relationships have been blessed by alcohol, strengthened by alcohol, hallowed by alcohol. I uploaded the photo to Instagram with the caption, 'Today is my dad's birthday'. On my fifteenth birthday my father gave me the first bottle of tequila I ever received.

3. From the doorway, on the way to the kitchen, I watch my daughter studying at the dining-room table. From the doorway means: my body split, exactly half of me is hidden safely behind the wall, the other half exposed, my eye peeled, on the lookout. A sight fixed straight ahead and a ditch to take cover in. Sometimes my husband is right, I'm a cat. Sometimes Wisława Szymborska is right, I'm a cat. My daughter looks up and smiles at me. I smile at her phone on the table and she says that she's using the calculator for some

homework. I tell my daughter that I can't control everything. I tell her that I don't care if she's lying to me. I tell her that if she's not lying, and bad things happen to her, it won't be her fault. I tell her what we're having for dinner tonight.

4. In general everything seems fine, except stopping.

5. In 2016 my father decided that I was (am) anorexic. He decided, just like that, that in fact I always had been. My daughter had come to the same conclusion much sooner. Of course, neither my father nor my daughter knows what anorexia is. The truth is that for some reason they're uncomfortable about the weight I choose to carry, and the label appeals to them. They don't know what they're saying but it doesn't matter one iota to them that an anorexic would glance at me in disgust and, at best, mumble 'wannabe'. This scenario doesn't interest me in the least.

My father, in 2015, via WhatsApp: 'What do you mean *small*, aren't you *extra small*?'

My father, in 2016, via WhatsApp: 'I have the dress in my hands, it's one of those doll-sizes you wear.'

Before deciding that I was (am) anorexic, when he was approaching his sixtieth birthday, my father had decided that I was old. Fortunately after a few months (with my current husband) we announced our (then future) wedding, and he got over it.

6. If a quote from a (published) text of mine were read to me at random, I'd know without question whether or not it had been edited (certainly with corrections).

7. I'm in the dark watching twelve Instagram notifications appear on the screen of my phone – they mean my dad misses me. My dad chooses twelve of the seventeen photos I've posted since the

last time he checked my account, when he sent me heart-shaped, digital smoke signals of affection. I follow his lead, and linger over the five that he (didn't) choose.

A few months ago my mum opened a Facebook account and at first she refused the Friend requests people were sending her; she said that she didn't want to Friend them because she had created the account just to keep an eye on my sister, who had slipped away through the open veins of Latin America, addicted to backpacking. (In the end my sister told me she had not threatened to start begging, as my mother had said, but that she had raised the possibility of selling pancakes on the street in some town in Costa Rica.) There are days when my mum 'likes' the things I share on Facebook, which are few and far between. Recently she shared a link to an article that explained why intelligent people don't have many friends.

8. When he's alone in a room, when he's doing something like getting dressed, shaving, washing the dishes, packing a suitcase or pan-frying something, my husband sings. My husband doesn't generally sing, and to some extent our relationship is based on a mutual abhorrence of music. There are exceptions: in altered states of mind I like to dance. Perhaps a burst of hypomania on the eve of my birthday or a tune by Kesha playing on repeat while I'm making a cake. When I met my husband and he came to pick me up in his car, the radio was always tuned to the same station, a little too loud for my taste. I also like to listen to music in the car. And I need it when I'm working out. Sometimes I get obsessed with a song by Eminem or Cypress Hill and I have to learn the lyrics, which can take me a while. I know the lyrics of all the songs I like by heart. I had nineteen CDs by the Ramones. There are nights when Spotify repeats a playlist of twenty or thirty new-wave tunes from a time when my husband and I didn't know each other. We dance to Babasónicos in the kitchen after we've turned out the lights.

But music annoys us. We have no desire to go to concerts. We can't understand people who go to concerts. We spend a lot of time trying to figure out what enables them to enjoy something like that. When he's doing something alone in a room, my husband sings. He hums different melodies I don't recognize, and when I can't take it any more, when I just have to know, when my curiosity is such that I no longer care about existence, and thus become one of the things in the world that prevent my husband from singing non-stop, I ask him what he's singing. He pauses a moment and says: 'Something or other.' At that moment I almost always understand why he's singing that particular song.

ATTENTI AL CANE

As first-born children, and rational beings, we're offended by the unbridled and anthropomorphizing affection – over the top by any standard – with which three of our four progenitors treat their pets. We analyse their excessive behaviour carefully: we gather irritating proof. We say terrible things like 'The mere act of forgetting that an animal has more in common with an object than with a human being . . .' and then we go to sleep. In the morning I remember that my mother is incapable of loving anything, even a dog. Then it becomes easy to try to withhold judgement, temporarily, until we witness the next outpouring of affection.

DEAD BABIES

The only thing I know about hamsters is that infanticide is habitual among their kind, and they are frequently given to children as gifts.

UNLUCKY MAMMALS

You could say that I never had a childhood: intense gaze, serious expression, more likely to have a conversation or sit thinking in a corner than submit to the taunts of some game. As the oldest I never had the luxury of being silly or weak. My father, just under six foot one, criticizing me from on high when, standing on their bed, I tried to make a joke, counting to ten out of order: that's not *funny*, that's *stupid*. My mother, when I was eight, stopped at a red traffic light on a curve around the Plaza Francia: what mattered to us – to my brother (aged two) and to me – was that she was happy, right?

At nineteen my perspective changed when I became a mother and had a daughter of my own. I had no contact with the woman who gave birth to me from the time I was eighteen until I entered my fourth month of pregnancy, when I was nineteen and a half. Later, when I was twenty-six, we stopped speaking for another ten years or so. During this time she was dead to me and the truth is that I thought very little about her, yet I was reminded of this situation a few times a year when I'd mention her in passing and a friend more fortunate than me would ask sadly if I still hadn't reached out to her. Going through life without a mother was like acknowledging to the world that I was handicapped. Periodically exposing my stump for the person at hand to see whether the injury was due to deep flaws in my own character or my mother's: victim or victimizer? Amputee, cripple, I kept a list of other people's mothers' faults: missing mothers, family stories, statements which made me certain that, in their shoes, I would have been obliged to stop speaking with their mothers as well.

Shortly after turning thirty-six, in the process of re-establishing our relationship, I asked my mother for photos of me and my brother when we were little, so I could copy them. I wanted to show them to my (not-so-little) girl, who had seen very few. I remembered myself dressed as a Hawaiian on the patio of the two-year-olds' room at the same nursery school my daughter later attended: surely it would make her laugh to see me like that, we could see how alike we looked, I could tell her about life before her arrival and, most of all, it was high time I made a serious effort to assemble an archive of my life to date.

It was the day before my husband's birthday, which we celebrated in the evening at home, and after beating around the bush, citing moves, renovations, broken pipes, my mother told me on the phone that she didn't have photos from back then any more. Bewilderment coupled with anger and confusion at this rediscovery: even after years of separation she could still exercise her unalienable right to make me feel like an orphan. Without these aids to memory I felt sick, senile, demented. I found it hard to sleep for days, and, for much longer than that, unless I had a specific task at hand my mind kept returning to this horrible revelation. I thought about the wickedest people in the world, and how it was impossible to imagine anyone capable of such a flagrant betrayal. So heartless.

But for my mother rules don't apply to her and everything she does becomes justifiable. In my desperation I thought of making a long list of all the photos from my childhood I could remember, describing each in careful detail, along with the memories linked to each one. My father, in a green blazer, holding newborn me on our balcony, a few days before he died. Me wearing tartan trousers and a pixie haircut, hugging a stuffed animal the three wise men had brought me on Epiphany. Sitting in a blue and white inflatable boat in the stock reservoir at my grandparents'. Just like in an Adam Levin story, I thought about trying to find all the photos of that unkempt little girl with a Coca-Cola moustache in the background of a Christmas picture in the albums of my aunts, uncles and cousins, a bystander at their birthdays.

I also thought often of insulting and reproaching my mother. I made internal calculations on how much never speaking to her again might affect my libidinal economy. The most important thing to me was not that she acknowledged what she had done, but that she understood the impact of it, the pain and the grief of feeling orphaned. But my mother, like the rest of the world, is full of recriminations for what has been done to her, yet she can't deny that her mother and her childhood existed, and are at her disposal. Before its time, the image of my childhood face is disappearing from memory and from history, just like what happens to most people, once they're dead.

The Days Gone By

GONZALO ELTESCH

Translated by Katherine Rucker

Tout suffocant
Et blême, quand
Sonne l'heure,
Je me souviens
Des jours anciens
Et je pleure

PAUL VERLAINE,
'CHANSON D'AUTOMNE'

I remember my first trip was on a bus like this, too, and that I kept pulling a little black notebook from the back pocket of my jeans to reread the instructions Alberto had given me. After twelve hours, I'd arrive at the main street of a small town, where all the passengers would get off. I'd have to walk two blocks north up that road then find a small yellow bus – I had underlined the word 'yellow' in my notebook – to take me to the lake where the boat would be moored.

That was the beginning. I was eleven years old and excited to spend the summer with my best childhood friend. No, that's not right. That's not how lives begin, much less stories. No, I understood a little later that everything really starts to happen once something breaks, once pain steps in.

I leaned back in my seat, turned off my phone and, in spite of my nerves, fell straight asleep.

I woke up when a ray of sunshine leaked through the curtains and hit my eyes. There was an old man sitting next to me. He nodded hello, I did the same. I settled back in my seat and opened the curtains a bit. It was a clear day, but I could tell from the condensation on the glass just how cold it was outside. I'd arrived. Again. The bus went down a narrow road with rock faces on either side. After a sharp curve, the thin blue line of the sea came into view. It calmed me, or at least left me indifferent. The lake where I was headed was different. It had the strength of the sea, that wildness, but it didn't give me the same peace. It kept me on edge: almost scared, not unhappy.

After a few minutes, the bus turned left and pulled into town. Nothing but a few wooden houses and some cafes and hostels for tourists who'd come to see the lake. It was eight in the morning. I was on time. The man next to me struggled up from his seat and looked for a parcel in the luggage rack. He departed with the same nod as before, went up the aisle and disappeared down the stairwell. This must be the place, I thought. The bus arrived soon after. First stop. About twenty minutes later, the second stop, and everyone piled off. I breathed deeply: the cold air entered me like someone clawing at my insides. I adjusted the straps on my backpack, put my hands in my jacket pockets, and walked towards the yellow bus visible in the distance.

The boat was moored at the jetty. Two iron decks with a white patina. I walked towards the queue of tourists waiting to get on while watching how a small crane arranged containers in the middle of the boat's upper deck. The queue started moving. When it was my turn I told the crewman I was going to Puerto Azul.

– Huh? he asked, seeming uncomfortable.

– I'm going to Puerto Azul, I repeated.

– No one goes there any more, he said.

Then, indifferent, he asked me to wait to one side; he'd deal with me later. I stood there while the tourists passed by armed with cameras; contented people, passing through. When the last one got on the boat, the crewman came over.

– I'm going to talk with the captain, don't move.

I didn't move. I'd felt this before, when I was just a kid, this shame of not understanding, of having arrived in an unfamiliar place.

– Where'd you say you're going?

I recognized the captain. Fatter, grey, same tone of voice, dry. He'd scared me when I was younger. He didn't seem to recognize me.

– Puerto Azul, I said.

– Is someone expecting you?

He knew they were: no one goes to Puerto Azul unless someone is expecting them.

– Leave your backpack on the deck next to the lifeboats, and don't wander off.

– Thanks.

– It's time to go. And careful getting up on the boat. If you fall in, we're not taking you again.

I smiled. Everything repeated in slow motion.

– What's in the containers? I dared to ask.

– The containers? Supplies for the people on the lake, fruit, vegetables . . . you really don't know?

I couldn't answer, because that's when the captain clapped me on the shoulder and said goodbye. The crewman invited me to get on. I left my backpack next to the lifeboats on the deck, then looked for a seat. It hadn't been more than five minutes when I heard a loud noise. The boat was pulling away.

Over the loudspeaker, they told us about islands, channels, giant trees, live but dormant volcanos. The boat moved slowly; it was hard to even tell you were cruising, that there were metres and metres of pure water beneath you.

I took my phone out and turned it on. Seven missed calls, all from Isabel. I should have called her when I got into town. Emilia would already be awake, eating breakfast in our bed with the television on. Breadcrumbs on the sheets, her smile dotted with blackberry jam. Isabel would smile and tell her that Papa was on a trip; she'd explain it to her calmly. She had all the answers, sometimes she had too many. By now, I imagine, she'd be thinking that this trip was all her fault, that I'd gone off without enough of an explanation.

The foghorn sounded and a slight rocking signalled that we were slowing down. The landscape had turned bleak.

I followed the crewman to the deck. It was raining and the wind was strong. That's the south for you, I thought. Clouds and rain, lots of rain. But I could see a launch moving towards us. Alberto. It had to be him. I looked for my backpack, went to the port side and got ready to disembark. I could hear the sound of the motor getting closer and closer. I pulled my phone out of my pocket and looked at the screen. When I got to Puerto Azul there wouldn't be a signal.

– Ready? asked the crewman as he opened the metal grille that served as a door.

Alberto reached out to take my backpack. Once I was on the launch I put on my life jacket and sat in the stern. I turned around to say goodbye to the crewman but he was already gone; all I could make out was the tourists' faces still pressed to the glass.

85

Alberto was thin, almost skeletal. He wore an old T-shirt that showed his firm arms covered in cuts and injuries. His face was gaunt, his skin leathery from the sun, and a long chestnut beard fell ragged down to his chest. He wasn't the same any more; neither was I.

As we advanced, the rhythm of the waves was constant, little uniform pitches, water in motion. I looked at the lake, blue, so blue that it was hard to believe we were approaching land. He kept his eyes low. His deep, black eyes. And the memory came back suddenly: the grey beach, the jetty that was no more than a pair of thick logs to disembark onto, Alberto's family waving at us. Back then his grandfather had been the one sailing the wooden boat, and a twelve-year-old Alberto waited for us on the land next to his grandmother, his mother and his sister, who'd appeared out of nowhere, running, excited for my arrival. María Paz. Our María Paz. The guilt that doesn't disappear with time.

Back in the present, I rubbed my eyes; tears were blocking my view. Alberto cut the motor and let momentum do the rest of the work. We'd arrived, everything so similar, so identical. But not. Alberto got out of the boat and tied the rope to an old tree trunk thrown on the beach. Then, as if I didn't exist, he started walking towards the house rising in the distance.

– Why'd you ask me to come back? I asked him.

He turned around, looked at me and came closer. The punch landed on my left cheek, but got my nose too. I was bleeding.

– Get out of the boat, the storm's coming, he said and kept walking.

I looked for the handkerchief in my pocket, covered my nose and followed him.

FROM THE NOVELLA *THE DAYS GONE BY*

Dead Hares

DIEGO ERLAN

Translated by Sam Gordon

A girl arrives in a town. She's by herself. It's midday. She's wearing a grey tank top and canvas shoes, and her hair is clinging to her forehead. It's completely still. Ten minutes earlier she got off the bus as though she had just woken up. Holding a bag in her left hand, she looks one way and the next, then walks into the bus terminal's cafe. She orders a fizzy drink before leaving by the glass door and heading to the toilets. The camera zooms in and follows her as she eyes the water puddled in the corners. There's a line of cubicles with metal doors. She opens one after the other until she finds a piece of toilet paper in the last one. She leaves her bag on the floor next to the bottle, pulls down her trousers and pants in one and sits on the toilet. She realizes her arms are sweaty. As the girl tries to piss, she scans the messages written in pencil, until she notices, in a corner of this, the last cubicle of these shitty toilets, another pair of white pants, scrunched up in a ball and stained with blood.

That's how it starts. In the next shot, we see the empty terminal. As the camera pans round we see the girl leave the toilets in the same tank top, with the same trousers and the bag now over her shoulder. Her hair is wet. The girl looks at the camera. On the other side of the road, a man is waiting for her.

'Who's this guy?'

'This guy's her father.'

She's still naked and buzzing as she looks at him in the gloomy bedroom. His arms are behind his head and his eyes are lost in the ceiling.

'Are you asleep?'

'How can I be asleep if my eyes are open.'

'Sometimes people can sleep with their eyes open. Or they open them once they're asleep.'

'Sure they do. What happens next?'

The van with the girl and the father in it stops outside a hut with a sign that reads *Atlantis Foods*. The father says he won't be long and tells her to stay in the van. When the man gets out and walks towards the store, she spots a long-eared hare in the distance. It's strangely white against the desert-like landscape and stares at her with that sinister look that white hares have. Right then, she feels the seat belt digging into her breasts, constricting her breathing and crushing her. She needs to escape it so she opens the door and disobeys the father. The hare scurries inside the hut. Some red and yellow plastic strips cover the doorway and through them she can see a pot coming to the boil on a gas cooker. The master bed, propped up by crates of beer, blends in with the fridges and the plasma TV and the computer where a ten-year-old boy is playing *Doom*. The gunshots and explosions are as artificial as the mood lighting that comes courtesy of the bricked-up windows. The father is sweating, as is the character standing there in nothing but a pair of shorts. You're just in time – I'm defrosting it now, he says as he pulls a piece of greyish meat from the fridge. This is my last one, he adds, giving the slab a pat before putting it on the plastic scales. One kilo four hundred.

She sits up and asks if he wants something to eat. He says he does and tries to pinch her bum, but she moves out the way and picks up her bra from the floor with her toes. Meanwhile she fills him in on the conversation she had with her daughter the day before. She wants to invite a boyfriend from school for a sleepover. So she suggested buying a mattress, maybe one of those blow-up ones: That way you can invite any girlfriends or boyfriends over and they can sleep on the floor.

Why the floor? the child replied.

Guests can't sleep in the same bed as us, she had explained.

Why? the girl wanted to know in return, and she hadn't known what to say to that.

'Don't you see?' she says in a low voice before opening the door. 'She's five. Five. What was I supposed to say? But that wasn't all. A few seconds later she turned to me and said: What about you? When are you going to get someone round to stay the night? I froze. Where did she get that from?'

'She must have overheard it somewhere.'

'It got worse: I want you to bring that guy from the other day to stay over.'

'She seriously said that?'

'No word of a lie. How much did you pay her?' Isabel laughs, crawling towards him and sitting on his now limp, blood-stained prick. 'I want you to bring him here for the night and make him your boyfriend, the little brat said. I want you to get pregnant. She's five and somehow she knew; and she said to me: Fuck, Mummy, fuck like the world's about to end.'

'No way she said that. She probably just wants a little brother, like most other five-year-olds want a toy.'

She puts his flaccid cock in her pussy but when he starts getting hard, she stands up and says I don't know, look, I don't know, but I feel like you two are playing some kind of trick on me.'

And then she says:

'You like screwing me this way, don't you?'

The girl who arrived in the town by herself is sleeping in a storeroom for tools, bolts and screws. Everything is covered in dust. At the back are some sacks giving off a nauseating stench. Nobody can see, but inside there are hares that have been shot.

'Why?'

'Why what?'

'The dead hares. I don't get that part.'

She explains that the father is living with a new wife and how they had a son ten years after she'd been born. They live in a town in the middle of the countryside where the father spends his time shooting hares. People pay five pesos per hare. The new wife can't bear the daughter from the first wife, who she calls a mad, low-life piece of shit.

At some point, as if to celebrate the visit, they head out to the town's only bar. It's called Mónaco. The father says hello to the man behind the bar who shows them to a certain table, even though the place is empty. The wife asks how her hair is and the girl replies: Hard to tell you've hardly got any left.

Why are you always so mean to me? the woman asks, what did I ever do to you? The girl shrugs and links arms with the brother as they make their way to the table in the middle of the room. She doesn't like that one – she'd rather be next to the window so she can look out over the square. When he joins them, the father says that the man he was talking to is the boss and he was glad to see her all grown-up and beautiful, and that if she'd come alone he would have given her a drink on the house.

The girl doesn't answer and just gazes at the window.

When she comes back to bed she says the food's still not ready, gives him a kiss, then asks why he got so angry the night before.

'Me?'

'Yeah, you. You had a sore head and when you've got a sore head you get angry about stuff. I know you.'

'Maybe.'

'So why?'

'Dunno. Maybe because I heard you talking to someone and afterwards you wouldn't tell me who it was.'

'That was why?'

Silence bursts into the room.

'You're a baby, baby. It was nothing. It was my half-brother.'

Music is blaring out from the CD player sitting next to the bare mattress. Life is one long song with changing melodies, the girl says. Until the disc gets scratched. The brother points out the flies on the other side of the window. Lying there face down, she turns her head and says maybe the world has started rotting. Then she looks back and loosens her trousers because they're cutting into her tummy. She asks if the mother's there.

The brother shakes his head. Then he looks at her and says: Here, have this T-shirt.

It's a black T-shirt that says *Ramones* in white letters.

She raises her eyebrows, acting all surprised.

It's a present, the boy says. It's good to see you.

She can't accept his favourite T-shirt. Then she adds that she likes the smell of his sweat.

The brother, still standing next to the window, doesn't take his eyes off the girl.

How many wanks do you have a day? she asks suddenly.

The brother hesitates. Someone yells in the wasteland outside and she switches questions: Ever wanked about me?

The brother looks down again and says: Yesterday, when you got here.

She smiles, then turns on the TV. The brother goes back to look- ing at the flies. The channels flip past until she settles on a scene where a horse is dying in a fantasy swamp.

How's that film going, the one you were talking about? the brother wants to know, and she purses her lips: You liked it, didn't you? Anyway. They're not boyfriend and girlfriend, they just fuck every now and again. At some point that night, the girl says:

'Am I hurting you?'

He looks at her, imploring. Then she starts talking again.

'You'll leave me, I know you will.'

He doesn't say anything and she gets up from the bed, struggles with her pants, then goes to the kitchen. She opens the oven door and then shuts it again.

'Why would I leave you?' he asks when she comes back to the bedroom and switches on the lights to find her skirt.

'Because I'm hurting you. That's why.'

It's always the same thing. They've spoken about it before. One day she or he will meet someone else, and how are they meant to know what that might become – a casual fuck, a friendship with sex, a half-open relationship, something that might give way to a less unconventional friendship, a more relaxed, more simple pairing between a man and a woman, without all the twists and turns.

'Maybe,' she says.

'Maybe,' he says back. 'Have you been with other people?'

She raises an eyebrow.

'What does it matter to you?'

'Have you or not? It's not a hard question.'

'I'm not saying.'

'That's worse.'

She sighs, then eventually says:

'Nothing. It's stupid.'

'I want to know.'

'It was just curiosity.'

'Curiosity about what?'

'We'd never done it. Look, it's not important. We both wanted it and now the mystery's over. Both of us have gone our own way.'

'So why won't you tell me if you know I want to know?'

'Because I was ashamed of it. That's why. Now that's enough.'

'Who was it?'

She tells him that he already knows.

'What was it like, then?'

'Please, I told you I don't want to talk about it,' she says abruptly. 'Tonight I just want to be happy. We were happy before.'

She leaves the room again. The lights of the passing cars suddenly illuminate the bed and he sits up to look for the trousers he'd left on the chair behind the desk. There are papers, a computer, pencils and an open notebook. He reads: *I don't know where everyone's gone. The flies are gathering at the windows and the girl is sleeping in a tiny room filled with bags. Hares? I'm not sure. It smells. There's something festering in every childhood.*

The Year of the Black Sun

DANIEL FERREIRA

Translated by Catherine Mansfield

THE TOWN THAT SMELLED OF WARM ROOFTOPS

Soon it will be night, where anyone can hide. It is a white town, attacked by erosion. Square blocks of streets lined with *macana* palm posts supporting telegraph wires where pigeons keep watch, and straight stone roads with a gutter along the middle for the rainwater to run down. Three hundred dazzling houses that smell of warm rooftops and look out on what will one day be the bottom of the sea. It will be night soon.

I'm leaving.

I'll die far from this place, where nobody knows my name.

The man is named after his stepfather.

He does not like his name.

THE LAST CARRIAGE

You ride away from the town in the open chaise pulled by the knock-kneed, mottled horse. It is the last Berlin carriage you will drive for an employer; the last you will see in your life, although you do not know that. Today you will return it to its owners, wealthy people from the other side of the walls built stone by stone by swarms of labourers, flaying the skin from their hands, shattering their fingernails between heavy rocks, exhausting themselves into hernias that inflamed their testicles and scalded their groins.

They worked for the local fat cats: *Conservative, rich and tight-fisted*, he thinks.

How do ants come to an agreement?

FENCED-IN HORSES

You call the horse Don Emilio and he lets you lead him by your hand and you know that he will miss you when he is locked away in the stable for days without anybody coming to take him out. He will buck with desperation and neigh and kick and turn round and round in circles and open his eyes extremely wide as if he knows something terrible is coming. And you will miss him too, because when a man spends a long time alone he can feel just like a horse.

You, who miss nobody, now believe that you will miss a poor, scrawny horse fed on guava fruit and green couch-grass.

Slavery is a habit too.

Is that why he will miss his miserable daily wage?

And what about the *mazamorra*, the bowl of milk and maize he used to eat almost guiltily with the other workers, hidden away at the table at the back of the kitchen at the hacienda to spare the master's daughter and partners the embarrassment of hearing the clicking of their palates, of seeing them swallow and slurp and belch?

THE AVENUE BETWEEN THE STONE WALLS

The four o'clock sun was golden, glossy as a ripe *lulo* fruit, and it cast heat and shadows over the town, stretching them out until they slipped inside the houses. The Berlin carriage passed by the dentist's clinic, the corner shops with foreign names, the barber's, a market crammed with orange-coloured pineapples, a ceramics stall selling stacks of clay pots, a sign that said 'I buy old gold' and the seedy bars selling cheap liquor. Further on, the main street swung north through a wide passage of flattened, yellowish land dotted with peeling buildings with straw roofs, before unfolding onto a vast stony avenue with a gutter running through the middle, surrounded by lime-whitened villas separated by stone and adobe walls. It was the widest street in town, created so that the few Berlin carriages that still existed in those days could pass by comfortably with their cargos of perfumed flesh.

You ride on with the sun falling on your left shoulder. The afternoon in three shades of red, amber and pearl stings your eyes. You will miss the animal troughs, the damp, earthy smell of warm clay, the stone walls, the tiled water tanks, the electricity arches, the waterwheel on the river, the weathervane rocked by the wind, the silos carved into the earth to store corn, barley and wheat. You will miss the perfumed blossoming of the orange grove, the insect green of the tobacco plants, the indolent sun that casts your shadow and that of the horse and the Berlin carriage and makes them slide like ghosts across that wall, which reveals its undergarments stitched in adobe and mortar. Just like that. A single moment.

What is it that still ties you to all this?

All that is here today will be gone tomorrow.

All that you see is not what it seems.

There is only you and these thoughts that you express to no one.

FAREWELL AT THE WATERING TROUGH

The carriage enters by the stone road, passes the orange trees and pulls up outside the stable. This time he does not walk straight to the door of the mansion, but instead begins uncoupling Don Emilio right there, in the place where each evening he finishes his working day as a common coachman.

Before the boss arrives to ask why he did not turn up for work, Don Emilio needs to be washed, his harnesses organized and hung from the hook, and put out to graze beside the watering trough.

He takes a wooden bucket, fills it with water from the tank and washes the animal down with a brush, while the horse frightens away flies by twitching his tail, rippling his hide and slowly lifting and lowering his hoof over and over again.

Yes, you will miss his flared nostrils that sniff you when you stroke him and the velvety softness of his long jaw.

After the bath he will lead the animal from the stable to the grassland and let him loose so he can feed.

Don Emilio tears away at the grass in search of ripe guava fruit that he will grind between his soft lips. He finds one. He bites it. Then he swings his head around and watches him from a distance, flicking his mane.

Goodbye. *Au revoir*, as the boss's daughter used to say before she went mad. And the horse whinnies and breaks into a run.

A discreet, familiar farewell, like that of a bird who hops onto your back to pull out a parasite: the mutual friendship between two companions who will never see each other again.

Then the horse swings his rump around and continues searching for guavas in the grass.

STABLE-BOY

Then the boss appeared in the stable. He is a sturdy, hard-faced man, accustomed to dealing with angry labourers, quick to resort to blows or strong words.

'I've been waiting for you,' he said.

He looked away and thought about the wasted hours he had spent that day watching people passing by while he waited for Duque at Inés's bar. It was as if he could still see him striding in suddenly with his raucous laugh, greeting everybody loudly, looking for him and then coming over and settling himself down on the bench, inviting him to ask if he had any news of Rosario Díaz.

'Nobody knows anything,' Duque replies, knocking back the shot of liquor that the landlady has handed him. 'Last night he passed through Lebrija, but today he might as well be up in the mountains as on the Chicamocha river or arriving at Matanza. Have you told them you're quitting yet?'

'No. When are we leaving?' he asks.

'The day after tomorrow. If that old bastard pays you, I suggest you buy yourself some boots.'

'What about a horse?'

'Forget the horse. Nobody wants to sell them. What we need is weapons. Rosario Díaz won't take volunteers without weapons. This is going to be a long war, as long as a week without meat.'

The landlady stops in front of the men to wipe the counter with an oily cloth and Duque stops talking.

She pours them coffee from a pot and walks away.

'What happened to the others?'

'They lost their nerve.'

He thought how the afternoon had seemed to drag on forever. He thought about Duque's restless fingers shaking a cup and tipping out some dice made of human knee bones for playing jacks.

He thought about the bird-like laughter of the landlady, Inés, who spoke at the top of her voice and flirted with every customer who walked into her bar. He thought about the endless cups of coffee he had drunk while he waited and how his eyelid had started to twitch uncontrollably.

Then he replied to his boss:

'I don't work here any more.'

For a moment he thought that he could look him in the eye and tell him the truth, free himself of his wounds, of the years he had served this man barefooted, his hands blistered by the hard labour of plastering adobe walls with clay and donkey shit when he was eight years old, until his hands became calloused and his boss made him work as a horse tamer at thirteen and a Berlin carriage stable-boy at fifteen, not because he wanted it but because his daughter wanted her own chauffeur at her beck and call. He thought about saying 'the age of slavery is over' and 'service is now voluntary', as Duque had suggested he could do that afternoon at the bar.

And why don't I say it? The question rose in smoke signals inside of him, as he realized that his mind had prepared everything he wanted to say but his mouth stayed quiet and his hands burned and the unexpected heat made his ears ring. *He knows it already, but he's playing the fool.*

He had been waiting all day for that moment, when he would say goodbye to a boss he had been tied to for years. But now that it was happening, there was no explanation to give. The ideas were not materializing into words.

'Well, fine. If you want to throw it all away then go ahead and fight amongst yourselves like the good-for-nothing Indians. Let's go to my office,' old Lausen said.

And they walked into the mansion, one behind the other.

From a window, the housemaid was watching them.

PORTRAIT OF A GRANDFATHER WITH A GOITRE

On the wall hangs a painting of great-grandfather Lausen, with his goitre, long moustache, spiderish eyebrows and dense sideburns. A rectangular table with places for twelve people stands on the raised floor of the dining room, and there is a full-length mirror where he can glimpse the scrawny figure of the housemaid, dressed in a cap and apron, awaiting the boss's orders.

As she becomes aware of the eyes watching her from a distance, the woman glares back at him, accusingly. Her grimace conceals a silent question: *Where were you, you fool? We're all in the doghouse because of you.*

He looks away.

The boss orders coffee without even looking up.

The servant bows her head and goes to the kitchen. Out of the boss's sight, her movements become rougher; she bashes and clanks the pans and dishes in an outburst of indignation aimed at the guilty party responsible for the boss's bad mood.

Then she returns and demonstrates her barely contained rage in the way she serves the coffee, letting it spill out from the cup to the saucer.

'Unbelievable,' says the boss, extracting a hair from his cup. 'Just leave it and go and wash your hair. Your head looks worse than a mop.'

The woman turns around and walks away, smoothing down the hair escaping from her cap.

'Come and sit down so we can talk about this.'

The boss rummages inside a wardrobe with mirrored doors. Next to his rifles he finds a wooden chest secured with a shabby-looking iron padlock. Then he comes back to the table, opens a black leather notebook, does some quick calculations and asks:

'Are you going to want the horse?'

'Don Emilio?'

'As part of your payment. I would estimate he's worth twenty pesos, because he's old, and I don't need him, since people will even kill you for a horse these days.'

You will miss his muzzle, his black eyes ringed with white, his ears that twitched as if they understood you.

'No. I need the cash.'

The boss takes five gold coins and fifteen banknotes out of the chest.

The coffee is smouldering, black and unsweetened, burnt and bitter, as if has been mixed with powdered beetles and deliberately left to boil over. He takes two sips and puts the cup aside.

Before paying him, the boss asks if it's bad.

'Is what bad?'

'The coffee.'

'No,' he says. 'It's fine.'

'Drink it. A war without coffee is not a war.'

The boss's request catches him by surprise. Without thinking, he lifts his cup and drinks the last mouthful. A drop runs down his chin and leaves its mark on his pale shirt. The coffee is so hot that it flays the walls of his throat on its way down.

The boss, who no longer has any of his bottom teeth, takes a sip from his cup and sucks in his lower lip when he feels the sting.

'Unbelievable! Just what you expect from these miserable old-timers.'

In between sips, the boss asks if he is sure about what he is doing.

'Hand on heart,' he says. 'I'm leaving.'

'Who are you going with?'

He could have asked 'where are you going?' or 'why are you quitting?' But, no.

'Who are you going with?'

'With Rosario Díaz.'

'I knew it! You let him get to you!'

If he knew, why did he ask?

'Do you know what? I don't give a shit. The time for prayers is over, boy. If I see you on my property one day with a weapon I'll have to put a bullet through your head.'

Or I might have to do the same to you.

From the painting on the wall, the grandfather watches them with his ball of flesh on his neck.

FROM THE UNPUBLISHED NOVEL *THE YEAR OF THE BLACK SUN*, THE FOURTH PART OF THE PENTALOGY OF COLOMBIA

The Southward March

CARLOS FONSECA

Translated by Megan McDowell

1.

At times, in the landscape's crowded calm, the only sound is the camera as it flashes. For that brief instant all that exists is him, the camera, and the impression that will be left to a future he still doesn't know, but on which he has bet it all. For that brief instant, nothing exists but him and his belief. Him and his future. Then, subtly, he is interrupted by that quick sonata that returns him to the middle of the jungle: the background sound of the roiling tropics, the cacophony of birds, the fluttering of uncaged chickens, the snore of a tired native, the hiccup of some drunken Englishman. Still further off, in a terribly singular and painful space, the sobs of the daughter whose plaints he only now hears again.

Only then does he take his eye from the camera and look at her.

Barely ten years old, she has an insomniac's heavy gaze and a terrible paleness that makes him think of Nordic latitudes he's never seen. Beside the girl, a thoroughly beautiful woman uses a left hand he knows well to soothe the girl's sobs. With her other hand, his wife labours over notes she makes in a small, reddish leather notebook. The same notebook in which she had written,

ten days earlier: 'Day 1, beginning of the trip.' Ten days since that inaugural meeting, and already the trip is starting to seem drawn out, weighty, routine. Ten days since a rusted-out bus left them on the threshold of what they now tentatively call jungle, but that at times seems like nothing more than a giant garbage dump dreamed up by an absent god.

The grunting rumble of a pig as it delves back into the garbage distracts him. And then he sees the panorama in its totality: the couple of drunken Brits on a corner finishing off the bottle of gold rum, the atmosphere of lethargy and siesta over which nature's everyday tyranny seems to loom, the drugged-out German again staging his monologue for a group of natives who, laughing, seem to enjoy the show. The rest of the pilgrims sporadically punctuate the scene of that brief comedy, resting under small tin roofs where the last drops of water drum monotonously. And beyond, in a background plane presaged by a faint soundtrack, a man with tired eyes and unusual strength returns to his indecipherable prayer. Ten days have passed since this same man, with his rough voice and unplaceable accent, promised them that at month's end they would reach the little seer.

2.

They call him the apostle. His arms are tattooed with allegories of war, and over a dozen plastic rosaries hang around his neck. His voice is hoarse but withdrawn. His speech has something of the delusional monologue about it, a private and endless prayer with which he fills out the empty hours. Just looking at him, it's clear he's not from here. *Gringo maldito*, the natives call him behind his back: the cursed gringo. He, meanwhile, refuses to say a word to them. Even so, everywhere he goes, five of them go with him. It's rumoured that he came to find drugs and stayed when he found the trip back was impossible. It's rumoured he comes from a moneyed family, and that when he was young he showed promise in theatre. It's rumoured that illumination came to him decades ago in the midst of the jungle, in front of that immense tree he claims to be guiding them towards. They call him the apostle because that's what he calls himself, but sometimes, when they look at him, the pilgrims have the feeling he's no more than a tour guide, a drugged Virgil on an absurd pilgrimage. A postmodern Virgil for credulous gringos. Still, all it takes is a second look, or just listening to him, immersed in his endless prayer, to know that he, at least, believes he is everything he's promised. Around him, three stinking pigs meander through the mud, while further on the natives play cards to win out over boredom. All of them wear shirts with gringo brands, and the ironic expressions of unbelievers. They call him the apostle because he promises things. Ten days ago he promised them, for example, that at the end of a month they would come to an enormous archipelago in the middle of the jungle, and that there, at the foot of an enormous fallen tree, the seer will show them the way. In his eyes, halfway between belief and madness, an entire era plays its hand.

Ten days have passed since they set off on foot, five since the little girl started to get sick. The whole time, the jungle has done nothing but contradict their expectations. Where they supposed they'd find naked natives, instead there are men wearing rock-band T-shirts. Where they expected to find the exuberance of nature, there are garbage dumps. Where they thought they'd find the absence of power, there is the omnipresence of the State. Everywhere they go they encounter police, solemn border agents who fight boredom by assiduously checking travel documents. Far from being the dreamed-of garden, the jungle is trying its best to show its most modern face: its ruinous, border-town face.

And nevertheless, they well know: nature is there, latent like a sleeping scorpion. They sense it at night, in the utter darkness that envelops them. They hear it before they see it: in the whisper of nocturnal animals, in the fluttering fowl, the croak of those frogs that seem like nocturnal birds, the murmur of the insects always poised to wage war against the mosquito net. He, however, has been brought along specifically to make nature visible: they've asked him, as a photographer, to document the trip. That's his place: halfway between participation and observation, halfway between belief and irony. Only five years earlier, he had earned a living taking photos of Broadway's most coveted models. Today, he is following a man who has promised an impossible thing. Two years ago he earned his living taking pictures of the most visible figures in showbusiness, and today he is chasing behind a drugged man's invisible dream.

3.

During the day, they cross villages full of sleeping natives and women who kill the hours in infinite conversations. Villages lost in the jungle, wrapped in the climbing vines of tedium. Insomniac villages where the men just watch them with utter indifference as they go by, as if the pilgrims have been invisible for a long time now. Indifference, the private form of contempt. They cross entire villages where they find only ruins of the peace they'd all thought they would find. On the third day, they understand that in these forgotten cities, tedium is the rule. In them, peace lies in the image of a mother who diligently whiles away her hours removing lice from the hair of a dozen sleepy children. They cross scenes of tedium with the distinctive steps of those still seeking something. The natives recognize them, and with a mocking gaze, let them pass. They cross the day like that, one village to the next, until the afternoon finds them and they stop in a place where the drunks seem jollier, and the tedium ebbs away. In those villages, they're ushered in with greedy eyes, since the natives know that at the end of the day, that's what these strange men bring: money. Then the hustle begins. Some policeman who gets up from his drunken stupor or chronic exhaustion to ask for their entry papers, his sole idea to interrupt these strange men's passage. The apostle, however, they don't touch. And that's the odd thing. How in these villages, too, the apostle seems to radiate an aura that makes him untouchable. They all present their papers and then he, beyond reach and age-old, crosses the scene as if he were the very leader of the tribe. He crosses the scene and disappears into the village, while the rest of the pilgrims return to their most vulgar pastimes, alcohol or drugs, yoga or prayer, sleep or sex.

And that's how they spend the day until the sun sets, when the apostle emerges from his penance and finally raises his voice in supplication. Usually he is accompanied by an indigenous woman, much younger than him, who takes care of feeding the fire's arabesques. And they all gather there around the night-time fire, waiting for the apostle to pronounce the first words. Sometimes hours can pass. Long minutes when the man refuses to say a word and during which only the moths fluttering over the fire can be heard. Sometimes hours can pass and he says nothing, but there they are, united by a dark belief, gathered around the fire of an unknown passion. It's a strange group they form. Drugged Europeans, Americans with shaved heads, Central European women with long braids who smile happily when they see the natives go by, young girls whose faces bear the traces of a tired illusion. Frayed shirts, one or another face painted, plastic rosaries and candles lit to saints. A great sect of tired men, credulous hippies who, as the evening falls, gather in an insomniac country to imagine a different world. And there, among the stinking pigs and the third-world garbage, there *they* are: an everyday family – father, mother, daughter – lost in an immense version of jungle, waiting for the prayers of a man whose arms bear tattoos of an inconclusive story: cataclysm and fire and a great tree amid a false landscape. They, however, believe. And that belief drives them to wait a little longer, to seek out the keys of the dazed monologue the apostle takes up again day after day, as soon as the sunset opens the way for night.

There they are, a postcard family – deluxe, straight out of a magazine – inscribed into the jungle. They, the same ones who five years earlier had appeared in all the fashion rags, the same ones who one day decided to shake off fame and delve into the labyrinths of pagan beliefs. They have managed to get rid of fame, to wrap themselves in the anonymity that the jungle confers, but they haven't been able to divest themselves of another, much more primitive layer that is beauty. That's why, while the pilgrims are congregated before the fire awaiting the apostle's words, as if hushing to hear the oracle, they shine like stars in an opaque constellation. A beautiful family, a model family, wrapped in a crepuscular world.

Maybe that's why when the apostle starts to talk, he begins by looking at them. He lets out a slight word that he leaves swinging in the air, and his eyes land on that girl with chestnut hair and dark eyes who now coughs again as she leans, with a shyness that seems ingrained, behind her mother. The girl has her mother's fragile elegance and her father's hushed conviction. And like that, looking at the girl who tries to hide behind her mother, looking at her as if his words were directed at her, the apostle begins his sermon. With his naked torso facing the flames, the fire lighting up that impressive tattooed torso, he speaks of a final storm in the jungle, a last whirlwind that will reduce everything to a single point. He speaks of endings and he cites, with a fluency far removed from his usual silence, the sacred scriptures. He finally takes his gaze from the girl, and with his eyes fixed on the fire he speaks of islands and prisons, of underground worlds and millenary disasters. Then he returns to his prayer, the pilgrims around him listening patiently, immersed in a belief that seems to devour everything in its path. He speaks in his invocation of a great fallen tree and a small seer, and his face takes on an unusual expressiveness, a terrible happiness that has something of madness in it. Then, the indigenous woman who has spent the afternoon with him brings a little bottle, and the apostle drinks something. After a few minutes his eyes become flexible, and his gaze is lost beyond the fire. Only then does his laughter begin, an enormous peal that rings out in the night. Then the pilgrims, on seeing him laugh, laugh too. They laugh as men rarely do, without reason or direction to speak of, while the night grows, fearful, cold, distant, around that ten-year-old girl who now coughs again like one interrupting a party.

FROM THE NOVEL *ANIMAL MUSEUM*

Lid / 1981

DAMIÁN GONZÁLEZ BERTOLINO

Translated by Lily Meyer

My first memory is like a graft.

When I was a year and a half old, I almost died. The story is one of my family's central myths, even now that my family has fallen apart. None of its members see each other much, and it's been over a decade since we all ate a meal at one table. But what we once were is still present, the way the sun is present for blind men who can't see its light, just feel its warmth on their faces.

The centre of the story is my mother, aged nineteen, alone in a house where she's rarely alone. She's holding me by my ankles with one hand, pounding my back with the other. I hang there naked, bruise-coloured, unable to cry. The only noise I can make is tiny, the sound of two consonants crushed together, *C* and *J*, *cjj*, *ccjj*, *cccjjjj*. Blood and spit run over my top lip, into my nose and eyes. The liquid smears my forehead like some horrible baptism, then thickens into a long strand of blood that swings between my body and the floor. It's a hot morning in November. My mother is eight months pregnant, and she's reached the limit of what her body can take. Her left arm is numb from my weight, but she can't change sides; she's right-handed, and she needs her good hand to hit me with as much speed, strength and aim as she can, which, she's just realized, is almost none. She's about to collapse. She's going to hit me one last time – there has to be a last time, she's just realized that too, and that *last* could be fatal. The question is how to find the right moment, the exact right conditions for her to gather up the rest of her strength and hit me so hard that I come back to life.

Now the sequence rolls back. I can't stop it from rewinding, restarting, repeating like one of those elusive dreams we never remember completely . . . The scene hasn't changed. My mother is getting ready to hit me for the last time. But it's hard to picture what comes next. The conditions she needs are impossible for me to remember, or to conjure. What I need can only be found in a place we could call the peripheral vision of memory, and even there, it's hidden by the scrim of other people's tellings. Other people: my mother, my father. My own memory doesn't count; it's not mine. It's like a borrowed suit, one that fits in some places, pulls and sags in others.

The house where this happened is in Montevideo, in the Nuevo París neighbourhood. It's the house where my mother was born, where my grandfather lived after he and my grandmother parted ways. My grandfather, Ángel Bertolino, died in that house at the end of the eighties.

But this was 1981, a hot spring morning, and my mother was home alone, changing my nappy. My father had left for work early that morning; he'd finally found a job on a construction site. My grandfather was gone too. The scene I'm describing was absolutely ordinary, one my mother had repeated over and over since I was born. She laid me down on my back so she could begin. In those days disposable nappies were hard to come by, and so she started by unwinding the strips of cloth she used to make my nappies. Nothing unusual, totally routine, but our routines blind us to tragedy, or else tragedy likes to hide in routine. When my mother talks about that morning, she always makes space for how normal it was. 'It was a morning like any other,' she'll say. 'I was changing your nappy, as usual.' Everything as usual, until the moment I reached for the lid of the nappy-rash cream (the famous Dr Selby's), wrapped it in my fist, and shoved it into my mouth.

Parents always move too slowly in moments like this. It doesn't matter how smart they are, or how agile. They're slow, and later they remember how slow they were, how inattentive and careless, even if it's not true, even if they weren't careless for a second. The stories always become stories of carelessness, and the more the parents relive them, the faster the children move. The poor parents are trapped in the memory, where they're eternally stupid and slow, and where the children become so fast they're unstoppable.

According to my mother, there was a moment when nothing happened. It took my tongue a moment to understand that the ridged thing in my mouth was small enough to lift to my palate, or maybe a moment for my throat to contract enough to get it down. But by the time my mother got her fingers into my mouth, it was too late. The lid was gone.

'I don't know what I was thinking,' she repeats on the phone. She's crying now. But imagine a lid that large, and a child that small. How could he swallow it? There's no way, or almost none, that the lid will get past his trachea. But it can get stuck there, between his larynx and his oesophagus, and that's enough for him to asphyxiate. All he can do to prevent it is cough.

My mother lifted me by my ankles with one hand and hit the middle of my back with the other. Nothing happened. Saliva welled between my lips. She burst from my room, shouting for help, but my father was at work, my grandfather and uncle had gone out, and the various grandchildren and cousins who often dropped by were nowhere to be found. My mother ran through the house, across the patio. She never stopped hitting me. (Sentences float into my head now, promising, It's all right not to tell the whole story. Not all the way, beginning to end. It's enough to describe the scene with all your senses, to get the image right . . . *My body became the tongue of a bell, swinging between its invisible walls, tolling the sound of death.*) My face turned red, then purple. Spit flooded my palate, ran down my cheeks, dripped to the tiles, hung in ribbons around my mother's legs as she carried me through the patio and onto the street, that street called then, and still called, Triunfo.

By then it was clear I was dying. I'd run out of air. My mother was preparing to hit me one last time. She didn't know why it was the last, only that it had to be, that she had to hit me so hard it would hurt me badly if I lived, so hard that if I died, she would know she couldn't have stopped it. But she was so tired. She was eight months pregnant with a daughter who, the doctors said, wouldn't be born healthy. A few months ago, while my mother was pregnant, I'd had rubella, and that had put her at risk. So I wasn't the only child whose life my mother feared for as she prepared to hit me, praying that I would vomit the lid out. She must have been thinking of my sister, but it's difficult to put her thoughts into words. I don't want to say what could have happened, or to be wrong, or unfair or unkind.

But after all, miracles, big ones and small ones (and isn't *small miracle* an oxymoron, anyway?) come from our bodies, don't they? What happens, or stops happening, inside us so that we can become greater than ourselves? Let's say, for the sake of the story, that two oxygen molecules collided inside my mother, attached themselves to some blood cell, and travelled down just the right capillary to just the right membrane, and let's say this happened at the exact moment when my mother hit me for the last time. 'I hit you so hard! I couldn't believe it. You were so little, and I had to hit you . . .'

I vomited out the lid in a rush of blood. Right away I started sobbing, and my cheeks returned to their usual pink. My mother collapsed, cradling me in her arms, and she, too, started to weep at the thought of what had almost happened.

The story has changed over the years. For a long time I thought this happened at night, when my father was home. In that version, my mother ran to him, me in her arms, so he could be the one who saved my life. It was like some ancient rite: the mother delivers me to the father, who brings me fully into this world with all its dangers, this world where I have to take care of myself. It was perfect. I must have forgotten some fragments of the truth on purpose, or refused to hear them, hoping to shape the story myself. But the last time I had a conversation about this with my mother, she reminded me that my father wasn't there, and for a moment I felt cheated; it felt like a loss.

Then I saw that the story didn't lose its symbolism. My mother, who gave birth to me, was the one who could have watched me die, and her hand was the one that brought me back to life. It's the core, too, of a great love story.

And it's a story with a happy ending – who can resist that? My sister was born a month later, in the last days of 1981, and she was perfectly healthy. She proved all the doctors wrong.

When I tell this story, I imagine my parents' lives without me. I imagine the world where I died before my second birthday, and I wonder how they would have talked about me, how they would have tried to keep me present. I imagine the fights they would have had about my death, the accusations, the slippery slopes, the *what would have happened if he'd lived?* As far as I can tell, my life – my real life – is the answer to that question. But over time, I've begun to wonder: is this the only way for me to live?

FROM THE UNPUBLISHED NOVEL *THE ORIGIN OF WORDS*

Scene in a Fast-food Restaurant

SERGIO GUTIÉRREZ NEGRÓN

Translated by Nick Caistor

By 2015, when Juan Carlos recalls that other afternoon in the same Wendy's thirteen years earlier, his ex-girlfriend Marielys is already dead.

In fact, a few months earlier he saw on Facebook that it had been four years since the tumour began to undermine her. He hadn't been there when it happened, but people said it was devastating.

'Like in the movies,' a mutual female friend commented, but he had never seen a movie where anything like that happened. Maybe a TV soap?

Anyway, this afternoon he is in the Wendy's on the corner of Road PR-1 and Luis Muñoz Marín Avenue, at one of the entrances to Bairoa, the neighbourhood where he grew up. For the first time in a long while, he has ordered a combo and not something from the dollar menu and sits on his own at one of the tables for two by the window. From there he can see the avenue.

It is then that he remembers the afternoon in question.

He can clearly hear Marielys speaking:

'What if it's positive?' she had asked, rubbing her eyes. She wasn't crying, and hadn't been, although it was as if she had. Her hands were shaking.

So were his.

They both looked down at the table. On it were two Frostys, a large portion of fries and a Diet Coke. They weren't looking at any of these, but instead at the plastic tube in the middle.

They had come into the restaurant about twenty minutes earlier. Marielys had gone straight to the restroom while he went to the counter to place their usual order. Unlike on other days, Juan Carlos had not been annoyed that she took so long.

Before that they had gone to the Walgreen's pharmacy next door. It was around twenty past two.

Marielys had left school early and he had gone to fetch her in his brother's SUV. That morning she had told her mother not to come to collect her because she was going with her best friend to practise a dance for a talent show taking place in a few weeks' time. In the pharmacy, Juan Carlos and Marielys had tried to make sure no one saw them, even though they knew that was almost impossible.

He was already in his first year at university, but had no lectures on Tuesdays or Thursdays. His brother thought it was odd he didn't go that day, because Juan Carlos always went to the campus, whether or not he had classes. Especially on Thursdays, when he had a reading group with people he had met at the only meeting of the Union of Socialist Youth he had attended. Neither he nor any of them belonged to the USY, but that was where he spoke to them for the first time. They were Maoists.

That week, as in the previous one, they were reading 'Serve the People', a 1944 speech by Mao Tse-tung. Because of what was going on with Marielys, Juan Carlos had not had a chance to look at it, but he went to the meeting where they talked – some more than others, and he didn't even open his mouth – about the coming revolution that would lead not only to Puerto Rico's independence but also to the downfall of capitalism.

Raymond, who had been at the university four or five years longer than him, had said that if what was meant to take place did take place, things would turn ugly, but that it would all be for love. Juan Carlos guessed he must be quoting Mao, but had no real idea.

Juan Carlos saw Marielys coming out of the restroom. She was a good-looker now, but at the age of thirty she'd be stunning. She looked pale. She was clutching the thing in both hands. He stared out of the window. Three black Honda Civics were parked outside. On the left beyond the last of them was a phosphorescent yellow car.

Marielys wasn't exactly brilliant, but then neither was he. Or at least not compared to his brother or his schoolmates. Neither of them pretended they were, although he would have liked to be. She was a hip-hop dancer and the following year after finishing school she would appear twerking in reggaeton videos. That was all she wanted to do. She had applied for university of course: her mother would kill her if she didn't.

Her mother might kill her anyway.

Marielys wasn't the slightest bit interested in politics. Nor was Juan Carlos. Or rather it hadn't interested him until he went to university. Now though he was starting to get it, or at least so he thought.

She sat down and threw the thing in among the food cartons, then covered it with a napkin.

He took the Mao photocopies out of his backpack and pretended to be reading them.

'Don't tell me you're going to read right now?' she said, exasperated.

'We have to wait anyway,' he replied.

'You can talk to me,' she complained. 'I mean, if you want to, if I'm not boring you.'

Juan Carlos put the photocopies down on top of the thing. He told her there were more important problems than the one they were facing at that moment. She asked him what could be more important than that. He said: the revolution. She said sorry, and he said not to worry, but she explained that what she meant to say was 'sorry, can you repeat what you just said?' so he did exactly that, telling her that the revolution was more transcendental than all this, that whatever happened, they would all be screwed if things went on as they were.

'What on earth are you talking about?'

Juan Carlos wanted to avoid a fight, but for some reason couldn't let the matter drop. He told her he was talking about really important things, about the country's well-being, about the future awaiting them. He told her they couldn't go on living the way they were, that being a colony was choking the life out of them, that capitalism was leaving them gasping for breath, that there had to be a way of life that went beyond simply surviving, beyond mere sordid reproduction; a way of life that was weighty, weightier than the Chinese mountain Mao talked about, or that Raymond said Mao talked about; and that he wanted to devote himself to that, he wanted to fling himself into the struggle without any illusions, to serve the people one hundred per cent. While he was talking, Juan Carlos could actually see all this happening.

He could see the country slowly grinding to a halt, falling to pieces, and then the bombs, the planes, the strong nationalist, independentist and anti-capitalist resistance withdrawing to the mountains and forests. From there they would unleash a heroic guerrilla war. Obviously it would be a tough life. It would be hard to live in the mountains, especially considering that he had been brought up in a gated community with air conditioning, cable TV and video games. He had never bathed in a river. But he would adapt. It would take time, but he would do it, and no one would ever suspect that deep down inside he had his doubts about the victory of their mission. He would push those doubts aside. He would be doing it for the country, of course, but also for the two of them.

The question was whether Marielys was willing to die for the motherland, if she would join him, and if she decided not to, could he break things off with her?

Marielys had been his first and only girlfriend, and he couldn't imagine himself with anyone else. And if he asked her there and then and she said no, that she would never serve the people as he imagined himself doing, would he be capable of taking to the hills with the forces of the national liberation army? His doubts worried him. Would he give up everything for her? It was possible he wouldn't. But then again, it was possible that, let's say, if in the small white circle of the pregnancy test covered by a napkin and the Mao photocopies there was a positive result, he would simply accept whatever she decided. Her mother would force them to get married; Marielys was so afraid of her she would do exactly that. And he would say that yes, he was ready to do whatever she thought best.

Years later, she would feel guilty for having forced him, but the truth would be that deep down he would be happy with the way things had turned out because he was longing for stability and would be delighted above all to see how the kid grew and who it looked like, but he'd also like to watch Marielys grow older, and to see what became of them. It wouldn't be easy. He would have to work longer hours if he could, and once he graduated perhaps Marielys's dad would help him get a job with the Electrical Energy union, and he would work hard and gradually get on, and they would be fine.

Or perhaps not. Perhaps over time Marielys would grow tired and frustrated, would decide none of this was worth it, that she had wasted her life, and then simply up and leave them without warning. What would he and the child do without her? How would they manage? Maybe he knew from the start that Marielys would be capable of doing it: she was strong and always got her way when she set her mind on something. Possibly.

'It's time,' said Marielys, suddenly bringing Juan Carlos back to reality. He took her hand: it was cold. Incredibly cold. He squeezed it. They both took a sip of their also very cold soft drinks, and peered at the result.

Thirteen years later, Juan Carlos laughs with a hint of sorrow. He quickly tells himself that this isn't nostalgia, even if he does wonder what has happened to all those desires, all that pulsing life.

Recording 1

GABRIELA JAUREGUI

Translated by Annie McDermott

We were crepuscular. No doubt about it. We ate croissants dripping with butter and then went to the gym with the grease still on our fingers. That's how it was with everything: coke, MDMA, 2CB, followed by weeks of fruit juice and smoothies. It was a symptom. It was an era. Crepuscular was the only adjective we could think of.

And meanwhile I couldn't silence the signal from beyond. It dictated to me, on and on, making me write even though I didn't want to. But what else could I do? I'd tried drowning out the signal with drugs, alcohol, sedatives, sex; I'd tried to stuff all my openings and pores, but to no avail. The signal still came. It told me the future; it told me what to say, and even what to think, about the things that were or weren't going to happen to people.

The most practical way of making sense of it was the most obvious and banal, but also the oldest in the book. Astrology. I have a job writing horoscopes, though I keep them deliberately vague, and sometimes slip in the odd mistake, so as not to reveal my gift. My gift – more like a responsibility, a weight on my shoulders. My voice that isn't mine. But then where does it come from? The universe?

I was like a copyist for the astral plane. Or at least, that's the sort of thing I liked to tell myself as I downloaded whatever came to me in the way of visions, words and feelings that were sometimes so intense I felt dizzy. In another century I'd have been called a witch; in another, a sorceress; in some cultures I'd be a shaman, and in others a devil. Here, the crepuscular majority (crepuscular – the commune's favourite adjective) just thought I was a good liar, and sometimes even wise. A skilled fabricator of futures, at best. But nothing more.

Sucking. The messages came from a long way off, and they sucked and licked at my brain as if it was a lollipop until I wrote them down. I don't know how else to describe it. It was like having a limpet stuck there, clinging to me, until my words on the page set it free. I wrote and wrote. But not all of it was for publishing in that glorified gossip rag; there was also my own writing, my notebook, a kind of book of prophecies.

What weighed on me wasn't just the feeling of responsibility for my visions, which were sometimes horrible and sometimes dazzlingly beautiful, but also the question of how to balance them with a crepuscular life. With a normal life, in the here and now. How to go for tacos with friends without the voice, the voices, coming at me out of nowhere. How to take a walk without breaking under the force of it. How to dance with someone and not end up deafened by the cries. Paralysis. Scales skewed by their own weight. Useless.

And in the answers to those questions, my journey.

The horse was a huge dog, a sacred dog. There was a short man next to him, a eunuch whose fingernails were the cosmos. The two of them worshipped a baby and licked the palm of my hand.

Sleepy-eyes and Burnt-legs sitting by a rock watching the mud flow past their feet. Miniature multi-coloured stones in the mud. Everything falling into a white lake of milk.

The visions came, and sometimes the interpretations took months, even years, to follow. Maybe it was my lack of experience. I had nobody to guide me. There were times when I cried and would have given anything not to have a vision. And other times, later on, when I was almost in tears because I wanted one so much. But visions come. You can't ask for them, you can't scare them away and you definitely can't choose which ones you want. And you can't hide. Visions come like the tide, like the sun follows the moon or a headache follows too many glasses of wine. There were days when I thought I was going mad.

A forest of snakes instead of vines and branches. Vipers, snakes, serpents of all colours and dimensions. Snakes writhing like a river. One bit me on my ankle.

When I woke up, when I emerged from the vision, my whole foot was swollen as if the snake really had bitten it. I was a teenager. The fake army boots I wore to school wouldn't do up over my puffy ankle. Sometimes the visions bled into reality – or, worse, they became even more real.

For a while I was sure something was following me. And one day, when I dropped my keys and bent down to pick them up (I was always carrying too many things, as if I needed to have my entire home with me at all times), I saw it. A sparrow. And I realized I'd been right. The sparrow was there every morning, afternoon and evening. If I went to get something from the corner shop, the sparrow would be picking up bits of rubbish or crumbs or insects in the entrance to my building. He'd take me by surprise when I was running in the park, perching next to me as I stretched my aching thighs. I'd go out to parties and then, no matter what time it was, I'd catch sight of him on the way home. It felt good to know my intuitions had some basis in reality. And so when I saw him hopping about at a different time each day, it was as if a weight was being lifted from my shoulders. I began to accept what looked like my destiny. And who believes in destiny these days? But who was I, little more than a sparrow myself, not to believe in it? The bird had passed his lightness onto me.

From a very young age I've been able to foresee what's going to happen to me, often with overwhelming intensity. My mother once crashed the car when she was taking me to school, and I'd known she was going to a few minutes before. Little by little these minutes became hours and then days, months, years. But other things were still as invisible to me as they were to anyone else.

As I sometimes say in my horoscopes: doing what you like is one thing, but destiny is something else entirely. I don't know what to think about that any more, after everything that's happened. Back then I wanted to feel as if I had power, but I didn't. My father killed himself. And there was nothing I could do. Mara and I had that in common as well: fathers who'd disappeared. The peso crisis was a taboo subject in our house from that point on, as were the Barzón's towering debts. My mother sometimes blamed one and sometimes the other as she scrubbed away zealously at the work surfaces and spoke on the phone to her sister or a friend of my father and polished every single loop of the telephone cord spiral. All I tried to do in those days was be a good girl, helping out and doing my schoolwork and putting my toys away, especially when my mother used to take out all the clothes and sheets and towels and unfold them, iron them and then fold them back up again. As if that would make my father arrive home from the office like normal, saying 'Oh, how lovely, you and Luisa ironed everything again? Even my shirt with the yellow stains under the arms that's been in the back of the wardrobe for the past two years? Oh, it's just wonderful to come back to a house like this.' That's what I imagined my mum was thinking. I couldn't see why she'd bother with something so pointless if not in the hope that magically, thanks to what she'd done, my father would come home again. But he never would. And there was nothing I could do.

The sword is being sharpened. It's made of gold. Now sharper still. It's offered, it's forged. It slices the air. It is the air.

In fact, as soon as I stopped living with my mother in that house where everything was so clean I never thought twice about eating food I dropped on the floor, so clean insects were afraid to come inside and where I never saw so much as a spider or an ant, let alone a cockroach, I let myself go.

There's a shell in a sea of blood but it has nothing inside. No pearl, no creature, nothing. It's clean. But empty.

I've never looked for my father in anyone else. He chose to kill himself. Things I have looked for, or am looking for to this day: messages in bottles on the beaches my mum took me to on holiday; my phone, which I always lose at the bottom of my bag; men or women who understand my visions; a teacher; the perfect pair of boots; the next rush of emotion that will silence the visions for an instant; the truth; my cat when he went off and climbed a tree or visited a neighbour's house and didn't come back for a week. Every day I stood outside and called him when I came back from nursery. I never stopped looking for a way to make my mother happy, and so I became a professional clown. I looked for friends and found them; I've always looked for a book that could explain the visions, a grimoire. They exist in fantasy films but not in the real world, or at least not the one I live in. Maybe some bookshop selling incunabula in London or Moscow would have one, but I've never been to London or Moscow. I'd like to go to London, but to Moscow not so much. One of Mara's and my favourite games involved making lists of the countries we wanted to visit. We'd each choose a country, dress up and put on a show with the help of sheets, carpets etc. Sometimes my mother was our audience. Sometimes Mara's brothers and sisters and grandmother, sometimes our soft toys and dolls. I chose Burkina Faso every time. I loved the fact it had once been called Upper Volta (which always made me think of high voltage) and that the name of the capital was Ouagadougou. It sounded like a song. For each performance I'd look at an atlas or encyclopedia or whatever else I could find, and I'd learn things that seemed incredible to me. That the national anthem was called 'One Single Night', for example. The soundtrack to my life, I'd joke later with Mara – before she was killed – and with Elena and Saratoga.

A dog and a candle. Under the dog's paw, a book of laws carved in metal. Sealed. The vision frozen. As if it's winter.

A hole that wasn't a window but a riddle. The eye of a lizard, only shut. A hurricane.

Pulled teeth, scattered and sown. Seed-teeth, stone-teeth, trash-teeth in an invisible landscape. Teeth looking for tongues. But they found an arch instead, went underneath it and disappeared as well. Then everything was invisible.

Out one night at a party where I was so high I was trying not to distinguish between the real visions and the ones caused by the candy flip I'd done a few hours before, I met Patricia. We started to dance. We kissed, we wound our arms around each other. It turned out Patricia had a son, Silvestre, a toothless little cherub in the photo on her phone, and was the editor of a pretty good fashion magazine. Between the kissing and the rubbing up against each other and the music, which was even more powerful than the drugs, I somehow managed to tell her I was a witch. I said it like I was joking. And she said she needed someone to write horoscopes for her magazine. 'But good ones, the kind that'll give me goosebumps.'

'Be careful what you wish for,' I answered, running a fingernail over her arm, and the skin prickled as far as her legs. We swapped email addresses and went back to dancing with our friends. The next morning, I still had her email address inked onto my arm. I only use my phone to speak to my mum. It gives me a headache. But seek me and you shall find.

FROM THE NOVEL *RECORDING 1*

Umami

LAIA JUFRESA

Translated by Sophie Hughes

Luz turns three years dead today. Mum fixes herself up a bit (she lets her hair down) but she's in a terrible mood. She burns the toast. I spill juice on the floor and she says 'Perfecto'. When she goes to brush her teeth she complains that Dad, who's just shaved, has left hairs in the sink. Dad and I mutter to each other, 'Patience', and when Mum finally announces, furious, that she's not coming with us, I think we're both relieved. Dad tries to convince her anyway, but she's unswayable.

'This year I have a stand-in,' she says to him. And to me: 'Pull up any weeds you spot, will you?'

Then she hugs me way too tight, as if she could pass on whatever it is I need to be her surrogate by osmosis.

'Come on,' I say from inside my headlock. 'Let's go say hi to Luz.'

But the name has an electric effect on her. In a flash, Mum lets go of me and walks off to her room, wrapping her hair back up in her rag. Today it's the black silk one. It's embroidered with silver flowers and in another lifetime it was her very special concert shawl. But tragedies take the shine out of objects. Ever since Luz died no one around here seems to care about clothes or furniture any more. Not even the instruments seem to matter much. Utilitarian things: the cello, the piano, the timpani. Just buoys.

I never knew my parents did this while we were away at camp.

'Every year?' I ask.

'Every year,' says Dad. 'And we always stop by that flower stall there.'

He parks, gives me some money and I go by myself. In fact they've only come twice, which isn't all that much. But the new life already feels old. We have new customs. The first time we went home without Luz I thought I'd never be able to walk into our room without expecting to find her there, playing with Bedtime Bear.

But now her bed is my chaise longue and Bedtime Bear is in a box somewhere and I don't ever expect to see her when I come home. If I think about her it's to imagine what she'd be like now: she'd be eight. Pretty soon she'd be wearing a training bra and I'd have to explain to her what to do if she gets her first period in school. I'd show her how to tie her sweater around her waist just in case, and tell her not to panic if she spots a dark stain in her knickers, to keep cool and to come looking for me in my classroom. We would be in the same school by now.

'And Luz,' I would say to her, 'don't you listen to those girls who say using tampons is like having sex, because they're eleven and they're liars.'

I swear some girls in my class talk about having learned to use a tampon like it was sailing across the Atlantic. All that's missing is the slide show, like the one Grandma Emma gave us when she came back from that cruise.

The flower arrangements at the stall are for old ladies. For dead old ladies or for old ladies who think their dead were really cheesy.

I take three sunflowers, pay for them and, getting back into the car, remember something basic: Luz isn't buried where we're going.

'Next year,' I say to Dad, putting on my seat belt, 'we'll bring flowers from our yard.'

Dad starts the car and corrects me:

'Our vegetable garden.'

Then, smiling, he uses the name, maybe to make up for Mum's reaction earlier:

'Luz would have loved your garden.'

The grave is small and made of cement, not too different from the planters in the yard I'm turning into a vegetable garden, only with a lid. The lid says: *Luz Pérez-Walker, 1995–2001.* And underneath: *Beloved daughter and sister.* Be-loved. Like an order. I've fantasized about this moment, about what I'd say to Luz. But in my fantasies it was raining and Luz was somehow able to listen to me. Now the sun is beating down and there's not a patch of shade in the whole cemetery. She's dead, and I have nothing to say to her. Was she beloved? She was my sister. 'Bina,' she used to call my friend Pina. 'Sana,' she used to called me (a mix between sister and Ana, although she didn't come up with it: our brothers used it before her). One time, Bina and I changed her outfit twenty times and put make-up on her: she'd let us do anything. Yes, I guess she was beloved. Her death certificate was made in Michigan. *DECEASED*, it says in capital letters. I hate this word. It sounds like diseased. But you can be cured from a disease. And, anyway, Luz wasn't sick. She even knew how to swim. She must have got caught up in something, that's what we think. Luz's body is in ashes in the lake. At the time it seemed logical, to cremate her and put her to rest with Grandad. But now I can't understand it: why would we leave her there? I wonder if my brothers think about her while they're out fishing. I wonder if they have anything to say to her.

I brought a big pair of shears with me, but I don't spot a single weed. I use them to cut the stems of the three sunflowers which I arrange on the grave until Dad and I agree on a nice composition. But almost straight away I mess them up again. If there was one thing Luz wasn't, it was tidy. Dad agrees.

'When she was really little,' I remind him, 'she used to get baby food everywhere.'

He laughs.

'One day,' he adds, 'I had to clean her mush off the ceiling. I never had to do that with the rest of you kids: that girl had arms like a baseball player.'

A blow to the chest, there, a few tears that come to my eyes but don't fall. 'That girl.' That's what we no longer have for Luz. What is it exactly? Irreverence? Cheek.

'You little shits,' Dad sometimes calls my brothers.

'Scaredy-cat!' he says to me when I refuse to eat chilli.

Being dead means this, too: nobody dares insult you any more, not even out of love.

I feel good when we leave. Sad but interesting. And clean. The only thing missing is the soundtrack. I ask Dad to sing something and who knows why but he breaks into '*La donna è mobile qual piuma al vento, muta d'accento e di pensiero*', a family classic. Mum used to sing it in the mornings.

'Now I feel like a pizza,' I tell him, and he passes me his phone.

I call Mum and she asks for a bacon-and-onion pizza, even though normally she refuses to eat anything that comes in a box. Dad cries at the wheel on the way to the pizzeria. Discreetly. No heaving chest, no little sobs, just tears running down his cheeks, like in the portraits the guy in our local park used to make: he would kneel down on the floor, and with a spray can and a spatula paint the same scenes over and over, in a matter of seconds. His favourite subject was a clown with a single tear rolling down his cheek. Now I realize I should've given him some credit: it turns out that there are actually people out there who cry like that, in my own home even. Isn't this called a revelation? Some people might call it that.

When we get home, Mum's not angry any more. She's sad and gentle: she eats some pizza and says it's good. Afterward, we flop on the sofa together and she strokes my head.

'It shouldn't be called an anniversary,' I say.

'That's what your dad always says,' she replies.

'I invented a word.'

'What is it?'

'Greycholy.'

'One of Marina's.'

'Yeah, I borrowed it. By the way, are you going to make up with her?'

'If Chela and Pina made up, why not, eh?'

'What's that got to do with anything?'

'Did you pull up the weeds?'

'There weren't any.'

'Hm. It must be because there isn't a body there.'

'What's that got to do with anything?'

'Could you bring me a blanket?'

Dad comes with us on our second trip to the garden centre, to oversee his investment. But he's his own budget's worst enemy. Pina and I watch as he falls prey, over and again, to the shop assistant, but we don't say anything. I'm glad Pina's back and that she seems as psyched about the plants as I am. It's another assistant today: not the pervert, but a young guy with dreadlocks. I feel awkward around him. I chew the inside of my cheek, then force myself to talk to him.

'I'm regenerating the oxygen in my mews,' I tell him.

'Nice,' he says, his eyes on Pina.

We leave the garden centre so overloaded with goodies that Dad decides to go and get the car. While we wait for him at the entrance, a lady comes up to us.

'How much for this?' she asks, pointing at our newly acquired cherry-tomato plant.

Pina butts in before I have time to answer.

'Two hundred pesos, *señora*. Go ahead, try one.'

The lady tries a tomato and buys the plant off us. I'm so impressed I'm lost for words. By the time Dad parks up and opens the trunk, Pina is already back, a replacement cherry-tomato plant and eighty pesos change safely tucked away in her pocket. She got back yesterday, but she still hasn't told me anything about her mum. She says to wait till she develops the photos. She took her old film camera, but now 'Chela has a digital one'. It makes me sad that she calls her mum by the same nickname we all use for her. I must have pulled a face because next thing she says, 'She asked me to call her that and I like it.'

'Okay,' I say. 'Okay, sorry.'

In total we have: two aloes, a lemon tree, a lavender plant, and various unidentified succulents. After today's trip we can add the cherry tomatoes and two specimens of a tall plant called *Monstera deliciosa*, but which for some reason has the nickname 'skeleton'. It has huge, dark-green leaves with roundish holes in them. I guess that's where the name comes from: the holes being the eye sockets in a skull. Or maybe it's subtler than that: the holes the dead leave behind, something you can't say. We also got a few other pretty plants: one of them looks like a red cabbage; the others are all green. I'm going to put those ones together in the planter nearest the house, because according to the dreads guy they like the shade. I already have the soil for the planters and next week we'll go buy the turf. I'm pretty excited about that as well. As I understand it, you just lay it out like a rug.

As soon as Dad leaves us alone in the yard, Pina lies face down on the picnic table. She's wearing a pair of hot pants so short you can see the smile of her butt cheek poking out on one side. It reminds me of last summer: we were sitting on a bench outside a shopping mall when a girl walked by and Grandma Emma said, 'She'll kill herself if she falls off that skirt.'

'Look!' shouts Pina pointing to the basil I planted two weeks ago.

Some little flowers have blossomed on it. I call Mum and she opens the sliding door. She'd been practising in the living room and has red eyes and a vague smile, like when she tells us she's sorry.

'You need to pull them off,' she says, pointing to the basil with her cello bow.

'Why?'

'If you leave them on the leaves fall off, and the leaves are the bit you eat.'

'Why?'

'Just listen to me, will you?' she says, and slides the door shut. One by one, Pina and I pull off the little flowers. It occurs to me that if I'd known, I could have taken them to the cemetery. It's a silly idea: they're tiny. But Luz was too. Tiny, I mean. She used to sit on my lap, hug her legs, then curl into a little ball so that I'd hold her.

'Squeeze!' she'd say.

Sometimes I was scared I'd hurt her or break something, and I always let go sooner than she wanted me to. We all did. My brothers held on a bit longer, but not much. Luz always wanted to be squeezed more.

'Squeeze, squeeze, squeeze!' she begged Dad, and he would squeeze her with a single arm.

I don't want to, but I can't help imagining her in her box, in the cemetery. But that's another silly idea because there's not even anything in that box. It was too expensive and complicated to bring the body back to Mexico.

'What?' I ask Pina, who's staring at me.

'Are you crying?' she says.

'Are you stupid?' I say, and she goes off in a sulk.

FROM THE NOVEL *UMAMI*

Work in Progress

MAURO LIBERTELLA

Translated by Nick Caistor

This is an urban horror story. The story of an innocent couple who one fine day wove the splendid golden tapestry of an idea. Let's do up a house! It was a moment of blind enthusiasm. The future shone bright before them; all that was needed was to knock down a few walls, put up a staircase, install a bathroom where the kitchen was, and to paint the facade.

The search for the ideal house had been exasperating. The one-storey condominiums, extending down a long corridor right into the lung of a Buenos Aires city block have become an object of universal desire at a time when there's money to burn, even though it's undeniable that almost all of them are crap. Dark, dingy and stifling, they are also the dramatic evidence of a former splendour: they are always houses that were once enormous but one day were split up due to demographic pressure and because no one could afford all that space. There is something unnatural about this type of building, as if it were impossible for that kitchen to be where it was, in the corridor, so close to the staircase. The heterogeneous nature of condos tends to make them ideal for constant refurbishing. In other words, a condo is always undergoing change: that is one of the few urban myths we can believe in.

With this conviction firmly established, we began our search. The few definite beliefs we set out with – budget, district, dimensions – set the parameters of what was on offer. The real-estate market produced the scandalous number of a hundred properties we could view. Where to start? Photos on websites offer the first clues: blurred thumbnail images, like shadows behind frosted glass. Photos of properties are the bastard progeny of the photographic art, a fraud in the history of the image. But nothing could deter us: the house we had in mind came out of the depths of the dream world.

I won't dwell on the details of the search, except to say that going into strangers' homes should be prohibited by law. The intimacy of these interiors is far too brutal. The smell, the chaotic array of objects, the revealing decor, the TV still on. No one can leave someone else's house unscathed; it's an unforgettable experience like reading forbidden love letters. And yet I think that these lightning forays into strangers' houses prepared us for the key experience of a building project: seeing things from the inside. It was a lengthy search, but one evening, just when everything seemed useless, when our initial poignant hopes were becoming a tangle of bitterness and resentment, *the* condo appeared. The photos were a disaster and we went to see it almost by chance, because we happened to be in the area. It was as if we saw lights on and went in. It was spacious, seemed solid enough, and was situated in a pretty tree-lined passage. It wasn't in a very good condition, and the layout of the rooms was debatable to say the least, but condos can be altered: we still clung on to that certainty as if it were an ideological banner we refused to let fall. We went round the house four times. We looked at one another like two old partners in a firm that no longer produces any profit, and decided to put down a deposit. 'We'll have to make a few small changes,' we told ourselves, and as we said it, something snapped.

What happened next was a chaos of masonry, unforeseen problems, poor decisions and wonderful moments of shared anguish. 'What have we got ourselves into?' we asked each other more than once, as though we were searching for the meaning of life itself. I write that sentence in the past, but it should be in the present: the work is still not finished, and possibly may never be. In this case, the confusion of tense is justified; if a life under construction destroys anything, it is the idea we once had of time, in its broadest and deepest meaning. The work itself starts with a lie: when the architect says three months, that means six. Paranoia is the only possible way to interpret this. You must never believe in other people's timescales, it always takes longer and longer and longer. Why should that be? Because of the unexpected problems, but also because of the matter. It also has its own time, which refuses to be rushed. Cement is slow to dry, it's not easy to cut iron, tiles are reluctant to stay vertical on the bathroom wall, as if the box they came in from the factory was the womb they never wanted to leave. And the people who work on a site have lost forever all basic notions of time. They are not necessarily lying when they say 'three months', they really believe they can do it, but the matter, the mother of everything that mankind has built, time and again imposes its own regime. Man says yes, matter says no.

Even though this is a horror story, the tale of how when two people put a deposit down on a house they opened the first cracks in the wall of their innocence, the most worthwhile aspect of a life under construction is beginning to see things from the inside. What is underneath the floor? What's between the wall and the street? Where do the water, light, gas and all the invisible things come in? I had no idea. Until recently all I saw were finished products, completed shapes. To me, a staircase was a succession of steps and a banister; a kitchen was a table, a sink and an oven; a room was a floor, a roof and four walls. What a fool. A house is everything this isn't, in the same way that a book is everything that isn't the cover and the author's photo. I remember that when I was little, a friend shaved his head and when he came to school next morning I asked him where his scalp was. His skull was white, nothing but skin untouched by the sun, and to me a bald person was someone whose head was tanned. 'This is my scalp: there's nothing underneath,' he said, showing me, and I skulked off. It's the same with a work in progress. It became an obsession with us to see everything from the inside. One evening when we were having dinner in a restaurant, my wife came back from the toilets and said to me: 'Go and take a look in the Ladies. They put the extractor fan behind the mirror and left a sill in the doorway so that water won't leak out.' Had I been in a position to do so, I would have handed her an architecture degree there and then.

The word 'work' has many meanings, and I don't think it's a coincidence that's also what we also call artistic objects. When literary critics talk of a text, they say it is 'constructed' in one way or another. Before it has a style, a book has a 'structure'. These are concepts borrowed from architecture, which is all about imagining something that does not exist and bringing it into the world. One of the most frequent warnings our architect gave us was that you cannot put heavy work on top of light work. First you have to build the walls, and then do the finishing and details. Isn't it the same with a book? Don't you write a rough first version that's somewhat hasty and clumsy, the inadmissible version, and then you set about reshaping it, polishing it, fine-tuning the details? One of the most horrific episodes of our life under construction concerned the staircase. Following arduous consideration about where to put it and what shape it would be, it was completed in a week. Once the staircase was finished, it was plain to everyone that this vertical construction was a mistake. The golden ratios had been broken, physics guffawed from the university cloisters. Walking up it was like driving a car along the edge of a mountain: the abyss was right there, seductive and terrible, gnawing at the wheels. With aplomb, and feigning a calm he did not really possess, the architect told us that it would need 'correcting'. He used the set phrase of my profession. That afternoon, thanks to the semantic equivalence between two professions, a common bond was created.

But there's more. Whoever dreams up the names for the colours of wall paints? That man is either a genius or a sadist. There is such a huge range of yellows that they gradually become increasingly abstract, until it's no longer possible to determine the original colour. Sunset yellow, vertigo yellow, tumultuous yellow, yellow plenitude, eggshell yellow. Borges once said that when he lost his sight what he missed above all was the colour red because of how beautiful that word was in different languages: '*Scharlach* in German, *scarlet* in English, *escarlata* in Spanish, *écarlate* in French. All words that seem worthy of that splendid colour. But *amarillo* sounds feeble in Spanish; *yellow* in English is very close to *amarillo*, I think that in ancient Spanish it was *amariello*.' What language do we have to adopt to talk to the painter when we're trying to explain exactly what orange we'd like for the patio? It's a conversation destined to fail. We ought to invent a translator, someone trained in the most advanced schools, who would be able to describe precisely what shade of orange we want for our patio when we ask the painter to mix 'revolution orange'.

Months and years have passed since all this began. Leticia and I have moved to a small apartment some friends lent us on the outskirts of the city. We lead a tranquil life: we read the newspaper, wake up early, occasionally go to the movies. Every so often we remember that there is a building project we started a long time ago, in the days when we had an iron will. Then we take a taxi to the house. There are always people working there; we don't know their names – they're no longer the ones we began the reconstruction with. None of them knows what they're doing or why they're doing it. The original plans have been lost and these workmen are simply refurbishing. It's like a huge research laboratory where nothing makes sense. When someone finishes something – a bathroom, a fitted wardrobe, a utility room – somebody else comes and redesigns, destroys, or alters it. So the work is constantly in progress, but never finished. The other day on our way back from there we sat and had a coffee. As we were laughing over past schemes Leticia suddenly became self-absorbed and began to stare out of the window. I imagined she must be thinking about all we had thrown away, the money and wasted energy, how everything had turned out in our life. Not a bit of it. She told me that the window frame was very well made and that we ought to aim for something similar in our work.

How Do Stones Think?

BRENDA LOZANO

Translated by Lucy Greaves

A lot of words rhyme differently and those are the Other Rhymes, that's what I explained to Mr Policeman. For example: purple and butterfly. With rhymes the words finish the same way just like two stories with happy endings. For example: slow and glow, grass and vast, never and forever. I know rhymes are like the happy endings of words because the letters hug each other, but I also know happy endings are made up because it's not true that all stories end happily ever after because as well as that I know things never last forever. Grass is always vast, except outside people's houses which have little squares of grass for dogs to poo on. And anyone who's seen Dila when she's slow will know she sort of glows. I think there are lots of words which are similar because they rhyme differently, just like there are sisters and brothers who look totally different, and these are the Other Rhymes. For example: blue and dolphin. That's why I really like the Other Rhymes T-shirt that Tatul gave me. I wear it almost all the time because it's got a dolphin in the middle and the fabric is blue. That's what I said to Tatul before he gave me the T-shirt and that's why he gave it to me. He has Other Rhymes, too. One of Tatul's examples: stone and quiet. That's what I explained to Mr Policeman: Tatul used to find Other Rhymes with me, but Mr Policeman didn't get it at all and wanted to know why me and Dila live in the car. Mr Policeman said: Who's Dila, who's Tatul. I said: Dila is my mum and Tatul gave me this T-shirt I'm wearing, and I explained why dolphin and blue are Other Rhymes and I also explained why Tatul says stone is the Other Rhyme of quiet. Mr Policeman went ha ha and started drawing hopscotch with chalk on the pavement while another Mr Policeman was asking Dila questions and that made me go ha ha too because policemen drive cars and shoot guns and don't chat or draw games with chalk on the pavement.

Me and Dila used to live at Tatul's house, but Dila got slow and went into the bedroom with a Man with a Moustache who wasn't Tatul. A few days after that I was in the kitchen with the Boring Book and Dila came in crying and I got scared because I get scared when Dila cries and she told me to say goodbye to Tatul because she was going to wait for me outside in the car. Dila said: We're going to hell. The Boring Book doesn't have the words Dila uses when she's angry, even though she uses the same ones when she's slow or happy too. It's impressive how Dila says the same word when she's slow, angry or happy and that same word means something totally different if she's slow, angry or happy. For example: Dila says I'm fucking A and if she says it slow I think she's contented, if she says it angry I get scared, and if she says it happy it means she's happy-happy. But the day we left Tatul's house, Dila was fucking A angry and that's why she didn't pack all my things. Luckily I was wearing the T-shirt Tatul gave me which I was also wearing when Mr Policeman asked me the questions and he was the one who told me that dolphins are the cleverest animals, I didn't know that because the Boring Book is really boring.

We haven't always lived in the car because things never last forever, that's what I explained to Mr Policeman while he was writing the numbers with chalk inside the hopscotch boxes on the pavement. Dila works and I work in the Boring Book which was one of the few things Dila didn't leave behind at Tatul's house, but I would've preferred it to be the other way round, that Dila left the Boring Book behind and brought Tatul, that's why one day I'm going to figure out where Tatul lives so I can carry on finding Other Rhymes with him. It's really fun, it used to make us go ha ha a lot and I imagine that the people who made the Boring Book don't go ha ha they go no, thousands of times. For example: you ask them if they want to go to the park and the people who made the Boring Book all say no at the same time or you ask them if they like the person who makes the Fun Books and they all say no at the same time. So my job is to fill in the Boring Book, sometimes in the car and sometimes in the park, on the green tables near the toilets and the playground, while Dila's job is at the restaurant. When I finish I go to the bit of the park where the grass is vast and the dogs are off their leads. Normally my answers to the Boring Book are right, I know that because I check the pages at the back, but if I've gone wrong I do it again and then the Boring Book is right. I was explaining this to Mr Policeman who was finishing drawing the hopscotch with chalk on the pavement and Mr Policeman went ha ha, while the Other Mr Policeman was bringing a cup of coffee from the shop because he was going to chat to Dila who was sitting on the car bonnet with her phone in her hand because a neighbour had called the Mr Policemen to tell them to come. I said the Newspaper Man makes up stories, I explained this to Mr Policeman and I told him that me and Dila have jobs, but Mr Policeman said his job was to explain to me how you play the hopscotch he'd drawn with chalk on the pavement while the Other Mr Policeman was talking to Dila who was sitting on the car bonnet without looking over at me.

I asked Mr Policeman if he thought I could have a job where I taught games to children and he went ha ha and crossed his arms and told me that a lot of the time Mr Policemen don't drive cars and shoot guns, he told me that at Mr Policeman School there are games instead of Boring Books. I said what games are there in the Mr Policeman School and he said there are monkey bars, ropes and obstacles they had to get round so they'd be strong and capable. I said: What's capable. Mr Policeman said: Dolphins are capable because they're the cleverest animals. I said: How do dolphins think. And Mr Policeman made a face like I'd just hit him with a stone. I said: How do dogs think, how do birds think and how do stones think, why are dolphins cleverer than stones. Because I think stones are cleverer than dolphins because they don't move or make noises, but Mr Policeman made a face like I'd hit him with another stone. He crossed his arms over his belly and carried on telling me that in Mr Policeman School they sometimes make pyramids, too: about five Mr Policemen kneel down, four Mr Policemen kneel on them and then three and then two and the Mr Policeman who ends up on top lifts his arms and wiggles his hands, then the Mr Policeman who was telling me this lifted his arms and wiggled his hands as if he was on top of the pyramid of Mr Policemen and that made me go ha ha a few times. So now I know that Mr Policemen play games and that sometimes they make pyramids of Mr Policemen, too, and they don't always drive cars and shoot guns because this Mr Policeman told me about the games in Mr Policeman School and showed me the rules for jumping on the hopscotch he drew with chalk on the pavement.

He took out a key ring with lots of keys that made a sound like bells which fell on square one, he hopped to square two, three, four, and up to ten and he hopped back without his other foot touching the ground, and I saw that Mr Policeman is capable because he picked up the key ring with lots of keys that made a sound like bells, hopped off the hopscotch he'd drawn with chalk on the pavement, threw the keys onto square two and said it was my turn. Before I hopped,

Mr Policeman said that me and Dila aren't allowed to live in the car, he said the Newspaper Man told on us because I'm supposed to go to school and they were there to sign me up for school and take us to a shelter. I said: What's a shelter. Mr Policeman said: It's a big house where lots of people live. I said we're living in the car for a few days, but that's not forever because before we used to live at Tatul's house and before that at Tato's house and before that at Dila's mum and dad's house, but I don't remember them because I was a baby and babies don't remember anything. I explained to Mr Policeman that when I finish the Boring Book and Dila finishes her job at the restaurant we won't live in the car any more, and I'm going to go back to school because Dila's supposed to sign me up and not Mr Policeman, and then Mr Policeman said: It's my turn, and jumped two boxes, picked up the key ring with lots of keys that made a sound like bells. Mr Policeman was falling over, he was wobbling because he was going to fall over and he didn't want to fall over because he's really big, his foot was wiggling like a chicken, he managed to get to square ten without falling and I went ha ha because Mr Policeman's uniform is so heavy that I imagined he was on top of the pyramid of Mr Policemen and knocked them all down and I went ha ha a lot.

I didn't tell Mr Policeman that yesterday Dila was slow and both of us lay down in the back seat, except she was folded up because Dila doesn't fit in lying down, that's why she sleeps in the front with the seat lying back, I was beside her and she showed me photos on her phone. Dila was stroking my hair and was happy-happy, she called me My Angel, because Dila always calls me My Angel and if she doesn't say My Angel I get scared because it means she's fucking A angry, but I was happy too looking at photos of the galaxy with her on her phone. I didn't ask how they take photos of the millions of white stars which float in circles squashed between phosphorescent green, purple and blue because Dila

146

didn't take the photos of the galaxy with her phone. Since we've been living in the car, Dila started to have more and more photos of the galaxy and astronaut men floating in space, and when I saw the photos of the galaxy that she's got on her phone it made me want to wake her up so she'd go out with me and see the stars in the park, I nudged her shoulder and she smiled without opening her eyes because Dila was slow, then I felt like saying I love you Dila and I said it, she stroked my hair without opening her eyes which was how she said me too. When I got out the car lights came on and that made the lights of the house opposite come on as if I'd broken their windows with a stone and a person came out, said something I didn't understand, but I didn't think it was the Newspaper Man because newspapers are things and not people who make up whatever they want. Anyway, yesterday I didn't see a single star, the night was big and black.

I asked Mr Policeman why the Newspaper Man told on us if we hadn't done anything wrong. Mr Policeman said: People aren't allowed to live on a public highway. I said to Mr Policeman: We don't live on a public highway, the Newspaper Man makes up stories because we've been living in the car for a few days and things never last forever. But Mr Policeman crossed his arms and said we're here to help. I wanted to see Dila but she wasn't turning to look at me because she was leaning back on the car bonnet talking to the Other Mr Policeman who was drinking coffee from the shop. Then I said to Mr Policeman: you drew the hopscotch on the pavement with chalk so I wouldn't listen to what Dila and the Other Mr Policeman were saying. Mr Policeman took the key ring with lots of keys that made a sound like bells, stayed quiet but not like stone because Mr Policeman clasped his hands and said: Do you know how the dolphin on your T-shirt thinks? I said: It doesn't think because it's not a dolphin it's a T-shirt. Mr Policeman said: You're cleverer than the cleverest dolphin. Then I looked at Dila so she'd turn and look at me and when she turned I pointed at my T-shirt which was how I said call Tatul, I pointed upwards which is how she'd said last night that we were going to travel the galaxy and she winked at me which was how she said Tatul's on his way.

FROM THE SHORT STORY COLLECTION *HOW DO STONES THINK?*

Fictio Legis

VALERIA LUISELLI

Translated by Christina MacSweeney

The Roman jurist Modestinus describes marriage as the lifelong union of a man and a woman – comprising divine and human law. Lavish gifts from the family of the woman are an obligatory accompaniment to the celebration of the alliance. However, according to the law enacted by Caesar Augustus, if the woman marries a eunuch, her family is exempted from paying the costly dowry. In the opinion of the father of Tachi's wife, the man who had wrested his divine jewel from its crown was exactly that, a eunuch. In his own words: a frigging *mayate*. But Tachi is just pale, short and a little melancholic.

With some anxiety, I note the Y of a blue vein springing up – rich with aristocratic blood – along his translucent neck as, with great effort, he vainly tries to lift his backpack and place it in the overhead compartment – in aeronautical jargon – or up there, according to his wife, who has to come to his aid with the stuff: Tachi, she says, why do you always bring so much stuff?

The couple sit down directly behind us. The four metal buckles – almost simultaneously – click. A fifth buckle clicks, belonging to a passenger sitting in the seat opposite her – on the other side of the aisle.

Just as soon as the flight attendant – an authoritarian Sevillian woman, a bit overweight and definitely too old to be wearing braces on her teeth – has passed for the last time, I unfasten my seat belt and drape the blanket over myself.

In Mexico, is this little blanket called a rug? I ask my husband.

It's called an airline blanket, he replies.

The Sevillian woman announces our imminent departure. The flight time will be ii hours 55 minutes – smoking is strictly prohibited even, or especially, in the toilets – we should turn off our electronic equipment immediately.

Before switching off my telephone, I open the Instagram app. The hipsters in Mexico City now read Allen Ginsberg in editions they buy second-hand – the world out there is better than in here – and use words like 'roomies' instead of room-mates – a world in which room-mates exist – light of the summer of 1968 – a perpetuated world – frozen – converted into an app.

The plane advances heavily along the runway.

Tachi had had a moment of glory, we learn at the zero hour of the flight, when the instructional video about possible disasters begins. At the age of twenty-three he worked for six months in a radio studio. The emergency exits are on both side of the plane – right – left. Not so much in the studio as close to it – more outside than inside – in backup and production to be exact. Children's oxygen masks should be put on after, never before, fitting your own. But on one particular occasion he'd interviewed a politician. It hadn't really been an interview – but almost, Tachi adds. Next comes the video animation about the yellow inflatable slides, which have always made me wish an unexpected disaster would occur during the flight – a landing on water with a happy ending. Tachi had expressed his admiration and the politician had – in exchange – patted the edge of his left shoulder. This selfsame politician had been everything: local representative, parliamentary delegate, secretary of state, governor of an important state and very, very nearly a presidential candidate. He couldn't now remember which state he'd headed – but thought – was almost certain – that it was a very prosperous – big – important – one. His wife agreed – but she couldn't remember the name of the politician either, much less the name of the state. A disembodied voice hopes we will enjoy our flight.

I wonder what politician he's talking about, my husband whispers in my ear. He's in in the seat next to mine, halfway through a Spanish newspaper.

I don't know, I say, maybe Hank González.

Poor Spain, he sighs – turning the page.

Are you sure this thing isn't called a rug? I ask again.

In Mexico it's called an airline blanket. But then it's a country that has politicians called El Profesor and La Maestra.

I refasten my seat belt under the blanket – I don't want the Sevillian woman to come around again and tell me off.

Not that the name of the politician or the state are important since the person listening to Tachi's story is Hans, a passenger somewhere in his early sixties – judging by his grainy, self-assured voice – who is sitting on the other side of the aisle, in the first seat of the terrifying middle block. Nobody should ever travel there: if the plane crashes and you're in that block, it's certain death – you end up squashed under the overhead compartments crammed with stuff – everyone knows that.

Tachi in the window seat – his wife – the aisle – and a passenger called Hans. We two – I'm in the aisle and he's by the window – in the seats directly in front of the couple.

Hans confesses that he doesn't care what the name of the politician in question is, because he thinks politics is beneath contempt and he hasn't read a newspaper in years. She agrees. But Hans admits that the actor showing us how to fasten our seat belts could be a PRI politician.

From the old Partido Revolucionario Institucional, Hans speci-fies, the good PRI: resolute men with those bushy Spanish eye-brows – President López Portillo eyebrows – President López Mateos eyebrows – but not President López Obrador ones, he hasn't got eyebrows or a National Project. So says Hans, who also says he despises politics.

The plane turns slowly onto the main runway, accelerates, and as if it were weightless – I put my hand in my husband's – rises up.

They formally introduce themselves seven seconds after take-off (0.07). Tachi and Pau – Hans. Hans tells them he is Swedish-Mexican, so both my husband and I have the impression that he is definitely Mexican. The obligatory question should have been why – how – Tachi got to be nicknamed Tachi. But it was a difficult question for the Swedish-Mexican to formulate since he had no sense of humour. My husband turns to me to say:

That's what they call taxis in Barcelona: Tachi.

I laugh, say it's wrong to make fun of the poor Spanish these days – but he stops me short:

It's absolutely true, that's what they call them.

The Sevillian woman apologizes – in Spanish – to the passengers of flight 401 in the name of the airline: Our entertainment system is not working – I repeat – I repeat again – our entertainment system is not working. However, she tells us that the passengers can make use of the synchronized map showing the flight path. She then repeats the same thing all over again, but in English.

At 3.04: Chicken or pasta. Chicken or pasta at 11.14 a.m., Spanish time. Altitude: 10,400 metres.

Another Roman jurist, Ulpianus, specifies that there is a sig-nificant difference between eunuchs who have been castrated and those who are born without reproductive organs. In the former case, the law holds: the family of the woman is exempted from paying a dowry. In the latter, however, they are not. The natural-born eunuch has an irrevocable right to a dowry.

The fact was, as we learn later from a comment by Tachi's wife – whose name I find it difficult to pronounce without giving a slight shiver and who, at 12.47 a.m. Spanish time, 4.37 in-flight time, is drinking her third plastic glass of wine – that they had just got married, and that her father hadn't given them any kind of present, not even a bit of help in setting up the marital home. They had a flat in Calle Platón, very nearly on the corner with Ejército Nacional. And, partly due to the father, they were having a hard time making ends meet and had to skimp on important details of the renovation of the flat. There's no need to repeat the exact words Tachi's wife used to say just that: skimp. What is important is that, as a result, they didn't know what to do about the kitchen. And there, the motive for the trip to Spain. 4.55. She wanted a pre-designed, fitted kitchen, to save a little money – but he, Tachi, preferred something tailored to meet the needs of the future family. That's why they had travelled to Spain: they had IKEA there and she wanted to 'see the kitchens in person'. Also, because they had Air Miles and friends in Madrid.

Hans, who confesses that he has never finished any degree, is, definitely, an expert in design history: The first fitted kitchen, he says in complicity with Tachi's wife, was invented by a brilliant woman: Margarete Schütte-Lihotzky. Judging by the way he pronounces the name, Hans clearly speaks German well. My husband looks at me, his lower lip pouting and his eyes turned up – I pinch his shoulder, acknowledging receipt of that expression I know so well, which means: I couldn't give a fuck. She, Tachi's wife, however, is very interested in this Margarete Schütte-Lihotzky. She asks for more information. Her row-mate passes it across – in torrents – from his side of the aisle to the other.

Hans – 5.14 – 5.42 – her.

I lower the plastic blind, stretching my arm across the space occupied by my husband's body. The dazzling Atlantic light outlines the rounded shape of the window. A stabbing pain in my right eye warns me it is just the sort of light that sets off my migraines. I try to close my eyes. My husband reads – dozes behind the newspaper – perhaps a primitive form of reading – and Tachi reads too. Hans asks him what he's reading. It's an action story, he says, about the situation in Mexico. That's what he says: an action story with a bit of sex about the Situation in Mexico. I suppose, in essence, Tachi is right.

Hans, who's also an expert in literature, compares Tachi's novel with the work of Kertész and the duty not to remain silent in the face of such horror, then he talks about Conrad's Horror Horror. After that, Dostoevsky, Beckett and then even Plato – which in fact is the street where you live in Mexico, says Hans condescendingly, turning towards Tachi's wife. She knows very well who Plato is.

Plato's my favourite author, she declares.

Hans names, and he knows a lot of names. He thinks it's right that Mexican writers – all of them – talk about the horror. It's our horror, our holocaust. And it's our duty to talk about it with every means available to us. That's what Hans believes. Tachi's wife, presumably, nods and raises her eyebrows. But neither of the two offers an opinion. When she manages to find a gap in the conversation, she leaps in and asks Hans about the relationship between Frankfurt kitchens and the Taylorism thing. She'd been really interested in that and wanted to know more about it. Maybe they could contract a specialist builder to copy Margarete Schütte-Lihotzky's kitchen designs for them – with a little upgrade.

I try to memorize that impossible name: Margarete Schütte-Lihotzky.

Perhaps that's what the original kitchen in our rented apartment on the top floor of a building on Avenida Revolución was like – like the Frankfurt kitchens. It's a tiny space – our kitchen – and a bit dark. There is just one window that opens on to a T formed by two very narrow streets at right angles to each other, crammed with formal and informal businesses. More – in number – informal than formal. Which means that the street functions not as an exterior but an interior – a never-ending, dizzying market, roofed with blue and pink canvas – the ground carpeted in chewing gum, gobs of spit, seeds, fag ends, fingernails, hair, insects, ten-centavo coins, vast archipelagos of cat and dog shit. Originally, when the streets surrounding the building were really streets, the Ermita had the 'porous' peculiarity – as one historical guide to the city puts it – of opening the private space to the outside world, and vice versa. On the ground floor there were pharmacies, cafes, agencies. The first functionalist building in the city, the first project of a fully modern, urban middle class. We have – they had – we have all had – a project for happiness. We moved there as newly-weds – very young – because a friend told us that Tina Modotti had lived in that very building – though we later discovered that this wasn't true – that Modotti had lived in a colonial house a few blocks away.

Hank González! cries Tachi. Agonizing 6.57 in-flight time. The conversation between his wife and Hans has just come to the point of opening a window to exchange emails and he is experiencing a stab of rage or terror. They scarcely register Tachi's howl – Hank González! That's what the politician was called! – and go on spelling out their electronic addresses. Hers: sleeplessnights@hotmail. com. His – life's full of amazing coincidences: wakefulslumber@ hotmail.com.

It was Hank González! I say with a little nudge to my – sleeping – husband.

We also moved to the Ermita because that's where the first sound cinema in the city was opened. And we liked that idea – living over a cinema. There was a project there for us. No matter that, in fact, the cinema had, for the past twenty years, been for adults only – that is, for decrepit fifty-somethings and curious teenagers. It was a cinema, and that's what counted – a cinema integrated into the building but structurally separated from it by a sort of Schrödinger's box. In other words, a hypothetical box, because while we are cooking above that cinema several actors and actresses are fucking noisily – like cats – all at the same time. To be honest, they don't fuck and we don't cook: they get hot and we reheat – because there's no place for sex in pornography and no room for a stove in our kitchen. But we do have a good microwave. Last year, while we were listening to the serialized adventures of the Savage Cowboy – a gringo who whips Mexicans for Richie (as he calls his sexual organ) – we invented Tupperware eggs Benedict. We absolutely adore them – even if ours are made with mayonnaise and my husband now thinks that I use it too liberally.

Tachi's wife suggests to her travelling companion that she show him the plans of her house – perhaps he might be able to think up better solutions than theirs – than her husband's in particular, she ought to say – but doesn't. My seat shakes slightly – a handrail for the woman who now stands up to take the bags down from up there to examine the plans of the house with the Swedish-Mexican, who, to her, seems to be most of all Swedish and only a little Mexican. She asks her husband to exchange seats with Hans, because it'll be awkward to study the plans across the aisle – and they'll annoy the other passengers – and the flight attendant will tell them off, and so on.

Tachi looks reluctant – he never travels in the middle block, she should know that by now.

Well, it's for our little home, she counters.

Hans moves to the window – she needs to stay in the aisle because she can't bear to imagine the abyss beyond the plastic blind. Hans thinks this is ideal, because he likes nothing better than the window seat. In fact, if they let him sit there for the rest of the flight, he'd be very grateful because nothing moves him more deeply than seeing the urban sprawl of Mexico City from the air, minutes before landing. It is so, so very much like landing on water. The Swedish-Mexican shares what he considers to be a fascinating datum: the very first map of Mexico City – water, nothing more – is in a Swedish museum.

Landing in Mexico City at night is like alighting on a mantel of stars – she rounds off, very much the mistress of her words.

Ulpianus also spoke about the 'rights of the husband'. If he discovers that his wife has committed adultery, he is urged to sue for divorce and it is recommended that he submit evidence against her. The only problematic situation is when the adulteress is under twelve, says the wise, cautious Roman, because, since she is legally underage, this represents an ambiguous case. But Tachi's wife, despite her twittery-bird voice, does not really personify the ambiguous case Ulpianus sets out.

Hans's first recommendation, at 7.00 in-flight time, is the Charlotte Perriand dining-room suite. Such a large room is crying out for a Perriand.

I try to read the first page of the Martin Amis novel I've chosen for the journey – as if I'd ever managed to read more than two or three pages on a plane.

And neither is Tachi making much of an effort to protect the lifelong nature of his conjugal union at 7.04 in-flight time – when Hans has already moved into the master bedroom and is suggesting that the south window be enlarged by a few centimetres and they install sliding windows.

The first lines of the novel are beautiful and a little sad. They speak of cities – cities at night – when couples are sleeping and some men – asleep – cry and say Nothing. I think about Martin Amis's teeth. I look at my husband's slightly open mouth and think that I don't know exactly what his teeth are like. Years ago I had a boyfriend who used to grind his teeth in his sleep. The Perriand dining-room suite is a work of art, Hans insists, while making a sketch of it. The point of his pencil squeaks on the paper – presumably the airsickness bag provided in case of turbulence. The persistent grinding of those teeth when I was fast asleep used to cause me a certain amount of angst. Sometimes – unjustifiably – that sound – even – really annoyed me: it seemed to indicate that the man, in essence, was sleeping very far from me. I used to wake him up and ask if he was feeling all right. Nothing, he'd say. Amis is right – they say Nothing. The decision is taken: the dining-room suite will be a Perriand. I close my book.

7.12 in-flight time. Tachi announces that he's going to the toilet.

Yes, she says.

Hans asks if she'd like a mint – 7.13.

Yes, she says.

Tachi walks to the toilet, perhaps to wash his face, perhaps to clean his teeth, perhaps to have a pee. Perhaps to cry. He'll undo the button and lower his trousers. Like they taught him to as a boy. Perhaps he grew up surrounded by women who liked clean toilet bowls – no splashes. He learned to pee sitting down when he was very young. He covers the seat with two lengths of toilet paper and sits on them – his two thighs landing simultaneously – to press the paper onto the surface – so it doesn't move a centimetre – no way is his skin going to come into direct contact with even a drop of foreign urine. He pees, pushing back his penis with his index, middle and ring fingers. The same fingers he uses to masturbate. Just a few tears – more from rage than anything else.

Whilst Tachi is washing his hands, Hans asks his wife why her family disapprove of the marriage. She, for the first time, becomes a bit defensive. Her father doesn't disapprove – she assures him. It's just that he and Tachi aren't on good terms – so much so that her father hung up on her the last time they spoke, after telling her that her husband was a frigging *mayate*. She confesses that she had to look that word up in an online dictionary. Between the two definitions – 1. Beetle of various colours and regular flight; 2. Homosexual man – she knew her father was referring to the second. But she prefers not to think about it. Better to talk about the bathroom: bathtub or shower?

Ulpianus writes: 'It is not copulation but its marital consequences which constitute the marriage.'

Hans, at 7.25, talks about his nephews and nieces. He isn't a parent either but he's a very good uncle, he assures her. He adores them. And he's also godfather to his niece, the daughter of his sister, who lives in Connecticut.

She repeats: Connecticut.

I don't know exactly where Connecticut is, I think.

Where exactly is Connecticut? she asks.

Hans says it's not important – that Connecticut is close enough to New York. Because every time he goes to Connecticut he manages to slip away to New York. He's got friends there, in Brooklyn. She and Tachi know New York well, they like Times Square. But Tachi isn't really into walking – he gets tired. She, on the other hand, adores walking. So does Hans. In fact, he did the Camino de Santiago de Compostela last year. She really wants to do that one day, but it would be difficult with Tachi. Hans assures her that there's nothing better than getting into bed – in the nude – after a good bath and a glass of wine, having spent a whole day walking through that landscape.

Tachi comes back from the toilet. 7.29. He doesn't sit down – he wants to walk along the aisle a little to stretch 'the old legs'.

7.30

7.31

7.32

The emperor Valerian, at 7.33 in-flight time, in the year 258 before the birth of Jesus Christ, wrote that the man who is married to two women at the same time is steeped in infamy. That's not Tachi's case. But he knows infamy – he prods it with his tongue – between his teeth – he has it between his legs.

7.34 in-flight time – 10,600 metres above sea level – time at point of destination 3.23 a.m.

I lift the armrest and lay my head on my husband's lap – perhaps sleep a while. On the lobe of my right ear, I feel the seam of his flies – and on my cheek, his slight sleeper's erection. I can't see him, but Tachi is standing by his seat, resting a hand on the backrest of mine. He's talking to his wife. She asks how he's doing. Fine, he says, although his legs ache. She asks if his father's driver will pick them up at the airport. Of course, Tachi says, that had been agreed all along. I pull the rug up over my eyes. I run through the list: here, my tongue – my first, second and third molars – my cheek – the denim – the metal track of the zipper – the stripes of his briefs – the warm tip of his penis – the seat – the carpet – the various layers of metal – the guts of the aircraft – and then, 10,600 metres of nothing between us and the surface of the sea.

And the white – constant – light that the plane rips through like scissors through a piece of cloth.

For breakfast – 10.41 – there are eggs Benedict with lots of mayonnaise. The Sevillian stewardess wakes me and I wake my husband. I'm excited by the coincidence. He doesn't notice it. He smiles at me – yawns – vigorously kneads his eyes with his wrists. We eat.

Why are you called Tachi? asks Hans, his mouth full of Benedicts. 10.43 – the hour of cruel questions.

Who's going to meet you at the airport? my husband asks me.

I'll take a taxi, I reply. And you?

A friend's picking me up. If you want, I'll call you on Sunday and we'll organize it so that you don't have to be there when I come to get my things on Monday.

Whatever, I say.

It's a nickname, says Tachi.

But how did you get it? insists Hans.

Too much mayonnaise! she interrupts. They agree on this.

Just because, says Tachi. My name's Ignacio, but my little sister used to call me that when we were kids.

Ulpianus indicates that three conditions have to be fulfilled for a marriage to be considered legitimate: proof of fitness to marry; that the man has reached puberty and the woman is of an age to have sexual relations; the consent of both parties.

11.03. The Sevillian woman and a male flight attendant collect the trays.

11.17. The Sevillian woman collects the earphones, which no one has used. I pretend to have lost mine – I've put them in my pocket – in case they come in useful.

11.22. The descent begins.

11.30. Tachi doesn't want to sit in the middle block for the landing. It frightens him – he doesn't like it, he insists. Hans offers to change back. The city had dawned cloudy and wet, so the view from the air wouldn't be much to talk about anyway.

11.45. Tachi and my husband look out of the window in silence – the city blanketed in thick – milky – clouds.

The aircraft descends – touches down – bounces slightly – comes to earth again – moves forward – gradually brakes – and comes to a complete halt.

Titans on the Beach

ALAN MILLS

Translated by Delaina Haslam

When you see them running like that, completely naked along the Baltic Sea beach, the baby Teutons take on the appearance of ancient Atlanteans, or giant marble structures in miniature.

The north wind, at times too strong, shakes me and leaves me spinning like a weathervane, while it barely tickles these little Hulks. Truth is, I love watching them laugh. So healthy and wholesome.

Any of these chunky tots would easily have me in a wrestling match, and it wouldn't even be a great achievement for them. I've seen them at the Brandenburg lakes sizing up the swans or scaring them off, and I have no doubt that, if it came to it, they'd know exactly how to flip me onto my back.

'Right, that's it. I'm getting the new Mac,' Sue K. says to me as she lifts her hand from her shaded recliner to signal that we've finished the fizzy water.

Her movements create a fleeting shadow puppet – an iguana or salamander – on the sand.

'I can't work with this shit machine any more. Honest to God I can't,' she goes on, licking the tip of one finger to turn the page of her book.

Her voice mixes with the spasms of the north wind. Gusts of air drag tiny pebbles, transforming my mental images: an astronaut surfing through a wormhole, or a little buddha facing the rapids of a river.

My mind frames our scrap of beach like one of those magic drawing boards which those of us who grew up in the eighties had as children – Etch A Sketch, I think they were called: unwieldy contraptions filled with aluminium powder, like Egyptian tablets on which you traced your dreams – pretty much an early version of the electronic screen of a smartphone.

I shift the sand with my toes, rather like a trained monkey. I kick little stones towards the sea and, without having to employ too much conscious effort, begin to reproduce the solid frame of Sue K. in the sandy pictures of my imagination. I don't really know if it's my mind that's drawing her, or if the sea breeze has simply taken it upon itself to accurately interpret my desires. It's like I want to make a copy or clone her as confirmation that this goddess is really mine.

As I slide a glance at her washboard stomach I can't help but lament the inevitable deterioration that Sue K.'s body will suffer at the – as yet unforeseen – time we come to start a family. I wallow pre-emptively in the idea of what a shame it would be to see such muscle tone squandered by the merciless growth of an offspring – especially considering the massive size of the infants round here.

Seriously, what type of extraterrestrial vitamins do they put in these kids' bottles?

I see them running past my recliner. Then they dart out of focus and disappear. I listen to them skulking around like a gang of mutants. It scares me to think that, say, between turns, they could accidentally knock me down or knock me out. I watch their jerky movements, and their steps seem to make the earth shudder.

Then – and this may be a simple consequence of culture shock, or another of the many supposed delusions caused by huge post-migration stress, as Sue K. keeps telling me – the thing is that for a while here it's seemed to me that German babies are really giants landed from a parallel dimension. I don't just say this because of the obvious physical aspect, but also because of their attitude, a certain emotional rhythm, a mood, a tone of mind which makes them, in my eyes, abnormally hardy, mighty, hefty, masters of a sturdy air of domination.

I sometimes feel like I'm sleepwalking along the paths of a nightmare – or in a film: *Attack of the Behemoth Babies* – in which I'm pursued by acromegalic toddlers equipped with an affection as indifferent as it is overwhelming.

I haven't yet managed to find a spark. There hasn't been the slightest sign of chemistry between us, so all I can do is accept it. I've tried a thousand and one clownish antics each time I catch one of these little angels looking; I make funny faces, or try to start one of those cute games; I start whistling, or try to make some kind of silly noise. However, I hardly ever get a response.

Sometimes one of them gets a fright when they notice my thick brown body-hair, but nothing more: once they get over the initial shock, the best-case scenario is that one stretches out its fingers towards me as though reaching out to a talking teddy bear – with no further interest than a curiosity which borders on taxonomic. These unfortunate children of the Devil seem to come adapted to rational order from birth.

'Come on, give my back a little scratch, will you, Chewie? Don't be a grump,' Sue K. demands. 'At least it'll get you down off that cloud for a minute. Don't abandon us mortals, don't leave us stranded at sea.'

I listen to her as I continue to stroke my right foot. I take a deep breath, or rather, I sigh. I take an arm off my recliner ready to airlift it towards Sue K.

While I must admit that I don't enjoy scratching tasks as much as I used to, they're not exactly a hardship either. Although it's not like at the start of the relationship – when I'd practically be licking my fingers after performing this chore – I still get something out of these primate favours.

'A bit more to the left ... a little bit more ... that's it, *por ahí vas a toda madre*, my Chewie, give it to me hard baby, *así*, that's right, ah ... now lower, a tiny bit lower, there, right there ... *eso, eso es*, now give me a bit of nail, that's it, that's right, ahhh, that's what I like, we're going straight to heaven like that, Chewie, don't stop, carry on, don't hold back ...'

She's in a good mood this afternoon, my queen of hearts. She always calls me Chewie when she's happy. I'd rather she called me Chewie than Chewbacca, obviously, but in an ideal world she'd call me by my real name, Jesús – a name which, out of fundamental ecumenical respect, ought to be untouchable and incorruptible. No one in the once sacrosanct occidental world can deny that my name is the sacred name par excellence.

In any case, I'm not complaining. I knew from the outset that Sue K. was a non-believer, a scientist, as well as a literary type, so I couldn't exactly expect much different. In her view, my name is just a name. It could have equally been Mohammed or Krishna – it wouldn't make any difference to her. Maybe even, if I'd been named after one of her literary idols (let's say Günther, Salman, Umberto, Gabriel, Jorge Luis, Juan Nepomuceno Carlos, or her very favourite, Roberto), things would be different.

Moreover, it's understood that Sue K. calls me these nicknames because she's teasing me out of love. What I don't appreciate as much is when her friends turn up at our flat in Berlin and straight away start giving it Chewbacca this, Chewbacca that, or Chewie here, Chewie over there; Chewbacca above, Chewbacca below, Chewbacca everywhere.

'So you didn't go and look for work today either, Chewbacca?'

'The German's going a bit slowly, Chewie sir.'

'*Wie läuft's, Chewbacca, hast du den Fuchs schon gefangen?*'

'*Alles okay, liebe Freunde.*'

It's not that I don't appreciate their interest in my adaptation to the German culture, nor their well-meaning attempts to kick me into gear to finally find a job. It would be ungrateful of me to think they were asking me so many questions out of morbid fascination, or just to please my wife. However, I have to accept that I don't really like them taking the liberty of calling me nicknames that are meant only for my family or those I'm closest to. Maybe in time, God willing, we'll become closer, but for the moment let's be clear that I've been in this country just under two years, and I don't feel they have the right to call me names. Whenever I can, I ask them once again, plainly and simply, to do me the favour of calling me Jesús; again and again I try to correct Sue K.'s friends, but as sod's law has it they don't take a blind bit of notice.

My queen of hearts has told me I shouldn't take such things to heart so much.

'Relax, darling, don't be so sensitive,' she tells me. 'You look like the poor cripple girl in your *telenovela*. Don't get so angry – you know we all use your nicknames affectionately, don't be so stuck up.'

She always sounds so convincing, focused, well balanced. And, well, at the end of the day, she's got a point, right? It's clear that the change of country has left me a bit crotchety, since the truth is that before, I'd rarely get annoyed if someone I knew (or was acquainted with) called me Chewie.

Chewbacca is a different matter. That's another story that I don't feel like telling right now.

It's not even a big deal: let people call me whatever they like; let's just agree to make me the beast and have done with it. Because at the same time it's clear that I need to make a few friends, and also I've got to accept that I can't exactly be picky in this respect: either I lighten up in the face of Sue K.'s colleagues' banter or forget it. It wouldn't cost me anything to play along a bit more. It's about time I compensated in some way for all the arrangements my wife had to make to ensure that I'd settle comfortably in this country.

I think this over in silence while I continue to scratch, and I contemplate the radiant turquoise tones of the horizon.

'Ow! Be gentle, Chewbacca, don't attack me!' Sue K. interrupts me with a swipe. 'You're digging your claws in!'

'I got distracted, buttercup, I'm really sorry.'

'You haven't drawn blood, have you, you filthy animal?' She squeals. 'Look! Look what you've done to me.'

Her mastery of Spanish and her fiery handling of my country's slang shine even brighter when she uses them to curse. This is how Sue K. aces at being a drama queen of Spanish, this is where she demonstrates that she knows the language of Cervantes and José Alfredo inside out.

Her shower of slaps has left my right arm with a hot, burning sensation. It must be red, but I can't check because of the layer of hairs. It doesn't actually hurt that much, it's more of an intense feeling which is in fact quite nice.

Sue K. takes control of my right hand. She leads it up and down, trying to determine whether I've inflicted any deep wounds along her athlete's back. She gradually starts to breathe more calmly and relax when I take her compact from her bag to show her in the mirror that I've barely grazed her, it's a faint cat scratch which will hardly leave a mark; I give her one, two, three, four kisses along the trace of a blotchy line.

'*Sana-sana-colita-de-rana-si-no-sana-hoy-sanará-mañana.*' I say this little rhyme, but I don't think Sue K. is impressed as she leaps up like a panther, puts the Daniel Sada novel she's just finished into her backpack, leaves her recliner behind, pads across the sand like a lioness preparing to pounce on a gazelle, takes a few steps towards her bike then signals with her eyes that I should follow.

Going at the same pace as she rode to the beach, my queen of hearts starts talking to herself. She does this pretty much out loud – so that I hear her, of course – while it's clear that she's talking to herself; she doesn't expect me to respond and, what's more, what on earth could I say to her?

It's difficult for me to understand how these things work. She often tells me about her projects, her ideas and her movements in the academic world. She speaks in military jargon which sounds completely weird to me. I'm sure that if, say, a stranger heard her without having any idea of the actual context, they might think that the person speaking was the commander of a large army facing the pressures of fratricidal war.

My Prussian monarch goes on and on through her theatre monologue. This time she goes so far that I can't deny feeling a bit cheated: our stay in the Ostsee was supposed to be an oasis in the middle of Sue K.'s intense professional life. The aim was to switch off so that she could then go back to the university recharged. The plan had been to relax and chill out for a reasonable amount of time. The original idea was that we'd stay well away from real life, totally removed from work problems. And the original objective of the trip was to be completely calm for a while.

'Chew-ie, catch up! Pedal faster or you're never gonna work off that builder's belly!'

Her cries are like a white-hot worm boring through my ears like they were two apples.

And I'd like to do as she bids, how could I not, but my increased efforts are in vain. Between my construction worker's stomach and these Tweetie Pie legs, I wouldn't gain enough speed to catch an escaped circus dog on a unicycle.

Bitterly, I watch Sue K. getting further and further away. I watch her leave the beach at a constant speed, going into one of those dreamy little streets reminiscent of the town in *The Truman Show* with its utopian-designed houses that radiate well-being.

I'd like to call something nice to my queen of hearts, some quaint witticism to get her to wait for me, but I haven't got enough breath. I moan, spit on the floor and splutter, feeling like I've run out of air.

Didn't we come here to relax?

FROM THE UNPUBLISHED NOVEL *ZORRERA*

Come to Raise

EMILIANO MONGE

Translated by Frank Wynne

We didn't expect – though we should have guessed – that this one, too, would have stopped dead. This makes a hundred and thirteen, by my count. A hundred and fifteen, according to Laura, who heard someone say: *The one at the white tower still works.*

Now we have to go back. Or rather to go forward, but in the opposite direction. The words 'go back' and 'go forward' have long since lost all meaning. Or ceased to matter. When it comes to it, most words have lost their meaning. And yet still we cling to them.

The last few blocks – now the first few – will also be the least difficult. The drains are one of the few privileges left to us. Who would have thought? A job half-done is now our only protection.

But, like everything else, the trenches can suddenly stop. Or start. And Laura and I have to clamber from the depths. Sidestep a group of burn-outs, scrabble up and down mounds of earth as our shadows fade with the tracks we leave behind.

'Between the pipes!' I call to Laura as we reach the corner, hop over a plinth shorn of its statue, circle the rusted skeleton of a car and reach the pavement on the far side of the street: 'Keep down, stay between the pipes!'

I don't know how long it's been since a man and woman walked upright. Those of us who still move around do so the way we do. It not only keeps us hidden, it teaches us to use our hands again. These days, being able to grip is less important now than being able to move fast.

'Along the road or through the building?' Laura calls, suddenly stopping. A few metres ahead, the pipes shielding us come to a dead end. I don't know why she's asking, and tell her as much: 'Why are you bothering to ask?' Smiling, Laura says nothing but runs towards the entrance of the skyscraper from whose apex it seems night is being born.

In the few metres before we reach the hulking concrete behemoth, Laura and I jump several craters and dodge past another family of burn-outs: avoiding each other's eyes, as though unaware that they are huddled together, they are soaking up the last rays of afternoon.

This is how it began. Or at least it was the beginning of the end: a man left his office, stopped in the middle of the street, allowed every muscle in his body to go slack and whispered: 'I'm exhausted.'

Midway through the building, I catch up with Laura. 'Rooms', we called them many years ago, and I don't know which is more distant, the 'many' or the 'years'. 'Just the way you like them,' she says, smiling at me again. She's right. We're running through a vast, cold, empty gallery. A space that might have been anything.

'It wasn't designed to be a ruin,' I say to Laura for the umpteenth time and now it is my turn to smile. 'But we need to get a move on,' I say, racing across the raw concrete: 'We can't hang around, it's getting late. And we left our things unguarded.'

'Our *thing*,' Laura corrects, clenching her jaw as she, too, breaks into a run.

By the time we see the main door of the colossus, we can scarcely see a thing. The street is shrouded by a plastic tarp fluttering fitfully with the wind. The sun is dipping below the mountains that ring this last metropolis, shearing all things of their shadows.

On the steps leading down to the street, we once more come to a sudden halt. We hesitate, turning towards each of the compass points except the one from which we came. 'It's obvious,' I say to Laura a second later, as our eyes make out the contour of the bridges.

As we approach the point where the street arches its back, we dodge past a thicket of shrubs, another group of burn-outs and the remains of one of the defeated. I see mistrust engraved on Laura's face. It has been months since we came across one, months since we stumbled on one of the vanquished.

'Don't think about him,' I say, 'just keep running.'

But I am the one who cannot shut out the feelings of revulsion as we race uphill. Was he simply prey, or had he, too, been a malefactor?

Malefactors: this is the name we give to those who go beyond exhaustion, the burn-outs who, rather than seeking shelter, dried out like piles of salt: the dead-beats who rather than practising self-mummification, allowed themselves to rust like a mesh of cogs; those who, without realizing, stopped the clocks.

'Perhaps he was the first,' I let slip in a low whisper, and my words stop Laura in her tracks: 'Why are you still harping on about that?' She's right, why am I still brooding? Why is it always the same? Why am I so determined to believe that it was self-exploitation that made them suddenly grind to a halt. Why can't I simply accept what we've been told?

'You know perfectly well it was the sphere,' Laura whispers, coming closer and trying to hug me. She knows me, knows the thoughts that wound me most. 'The huge sphere that fell stopped all the clocks,' she says, trying to reassure me. She tries to put her arms around me, but they are not adapted to such gestures.

*

A moment later, Laura lets me go, steps back and smiles. 'You'll see, we'll find one that works,' she says encouragingly, as though it is her job to support me. As though I am not the one responsible for keeping the fire in her belly burning.

'I'm sure we will,' I say to my daughter, regaining my composure. Then, wiping my eyes, I point into the distance. We have reached the highest point of the bridges: despite the gathering dusk, it is still possible to see the vegetation devouring and destroying the ancient constructions built by men; seeing the plants reclaim what was always theirs brings a smile to both our faces.

In an attempt to strengthen the bond that the landscape has created between us, Laura and I turn and survey the other horizon visible from the bridge before we set off again. 'Security is your responsibility,' I say, decoding for my daughter these ciphers that once were letters over there on the factory tower ringed by the twilight, at the far end of a patch of waste ground that could be crossed in two steps or two hundred.

'Don't read it!' Laura screams. 'You always do that!' she says, suddenly angry, and turning on her heel, races down the road, 'I've told you, I don't want you reading them!'

Twenty metres before we leave the bridge, I hear my little girl's voice, quavering in the wind: 'A hundred and sixteen,' Laura says, snatching an old wristwatch off the ground without breaking her stride.

'A hundred and fourteen,' I protest, feebly clinging to my own calculation. Smiling again, Laura lightly tosses aside the useless lump of plastic. 'We're not safe, Papa.' Above our heads, lowering clouds have descended on the darkness: I cannot see them, but I can sense them – can I smell them?

'We're not safe, either of us,' my daughter says, running faster, her words becoming a premonition, warping the only two faces either of us have ever touched, ever admired. 'We're not safe,' she says again in a hushed whisper, and her premonition becomes reality: gradually we hear the sound, the sound made by those who live behind the huge white bars.

Every night they slip out in search of us. They want the one thing we have, they know that it is all that remains, that we possess it, they want to take it back to their translucent caves. But they do not know where we hide it. 'We have to make it back to the hideout,' I call to Laura. 'We have to hurry,' I goad her, turning our pace into a headlong flight.

'Head for the mouth,' I order a moment later, as we finally leave behind the ridge that begins where the bridges end and ends here, where the strange, inextinguishable arc of light soars like a temple to nothingness.

Despite my insistence – 'Head for the mouth' – Laura turns into the little alley that plunges into the earth: this is another route into the old city. The shortest route from where we are, but not the one that we usually take, the one we know best. Behind us, the noise of those who live imprisoned in translucent membranes grows louder.

'Turn right,' I yell angrily, 'that will take us there,' and watch as Laura obeys. We need to get back to our cave as quickly as possible, I think, and, as always when I do so, I am grateful to have happened on it one day; it is a place where my daughter can be safe; where the one thing we possess is beyond their reach; in that refuge, I can safeguard both.

'Thank you for leading us to the cave,' I mutter, switching on my flashlight and seeing the halo of light, or rather the thick ocean of darkness that encircles it, conjuring the image that comes to me on sleepless nights of what we once called gods. 'Thank you for leading me to this place,' I whisper as my daughter races towards the tunnel at which I am shining the torch.

'For showing us that this was what we had been searching for,' I mumble gratefully and, taking my hand from the walls, I pat the pocket in which I keep the talisman I was given: *Welcome to Paradise*, read the words on the billboard we stumbled upon one day; words that, as we drew nearer, were transformed into something else: _ _ _*come to* _ _*ra* _*ise*, read the letters over the cave that has become our refuge: some of the letters have faded. It is still some way off.

'Give it a rest with the gratitude,' Laura calls back, reading my mind yet again. 'Quit with the bullshit and run faster,' she says, swerving towards another tunnel.

'They're getting closer,' my daughter yells at the top of her lungs as we dash into one of the central shafts: only then do I hear them again – she is right, the noise has never been so close. I can feel the sound waves shudder down my back, my neck; the skin on my lower back is hissing, they're less a hundred metres away.

'They're going to find our hideout,' my daughter warns and, despite her fear, she stops in her tracks, switches off her flashlight and presses herself against the tunnel wall. 'They're going to take our things,' she says, grabbing my torch and flicking it off too. 'Our *thing*,' I correct as I, too, try to force the wall to open up and swallow me.

'Don't make a sound,' I say to Laura, silently, simply moving my lips. All we can hope is that they will lose their way, the noise they make is closer now, too close; it is upon us.

Petrified, attempting to become one with the stone, Laura and I stand motionless for a long time. But we cannot stay like this forever. To stay silent is almost to surrender, to allow exhaustion to seep in, to give up or give in, to lose track of time. We not only fear these creatures, we fear becoming those things they scarcely notice. My daughter would not know how to mummify herself, she would be filled with the awareness of self-exploitation. Perhaps this is what gives me the strength to draw myself upright. I notice that the noise is further off: 'Now!' I say and set off at a run.

When the noise finally fades, I look over my shoulder, I want to smile at my little girl, but though I scan the darkness I cannot see her, Laura is not following. Terrified, I stop, turn and begin to retrace my steps, my fear mounting.

'Laura!' I call out, 'Laura . . . Laura!'

I find my daughter, sobbing, rooted to the same spot where we tried to become one with the rocks. 'Get up,' I say, crouching down and pressing my lips to her ear. 'We can't do this, you know that.'

Despite my words, Laura does not react, does not move but for her trembling. I shake her, gently at first, then forcefully. She moves her head – no, just her lips: 'I don't want to any more.' Silently, I try to think of what to say to her: mentally reviewing what we have lived through together, recalling every word we've spoken, invoking every day we've lived.

In the end, I say nothing.

Having waited with my daughter for a moment, I try again: 'You can do it now,' I say as I wipe her eyes with the one hand still capable of making the gesture. 'We need to get back to the cave.'

Lifting Laura is not easy; I feel rust in my bones, the powerlessness of fingers that have not touched other fingers in an age; I cannot straighten my back to haul her to her feet.

In the end, I have to tuck my head under her arm to haul her to her feet.

Making it through the first tunnel is an ordeal. But gradually, Laura comes to herself again. And then, when I feel the moment is right, I bring my lips close to her ear: 'What would happen if they found our thing?'

I see something blaze again in my daughter's eyes. And though she continues to lean against me as we navigate the tunnels, by the time we reach the vast gallery where the wider tunnels converge, Laura is finally walking on her own.

A moment later, we are sprinting again. Glancing at each other from time to time. Sometimes even speaking in low voices: suddenly I tell her to turn, all that is pushing her forward now is the terror within her – they can't have found it.

Frantically we cover the final stretch, Laura is increasingly panicked, I am increasingly radiant. And so we come to the cave: *come to raise.*

No sooner are we inside than I rush to the corner and throw myself on the ground. I slide away the rock shielding it and cup the thing in both hands; I need to bring my little girl back to herself, to give her the strength that exhaustion threatens to sap from us.

We sit on the floor facing each other and I arrange the flashlight and slowly, carefully, unwrap our thing: it glitters in the palm of my hand.

'You turn it over,' I say to Laura. And my daughter excitedly raises her hand, brings it to my palm and turns time. The trickle of sand is barely audible.

Papi's False Teeth

MÓNICA OJEDA

Translated by Anna Milsom

Daughter took care of Papi's false teeth as she would a corpse, that is, with reverent, beyond-the-grave devotion. Dry round the incisors, rattling audibly, they materialized all over the house like a red-gummed ghost. The castanet click-clack of molars made her smile in the early mornings, and in the afternoons a tribal percussion, a chattering, soothed her until she nodded off across the pink pillow where fireflies spiralled down to die. Every night while she slept, Papi's dentures became her lover and bed-mate, slavering in her dreams and inconsequential nightmares with no sign of a moist, foul-smelling tongue, no rusty blade stabbing through her consciousness. And when she woke up, Daughter would sweep the dead flies from the pillow with her hair, sit on the patio steps to observe the dying garden, and take Godzilla out for a walk round the block. Together they barked at the other dogs that were muzzled, beribboned and dressed in little doggy outfits like two-year-olds.

The owners didn't like the way she barked louder than Godzilla.

They called her crazy bitch.

They looked askance at her feet.

Later, when she got home, Daughter would scrub Papi's teeth and put them up on the shelf like a trophy. She put them beside her on the sofa before switching on the TV. She took them to bed and tucked them under the sheet. She took them into the bath and sank beneath the water with them. She kept them in the fridge. She stashed them in a shoe. Daughter moved the false teeth all over the place, but hid them when Mami and Little Sister came to visit. They imagined they'd already taken all Papi's stuff because they didn't realize her home was a mausoleum patiently being constructed, bit by careful bit.

'You're neglecting the garden, completely killing it off.'

'How disgusting! It's full of dog shit.'

Mami and Little Sister paid no attention to the intimate architecture of her mourning, although they sniffed out the consequences easily enough.

'Do you think this level of squalor is normal?'

They stared at the garden like twins, simultaneously pursing their lips at all that disease. They had looked at Papi the same way when they left him with her – one ailing father dumped on the doorstep; one wheelchair, one drip stand, one oxygen cylinder. They left him even though they knew she was incapable of looking after anyone. They left him with her because she was the eldest: the Daughter. Meanwhile Mami dressed like Little Sister and drank too much. Little Sister would be leaving school soon and had a boyfriend she was always disappearing off to see bands with. They visited Daughter every Wednesday and Friday now, but when Papi was still alive they only came the last Saturday of the month.

'Everything's covered in dust.'

'The spiders will eat you.'

'For God's sake, cut your nails!'

During these post-mortem pop-ins, they'd change their clothes in Papi's room and get stuck into the cleaning. They put on long, tatty Nirvana T-shirts. T-shirts with pictures of drums and tigers on the front. Pictures of the Powerpuff Girls. Daughter watched them calmly because they never dared go into the garden where she'd buried the false teeth to make sure they wouldn't take them away from her. They had sent over a gardener three times to cure the sick plants, but she wouldn't let him in.

'You just love being surrounded by dying things.'

'You just love upsetting us.'

It had been Mami's idea to take all Papi's stuff. Mami, who considered herself to be in her prime. Mami, who was twelve years younger than Papi but now that he was dead would soon be eleven years younger, then ten, nine, and so on until she caught up and overtook him, finally dying older and sicker. More silent, more broken down, and with fewer teeth.

Daughter was surprised by how many of Papi's teeth fell out.

'The doctor says it's normal,' Little Sister told her, back when Papi was still living with her and Mami.

'What doctor? Doesn't that usually happen when you're very old?' Daughter asked. 'And he isn't that old.'

Week after week their father's teeth dropped like ripe fruit onto the parched earth of his tongue. He spat them out and they bounced off the walls, tables, chairs and sofas in Mami and Little Sister's house.

'Have you ever sat on a tooth all covered in blood?' Little Sister sobbed, trying to make her feel guilty. 'If you've never sat on a blood-stained tooth, you don't know shit.'

By the time their father died, his mouth was a pale tree with roots of dark spittle, but when he had his false teeth firmly in he drank and reeked of dead rat. Daughter knew what decomposing rat smelled like because it had taken them days to find one trapped in the hoses behind the washing machine. Their parents never noticed the creatures that died behind the appliances: they drank a lot and played at being other people in the room with the blue curtains, a shallow dish at the foot of the stairs, a dog lead, a muzzle and a yellow bone.

Papi suffered from tremors and sweating, he'd been knocked sideways by withdrawal symptoms ever since Daughter and Little Sister were eight and seven. He would curl up in a corner and whimper like a giant baby while Mami drank, her lips swollen, whistling for him every now and again.

'My girls, my poor little girls,' he used to snivel, his face all covered in snot. 'Forgive Papi! Forgive Papi's weakness.'

He never could manage more than a day without a drink. Neither could Mami. Daughter and Little Sister preferred them drunk because it meant they didn't cry or fight during their red sex. When they were drunk they used to giggle and titter and allow the girls to shut them in their room. When they were drunk they were better parents. They gave them presents. They spent the grandparents' inheritance on toys. They took them on trips by bus and plane.

Sometimes people didn't realize their parents were drunk.

Sometimes not even Daughter and her little sister could tell the difference.

Then Daughter turned eighteen and went to live on her own in the house that had belonged to her grandparents. She abandoned her sister, her mother and her father. She abandoned her sister to her mother and father. She didn't feel bad about it, because up to that point she'd always taken care of Little Sister. She had protected her from mosquitoes carrying Dengue fever, from cracked plates, from the puddles of piss on the floor and from Mami and Papi's grunting and red sex.

Sometimes, when Papi wanted to stop drinking and wept like a revolting grubby infant and clung to Little Sister bleating apologies nobody asked for, Daughter would hold out the bottle and say, 'Here you are, Papito'. And that's how she made him let go of Little Sister, who back then was afraid of the slightest thing.

Mami was far more together.

Mami never wept or tried to stop drinking.

Mami gave them each a glass of rum and Coke when Daughter was nine and little Sister was eight.

'See? It tastes awful! Never drink like Mami and Papi do, darlings.'

Daughter notices that her mother is never drunk when she visits with Little Sister and cleans the entire house, barring the garden which belongs to Godzilla and Papi's false teeth.

'That bloody wolf!' her mother yells when the dog barks at her and bares his lion fangs. His shark teeth.

'If the little bastard was any uglier, it'd kill him,' Little Sister says when she goes out to smoke and sees him tied up, slobbering over the sick earth.

Daughter liked Godzilla because she found him the very day she decided to move out and live alone, leaving her father, her sister and her mother. He was injured and mangy. It was raining and all she did was walk along the pavement ignoring him, but he bit her leg.

Pain, she realized that afternoon, could be enlightening.

Everything went white. She wasn't aware of the moment she fell to the ground. She didn't even kick the dog. And because of that, because she allowed him to bite her, Godzilla let go of her calf. Daughter remembered it perfectly: that moment of absolute clarity in the dog's jaws, in the piercing of her own flesh. And a vague image suddenly came to her from the past which made her realize this wasn't the first time she'd been bitten.

She didn't know how she had managed to get to her feet and continue her walk with so much light in her head, but the dog was behind her. He followed the trail of blood and rainwater. He followed Daughter, who was trembling all over. Daughter, who had never questioned her ability to remember before, but was now reconstructing herself with every step she took. And each one brought back a distant memory, painful and dim like the landscape of her house inundated by storm and spiders. Then she cried, with the dog at her back licking her blood. She let herself cry at the fear of knowing that if she had remembered this much she might remember worse things, things that had happened to her and crouched hidden in her mind like cockroaches that suddenly scuttled out of the bedroom to tell her who she really was even though she didn't want to know.

That's why Mami and Little Sister hated Godzilla: because he was a blood-licker.

That's why they cleaned the whole place except the garden.

'We know you need time and blah blah blah, but this can't go for ever,' Little Sister told her. 'You'll have to start behaving like a normal person some day.'

Godzilla respected Daughter because she'd let him bite her, or maybe because he'd tasted her flesh and found it salty and sad. Sometimes when she took him out for a walk he peed on her feet. When she got home she would leave them unwashed so that the smell of her father bloomed in her grandparents' house.

There were days when she didn't have the energy for anything other than Papi's false teeth, lovingly licked clean by Godzilla.

'Look, I know you left us and I don't blame you, don't think that I do, but you're going to have to take over now because your little sister and I just can't have him here any longer,' Mami told her over the phone.

So Daughter said, 'Let's put him in a home. We can pay somebody else to look after him.' And Mami said, 'Don't be thick,' like she did when she wasn't drinking much. 'We can't do that. You know he has other needs.'

But Daughter didn't see why they couldn't forget about his needs if he was ill and couldn't even speak properly.

'You've had your little holiday, now it's family time.'

Mami was nearly always drunk, but never when she visited with Little Sister to stroke Papi's head. He could barely move.

'Your sister can't do what needs doing, she doesn't respect the limits.'

'She's rough.'

'She goes too far.'

Little Sister told her that the medical diagnosis was slow in coming so Papi devoted himself to drinking more than ever and Mami to hiding out with her moderately alcoholic friends in what had been the grandparents' villa.

'If you don't help out, I'm going to explode,' she said. 'You have to take him or I won't be answerable for my actions.'

At about that time Papi began to stoop and couldn't walk more than a couple of feet without falling over. His illness was just like his drunkenness except that it didn't include Mami, dog leads, muzzles, barking, bones, beatings or hysterical yelping in the living room. It didn't include red sex.

Next came the wheelchair. The pills. The drip. The injections. The cylinder of oxygen.

'What bothers Papi most is that he can't drink any more,' Little Sister told her. 'That and the fact his teeth are falling out.'

Papi had always been proud of his looks. He was a man who despised ugliness and knew only too well how to use his teeth.

'At least I don't have to bear the two of them putting on their shitty little performance any more.'

If he took them to school, Papi would grin from the driving seat of his convertible and all the other girls would sigh.

'Your dad's so fit.'

'You're so lucky.'

Then Daughter would say, 'But he's a dog,' and only Little Sister would laugh because she knew just how true that was.

Papi liked people to admire his teeth so, long before he got sick – when gum disease from the booze threatened to hurt his ego – he went off to a wrinkled dentist who had the smile of a twenty-year-old. 'I'm going to look amazing after I've had the work done,' he told Mami. And he did look amazing, for a few years at least, until the illness took hold of him and he couldn't go to the dentist with the young mouth any more and his teeth started to fall out.

'It's just not normal for his teeth to drop out like this,' Daughter insisted, back before Papi came to live with her but when he had already lost the power of speech and used to goggle at her with wide-open eyes, as if watching a horror film.

'Of course it's normal,' Little Sister replied. 'What isn't normal is him spitting them out all over the house like a child.'

But a child only spits out milk teeth, the first set not the last, Daughter thought as she observed her father's eyes nearly popping out of their sockets.

'Mami doesn't do anything to help.'

Ever since Godzilla had bitten her leg, she didn't like being around her father.

'If things go on like this, I swear I'll run away.'

Little Sister's boyfriend wore a ripped black leather jacket even on hot days. He smoked Lucky Strike and had shown her sister how to blow smoke rings.

'You shouldn't let her smoke,' Daughter complained to Mami, back when Papi was still alive but could no longer drink or go to bathroom without help.

'So now you're telling me how to bring up my own daughter? Do me a favour. Concentrate on learning how to wipe your own bum, you moron.'

Daughter had frequently felt like a mother to her sister but she wasn't sure what being a good mother really meant and she wanted to be good, really good, like back in the days when she still lived with Little Sister and Mami and had never even considered moving into her grandparents' empty house.

She used to wonder how much her sister's boyfriend knew about Papi, how much Little Sister had been able to remember and talk about.

Once she asked her, 'Don't you find there are things that happened years ago you can't remember properly? And Little Sister glared at her as though she had a bogey dangling from her nose or a bit of food stuck between her teeth, 'No, because I don't know how to act dumb.'

Daughter often thought about what acting dumb meant in situations where being smart would have been difficult; a subconscious sacrifice, placing yourself outside your own mind.

When Mami and Little Sister handed over her sick father and she bathed him for the first time she found a recent cigarette burn, healing badly, a couple of inches above his knee. But Papi was now beyond speech and could only twitch the lids over his increasingly watery, bulging eyes.

'Ask your little sister about it,' Mami told her over the phone. 'I told you that you had to take him.'

That same afternoon, Daughter noticed her father's gums were swollen and blood sometimes dripped down his chin and onto his shirt.

'Someone's stubbed out a cigarette on Papi's leg,' she told Little Sister during a pedicure session. 'You used to bathe him, you must have known about it.'

Daughter, suddenly in charge of Papi's health and his good death, took him to a dentist who sorted out his gums and made him a set of false teeth.

'Of course I knew,' Little Sister replied, painting her nails the colour of flesh. 'Of course I know.'

And when the dentist asked, with the air of a private detective, how her father had managed to lose nearly all his teeth in a fall, Daughter answered so fast she was surprised by her own quick thinking. 'He fell down the stairs,' she said, while Papi's eyelids fluttered like a butterfly just doused with insecticide.

'You're insane, how could you?' Daughter burst out, feeling like vomiting from the smell of the nail varnish. Little Sister rolled her eyes, 'Oh, please. Don't play the innocent with me.'

Daughter sometimes floated in the full moon of her memory: circular, white, full of things she wanted to forget and did forget, though not permanently. Things like when Mami and Papi got drunk and Little Sister and Daughter would shut themselves away somewhere so they didn't see them playing in the living room. So they didn't see the red sex and their father on a lead.

Their father muzzled and on all fours.

Their mother wearing spurs.

So they didn't see him gnaw the bone mother threw him and then stepped on. So they didn't see Mami walking Papi down the corridor, chucking scraps on the floor for him, punishing him for peeing beside the sofa or pooing under the table.

But Little Sister still painted her nails the colour of Papi's skin.

'What's it to you if I burn him or take out all his teeth if he's just a dog?'

Daughter didn't want to think about how her sister had told her who she really was and she hadn't wanted to hear it. That's why she bathed Papi, fed Papi, took Papi for a walk. That's why when the false teeth arrived, Daughter put them in Papi's mouth and he stopped being afraid and smiled at her, baring new incisors that weren't his but looked as though they were. And Daughter combed his hair, sprinkled him with aftershave, took him out with Godzilla. And while Godzilla barked at other dogs, Papi slowly moved his jaw, stuck out his tongue and panted, quite content. And when Godzilla showed his teeth, Papi happily showed his too and it made Daughter angry because she remembered things she didn't want to. She remembered a straining leash, Papi barking like a lunatic, salivating, banging his kneecaps off the tiles, scratching the floor, staring at her and Little Sister – terrified, stunned – in the corridor, and Mami letting go of the lead.

'My girls, my poor little girls!'

'Forgive Papi!'

'Forgive Papi's weakness!'

Had it been her or Little Sister? Sometimes she wasn't sure. Sometimes she saw herself shutting the bedroom door just in time, saving herself from those jaws, leaving her sister outside to the mercy of their father's teeth. Other times, it was her in the corridor begging Little Sister to open up, let her in, and then came the bite.

'I don't remember anything of the sort, but if it did happen it must have been just the once, a booze thing, because your father was perfectly harmless when we used to play together,' Mami told her. 'That ugly mutt of yours is far more dangerous and I don't see you going around complaining about what he did to your leg.'

But Daughter knew Godzilla wasn't the first dog to bite her.

'You're the one who should be taking care of him,' she complained to her mother when her father started to howl and soil himself every night.

'I can't do it,' Mami replied simply, as if she were talking about shaking out a large rug. 'I only know how to punish your father, but you really know how to look after a dog.'

Daughter dried his fur with a hairdryer. She gave him chicken bones to gnaw at with his false teeth, she clipped on his lead and tied him up beside Godzilla in the garden to watch the sun go down. She let Mami stroke his head when she came to call. She made sure Little Sister didn't pinch his ears.

'You should punish him one day and then not the next, because that's what he likes,' her sister instructed her as she said goodbye. But Daughter was brushing Papi's dentures and watching them sink to the bottom of a glass of clean water.

She changed his nappies. She filed his nails. She shaved him. She whistled for him like she whistled for Godzilla.

She let him bark and howl in the night.

'That's what killed Papi off early. You know that, don't you?' Little Sister asked, leaning on her mop. 'Your obsession with being a good girl, when what he needed was looking after in a very different sort of way.'

Her sister's boyfriend wore black nail varnish and had swamp-coloured eyes. Sometimes, if she bumped into him waiting for Little Sister outside school with his ears pricked, tongue hanging out and fingernails curled in his pockets, Daughter imagined a pair of pliers and wondered how much he knew about the cigarette burn and Papi's teeth.

How much did he know about her sister's shameless, violent way of loving?

One Friday, when Mami was cleaning the windows, Godzilla dug up the false teeth and lay licking them on the lawn.

'I can't believe you kept hold of them,' Mami said, stroking Papi's dentures over her cheek. 'We should have buried him with these,' she wailed, make-up running. 'Oh, what's a dog without teeth?'

Daughter spent a good deal of time thinking about this: what *is* a dog without teeth?

Papi wet himself. He soiled himself. He howled in the night and Daughter never gave him the chance to really use his dentures. She never let him defend himself. Before bed, she took them out with a thrill of pleasure she wouldn't dream of admitting, watching how her father's eyes widened in horror at his denuded mouth. Reflected in those twin orbs, like eggs about to pop, Daughter saw exactly who she was, even though she never wanted to recognize it in the morning.

'You really know how to look after a dog,' Mami maintained, but Daughter wasn't so sure that the domesticated Godzilla would recall the enormous pleasure to be had in biting.

She didn't know whether, when she took him out for a walk and slipped off his collar saying, 'You've got to go, I don't know how to look after you or whether I love you,' the dog understood that she would have preferred him to leave and never come back, to use his teeth elsewhere, on other bones, to lick up another family's blood. But the dog just slobbered at her heels and, if he did wander off, if he let himself be taken for walks and pee on other feet, he always came home with a clean snout.

Teresa

EDUARDO PLAZA

Translated by Rahul Bery

Fernanda is my wife. Teresa is her aunt, her father's youngest sister. They're very similar, physically I mean. Fernanda is thirty-two. Teresa is thirty-six.

Teresa and I slept together once, in the beach house in Tongoy. Fernanda's house.

Fernanda had already returned to Santiago and I, with no work to go back to, and allergic to the warm Januarys in Antonio Varas, had decided to stay on the coast for a few more days. I'd brought four hours of recordings with me to transcribe, as well as my Xbox 360. I wanted to finish *Assassin's Creed 4*. That was how I was occupying myself when she showed up with a couple of friends. Teresa. They'd spend all day at the beach, returning home around midnight, always in silence. They were like timid little girls apologizing for the noises their footsteps made.

Teresa's friends were twins, blondes. They were twenty-five, twenty-six maybe. Their skin was white and opaque, like skimmed milk. There were pale-blue veins on their eyebrows and in the middle of their foreheads, as well as on the backs of their hands. One of them was pregnant and always wore a maternity belt, even when she put on a swimsuit and went into the sea. All of their extremities were stick-thin, like mosquito legs. Sometimes they mumbled things to each other. I'd get up at midday, turn on the console and play until I felt hungry. Then I'd go down to Negro El Cero, buy some seafood empanadas, take a short stroll down by the shell heaps and then go back home. Every time I walked past I'd see the three of them walking along the shore, letting the waves brush up against their feet.

Tongoy was the only place in the world I had actively chosen to be over this whole period of my life. Fernanda was a journalist and wrote for a travel magazine. I followed her to Recife, Cabo Polonio, Montañita, and also to San Francisco and Phoenix. I wanted to be a writer. The whole thing seemed like a good opportunity to quit my office job, sell the car, and, with my savings to live off, finally finish the fifty stories gathering dust on my laptop. I followed her to the Trans-Siberian railway, the Kungur ice caves, the white nights. I soon realized it hadn't been such a sensible move. I'd wake up late, still tired, while she would have done so early and full of energy. I didn't enjoy being with strangers. I became parsimonious. I started smoking. She hated it. My money lasted half as long as I'd estimated at the start, and I soon became a costly nuisance. We fought a lot. We were young. Every time we argued I got scared she'd leave, abandoning me there, lost and wretched in some country that was straight out of the pages of a glossy travel brochure.

When we returned to Chile, a year later, I hadn't written even two half-decent paragraphs. I had to put being a writer on hold again and focus on just trying to pay the bills. Finding work wasn't easy for me. Fernanda, on the other hand, was offered some teaching work at the university within a matter of days. The pay wasn't bad. I began doing transcriptions for students, psychology or anthropology mostly. I woke up at midday, played Xbox until five or six and then transcribed until three or four in the morning. I liked working at night, while she slept or went out with friends. With time we began to settle into this new life: things had just turned out this way and while it wasn't quite what we'd expected, nor was it some huge sacrifice. We tolerated our destitution and when the weather was good we'd go and stay in her house in Tongoy.

Teresa was not Fernanda. She didn't have her passport full of stamps, or her stock of witty and enchanting anecdotes. Her whole existence was like her visit that week when we slept together: anonymous and silent.

She arrived in Tongoy thinking no one would be there. When she was made aware of my presence, she called Fernanda to apologize, she'd thought I was with her. He stayed on by himself for a few days, Fernanda said, he needs peace and quiet so he can write.

Fernanda's whole family believed that I was finishing a book of short stories. According to her, it was best they didn't know that the work I was doing was more suited to an undergraduate. I didn't mind lying.

That afternoon I was watching films and drinking beers. I found out how to get Netflix on the Xbox. There were speakers in the lounge, which I brought into the room and connected to the TV. It was the closest I could get to having my own cinema. I watched *Deathwish*, and drank two or three cans. Then I watched *Public Enemies*, with Johnny Depp. Later on, I watched *Top Gun* and *Ronin*. I only left the flat when the beer ran out and I had to go out and buy some more.

As I walked, I saw three boys tormenting a cat by the quay. They'd stuck bits of sellotape all over its body – whole metres of tape, wrapped thousands of times around its back and belly. The cat was trying to move; it took one step before falling onto its side. It looked drunk. The boys were throwing it by its tail, spinning it onto the ground and laughing. The animal didn't make a sound. Maybe it was suffocating. The smallest boy, ten or eleven years old, watched it as he played around with some scissors. A woman shouted out of her window: Let that animal go! I'm going to call your father. Put those scissors down. The boys took the cat and went off towards the boats. I remembered the harbour in Coquimbo when we were boys: setting effigies alight on New Year's Eve, running from our fathers. Bursting tyres. Stealing car badges. Many of my friends from that time had ended up in Tongoy, where their children had been imprisoned by the Maritime school which, instead of educating them, turned them into the submissive hostages of the oyster industry. After a while we'd stopped seeing each other, and over time the town itself had also begun to lose its colour and dry up. El Niño changed the temperature of the water and the men had to get into their boats and go out in search of cuttlefish and mackerel. The oysters, which had promised to lift them out of poverty, which had painted their houses and paid for new trainers for their children, had gone away, leaving the dinghies empty and the town's inhabitants gathering seaweed.

In Negro El Cero I bumped into Teresa and her guests. They were eating empanadas and two of them were drinking beer. She beckoned me with her hand and greeted me warmly. The alcohol had relaxed her tongue, and her speech was elegant and graceful. She smiled freely and loosely. I sat down opposite her.

– Will you join us?

– I can't, I'm working on some texts, I said, lying.

– What do you write about? At the time I was transcribing focus groups for master's students.

– I go over old stuff, edit it.

The twins sat opposite each other, so that their side of the table was perfectly symmetrical.

Teresa was still married, at least on paper. She had run away from her marriage like a dog fleeing the scene after being hit by a car. One night she took her purse and left her apartment, her block, and the life she had been building. She never went back. For a few weeks she hid in friends' houses. Her husband called everyone, demanding to know her whereabouts. After a while the calls became less frequent, until one day he just stopped. Teresa came out of her hiding place looking as thin and stiff as a hat stand. She never said a word to anyone, and because so many people are happy to assume that issues disappear when they are no longer being spoken about, it soon ceased to be an issue. She quit her job formally and left for Tirúa, a small inlet in the south. Her brother, Fernanda's father, had a cabin down there. We lost track of her for several months. She came back from the south with the twins.

I ordered three prawn empanadas to take away.

– How long are you staying? I asked.

– Three or four more days. We want to go to Mamalluca, to the observatory. We'll stay in the Elqui Valley and then go a little further north. I haven't been to the valley for more than ten years! And it's one of my favourite places. I want to take the girls – they barely know Chile at all. Why don't you have those with us? she said, finally. I agreed and ordered a litre bottle of beer.

An orange glow began to spread over the roofs of the houses, at the same speed as the rising tide. Something both fell asleep and died at once, was suspended. People began to order their things and leave. The cars left, almost in synchrony, back the same way they had come earlier, like a line of ants leaving furrows in the earth, carried along by an impulse learned over generations. Silence settled over everything, filling up every crack, every hidden corner, reaching the places only the sand can reach. Soon you could hear the sound of the sea.

We went back along the quay. The twins walked behind us. One of them stopped suddenly and gripped her sister's hand. She shouted, pointing towards the pier. We turned and looked in the direction of her finger: the three boys were putting the cat in a bag and attempting to toss it into the sea. The animal was still wrapped in tape and didn't appear to be offering any resistance. They closed the bag.

Teresa shouted frantically, running off towards the boys. We all followed. The boys saw her. The oldest one took the bag and threw it, with all his strength, over the heads of the other two. The bag disappeared into the sea. The orange glow gave way to a greyish blue. The town's lights flickered on. The boys fled, towards the small boats docked at the quay, scuttling off like lizards.

In the sea there was nothing. Teresa was out of control. She was shouting, putting both hands over her face and looking out over the water, searching for the bag. One of the twins began to cry, with one hand on her mouth and the other on her belly. Her sister tried to make me do something. I waited eight, ten seconds before putting my hands in my pockets to take out my wallet and then removing my jacket. Without taking off my trainers I launched myself into the water. It was very cold. Find the bag, Teresa begged, please find the bag. They threw it over there. I counted to five, took a big breath and went under, going two or three metres down, letting myself fall in the same position, feeling my way with my hands.

A few seconds later I came up for air. Teresa was crying inconsolably and the twins had stepped back. I waited a few seconds, then went under again. Suddenly, submerged in that darkness, surrounded by the unknown, I began to hear the distant whisper of terror, like an approaching storm. Making its presence known. I'm looking for a dead cat, I thought. In total darkness, looking for a dead cat.

Then I felt it. Its claws scratching my left arm, like needles. The creature was attacking me. I began to panic. It was fighting, goading me on. It sank its claws in like a bear trap. It wouldn't let me go. I thrashed my right hand around and in vain ripped off bits of the bag without managing to get through to the body. I kicked furiously, trying to move away from the cat which was beginning to shake, still clinging on to my body. Then it stopped. I turned around to move off and felt it floating between my legs, empty now in the calm of death. Despairing, I came up. When I was above the water I took a breath and and let out an anguished wail. Teresa was still crying. She told me to come out. She begged me to come out. One of the twins was sobbing and the other was covering her eyes, wishing herself somewhere, anywhere else. I propelled myself upwards and climbed onto the jetty. Two women watched from the quay. Let's go, let's go, Teresa repeated. I'm sorry, please forgive me. Let's go, please. *Girls, come on, let's go home. I'm sorry. Let's just go, okay?*

Back at the house Teresa couldn't find any cotton or bandages, so she tore some kitchen roll into shreds, soaked it in alcohol and fastened it over my wounds using a couple of knots. Her eyes and nose were still red. I told her to be calm and, half smiling, she told me she was okay. It's okay now. The pregnant girl had gone to lie down and her sister, now recovered, was making tea for her in the kitchen. It was maybe two or three in the morning when I switched off the TV. I didn't manage to finish *Assassin's Creed*, as I had planned. I wouldn't finish it in Tongoy, but in Antonio Varas, four days later.

I was drifting off to sleep when I heard the door creak. Teresa got into the bed quietly and carefully, almost brushing against my back. After five or ten minutes, she began to sob, silently but deeply, muffling the sounds with the pillow. I thought about turning over and embracing her, consoling her, telling her that she could count on me, but my timidity got in the way. My timidity, and maybe hers as well. I wasn't sure. She lay awake, sobbing, for an hour. After that, I felt her body finally beginning to give in to rest. I stayed awake until she was asleep.

When I woke up she'd already gone. There was a thank-you card, signed by all three of them, on the kitchen table. They'd left for La Sirena at midday and hadn't wanted to disturb me. After making coffee I grabbed my trainers and went out into Tongoy for a walk. I wanted to see the ocean.

Suffering Creature

EDUARDO RABASA

Translated by Christina MacSweeney

I know they're coming for me. They'll be here any time now. I can visualize them bursting into this pigsty, or, in a few days, into the next pigsty. Or it could have been any of the previous ones. I see them with bulletproof vests and shotguns, so fucking gutless they have to come in packs. They're wearing helmets and have LED masks, because the cowards will come at night. I'm certain of that. When I manage to think of something else, to stop seeing them, then I hear them. Helicopters. A lot of helicopters. Flying in concentric circles, stalking me, enjoying the profile of my panic. They descend lightly, as if they were metal flies, come unbearably close, and then vanish at the last minute, only to take up residence in my head, where their blades sound with renewed fury. The din drills into my neurons. It can go on like that for hours. The only way to silence it is by getting off my head, as can be seen from the empties and the half-used packets of pills I've been leaving behind in the pigsties. Losing myself in video games the whole day long. Imagining that this time the bloodbath is justified by a noble aim, a mission framed by the eternal struggle between good and evil. Evil. Am I really the personification of evil they all claim? Bloody journalists.

Always sticking their fucking noses in where they know they don't belong. What do they expect to happen to them? None of the boys from my former realm are the sort to pussyfoot around. But it's always me, me, me. We, the chosen few, were groomed to shoulder the burden of guilt for the weak, those people who need us to govern them with an iron fist, so they can turn against us, when we did nothing more than what, in their hearts, they were crying out for us to do. The Cuban *santero* prophesied it when the old man took me to the ritual handing-over of the baton, to prepare me to succeed him as headman of the clan, to become him: after anointing my face with the blood of a dead cockerel, the *santero* turned to the old man and, in that clipped Cuban accent, pronounced, 'This kid's got the balls of a ruler. He'll choose between his enemies and himself. Many heads will roll. Many heads.' Shame I had to travel with the old man, listening to his drivelling lectures. While he was training me, I was watching the hot little Cuban girls go by, well aware that for a few sticks of gum or a couple of tampons I could fuck any one of them. But the old man would be going on and on about the dangers of encouraging false hopes in the populace. 'What use were the ideals of the beardies, my boy, when everyone, except for just a few, ended up in the same shit at the bottom of the heap?' Naturally our lot paid lip service to their duty to the people, but during that interminable trip, the old man repeatedly warned against believing the stupid stuff I'd be obliged to spout if I wanted to become a distinguished member of the clan. I believe the bastard was jealous of all the possibilities my youth offered me, so he had no problem with fucking me about during our stay in Cuba, keeping me with him night and day, but it was also because he'd arranged that, as soon as we got back, I was to go to Europe with the sons of the faction. So we'd get to know each other, become brothers, go drinking and whoring together, prepare ourselves for the generational handover. I can hardly remember the details of all those cities with their decadent beauty, their boring museums, galleries and cathedrals, the terrace cafes where people spend hours sitting around looking superior, just because over there you can have a coffee or a beer while chatting in a civilized way with anyone who turns up. That's why they felt sorry for us when we approached them warily, with our feral air, and it was much worse for those of my comrades burdened with the curse of dark skin, flat noses and thick lips. When I saw them, rat-arsed, trying it on with the dumb little princesses, even I'd have felt disgusted to be in those girls' shoes. The amazing thing is that some of those motherfuckers got lucky, and ended salving the social consciences of the frigging compassionate airheads. I had no time for stupid stuff like that. The old man had trained me to watch the others carefully, to set them tests and lay traps to check who was loyal, who was a bootlicker, who was a fool. It would all come in very useful one day, he told me. And he wasn't wrong. If I managed to escape by the skin of my teeth in the plane, it was because after that trip I was able to identify who I could rely on in a tough spot: it was my faithful lifelong subordinate that got me out. Thanks, frigging Humberto. You'll see; when the mad dogs stop barking, we'll get out of all this together. Just wait patiently and don't give up hope. Like the time we left those snot-faces thinking they were Juan Camaney in the bar in Prague, playing the highbrows with some university girls while you and I were downing God knows how many litres of beer. I caught your eye, and we were outside in a flash, on one of those cobbled streets lined with buildings so old we were wetting our-selves laughing, saying that Dracula must have been born in one of them. You hailed a taxi and I'm not sure how, but you managed to tell the driver to take us to the whores. I still remember how elegant that brothel was, its heavy, red velvet curtains, and especially the goddesses walking around in their fine lingerie, so different from the ordinary pros we were used to. You chose me a skinny one with the face of an angel, the way you knew I liked them. She led me to a room with the sort of bed that looks like it belongs in a fairy tale. The sweet scent of her perfume filled me with infinite sadness, the sadness of knowing that for all we were able to get a glimpse at the luxuries of those worlds, we'd have to go back to our lives in third-rate reality. I thought about biting her, beating her up and fucking her in the ass, so she knew just who she was dealing with, so she had it clear that I wasn't one of those Mexican hicks, so easily impressed when they let them off the farm. Luckily, something stopped me, warning me that it wouldn't be as easy to get out of that sort of mess there. Trembling with rage, I grabbed her by the scruff of her neck so she wouldn't even think about not sucking me off. I pulled that whore in so close she had to cough just to take a breath. When I was ready to come, we tussled to see which of us would win out. The bitch managed to pull herself away and I remember letting all my cum spill over her golden hair. She ran to the bathroom, shouting in her weird language, and I took advantage of her absence to dress and get out of the room as fast as I could, leaving on the bed a wad of that dull paper money they used to have in those countries. When I got back to the lobby you were waiting for me. From just a single nod of my head, you knew you had to find a taxi and not ask questions. Ah, frigging Humberto, I'll be dammed if we don't go whoring together again when this whole mess calms down. In the meanwhile, it's a matter of hanging on in there. A few days ago I'd had it up to the eyes with the video games and I asked the slut who comes to do the cleaning if she knew anywhere a man could go to find a little female company. Since she didn't understand, or was playing dumb, I looked her up and down to see if she'd serve for a bit of physical relief. Compared with some of the maids I've used when I've been super-horny, she wasn't so bad. I told her to go to the bedroom and wait there until further orders. Then I went to the bathroom, where I keep the stash of medication, and hunted among the frigging tranquillizers for the blue pills that help me to ward off the stress in those complex moments. I waited the prescribed time, imagining the slut scratching and begging for her life, but when I was about to give it to her the noise of the helicopters returned, the kicks at the door, the drawers thrown to the floor, the lamps broken, the shouts of don't make a move you son of a bitch, and there are no blue pills that are any use against all that. By sheer force of will, I set myself to finishing what I'd started, squeezing my eyes tight shut to keep reality at bay until I came. It was so dismal that I didn't even have the strength to clean myself up. Just pulled up my trousers and went back to the limbo of video games, vodka, and the other pills. At moments like that, I'd almost prefer the arseholes to come for me, so we can all – the lawyers and the network of friends – get started on the next phase, the battle to clear my name. When I came back from the European trip, the old man had found me a place in the Ministry of Finance, in the Office of Public Works. 'So you get to know every corner of the state, so you learn the reality they didn't teach you in that frigging tight-arse university in the capital you decided to go to.' He left me in the care of his former protégé, Ortega, a university man too, now minister of finance, whom the old man thought had what it took to become the next state governor. As usual, he was quite right. Those were the years of my real political education. Ortega crammed me full of principles and loaded me with responsibilities. I wasn't aware, because I was still a dumb kid, but he'd been testing me from the very first. Look where I am now, Ortega, and tell me if I didn't pass with flying colours. If I'm guilty of anything, it's of having learned his lessons too well. Behind that affable exterior, the impeccable guayabera, the complexion weathered by so many battles fought under the sun, the bald scalp with its wings of wavy hair that made him look like a Greek sage, Ortega was a wily old bastard, the sort that are born to achieve whatever objective they set themselves. When we were touring the state, we'd stay up drinking until dawn, me listening, him speaking, sussing me out to see whether I was actually one of them. Which, of course, I was. Ortega's teachings impregnated me as if I'd come into this world bathed in those waters. In fact, they were just a few sacred principles that all the others followed from automatically. Ortega was well versed in history. 'Unfortunately,' he told me in a paternal tone, 'from the times of our earliest ancestors, our country has been populated by brown-skinned, bean-eating yokels. And just to make matters worse, we were conquered by a bunch of avaricious brutes whose only thought was to destroy everything and take the gold, always sheltering behind the shield of the cross. After five centuries of servitude, there's nothing we can do but maintain the old structures. Don't forget, my boy, that even before the conquest, the power of the Tlatoani rulers was a source of pride for the rural *macehuales*. They used to honour those Tlatoanis with one quetzal feather after another, never even thinking to wear those feathers themselves. And for a land of barbarians like ours, in politics, form is everything. So to make yourself respected, the cardinal rule is not to sink to the same level as the losers.' The more pissed Ortega was, the more philosophical he became. 'It isn't the fault of this accursed race. When has it ever produced a Shakespeare? Or even a Frank Sinatra? Remember this, my boy, every peso invested in those of us in charge ends up benefitting them too.' How those words have drilled in my mind during every single instant in the pigsties. Later, what the old man had predicted came true: Ortega was anointed as the chosen candidate. I became the youngest campaign manager in the history of the state. Rally after rally, promise after promise, hand-out after hand-out, we visited every municipality. Even though losing was out of the question, Ortega never allowed us to rest. The gears have to be oiled for those who come afterwards. Right, my boy? With a wink from him, I knew what the future would hold for me if I had the necessary mettle. Installed in the governor's office, all I needed to complete my profile as Ortega's appointed successor was a wife who would give me a family. Stability. Progeny. A shared future. And here's the outcome of an overdose of future. I wonder where you are now, you miserable bitch. Do you think you're above our present situation? Your loyalty was as short-lived as the coats you discarded by the dozen. In fact, it's better this way. The children aren't to blame for anything. I just hope you manage to keep them out of the picture. Protect them from the lies of those shit-shov-elling journalists who were on the state payroll not so long ago. And your sagging boobs are past help now, no matter how many operations you have. God bless the women who have been capable of giving me what you refused through all those years. You were a disposable womb, interchangeable with any other, conceived to give me descendants, male offspring I too would mould in my own image. Until everything went up in smoke. It's the rebellion of the barefoot Indians. They have no idea what a Pandora's box they've opened. No one better than us for keeping things where they belong. No one like us for keeping the rats in the sewer. And now those sewers are clogged with their mutilated heads. That's what you get for not believing in us. For not having understood that our imperfect order was as good as this damned country gets. And now I've had to go into hiding. I can sense them creeping stealthily towards me. Traitorous lizards, sent by people who don't respect blood pacts. But I won't fall alone. I know enough to pull them down the drain-pipe with me. The helicopters are descending. I can see it all. The pigsty will shake under the whirlwind of their blades. They'll soon destroy everything. They'll take the photos they need to keep up the farce. And then that will be gone too. The hatching is inevitable. A new brood will emerge from the ruins, one that will make them yearn for our rule. I hope they will at least let me have one last match with the video games that have been with me to the end. The pills, the vodka, the sounds and images are all mixed together. If I could only find a way to make the commando I control with this remote come to my rescue.

The Art of Vanishing

FELIPE RESTREPO POMBO

Translated by Daniel Hahn

Umaña discovered a feeling of comfort here that was new to him: although he rejected families, this one – with its evident tensions and reproaches – seemed somehow to provide him with a sense of calm. He was a spectator to a work of dysfunctional theatre. He was particularly moved to see the boy. The illness had already reached a very advanced stage in the child's body; he found it hard to move, speak or take any food. Umaña had never paid too much attention to children, those misshapen, slobbering creatures. The truth was, they disgusted him: they were repulsive, whichever way you looked at them. But there was something different about Luciano. Perhaps it was the unanswerable image of fragility that he projected. Whenever Umaña gave him sweets or made any gesture towards him, the boy, in his utter defencelessness, would smile. At night, the man would tell made-up stories about pirates that the boy would follow almost as though hypnotized. It awoke a paternal instinct in Umaña that he would never feel again.

*

The night everything changed it was nerve-wrackingly cold, the kind of cold that clings to your skin furiously. Every mouthful of icy air made your lungs burn.

The two men went to Skál, same as every evening. It had been an exhausting day and Umaña grumbled the whole way. They settled close to a group of Russians who were celebrating some special occasion or other with a huge amount of noise. Zárate was tipsy after two drinks and announced that he'd be leaving soon. Umaña watched him and then, from nowhere, his eyes lit up. 'No, stay, please. These guys are just about to shut up,' he said, gesturing towards the Russians. He walked, somewhat theatrically, over to the next table. He touched one of the men on the back with his index finger and said, 'I'd like to ask you and your friends to shut up. You're bothering my friend.' This man, who was nearly six foot six, immediately turned around; he looked astonished for just a moment then burst out laughing. All his friends laughed at the same time, they clapped one another on the back and clinked glasses, as all the while Umaña stood there in front of them, undaunted.

The Russian continued to ignore him and Umaña returned to his seat. But he didn't stop watching the group, jiggling his leg nervously. Before long, one of the men came over to him: 'Don't be like that, pal,' he said warmly. 'Why don't we share a vodka and sing a song together instead?' When he wrapped his tattooed arm around Umaña's neck, the other men cracked up. The drunk sang a song and tried to hug him. That was all it took: Umaña picked up a bottle from the table and smashed it onto the head of the Russian, who fell to the floor, his skull fractured. His friends hurled themselves at Umaña like a pack of raging hounds. It took Zárate a while to understand what was going on, but then within a second he'd leaped from his seat, propelled by an uncontainable fury, yelling a kind of war cry. With his fingers clenched into tense fists and still shouting, he threw himself onto two guys. One of them received him with a knee to the gut. He rolled onto the floor and the other started to stamp on him.

The bouncers tried to get them all out. But in next to no time the Russians had tired of beating up the two Latins and helped their friend back to their table. Zárate and Umaña walked as best they could towards the door, and sat out on the sidewalk to catch their breath. Umaña's nose was broken, he had a deep cut in his right leg, his lips were split and he was spitting blood. Zárate couldn't move three of the fingers on his right hand and one of his teeth had been pulverized.

While he was rearranging his nose, Umaña asked for a drink. Zárate crawled over to the next-door liquor store and bought a bottle of common gin. They drank half of it as though it was water, and used the other half to clean their wounds. Zárate, as though possessed, was reciting a poem he'd suddenly remembered about the inexplicable happiness some soldiers feel after losing a battle.

Once he had calmed down, the architect suggested they ought to go to a clinic. Umaña didn't agree, but his friend managed to persuade him. When they arrived, the emergency room was full. It was Friday night, and there were all kinds of emergencies. The place wasn't able to keep up with demand, and a nurse on reception was dealing with the patients as they arrived and assigning them positions in the queue according to the severity of their case. Zárate told her the two of them had been injured in a street brawl.

The woman looked at them and, somewhat contemptuously, said they should wait; a doctor would see to them in the next three hours. She tossed them a form to fill out and said they were to sit and wait on a bench out in the hall. After filling out the document, grudgingly, Umaña went over to the woman and handed her the sheet of paper. Barely looking at it, she said there was some information missing. Umaña shook his head and answered that he wasn't in the mood for these kinds of formalities. Then the woman said that if he didn't go through the admission process properly she would have to throw him out of the clinic. Once again Umaña went nuts: he jumped over the desk and attacked the nurse. With uncommon speed he put his hands on her neck and tried to asphyxiate her while screaming that she was an 'insensitive woman'. A doctor who was standing nearby tried to separate them, but Umaña was gripping the woman's neck viciously. Zárate decided to join the fray and bit one of the doctor's ears. The clinic security threw them out at once, threatening to call the police on them.

Back on the street, the two friends weren't ready to give up. They decided they were sober now and that it was time to find a new adventure before calling it a night. So they took a taxi and headed for a brothel in a street buried somewhere in the Lavapiés neighbourhood. Zárate had heard about this filthy dive from an Ecuadorian he knew, by the name of Fred Cifuentes. In addition to selling drugs, running prostitutes and managing a long list of shady businesses, Cifuentes made his money dealing in sex dolls, some of which could cost thousands of dollars. The Ecuadorian was a partner in a number of whorehouses, among them the one in Lavapiés called Nautilus.

The place blended into a corner between sex shops and crappy bars. Several Colombian, Ecuadorian and African girls standing outside received the guests and invited them in. A Galician guy, who wasn't tall but was very muscly, dressed in a black suit, stood guard at the door. He looked at the two new guests with a certain amount of misgiving, but once Zárate had mentioned Cifuentes he allowed them in.

The decor of the Nautilus was maritime, hence its name. The barman wore a cheap imitation of a ship captain's uniform, and the waiting staff were pretending to be buccaneers. The whole thing was in overwhelmingly bad taste: the flimsy plastic chairs, the blinking coloured lights, the grubby, greasy floor. The prostitutes sitting at the bar, however, just wore outfits that were light and summery. They watched the two newcomers eagerly: they looked like easy prey.

Suddenly the lights went out and a small stage at the back of the room, which up till now had been in darkness, was lit up. The man who had previously been acting as barman got up onto the stage and began to talk. 'Welcome, distinguished customers, to the Nautilus, where the secrets of the deep are hidden,' he said, as a little elderly man seated right beside the stage applauded rapturously. The host, totally immersed in his role, went on flattering his illustrious audience and cracking double entendres, about seamen and chasing tail and booty and much more besides. Then he announced the main show of the night: the dance of the god Neptune and his naughty nymphets. The curtain opened and a huge black man appeared in the middle of the stage, dressed only in white briefs and a pair of studded leather boots. In his hands he held a plastic trident. At once a variety of women came out wearing bikinis with plastic tails that mimicked those of mermaids. As they appeared on stage, the nymphets threw themselves at Neptune's feet and stroked his body.

The show went on, while the black man stripped his girls, one by one. Then he inserted his fingers into their vaginas, and his tongue, and his huge dark penis and, finally, the plastic trident. It all looked painful but the women moaned as though experiencing a very pleasurable orgasm. What few customers were still there came up close to the stage and shouted all kinds of obscenities. Zárate sweated and salivated like a horny adolescent. Umaña just wiped away the drops of blood that were still flowing from his wounds. The scenery, made out of cellophane and cardboard, was gradually collapsing as the performance proceeded: the grand finale included a marine orgy.

Zárate and Umaña had had enough, and it now being past eight in the morning, they decided it was time for them to go. Before leaving, they went from table to table drinking the dregs that the other patrons had left behind. When they arrived back home, day-light already falling on their weary bodies, it took them a while to understand what was going on. The street where Zárate lived was blocked off, with a police guard. Dozens of curious bystanders were loitering around the area. There was smoke clouding their eyes and a smell of burning that was unbearable. Firemen ran back and forth.

The fire had started around ten that night, the same time the Russians were beating up its victims' husband and father.

Mirna had gone to put Luciano to bed and then collapsed onto her own. She forgot that, on the first floor, the fireplace was still alight. The carbon monoxide that was escaping – it was an old fireplace with structural flaws – must have knocked her out. The sparks began to fly and one of them landed on the bookcase. The cheap wood and the dry paper burned at once. According to the investigations that followed, the burning of the first floor didn't take long. It was impossible to determine whether the woman and the boy managed to wake up or whether they died in their sleep. Nor was it clear whether they had asphyxiated or burned to death. In any case, they told Zárate, they wouldn't have suffered much, just a few seconds. The mere fact of imagining these fragments of time caused Zárate a pain in his belly that made him double over, vomiting up bile.

The apartment was turned to ash and there wasn't much that could be recovered. They didn't let Zárate near the accident zone. He tried for the first few days, but bit by bit he lost any desire to move. He spent his time going through all kinds of procedures, talking to the police, to the forensic scientists. He tried to imagine what had happened in his wife and son's last hours with the minutest precision: he wanted to know everything, every detail, to reconstruct each moment with as much realism as possible. When there was nothing left to do and the case had been closed and filed away as an accident, he checked himself voluntarily into a public psychiatric clinic. He was tormented by the temptation to throw himself off a balcony or onto the rails of the metro. But he couldn't do it. Umaña kept him company, with an older brother's resignation. They didn't talk: they just sat in the clinic's small lounge in silence. Occasionally Umaña would ask his friend if he needed anything and his friend would answer no, nothing.

Two more months went by in this fashion. The intense winter finally faded and gave way to a feeble spring. With the change in climate, Zárate's spirits picked up slightly: he was accepting food, bathing, speaking a few words. At this point Umaña said goodbye. On their last afternoon together, he told Zárate he couldn't stay with him any longer. That, once again, he was feeling that incurable need to get away. Europe felt like a place in decline, its centuries of history weighed too heavily on him: he could sense the tiredness of those cities in the very air he breathed. He wanted to be a witness to the collapse of his own country: Colombia. He needed to know whether he was able to bear the vertigo of that fall. He also fancied setting the world on fire, before the world set all of them on fire. He patted his friend on the back – taking no notice of his phobia of physical contact – and murmured a 'goodbye, Juan Manuel'.

Gradually Zárate began to accept his destiny. The doctors discharged him, as he was now out of danger and they could see no reason to keep him in the psychiatric unit. All the same, the guilt was a weight that made it hard for him to move: as a matter of fact, in one of our conversations, he told me that he would never stop believing, despite all the evidence and everybody's opinions, that he was responsible for the death of two innocent people. The day after coming out of the clinic he took a flight back to Colombia. He understood that the only way to survive was to surrender himself entirely to a professional discipline, so he sought work as a teacher and thought of nothing else. The pain would never go away, but at least he had something to keep his mind occupied. He didn't blame Umaña at all. As a matter of fact, he was grateful for his friend's silent support: he knew this was the greatest expression of generosity his friend could have given him.

Valentina in the Clouds

JUAN MANUEL ROBLES

Translated by Sarah Moses

He was walking ten blocks behind her. Though he didn't want to run and create a scene, he didn't want to lose sight of her either. It had been a long time since he'd seen her react this way. This is ridiculous, he thought. He called her name, but only a few times – if he kept at it, he'd draw attention to them and raise a red flag. And that was something he couldn't let happen. He was acutely aware of the route they were taking, saw it sharply as he imagined the aerial view: two red spots on the grid, on the map, and in this way, visualizing it perfectly, he kept the targets under control and felt he could avoid any excessive display of emotions. They were already far from the cineplex; she'd left the theatre right after the movie began (her sudden silhouette had blocked the screen). And he went after her. They walked along the main road, then turned, one after the other, onto their street. At this point, she sped up; always aware of the aerial view – that of a vulture, of God – he followed suit, making sure to maintain the distance between them: neither chasing her nor losing her. He loved his wife. Now he could barely see her: a distant spot, almost a target to shoot at, a duck. How long had it been since he'd had so perfect an image of her, so tiny and panoramic, no more than lines?

He saw her go into their house and stopped. Then he slowly moved towards it. The door was half-open. He went into the living room and saw her sitting on the sofa. She wouldn't look him in the eye, but the urgency of her hatred was gone. On her left, sitting so calmly that he blended in with the furniture, was their son, holding his tablet. The boy was their buffer zone. The confirmation that they had long lost the right to become exasperated over trivialities. The child was surprised to see them home from the movies so soon. But he didn't ask for an explanation. He went back to what he was doing on the screen with fingers that were long, dexterous, elastic. Suddenly, he seemed to remember something.

'My homework, Mum . . . Your photos!'

His mother nodded, as though to show she was already on top of things. 'I'll take care of it now,' she said.

The boy's father hung up his jacket. He was about to leave the room but what he heard had caught his attention. 'Photos?'

She was still silent, more out of annoyance than any desire to be secretive. Eventually, she answered. 'His teacher. She asked him to bring in photos . . . of me.'

'From when you were twenty-three, Mum,' said the boy.

'His art teacher,' she added. 'She's turning twenty-three tomorrow and has asked them to bring in photos of their mums at her age as a way of working her birthday into the class. Sweet girl, don't you think? To remind me of how I looked two decades ago.'

'Sounds like fun homework,' the boy's father said.

'Really? I think so too. But there's a problem.'

'What's that?'

'There are 7,441 photos.'

They both raised their eyebrows.

215

He thought about the number and pretended it didn't matter much. 'So what's the problem? We have enough access, don't we?'

'We have ten minutes of access, that's all. It's what you get per month without a plan. Ten minutes for more than seven thousand photos.'

The boy continued to watch them.

His father smiled. 'That's more than enough, isn't it?'

She replied in a hurry. 'No.'

'What do you mean, no?'

'That won't be nearly enough time to choose. His teacher asked for a selection of photos and I'll have to include the first ones that appear. How will I look in those shots? Which ones will come up? I've had a lot of stupid photos taken. It's so little time.'

He understood what was going on. The teacher was young and beautiful. At five foot eight, she was a babe with perky breasts and a huge rear end without a millimetre of cellulite – he knew this because he'd snooped around her profile – and his wife, the boy's mother, was someone whose best days were behind her.

'Well,' he said, as though blaming her, 'you told me you didn't want to—'

'I don't want to,' she said right away. 'I don't want to give them another cent. You know there's no end to this. You pay for one package, then another. And another. It's a vice. I've seen people go into debt.'

'So what do you want to do?'

She looked tiredly out of the window.

'Well,' he went on, lowering his voice, 'there's also the other option.'

The other option was shady. Friends of theirs could get them the name of a good 'astronomer'. These were adept blokes who knew how to track down photos containing your face, those stored in networks over the course of your life, in your city and in the whole world: high-school trips, concerts as a teenager, vacations when you were young, images consolidated in distant server farms. Astronomers could recover, copy and upload the images to a secure cloud that was difficult to locate.

'Forget about it. I've heard awful stories.'

He made a face, mocking her. 'What stories?'

'The pictures they send you . . . I've heard things.'

'Oh, please. You can't possibly believe they keep private photos. Don't act like a child.'

'No, it's not that. I've heard they *play* with the photos – change their order, make up stories, rearrange them.'

'They rearrange photos? Make things up? Who? Why?'

She wasn't sure, but she'd heard stories on more than one occasion. It had happened to a friend of hers. An astronomer had compiled photographs from all of her teenage years, two thousand of them had been organized to create a sort of comic strip, an entertaining book. No one ever found out what she saw inside it, what horrible story those snapshots or vignettes told, what plot, what lesson, but the fact is that overnight, she packed up all her things and went away, far away, never to return.

He started to laugh. 'Someone's been watching a lot of movies,' he said.

'That's not true.'

'So then let's just pay for a package. We don't have to spend a lot. The premium option is on sale and it includes aerial shots now.'

'Yeah, I know,' she said. 'My sister was sent one that had been taken from the sky when she was at the pyramids in Egypt years ago. She was still thin and looked amazing. She was happy to see herself like that, the muppet.'

'It's an option,' he said. 'Not a bad one.'

'No,' she said sharply. 'We don't need the package. I'll deal with it.'

*

The next day he awoke more tired than usual. She got up first, to make breakfast for the boy. He stayed in bed: he felt their steps, the bustle that broke apart the world of sleep. He got up. When he walked downstairs he discovered his wife grumbling into the landline.

'I've already told you I'm not interested in your offer.'

The boy was using his tablet with one hand and bringing pieces of omelette to his mouth with the other. He did this skilfully. His fingers were so long and nimble. He looked like a card shark shuffling a deck in Las Vegas.

'I understand,' she continued. 'It's your right, but it's *my* life. I want to speak with your supervisor this minute! Hello . . . hello?' She threw down the phone.

'What happened?'

She held out her mobile phone and showed him what was on it: a horizontal photo filled the screen. When she touched a button, the same image appeared on the television. The three of them turned around to look.

They'd sent her an aerial image. It began as a wide shot and then moved in close. The boy was clearly fascinated with the way the screen zoomed in. Suddenly, the frame closed up around an image that was a little blurry at first, then very sharp.

The boy's father recognized the location in a few seconds. He smiled. It was the Bow Bridge, a pretty arched walkway that crossed the Lake in Central Park. The image was from the second trip they had taken to New York City together, the last before they were married. Both of them were in it, on the south side. He remembered the bridge's wooden deck, so solid that the planks barely vibrated under his feet. He remembered the balustrade of sculpted stone, a row of circles, each with a hole in its centre. He remembered the pots of lilac flowers at each end of the bridge. He remembered the wind in her hair, and her face, which radiated confusion more than happiness, and behind them, the imposing sight of the San Remo building, with its two orange towers. On the screen, those towers were now charmless rectangles, devoid of all their splendour because of the picture's perspective. She had on a turquoise dress that set off her black hair. He was wearing a checked shirt with the sleeves rolled up. The filter's effect had brightened the green of the broccoli-like trees surrounding them and lit up the turquoise of her dress, and their faces: hers appeared salmon pink, his milky white. They stood very close to each other.

Had the photo been taken before or after? he asked himself. If he looked at her closely and discovered a gesture, something revealing in her behaviour, he'd know. He'd always enjoyed the challenge of trying to guess someone's emotional state with only an aerial view of their body. There were times, during his paragliding years, that he thought he could do it: arms and shoulders, if one looked carefully, revealed two men to be arguing instead of just talking, even made it possible to distinguish a chat between friends from one between business partners, or to be relatively confident that a teenager was dying of love for the girl walking by his side (tiny, almost imperceptible jumps gave him away). It was all a question of concentrating on the right lines.

They'd just arrived in New York. He'd planned on proposing to her in the Empire State Building, with the city below their feet, but when they got to 34th Street in Manhattan, an announcement informed them that the observation deck was under maintenance. Unexpected events completely rattled him and he began to panic. He grabbed his mobile phone; he didn't want to do it, but he had no choice. Desperately, he looked for unique locations where a man could give his girlfriend a ring. The search engine came up with the Bow Bridge and four other options, but he'd have to pay to see them, so he went with the quickest solution. He looked at the map, reading testimonials on the fly to see what couples who had professed their love on the bridge had to say, and figured it would work. They walked on.

Now he knew. The photograph captured the moment right before he'd proposed: the ring hadn't yet been taken out, but it was about to happen – he knew because his wife's youthful body was upright, haughty, mocking. She hadn't been surprised. Instead, her gestures revealed the banality of the scene. This is the best you could come up with? The Bow Bridge? It's so run-of-the-mill. So cheap. She didn't say this out loud, but her face made it clear. So did her rigid back (which was visible even now, in the picture). But seconds later her eyelids relaxed: she looked at the ring closely, saw him getting down on his knees. Below, in the lake, a couple of blokes in a boat whooped, gringo-style. In the aerial shot, the rowboat was still off in the distance, towards the south (above them).

A message appeared on the screen: 'Click now and you'll get 189 photographs from this day. We know it's a special one.' The premium package.

Angrily, she picked up the phone again.

There was no need to waste time asking themselves how the company knew it had been a special day. It was obvious. Both of them had taken a ton of photos. And minutes after she'd said yes, they'd announced the news. The congratulations poured in. The vibrations on their mobile phones came faster and faster, like a heartbeat gone wild. New status: engaged.

On the phone, she asked to speak with an operator. When he saw her like this, furious as she clutched the receiver, he approached her and tried to calm her down.

'Look, it's not that bad,' he said, pointing to the screen.

'No? Well, I'm not okay with it. Who do they think they are? We're having breakfast.'

'It's a good photo, don't exaggerate.'

'And what makes them think I want to see it right *now*?'

'They haven't done anything wrong. It's exactly what they're going for – the surprise factor. Besides, they're careful about which photos they send. We're not going to get any old shot, you know that. They won't choose something that'll upset us. A lot of money is invested to prevent that from happening.'

It was true. They had several means of preventing the system from sending, for example, images of their wedding to a couple who had recently separated. Or from suddenly bringing up someone who'd caused pain. Sons or daughters who'd died as young children. Sleazy blokes on trial for sexual abuse.

'That's exactly what that idiot told me,' she said. 'But it's beside the point.'

The boy had taken the mobile phone and was zooming the image in and out with his index finger and thumb. With his other hand, nimble-fingered, he searched for the Bow Bridge on his own tablet and the screen filled with photos. Hundreds of photos of men on their knees, proposing.

'Your father, a true original,' said his mother. The boy opened his eyes wide like plates. She dialled the number again.

'You're going to keep trying?' the boy's father asked.

'I'll send them a formal complaint.'

'Forget it, that'll take months,' he responded, annoyed. Did it bother her that much? This party-pooper attitude was beginning to bug him. He had an idea. Something stopped him for a second, but then he went for it. 'Look, if this is really bothering you, why don't you register yourself as an "at-risk subject"? That way they'll leave you in peace on the spot.'

'At risk? What are you talking about?'

'You register and then—'

'Do you think I'm crazy?'

'That's not what I said.'

'Why would I do that? I haven't been traumatized. I don't take pills. That's for people who are disturbed by their past. I'm not one of those.'

'Okay, okay, calm down, don't attack me. It was just an idea.'

A tense silence set in. She looked at the time. In a hurry, she told the boy to grab his things for school, then went into the kitchen to get the keys. And when he thought she'd leave without saying another word, he saw her stop.

'One hundred and eighty-nine photos. Did they say one hundred and eighty-nine photos? How much did we even do that day? Doesn't it seem like a lot?'

She closed the door, leaving the question in the air. He thought the promotional message had been an intriguing way to advertise: it was like giving you a gift wrapped up in a bow – the black box from a flight you took with your wife, but one that contains nothing shocking. The black box is what's shocking. He got ready for work. From ten to seven, five days a week, he was a productive man.

FROM THE SHORT STORY 'VALENTINA IN THE CLOUDS'

Family

CRISTIAN ROMERO

Translated by Anne McLean

'We are family,' says our mother after the prolonged silence of dinner.

'We are family,' we all respond as if it were a mantra.

The sticky, bitter smell of our father's illness begins to float in the atmosphere, and its punctilious pain, fainter than in other periods, attacks me on my left side. I look at all my siblings, each showing their pain in their own way. Our mother has her eyes closed and barely moves her lips. The servants clear the plates with a fear difficult to hide: on their faces we see the disgust they feel for us. Sara gives silent orders, points with her hand, raises her eyebrows, tilts her head. Lovely, of course.

The night, like every year, is the same colour. A cold, thick sound slips in through the half-open windows and outside the sugar-cane fields fade. When I turned off the main highway and drove up to my father's hacienda everything froze into the same instant, as still as a fishbowl. It doesn't seem as if a year has passed since the last Communion. The image of the house is a blurred photo with the same opaque colours, the same aged wood, the same dust-covered furniture. And Sara, with her porcelain skin, remains intact, as if the years could not wear down her humanity.

Our mother opens her eyes as she rings the little bell she carries in her hand. The servants withdraw from the room. Sara closes the doors as soon as they leave and remains in the semi-darkness, with her hands behind her back and chin held high. She has barely looked at me all evening, but on her chest she is wearing the necklace I gave her as a child and that makes me feel calm.

My siblings stand up and begin to undress. I do the same, reluctantly, without taking my eyes off Sara. Mateo, Jacobo, Tomás and Susana can barely hide the devastations of the illness; their famished bodies, their pronounced bones and withered breasts reveal the good condition of the infection that survives within us keeping our father's memory alive. Once more I'm struck by the foggy memories of those times so distant now, when the illness that kept our father in bed for so many years, coughing and cursing, did not make him lose the authority in his impetuous voice and the sudden pounding of his hands on the table, again and again, when he gave an order.

The wound in my side begins to palpitate and fester beneath the dressing. It hurts, it hurts a lot. For a moment I feel frightened at the thought that the wound is rejuvenating and that all my efforts have been in vain. I think of how many times I've promised myself I wouldn't return, how many times I've sworn to never again set foot in this house, not attend this Communion, renounce this surname. But I hope this will be the last time I see them and finally Sara and I will be able to be free.

Mother begins to walk around the table, repeating the movements of the ritual. Behind her goes Sara. She carries a punchbowl filled with water and has her eyes fixed on the bottom of it. Each of my siblings shows a part of the illness to Mother. Mateo begins to pull out clumps of hair, which his scalp sheds as if they were wool, then he drops them into Mother's hands and she sniffs them before depositing them into a glass in the middle of the table. Immediately afterwards, Mother washes her hands in Sara's bowl. Jacobo exposes the enormous wound that crosses his chest, as if it had been opened by a hot and dull knife, and a greasy liquid oozes from it. Mother passes a finger over it, collects that slime and puts it in the glass. She washes her hands.

As she continues her tour of my siblings' wounds, I feel mine awaken from a long lethargy and pierce me from inside with desperation. I take a breath, clench my teeth and think: All this is worth it for Sara, only for her; soon the illness will leave my body, very soon. Then I remember those afternoons we ran through the crops, played together naked and swam in the river. Father told Mother to keep an eye on us, that we shouldn't spend so much time together, but she said we were just children, and we always managed to take our clothes off and touch each other.

Susana squeezes her haggard breasts and, after a smothered moan, out comes a liquid as thick as honey. Then, Tomás takes off the face mask he always wears, opens his foul, purplish mouth and pulls out a tooth, which, as it comes out, leaves a fine thread of putrid blood. I feel I might vomit. I've never been able to get used to this smell, the one that took over everything when the curse began to float over our lands. It arrived just like that, all of a sudden, gave no respite. Father made a pact and did not fulfil it and now he had to pay the consequences. First, as if it were an atrocious warning, it rained for entire days. Then, the cattle fell ill and died vomiting blood and birds began to crash into the windows, desperately, leaving blotches of their guts on the glass, while the dogs fled with their heads bowed down. They were strange days, everyone forgot about us. And Sara and I, the youngest in the family, hid to give encouragement to each other.

When Mother arrives at my side she does not look me in the eye. I feel afraid. For a moment I think we've been discovered. Then I take off the dressing and she and my siblings choke back a cry. Her hands fly to her mouth, while her head shakes back and forth.

Sara opens her eyes as wide as they'll go. My wound looks much smaller than it did a year ago and, of course, they don't like that. I've broken the promise, letting my inheritance die. Luckily, since the beginning, the illness did not find in my body the same comfort it found in those of my siblings. It has barely been able to sustain itself, so with a bit of effort and some healing rituals it has gradually all but disappeared. It's not my fault my body has resisted, just as it's not Sara's for never having contracted the illness. I remember those days wrapped in constant cold, when she took on with some culpability the fact of not perpetuating that infection in her body, as if it had been a sign, a cruel irony.

Finally Mother looks me in the eye. I don't know how, but I am able to hold her gaze. Some seconds go past and dilate in the silence and, suddenly, she strikes me. The slap resounds throughout the room. Sara closes her eyes. I stand with my cheek turned. Only for Sara, I do it only for her.

'What have I done to deserve this, what have I done?' says Mother between sobs. 'What is your father going to think?'

I remain silent. My siblings look at me over their shoulders. Their bodies disgust me, but I'm more disgusted by the fact that we have accepted the order to sustain father's illness, to keep it alive in our bodies in exchange for continuing to flaunt the family wealth. Mother sticks her finger into my wound and begins to scratch. It feels as if she's sunk a red-hot iron into me. I resist. I search for solace in Sara's eyes, but she ignores me. Mother deposits the little she can get from my wound in the glass and washes her hands.

Then, in silence, we continue with the next phase of the ritual. I notice my siblings' nervousness. Mother looks at me out of the corner of her eye, without even trying to hide how ashamed she feels. Sara's eyes shine with confusion, which she cannot hide either.

Mother lights the glass on fire and a magenta-coloured flame flashes up before us. The French windows open wide and gusts of wind, heavy with a humidity that seems eternal, blows in through them: ricochets off the walls, knocks down paintings, breaks glasses. It is much stronger than on other occasions and that can only mean one thing: Father is furious.

Clouds of dry leaves blow in through the open windows and swirl around the table, like furious crows, while the flame sustains itself in the middle of the circle. Mother holds up her hands and says:

'I guard your lineage. Your lineage guards your lands.'

Then she begins to pronounce words in that secret language from distant worlds, the codes to the pact, the codes to the ritual. Those words hide a power beyond our understanding, something that has taken over our whole existence with the implacable patience of a terminal illness.

Sara is in a corner of the room. She squeezes her eyes shut, seems frightened. I watch her, fascinated by her beauty. But it is one of those moments when I don't seem to recognize the Sara with whom, when the skies turned strange, I used to hide in the stables, in the attic, under the tables and the beds. The Sara I fell in love with.

'Our destiny. Our pain. Our passion. My blood is your blood,' says Mother.

Then we all respond, one at a time:

'My blood is your blood.'

The words hurt my throat. Then Mother says:

'Your blood is my blood.'

We repeat the phrase. The atmosphere hardens. My ears buzz. The back of my skull begins to palpitate, as if my head has filled up with hot water.

'Our blood and our bodies belong to you,' continues Mother, followed by the echoes of my siblings, which resound like an invocation. I look at Sara, who still has her eyes closed. I just want to steal one moment of her gaze, which will tell me I'm doing the right thing, that soon we'll go away from here. My siblings hold hands and I prepare to leap into the void, my only hope of escape.

'*Uoy ot gnoleb seidob ruo dna doolb ruo.*'

The silence arrives like a bomb of air that fills the whole room. For a moment the screams of my mother and siblings emerge from their mouths like slipstreams of colours that float up to the ceilings, soundlessly, all swallowed by whatever has come out of that fissure I have just opened. Finally Sara looks at me, dismayed. I see fear in her eyes and that worries me.

Then the windows smash. The walls crack. The floors open like wounds. And the sound returns, invades my ears and then all is chaos: something in the immutable logic of this home has broken. The house begins to collapse. The curtains go up in flames and the faces of my siblings and mother fill with pustules. I run to embrace Sara, but she, in the midst of the confusion, runs away down the hallways of the house. All around me is an inferno swallowing up the walls on which are written the histories of my lineage.

Something is trying to escape the wound. A blaze flares up in my side and a trail of smoke floats before my eyes: the illness has abandoned me. I feel that part of my existence has been torn out. I turn my head to see the only thing I don't want to see: the bodies of my family roasting in an implacable fire. In their screams I recognize my father's voice, and that fills me with panic.

I run through the house, calling Sara, desperately. The smoke fills my lungs, robbing me of breath. I find her in a corner, coughing.

'Let's go,' I say.

'What did you do?'

'Let's go.'

A piece of the ceiling falls behind us. I turn and at the end of the hallway I see an enormous ball of fire bearing down on us. Hand in hand we run out of the house. Outside, even the thistles are in flames. Without even thinking we run into the blackness of the night.

I feel dizzy, I want to throw up. Sara keeps up with me, but a familiar cough has seized her. We cross the garden and I see her weaken, her breathing damp and laboured, as if her lungs were full of mildew. But she wants to carry on anyway, like the strong woman she has always been. In the sound of her cough I sense something that worries me, an idea I insistently ignore. She falls to the ground. I help her to stand up and see a small blister at the corner of her mouth. I recoil, startled, but I go back and approach to help her up from the ground. She covers her mouth as she coughs and when I clutch her hands, a smear of coagulated blood floods over our fingers. We look at each other, like a pair of injured animals. I avoid her eyes, overwhelmed, and stand watching our house engulfed in flames.

The fire climbs full of arrogance.

Children

JUAN PABLO RONCONE

Translated by Ellen Jones

I was late for the meeting. The group facilitator was waiting at the school entrance. I introduced myself and left my umbrella in a sky-blue bucket by the door.

'It's nine,' she said, adjusting her thick glasses. 'I thought you weren't coming.'

That same afternoon I'd argued with my dad and had almost stayed home, but I didn't tell her this.

'Sorry. It's Monday and I had classes.'

'A lot of people call me to say they'll come,' she claimed, 'but then they change their minds and don't show up.'

For some time I'd been in the habit of joining a random assortment of gatherings: trade unions, self-help conferences, free literature workshops, film screenings, youth wings of political parties, support groups for addicts. I didn't mind what they were, or who was there, I just wanted to be somewhere, surrounded by people, to let myself be carried along by other people's voices, other people's company. I'd got the idea from a North American film where a guy visits groups of cancer patients. Desolate people, but when he's around them the guy feels good, liberated. When I told my sister what I was doing, she said there was another film, much older, full of Cat Stevens songs, about a teenager and an old woman who go to funerals and wakes of people they don't know – but I never did that, out of respect for the relatives.

I'd spoken to the facilitator on the phone and was surprised she was so young. She was short, chubby and ruddy-cheeked. She had brown hair pulled back in a bun and was wearing a long dress. We went into the school through the back door. We walked through an empty playground and then down a dim corridor.

'We meet here because the headmaster's part of the group,' she said, 'and doesn't charge us rent or anything.'

My dad and I had argued that afternoon because I'd told him I was dropping out of university. It was a short but intense argument. I want to be an actor, I told him. A theatre actor and director. I'd given it a lot of thought and was firm in my decision. I didn't know much about theatre – I'd barely read two plays – but I *was* sure I didn't want to be a doctor, like my dad, my mum and my sister.

The facilitator stopped outside a door with a little sign stuck on with sellotape: 'Meeting room. Reserved next week for Scout Group.'

'Try to relax', she said. 'The first time's always special.'

We went into a small room. The parents were sitting on school chairs in a circle. No more than ten of them. There was a whiteboard and a wall calendar showing all the school activities. The floor was yellow and the walls a watery blue.

'Welcome,' somebody cried out.

I thanked them, and sat down next to a man of about fifty. He had eyes like a cat and a flat nose. In his hands he had an old photo of a thin, hollow-eyed boy who was smiling.

'We all bring photos of our dead children,' the leader said. 'They help us make contact.'

I don't, of course, have a dead child. At twenty years old I hadn't even thought about the possibility of having children. But there

I was, sitting with all these people, eagerly awaiting the beginning of the séance.

'How old was your son?' the leader asked me.

'Five,' I lied.

'You had him very young,' commented a man with a thick white beard. He was the oldest, and the leader had told me on the phone that he'd been communicating with his son's spirit for more than twenty years.

'Yes,' I said, 'in fact I was still at school when he was born.'

'How did he die?' asked the cat-eyed man.

I looked around. Everyone was waiting for my response. They looked like children, lively, eager children, like they were waiting for the start of a snowball or water-balloon fight.

'He drowned in a swimming pool,' I said. 'He couldn't swim.'

'We're here for you,' said the man with the beard.

The purple curtains were open. Outside a woman sat on a garden bench, her profile visible from the meeting room. She was even shorter and fatter than the facilitator. The light from the streetlamp was fending off the night and I could see she was concentrating, her head bowed.

'That's Doña Marta,' the leader said. 'The medium who connects us.'

'She's preparing herself,' Cat Face explained. 'She needs to concentrate before making contact.'

'It's important that you relax and that you trust her,' the facilitator said.

'It's all about trust,' somebody agreed. 'The spirits appear when there's a welcoming atmosphere.'

In the corner of the room was a fan. It was very small and not plugged in. There was also a bookcase locked with a padlock, some empty plant pots and two brooms propped up in a corner.

'Everyone remembers the first time,' said Cat Face. 'Do you remember my first time, Don Luis?'

The man with the thick beard shifted in his seat and smiled happily. He had little eyes and deeply tanned skin. He said:

'Yes, yes, of course I remember. I've seen many parents come and go, and many facilitators.'

Doña Marta left the garden and came into the room. All the parents were quiet, watching her approach. The woman sat down on one of the chairs in the circle. She had a round face and dyed blonde hair. She was blind, but didn't have a white cane; I thought she must be about fifty. The leader stood up, lit three candles and put them in the middle of the circle. Then she turned off the light and went back to her seat.

'You can only talk when she does,' Cat Face whispered in my ear. 'And don't overdo it with questions or you'll tire her out.'

We held hands. Doña Marta took off her dark glasses and took the hands of the parents sitting beside her. She had pale eyes, like they'd fogged up, and sitting there in the gloom, the yellow of her dress barely visible by the candlelight and the streetlight filtering through from the garden, it seemed to me there was nothing special in her face, nothing to make me suspect what was to come.

Doña Marta opened her mouth and left it like that for a minute or two. Then she started to move her head, like she was nodding. All the parents had taken out the photos of their children and put them on their laps. Doña Marta closed her mouth and started making noises – a kind of intermittent purring – and her head movements became more frequent and frantic. Finally she stopped, leaned forward slightly and began to speak.

I left the school a little disturbed. I didn't want to go home and see my parents and my sister, all so perfect, talking about patients or telling stories from the hospital. The night was cool and it had begun to rain. I decided to take the facilitator home because I saw her at the bus stop, without an umbrella, and because I didn't want to be alone. The woman got into my car and sat down with her legs pressed tight together.

'You probably feel weird,' she said after a couple of minutes. 'It's difficult at first to get used to the idea that they're still here, with us.'

The séance had impressed me, in a way. Doña Marta had spent the whole session communicating with my supposedly dead son. She recounted in detail the story I'd invented when I'd decided to participate, the story I'd duped the parents with. She said she could see a five-year-old boy. A pretty, skinny boy. She said she could see water, and at that moment all the parents turned to look at me. Cat Face looked so edgy and out of control emotionally, like he wanted to get up and start shouting. I can see a child dipping his feet in the pool, said the woman, without moving her small head, looking straight at me with those enormous pale eyes. I felt a degree of anxiety, but tried not to let it show. The boy falls in the water, continues Doña Marta, and no one hears. No one is there to pull him out, to help this child. Cat Face whispered that I mustn't feel guilty. Doña Marta made an abrupt movement with her head and her tone of voice changed. Now it was rasping, harsh. Everyone looked at her, worried. I want you to know that I love you, said Doña Marta, trembling. I love you so much. I'm your son and I'll always be with you. Some of the parents started to cry. Papi, I'm in heaven, said Doña Marta, and heaven's so pretty. Then the trembling stopped and the session came to an end. The facilitator, in silence, blew out the candles and turned on the light. Cat Face hugged me with his left arm and waited for me to say something, but I couldn't think of anything at all.

The facilitator gave me directions to her building, in a neighbour-hood on the outskirts of Santiago. I didn't know what to talk to her about, so I told her about the fight with my dad and said I was dropping out of university.

'I used to dream that my son would be a doctor,' she said. 'Every mother wants one doctor child.'

'But in our house there's already a doctor child,' I told her.

The streets were wet and the colours of the trees looked brighter, sharper.

'You were lucky,' said the facilitator. 'I've spent five years trying to communicate with my son and he's only appeared three times.'

'And what did he say to you?'

'He said he forgave me for leaving him alone the night he died. That it wasn't my fault.' The facilitator stopped for a second and looked out of the window. 'That he knew I wasn't there because I was working, working for him and for his grandma.'

By the time we got to her building it was raining heavily. I switched off the engine and we sat in silence, looking ahead.

'Don't drop out of university,' she said, but I didn't respond. In truth I didn't really care whether I finished my degree or not. 'That's my place.' The facilitator pointed to a brick building with an external staircase.

For a second I thought about doing something crazy.

The woman was there – with those thick glasses and that long dress and that heavy figure and red face – sitting by my side, and I imagined asking her to have a child with me.

A child like her dead child.

A pretty, skinny child who we would teach to swim really young and who we would never leave alone because my father would give me money to hire a nanny. A child who we would bring up to be a doctor, I thought. A well-behaved child, a child who looked like me. We could be really happy. I could even knuckle down, I said to myself, and finish my degree as quickly as possible. The facilitator and I, together, in a warm home. She would never have to go back to those sessions because now she'd have a new child, and she'd also have me. And we'd grow old together and maybe we could even have more children.

'It's been a pleasure,' said the facilitator. 'Thanks for the lift.'

'Goodnight.'

'Goodnight,' she said, and was lost on the path that led to her building.

The Summer of '94

DANIEL SALDAÑA PARÍS

Translated by Christina MacSweeney

Teresa left one Tuesday around midday. I can't remember exactly which month, but it must have been the end of July or the beginning of August because my sister and I were on holiday. I always hated being left in the care of Mariana, who systematically ignored me for the whole day, barricaded in her bedroom with the music playing at a volume that even to me, a boy of ten, seemed ridiculous. So, that Tuesday, I felt resentful when Mum got up from the table after lunch and announced she was going out. 'Look after your brother, Mariana,' she said in a dry monotone. That was the way she generally spoke, with hardly any intonation, like a computer giving instructions or someone on the autism spectrum. (I sometimes imitate her now: remembering, or making an effort to remember, that remote, neutral voice and trying to reproduce it.)

Teresa, my mother, gave me a farewell kiss on the crown of my head, and then turned to Mariana, who received her kiss on the cheek without the least show of emotion, or any attempt to return the gesture. 'When your dad gets home, tell him there's a letter for him on the desk,' she said from the door, in the same robotic voice. Then she left, turning the key behind her. She was only carrying her bag; a holdall whose bulk my father used to make wisecracks about whenever we went somewhere together: 'Just what have you got in there? It looks like you're going camping.'

That evening, when he got back, my father read the letter. Then he sat with us in the living room (my sister was watching music videos while I was trying to make an origami figure) and explained that Mum had gone away. 'Camping,' I thought. One Tuesday in July or August 1994, she – my mother, Teresa – went camping.

My interest in origami had begun that same summer, not long before the events just mentioned. At school, during the break, I used to perch on one of the planters and pull leaves off the shrubs. I'd fold each leaf down the middle, hoping to achieve perfect symmetry. Then I'd attempt to extract the petiole and the midrib. (I liked calling the central axis of the leaf the 'petiole' and the 'midrib'; I'd just learned those terms in class and thought using them made me sound mature and knowledgeable.) I'd remove the midrib and the petiole, put them in my trouser pocket and forget all about them. In the evening, when I was back home, I'd empty the contents of my pockets and line up the petioles on my table. Sitting before my botanical booty, I'd take out my sheets of coloured paper and my origami manual and, with a patience I no longer have, start folding. In some way, I saw my compulsion to fold the leaves of those shrubs as a form of entertainment, a ritual practice I could carry out in secret, one which would help enhance my manual skills.

The frog was, in theory, one of the simplest origami figures. According to the manual, it was a 'beginners' exercise, and was the second to be explained, coming after only the general advice on how to make the basic folds and the crane. Mine, however, looked like frogs that had been run over by a car on a federal highway after a rainy night. I wasn't aware of that then, because I'd never seen a dead frog in such a condition, but life would take on the task of offering me the comparison I now employ.

On Monday, almost a week after Teresa's disappearance, I made, or tried to make, four frogs with the coloured paper that came with my origami manual. Partially frustrated by the results, I read a chapter of my Choose Your Own Adventure book, and later, having had enough of being cooped up indoors, and of the silence in which the last six days of my life – and more importantly my holidays – had passed, I decided to take a walk to the Rec, as we called a section of the park that split the Educación neighbourhood in two.

My father nodded his permission distractedly. After Teresa's departure, he had taken his minuscule annual leave and was spending the whole day in his bedroom, at his desk (in a corner of the enormous room that he had christened his 'study'), or in the living room, staring at the blank television screen. I put my head around the bedroom door and told him I was going out to play football. It was an unlikely story, one that I invented to capitalize on the complicity that had grown between us while watching the World Cup semi-final between Sweden and Brazil, but he displayed not the slightest interest, not even congratulating me on my initiative: apparently busy working on some document, he was sitting in front of the black screen and glowing green letters of the computer.

The Rec, or recreation area – to give it its official title – had a single basketball hoop and two rusting goals, around which gathered the most noteworthy local teenagers who, to me, seemed like hostile, feral adults whose only interest was in harassing the younger kids. I tended to avoid the Rec; the nearest I got was to pass it when accompanying Teresa to buy the newspaper. On the psychogeographic map I had drawn of Educación, the Rec was not very far short of Hell: an abominable region in which there was nothing for a child like me – addicted to origami and the shadows, with no love of sport or getting into scraps – to do on a Monday during the school holidays.

As I came closer, I spotted, among the group of adolescents standing around the goal, the Rat: the leader of a gang of rowdies, famous for his precocious consumption of illegal substances.

In 1994, the word 'drug' meant little more to me than the temporary tattoos, kinds of transfers, that came with the wrapping of certain brands of chewing gum. In the Celestino Freinet primary school – which my sister and I attended – the rumour had gone around that those chewing-gum wrappers were sometimes impregnated with drugs, so that when the temporary tattoos (of pirates and dinosaurs) were applied to the skin, children experienced sudden, disturbing fits of madness, and on occasions even died or ended up living in the tunnels of the number 2 Line of the metro. These stories, however over the top they might now seem, were for me, at the age of ten, the indisputable Truth, and every time I saw the Rat, I imagined him smothered in temporary tattoos of diplodocuses and corsairs, tied down to a hospital bed, blood seeping from his eyes. That is why I changed direction.

As I walked, I was folding leaves from the shrubs down the centre, following the midribs. In contrast to my usual practice, I didn't throw away the two halves of the leaves, but decided to keep them in my pockets with the petioles (one half in the right pocket, the other in the left, so as to preserve on my person the fundamental symmetry demanded by origami). Absorbed in this meticulous activity, I didn't notice that I had arrived at the corner of the avenue on which stood the newspaper stand Teresa used to frequent each and every morning. The sound of the vendor's voice snapped me out of my reverie: 'So why hasn't your mum been around lately? Is she on holiday?' I looked at him in stupefaction. That a nameless newspaper vendor should notice Teresa's absence felt deeply sad, and even now, twenty years later, I find it difficult to explain why.

I considered telling him that Teresa had gone camping, but my voice stuck in my throat, as if I'd swallowed a small balloon and it was there, blocking half my trachea. The newspaper vendor must have noticed that something was not right, because he didn't ask any further questions and, instead, with a solemn expression, handed me a copy of the paper my mother used to read right through in the living room while my sister and I were doing our homework. On the front page there was, yet again, a photo of the man in a balaclava, with a pipe in his mouth, standing in front of a huge crowd. 'Subcomandante Marcos giving a speech during the opening of the National Democratic Convention,' I read in the tiny letters of the caption. There was no way I could have known it then, but Teresa was one of those dots of ink in the press photograph, one head among many others.

On my way back home, newspaper in hand, I decided to make a detour to avoid the Rec, where I guessed the Rat's gang would be still loitering, holding spitting competitions, whiling away the time before a victim turned up to give them the chance to swap boredom for cruelty. I progressed along the avenue – the limit of where I had permission to go on my own, according to Teresa's stipulations – passing a number of taco restaurants, the local pool hall, and the cafe where Mariana used to meet her girlfriends to drink cappuccinos and feel grown up. On almost every lamp post, every public telephone, there was at least one election campaign poster: a smiling, basically menacing face with eyes gazing out at the pedestrians and motorists from the rigid laminate, from its clumsy attempt to seem friendly.

I left the newspaper on the coffee table in the living room and threw my trainers, as was my custom, into the hall. Then I speedily checked out the house to ensure that my father had gone out. He would most likely have told Mariana where he was going, charging her with the responsibility for communicating this to me, but my sister was on the telephone in her room (a few months before they had given in – unfairly, I considered – to her demand to have one of her own in there) and I grasped the opportunity to root around in my parents' room.

Their bedroom was always in semi-darkness, with the thick curtains invariably drawn and Teresa's reading lamp perpetually casting a dim light. On the desk, I remember seeing the china dog my grandmother had given Mum, and about which my father had made dopey remarks for several days after its arrival. It was one of those long-eared hunting dogs, lying in a resting position, looking up with an expression of supreme tenderness in its huge eyes. Under the dog, folded and unfolded several times – like my unsuccessful origami frogs – was a sheet of paper on which, even from a distance, I thought I could make out Teresa's elegant handwriting, with its elongated *l*s and *d*s that almost overlapped the tails of the *q*s and *j*s of the line above. I approached the sheet of paper with my knees trembling and, very carefully moving the china dog, read a line at random. But before I could continue, I heard the front door opening, and my father's voice announcing, with forced joviality, that he'd dropped by the video store for a couple of films.

FROM A FORTHCOMING NOVEL

An Unlucky Man

SAMANTA SCHWEBLIN

Translated by Megan McDowell

The day I turned eight, my sister – who absolutely always had to be the centre of attention – swallowed an entire cup of bleach. Abi was three. First she smiled, maybe a little disgusted at the nasty taste; then her face crumpled in a frightened grimace of pain. When Mum saw the empty cup hanging from Abi's hand, she turned as white as my sister.

'Abi-my-God,' was all Mum said. 'Abi-my-God,' and it took her a few seconds longer to spring into action.

She shook Abi by the shoulders, but my sister didn't respond. She yelled, but Abi still didn't react. She ran to the phone and called Dad, and when she came running back Abi was still standing there, the cup just dangling from her hand. Mum grabbed the cup and threw it into the sink. She opened the fridge, took out the milk, and poured a glass. She stood looking at the glass, then looked at Abi, then at the glass, and finally she dropped the glass into the sink as well. Dad worked very close by and got home quickly, but Mum still had time to do the whole show with the glass of milk again before he pulled up in the car and started honking the horn and yelling.

Mum lit out of the house like lightning, with Abi clutched to her chest. The front door, the gate and the car doors were all flung open. There was more horn-honking and Mum, who was already sitting in the car, started to cry. Dad had to shout at me twice before I understood that I was the one who was supposed to close up.

We drove the first ten blocks in less time than it took me to close the car door and fasten my seat belt. But when we got to the main avenue, the traffic was practically stopped. Dad honked the horn and shouted out of the window, 'We have to get to the hospital! We have to get to the hospital!' The cars around us manoeuvred and miraculously let us pass, but a couple of cars up we had to start the whole operation all over again. Dad braked in the traffic, stopped honking the horn, and pounded his head against the steering wheel. I had never seen him do such a thing. There was a moment of silence, and then he sat up and looked at me in the rear-view mirror. He turned around and said to me:

'Take off your underpants.'

I was wearing my school uniform. All my underwear was white, but I wasn't exactly thinking about that just then, and I couldn't understand Dad's request. I pressed my hands into the seat to support myself better. I looked at Mum and she shouted:

'Take off your damned knickers!'

I took them off. Dad grabbed them out of my hands. He rolled down the window, went back to honking the horn, and started waving my underpants out of the window. He raised them high while he yelled and kept honking, and it seemed like everyone on the avenue turned around to look at them. My underpants were small, but they were also very white. An ambulance happened to be a block behind us. The driver must have seen our distress flag, because its siren came on, and it caught up with us to start clearing a path. Dad kept on waving the underpants until we reached the hospital.

They left the car by the ambulances and jumped out. Without waiting, Mum ran into the hospital with Abi. I wasn't sure whether I should get out or not: I didn't have any underpants on and I wanted to see where Dad had left them, but he was already out of the car and slamming the door, his hands empty.

'Come on, come on,' said Dad.

He opened my door and helped me out. He gave my shoulder a few pats as we walked into the emergency room. Mum emerged from a doorway at the back and signalled to us. I was relieved to see she was talking again, giving explanations to the nurses.

'Stay here,' said Dad, and he pointed to some orange chairs on the other side of the main waiting area.

I sat. Dad went into the consulting room with Mum and I waited for a while. I don't know how long, but it felt long. I pressed my knees together tightly and thought about everything that had happened so quickly, and about the likelihood that any of the kids from school had seen the spectacle with my underpants. When I sat up straight, my jumper stretched and my bare bottom touched part of the plastic seat. Sometimes the nurse came in or out of the consulting room and I could hear my parents arguing. At one point I craned my neck and caught a glimpse of Abi moving restlessly on one of the cots, and I knew that, at least today, she wasn't going to die. And I still had to wait.

Then a man came and sat down next to me. I don't know where he came from; I hadn't noticed him before.

'How's it going?' he asked.

I thought about saying 'very well', which is what Mum always said if someone asked her that, even if she'd just told me and my sister that we were driving her insane.

'Okay,' I said.

'Are you waiting for someone?'

I thought about it. I wasn't really waiting for anyone; at least, it wasn't what I *wanted* to be doing right then. So I shook my head, and he said:

'Why are you sitting in the waiting room, then?'

I understood it was a great contradiction. He opened a small bag he had on his lap and rummaged a bit, unhurried. Then he took a pink slip of paper from his wallet.

'Here it is. I knew I had it somewhere.'

The paper was printed with the number 92.

'It's good for an ice cream. My treat,' he said.

I told him no. You shouldn't accept things from strangers.

'But it's free, I won it.'

'No.' I looked straight ahead and we sat in silence.

'Suit yourself,' he said, without getting angry.

He took a magazine from his bag and started to fill in a crossword puzzle. The door to the consulting room opened again and I heard Dad say, 'I will not condone such nonsense.' That's Dad's clincher for ending almost any argument. The man sitting next to me didn't seem to hear it.

'It's my birthday,' I said.

It's my birthday, I repeated to myself. *What should I do?*

The man held the pen to mark a box on the puzzle and looked at me in surprise. I nodded without looking at him, aware that I had his attention again.

'But . . .' he said, and he closed the magazine. 'Sometimes I just don't understand women. If it's your birthday, why are you in a hospital waiting room?'

He was an observant man. I straightened up again in my seat and I saw that, even then, I barely came up to his shoulders. He smiled and I smoothed my hair. And then I said:

'I'm not wearing any underpants.'

I don't know why I said it. It's just that it *was* my birthday and I *wasn't* wearing underpants, and I couldn't stop thinking about those circumstances. He was still looking at me. Maybe he was startled or offended, and I understood that, though it wasn't my intention, there was something vulgar about what I had just said.

'But it's your birthday,' he said.

I nodded.

'It's not fair. A person can't just go around without underpants when it's their birthday.'

'I *know*,' I said emphatically, because now I understood just how Abi's whole display was a personal affront to me.

He sat for a moment without saying anything. Then he looked towards the big windows that looked out onto the parking lot.

'I know where to get you some underpants,' he said.

'Where?'

'Problem solved.' He stowed his things and stood up.

I hesitated. Precisely because I wasn't wearing underpants, but also because I didn't know if he was telling the truth. He looked towards the front desk and waved one hand at the attendants.

'We'll be right back,' he said, and he pointed to me. 'It's her birthday.' And then I thought, *Oh please Jesus, don't let him say anything about my underpants*, but he didn't: he opened the door and winked at me, and then I knew I could trust him.

We went out to the parking lot. Standing up I barely cleared his waist. Dad's car was still next to the ambulances, and a policeman was circling it, annoyed. I kept looking over at the policeman, and he watched us walk away. The air wrapped around my legs and rose, making a tent out of my uniform. I had to hold it down while I walked, keeping my legs awkwardly close together.

He turned around to see if I was following him, and he saw me fighting with my skirt.

'We'd better keep close to the wall.'

'I want to know where we're going.'

'Don't get persnickety with me now, darling.'

We crossed the avenue and went into a shopping centre. It was an uninviting place. We walked to the back towards a big clothing store, a truly huge one that I was pretty sure Mum didn't go to. Before we went in he said to me, 'Don't get lost,' and gave me his hand, which was cold and very soft. He waved to the cashiers with the same gesture he'd made towards the desk attendants when we left the hospital, but no one responded. We walked down the aisles. In addition to dresses, trousers and shirts, there were work clothes: hard hats, yellow overalls like the trash collectors wore, smocks for cleaning ladies, plastic boots, and even some tools. I wondered if he bought his clothes there and if he would use any of those things in his job, and then I also wondered what his name was.

'Here we are,' he said.

We were surrounded by tables of underwear for men and women. If I reached out my hand I could touch a large bin full of giant underpants, bigger than any I'd seen before, and they were only three pesos each. With one of those pairs of underpants they could have made three for someone my size.

'Not those,' he said. 'Here.' And he led me a little further to a section with smaller sizes. 'Look at all the underpants they have . . . Which will you choose, my lady?'

I looked around a little. Almost all of them were white or pink. I pointed to a white pair, one of the few that didn't have a bow on them.

'These,' I said. 'But I can't pay for them.'

He came a little closer and said into my ear:

'That doesn't matter.'

'Are you the owner?'

'No. It's your birthday.'

I smiled.

'But we have to find better ones. We need to be sure.'

'Okay, darling,' I ventured.

'Don't say "darling",' he said. 'I'll get persnickety.' And he imitated me holding down my skirt in the parking lot.

He made me laugh. When he finished clowning around he held out two closed fists in front of me, and he stayed just like that until I understood; I touched the right one. He opened it: it was empty.

'You can still choose the other one.'

I touched the other one. It took me a moment to realize it was a pair of underpants because I had never seen black ones before. And they were for girls because they had white hearts on them, so small they looked like dots, and Hello Kitty's face was on the front, right where there was usually that bow Mum and I don't like at all.

'You'll have to try them on,' he said.

I held the underpants to my chest. He gave me his hand again and we went towards the changing rooms, which looked empty. We peered in. He said he didn't know if he could go with me because they were for women only. He said I would have to go alone. It was logical because, unless it's someone you know very well, it's not good for people to see you in your underpants. But I was afraid of going into the dressing room alone. Or something worse: coming out and not seeing him there.

'What's your name?' I asked.

'I can't tell you that.'

'Why not?'

He knelt down. Then he was almost my height, or maybe I was a couple of inches taller.

'Because I'm cursed.'

'Cursed? What's cursed?'

'A woman who hates me said that the next time I say my name, I'm going to die.'

I thought it might be another joke, but he said it very seriously.

'You could write it down for me.'

'Write it down?'

'If you wrote it you wouldn't say it, you'd be writing it. And if I know your name I can call for you and I won't be so scared to go into the dressing room alone.'

'But we can't be sure. What if this woman thinks writing my name is the same as saying it? What if by saying it, she meant letting someone else know, letting my name out into the world in any way?'

'But how would she know?'

'People don't trust me, and I'm the unluckiest man in the world.'

'I don't believe you, there's no way she'd find out.'

'I know what I'm talking about.'

Together, we looked at the underpants in my hands. I thought that my parents might be finished by now.

'But it's my birthday,' I said.

And maybe I did it on purpose. At the time I felt like I did: my eyes filled with tears. Then he hugged me. It was a very fast movement; he crossed his arms behind my back and squeezed me so tight my face pressed into his chest. Then he let me go, took out his magazine and pen, and wrote something on the right margin of the cover. Then he tore it off and folded it three times before handing it to me.

'Don't read it,' he said, and he stood up and pushed me gently towards the dressing room.

I passed four empty cubicles. Before gathering my courage and entering the fifth, I put the paper into the pocket of my jumper and turned to look at him, and we smiled at each other.

I tried on the underpants. They were perfect. I lifted up my jumper so I could see just how good they looked. They were so, so very perfect. They fitted incredibly well, and because they were black, Dad would never ask me for them so he could wave them out of the window behind the ambulance. And even if he did, I wouldn't be so embarrassed if my classmates saw. *Just look at the underpants that girl has,* they'd all think. *Now those are some perfect underpants.*

I realized I couldn't take them off now. And I realized something else: they didn't have a security tag. They had a little mark where the tag would usually go, but there was no alarm. I stood a moment longer looking at myself in the mirror, and then I couldn't stand it any longer and I took out the little paper, opened it and read it.

I came out of the dressing room and he wasn't where I had left him, but he was a little further down, beside the bathing suits. He looked at me, and when he saw I wasn't carrying the underpants he winked, and I was the one who took his hand. This time he held on to me tighter; we walked together towards the exit.

I trusted that he knew what he was doing. That a cursed man who had the world's worst luck knew how to do these things. We passed the line of cash registers at the main entrance. One of the security guards looked at us, adjusting his belt. He would surely think the nameless man was my dad, and I felt proud.

We passed the sensors at the exit and went into the mall, and we kept walking in silence all the way back to the avenue. That was when I saw Abi, alone, in the middle of the hospital parking lot. And I saw Mum, on our side of the street, looking around frantically. Dad was also coming towards us from the parking lot. He was following fast behind the policeman who'd been looking at his car before, and who was now pointing at us. Everything happened very quickly. Dad saw us, yelled my name, and a few seconds later that policeman and two others who came out of nowhere were already on top of us. The unlucky man let go of me, but I held my hand suspended towards him for a few seconds. They surrounded him and pushed him roughly. They asked him what he was doing, they asked him his name, but he didn't answer. Mum hugged me and checked me over head to toe. She had my white underpants dangling from her right hand. Then, patting me all over, she noticed I was wearing a different pair. She lifted my jumper in a single movement: it was such a rude and vulgar act, right there in front of everyone, that

I jerked away and had to take a few steps backwards to keep from falling down. The unlucky man looked at me and I looked at him. When Mum saw the black underpants she screamed 'Son of a bitch, son of a bitch,' and Dad lunged at him and tried to punch him. The cops moved to separate them.

I fished for the paper in my jumper pocket, put it in my mouth, and as I swallowed it I repeated his name in silence, several times, so I would never forget it.

Naked Animals

JESÚS MIGUEL SOTO

Translated by Emily Davis

The red car stopped on the sidewalk and the driver got out, clearly relieved to have finally found a place to buy cigarettes. He left the engine running and didn't even close the door behind him. I know because just minutes earlier I had parked my car a few metres away to buy two packs of cigarettes and a case of beer that would make it easier for me to bear the inevitable defeat of my team in the football match that night.

As I took a second drag on my cigarette I saw the woman in the back seat of the red car. She sat with her hips turned and she was craning her neck. She seemed to be focused on watching the cars go by, as if she were trying to find some sort of migratory pattern among the models and colours that came and went along the cactus-strewn road.

I gathered that the woman had just been crying, not for a few minutes, but for weeks or even months. Her face was not in tears, but it had been shaped by tears. It wasn't sad, even – instead it was petrified in a past where it had been accustomed to crying. It was a face that seemed to have been redrawn with that unique effect of copious tears that have carved out their own courses, with their pools and their tributaries.

The man from the red car decided to smoke his cigarette just outside the store, with ceremonious drags, as if he were immune to the raging sun that would soon warm the beers I had just bought. I couldn't stay there any longer myself, and I drove off so the wind would cool me off even though it meant my cigarette would burn out faster.

A few blocks later the memory of the woman was fading away and when it had nearly vanished into thin air I took one last drag on the cigarette. The tobacco – and her face – left an acrid aftertaste that eventually dissolved into the heat.

Several traffic lights later the red car passed me. It wasn't going excessively fast. Probably the driver had made a series of small decisions (running a yellow light, not letting another car in, cleverly avoiding a pothole, changing gears at just the right moments) that allowed him to close the gap and again place the woman in my field of vision, this time at a diagonal. She remained in the same posture, but now I could see her from a new angle. I might say it was more beautiful, although I don't know if it was because of my point of view, or the re-emergence of the sun's rays, or because it was the second time I'd seen her: that second glimpse that – now free from the euphoria of the first encounter – allows for an unhurried pleasure of the senses. But it wasn't her beauty that interested me. It was her posture, which was even more striking; she held herself with such elegant simplicity. And even more than her posture, what intrigued me the most was the way she kept looking backwards, ignoring the road that stretched out ahead, clinging to the wake of images that were seamlessly superimposed in a perfect inverted progression.

For the next half hour the woman remained in my sight. I wasn't following the red car. We were just taking the same route. And so were lots of other cars, only the rest of them (since they didn't have a woman in the back seat trying to resist the bonds of time) were merely decorative spectres. At times those cars would move forward and block her from view, and then they would retreat and the woman would emerge again. And every reappearance, like a stubborn miracle trying to prove itself not by being spectacular but just by being obstinate, made me crave another hit – so much so that when the red car began to slow down to turn onto a side road that wasn't on my way home, I slowed down too. Not because I wanted to follow them, I told myself in an absolving whisper, but because I sensed that the woman needed to see something and – I said to myself, silently this time – I wanted to know what it was.

Now that I was following them on purpose and not just with the ebb and flow of chance, I was overcome with the feeling that I was committing a crime. I decided to maintain a sensible distance, which I'm not sure was necessary because the man was glued to the steering wheel, and the woman, in her petrified state, ignored me. Although I believe she noticed my presence a couple of times, she did so as if I were just another object in the scene, and in effect I was – we all were.

After another half an hour of driving, the red car stopped on a street lined with topiaries. The man got out. He rang a doorbell, the door opened halfway and across the threshold he had a short conversation with someone I couldn't see because this time I stayed back a considerable distance, nearly a full block away. As the man walked back to the car I got ready to go again, and to avoid suspicion I passed him before he could drive away, just like I'd seen in movies that illustrate the art of pursuit. But the tactic failed me: in my rear-view mirror I saw that the woman had got out of the car and was standing on the sidewalk.

I turned at the next street and drove around the block to end up exactly in the spot I'd been parked in minutes earlier. The red car was gone and the woman was still standing there, looking in the same direction she'd been looking when she was sitting in the car – backwards – towards the done and the undone. She had a large cloth bag over her shoulder and across her chest. It was threadbare and with one of her hands she was clutching the strap with what seemed like excessive care. Standing there she looked less elegant than before; she'd lost the sculptural posture I'd become accustomed to. It was like seeing Michelangelo's David buying a metro ticket or pushing a shopping cart.

I decided to turn off the engine and light another cigarette. When I closed my eyes to take the first drag I feared that when I opened them the woman would be gone, which would almost have been a relief because the safety of my apartment walls, my now warm beers and the match awaited me.

But when I opened my eyes the woman was still there. Since I didn't have a radio or a newspaper or a donut and coffee to pass the time, I just kept smoking my cigarette meticulously. When it was half-gone I decided that when I finished it I would light the next one, and then another, and another. (Predicting minuscule future actions distracts me from the impossibility of foreseeing big life events.)

Before I could get to the last drag a black car stopped in front of the woman and she meekly climbed into the back seat. I perked up, loosened my tie, tossed the unfinished cigarette out of the half-open window and started the engine. I followed the black car without hesitation, as if my usual routine were to follow cars that pick up women who look backwards, a job I was performing with a level of efficiency that made me slightly proud.

After half a dozen kilometres the black car abandoned the woman on another street. The driver knocked on a door and left, and she waited with her cloth bag. About ten minutes later a beige car pulled up and she got in without any signal from anyone. Cars of various makes and colours repeated this chain of events over and over with the density of a nightmare, one where you want to wake up but you also want to find out how it ends. In my car I repeated myself as well, cigarette after cigarette: start the engine; follow the car.

After seven cars I decided to put an end to this series of nearly identical episodes. And just as I've managed to do before in disturbing dreams, I chose to speak, because the sound of words can sometimes tear through veils.

While the woman was waiting, I pulled forward in my car and parked just on the other side of the intersection, several metres ahead of where she was. I was afraid inertia would compel her to climb into my back seat and turn her back to me while I drove, glued to the steering wheel, only to abandon her on another street after a few kilometres.

I shut off the engine and walked towards her. The furrows on her face were very deep, and her expression of lament, far from moving me, terrified me. It scared me in the way that someone else's pain sometimes does: as if I'd seen a mirror covered in boils. I didn't manage to say anything meaningful to her. 'Waiting for someone?' I muttered. 'I don't understand,' she said. Her posture relaxed slightly and although out of the corner of her eye she continued to look behind her, which was where I usually was with respect to her, she was paying attention to me. She wasn't completely gone – some thread of sanity kept her tied to a plane where we could commune.

I told her that if she needed to go somewhere I could take her and she said no, what she needed was several changes of clothing. 'Clothing?' I repeated like a diligent echo. She explained, clutching her bag to her chest, that she had found them naked like this, that right now it didn't matter because it was warm, but at night the temperature would surely drop, and she was worried because she didn't know if they could survive the cold. 'I don't think it will get that cold,' was all that occurred to me to say to follow the same line of thought she'd extended to me. She seemed bothered, as if my observation were just nonsense that was meant to trick her. She opened her bag and indicated that I should lower my head to see the contents it was protecting. Although they appeared to be a pair of tiny, sweaty and trembling puppies, it was impossible to say for sure that it wasn't actually a single body with two heads; it was also impossible to look at the palpitating, whining jumble and be sure they were even dogs. I think my indolence upset her. She told me, raising her voice, that the cold was going to kill them. 'Look, they're not wearing anything, they can't stay like this.'

More to comfort myself than her, I went to my car to look for some sort of cloth or rag in the glove compartment. In the meantime a silver car picked up the woman. I followed them and the nightmare resumed, only now the knowledge that she had company filled me with much greater apprehension. I began to wonder about whether the right clothes for those puppies would be the same as what infants wear or if it would be better to get something from a special shop for animals.

I decided that at the next stop, when they abandoned the woman on the street, I would make her come with me and we would solve her immediate problem, which – besides her pained face that had been shaped by tears – was those tiny trembling animals' lack of attire. But then the grey car abandoned the residential areas and started down the road that leads to the border checkpoint, and I wouldn't be able to go through. I stopped on the side of the road and didn't turn back until the silver car had shrunk to the size of a fly and was swallowed by the horizon. On this side of the threshold I had football waiting for me, clothes in my wardrobe, and feverishly hot drinks that I'd have to chill with ice cubes – a handful of small certainties, a somewhat clean mirror.

56 (the Fall)*

LUCIANA SOUSA

Translated by Peter Bush

The last thing on Oscar's mind when he picked up the phone was that, in a few hours, he would be extracting his Uncle Agustín's corpse from the modest flat where he had spent the last fifty years.

He'd not seen him since that day four years ago when the old man had asked Oscar to return the spare key to his security box. He was going to take his money out of the bank.

'What will you do with it all?' he'd asked.

'I'm going to spend it.'

'You old shit,' thought Oscar. His uncle had a good pension, no family and almost never left his house.

They'd not spoken since.

When he received the call from a neighbour alarmed by the smell from the old man's flat, that money came to mind once again. He thought about it and wanted it as he might desire a beautiful woman. Then he fantasized endlessly about the pile of cash. A flat and a nice windfall would come just right to help him break up

---

* Each number on the Argentine betting card has a meaning.

with Malena and start afresh. He might even be able to leave his office job and open the wine shop of his dreams. His children had grown up.

He switched the sombre, tetchy expression he adopted when working at his window at the National Car Registry for a beaming smile that he paraded through the office, several underground stations and the three blocks he had to walk. A few metres before reaching the building where the old man lived he rehearsed a look that went from worried to sad. He cut diagonally across the road towards the corner of the street and bet a few pesos on number 47: *the dead man.*

When he finally arrived, he was met by the distraught neighbour and two policemen who gave their condolences and told him they'd have to move the body to the morgue. Oscar dealt with the formalities with the sangfroid of a butcher and, once the police returned the body to the family, they buried it in the Chacarita cemetery.

Oscar moved into the flat that same weekend. He'd not been inside for years, but he could remember everything in minute detail. It was a two-room ground-floor flat with a gallery, the large windows of which overlooked an inner courtyard. The spacious living room had suffered an invasion of angular, brown armchairs that matched the wallpaper striped in different hues of maize yellow. A modular furniture unit stocked with sets of glasses filled the whole wall opposite the main armchair.

The bedroom was less out of the ordinary, the walls were painted white and it had a large wrought-iron bed with an elaborate headboard Oscar thought would fetch a good price, a smallish wardrobe stuffed with clothes, and a bedside table with two drawers he checked straight away – an unloaded revolver, some cash, boxes of pills and two valuable watches he pocketed there and then. Oscar counted 1,200 pesos. He didn't immediately decide what to do with the weapon. He left under the window a photo of his uncle and his mother he knew they'd taken one summer in the seventies in Mar del Plata.

The kitchen looked new; the thinnest layer of dust covered the huge granite top that extended to the first-rate cooker. He imagined the old man probably didn't cook very much. In one corner, envelopes with unpaid bills and a few advertising flyers. In the fridge, an empty carton of milk, some eggs and half a kilo of ham that was beginning to turn green. Newspapers from the last two years were piled up in the tiny utility room.

Oscar started to get rid of the furniture. He sold the practically unused kitchen furniture and the crockery from the modular unit in the living room to a trader from the flea-market to whom he promised the bed, once they moved out for good. He gave away some worn-out clothes. He decided to keep back for himself a dozen pristine shirts and trousers.

It took him two weeks to find an important stash of money. He found it in an empty tin of paint in the utility room. He counted the money in just a few minutes – almost $70,000; they'd been stuffed inside a stiff brown-paper envelope. He experienced the mean, calculating satisfaction of someone who lays a bet and knows he's going to win something at every attempt. He immediately thought that wasn't enough, that there must be more, but even so he rapidly bought a flat in a block about to be built in the leafy area of Barracas. That same day, before night fell, he placed the bet he'd been wagering on for years; 100 pesos on 32, *money*. He kept the rest back for a blow-out and a bottle of good wine in a bar he usually went to with Malena.

A week later, when things had begun to go badly with his ex-wife, Oscar left the flat he had rented in Colegiales and moved into his uncle's place for good. He still hadn't found a large slice of his money. He had a hunch. And when he had a hunch, he was never wrong. He didn't let anyone help him and, after his first painstaking search, he started tapping on every single kitchen and bathroom tile. He removed the skirting boards, dismantled furniture and opened and inspected every box his uncle kept in the trunk room.

The place was soon a complete mess. Dust darkened the furniture and added a brownish filter to the windows that let in less and less light. He heaped up everything he couldn't sell in the middle of the living room. He bolstered the pile with books, lamps and other small things, and in no time a mountain of items divided the room into four. Rubbish, papers and objects of no value would end up in the street.

Within days Agustín's place looked like a building site in reverse. Oscar laboured away every night with destructive energy, as if starting from zero again. He spent his day-time at the office in a state of exhaustion. He let his beard grow, didn't eat properly and slept in two-, three- or four-hour siestas; one in the evening and one at dawn.

Oscar went along with what they said at work; he agreed that he looked poorly. He couldn't recognize what he saw in the small bathroom mirror every morning. High, scraggy cheeks, blue bags under his brown eyes, and a white, elongated tongue he stuck out completely when he was cleaning his teeth. His thin neck was hard put to support a head that had more hair than anything else. But he wouldn't relent on the missing money, and believed that once it did appear – which he calculated would be any minute – he'd be able to give up work and take a much-deserved holiday on a southern beach where he could recover his energy.

But the money didn't appear.

At the end of the month they cut off the electricity and gas because he hadn't paid his bills. Then Oscar sharpened and applied his five senses like a wild animal. He stopped going to work, which wasn't the result of any rational decision, he simply couldn't get up after spending the night searching for clues. He inspected everything so carefully he could soon identify individual rats nesting in the box for the shutters of the window that looked over the yard, and the three cockroach nests he discovered after leaving bait in different parts of the house and vigilantly waiting for them to appear. He didn't bother to poison the rats or kill the cockroaches even though the old man had kept supplies of poison; it sufficed to know that nothing was hidden in those small hollow spaces.

A week later he collapsed and slumped down on his bed; his skin was yellow and his liver shattered. He didn't need the fingers of one hand to count the number of times he got himself up. The same neighbour who had found his uncle's corpse called the ambulance after hearing Oscar's terrible wails. Analyses diagnosed advanced pancreatic cancer. He barely had time to talk to his children, decide who would inherit his flats, and finalize a will detailing all the goods that they found in Agustín's house. His last wish was a huge bet on 17, *misfortune*. Malena, his ex, decided to keep that money.

Oscar was buried some thirty metres from the old man.

Malena quickly refurbished the flat. She gave what clothes were left to the church, removed the carpets and had a new bathroom fitted. She decided to rent out the flat while her children were at university, and eventually, Emilia, one of her second cousins who'd just come to the city, moved in.

Emilia was a nurse: every day she left the house early and the moment she got back she had a hot shower and watched television in bed with the huge cat with shiny fur she'd inherited from her mother. She was pleased with the flat; she bought a garden set and filled the yard with plants she organized according to size and colour.

She also liked the neighbourhood; it was quiet by day, even though it was central; everyone seemed to be just passing through. At dusk when the sky was turning into a purple awning, people opened the enormous windows of their low houses, and you could smell what they were cooking or watch the game on the television through their wrought-iron bars.

Emilia invited Malena to lunch on her first free day. Her children were on an excursion so they could talk at their ease and catch up. Malena brought a bottle of wine to accompany the stuffed joint Emilia was going to roast in the oven. She had yet to cook a meal in the flat and decided she ought to celebrate her occupancy of her new home.

It was a cool, sunny day but they were both happy to sit in the yard and use the plastic furniture for the first time. In a way, though neither said as much, both felt they were starting afresh. They had a laugh over the news about the duty doctor who'd invited Emilia out and that was probably why they didn't notice the thick black smoke issuing from the kitchen. The smell reached the yard, and Emilia leaped from her chair like a jack-in-the-box, while her cousin felt tempted to laugh. You could hardly open your eyes in the kitchen. Emilia was furious. It was the first meal she'd cooked in the house and that wasn't a good sign.

She struggled to switch off the oven and then opened the kitchen doors and windows to ventilate the space. A few minutes later she extracted the tray with the roast. It was covered in black dust, but still looked raw.

The oven was slow to cool down. She took out the roasting tins and cleared out the inside. She found it was carpeted with oddly shaped bits of green paper it took her until nightfall to empty out with a spatula.

Roots

MARIANA TORRES

Translated by Lisa Dillman

They never tell you whether the place chooses its inhabitants – entices them somehow, until they turn up with their belongings from other lives and cast their children down there – or the emigrant is the one with the ability to choose. I elect to be born. I elect to be born here. I choose this territory and its islands covered in tiny crabs for my children to grow up and put down roots. Long, fleshy roots born from the soles of their feet that reach down into the earth. Sinking into the sand, mixing with the salt, the sugar cane, the mosquitoes.

Another thing they never tell you is that moving those roots hurts.

And they don't tell you that uprooting them leaves a mark, that it's something you carry all your life.

I was born in Brazil because everything grows in that soil. All you have to do is drive a broomstick into the ground and it will sprout leaves. I was born quickly, with no fuss. My mother says she started having contractions while picking lettuces in the vegetable patch and, because she assumed it was one of her stomach aches, she kept working. When we got to the hospital they anaesthetized her and pulled me out, caesarean. I was a girl and weighed less than a stuffed turkey. The day I was born my father ate an apple and buried the seeds. One of them took root and from those roots grew an apple tree, a gangly apple tree that in a year was already several centimetres taller than I was. My parents set wooden stakes all around its trunk to make it grow straight, without bending.

At the time we lived in a too-perfect place, though I didn't know it then. To me it was normal to have a beach twenty metres from the door, and banana and guava and lemon trees, and land to plant lettuces on, and a white house, and a warm, stable climate, and big rocks to climb in the garden and a town a few kilometres away where people whistled songs on dirt roads.

I was almost one when I dared to lift my feet from the ground and pull up my own roots. I raised my right foot for the first time and my roots hung in the air. I felt a cramp that began in the middle of my foot and surged up my body to my belly button. Like the lash of a whip. Painful and yet, at the same time, comforting. I got used to the feeling and, carefully, took my first steps. And I saw how the roots re-took in the earth when I rested my foot back in the hot sand. The sand on which I took my first steps was hot and humid.

Because everything in Brazil is hot and humid.

The apple tree was growing well and, since my parents knew about trees and wooden stakes, it also grew straight. I learned to climb it. I would place one foot on the stake, the other on the trunk and climb up to the lowest branches. From the apple tree's trunk I could touch the sea with my fingertips. A dark-blue sea, speckled with islands. And smell our beach and our stretch of sea. Because everyone I knew had their own beach and stretch of sea.

Angra dos Reis, back then, was almost-wild territory, and though it's hard to build on the jungle, if you keep insisting, the jungle gives in. There was a time when it was overrun with European buyers invading the land with cement mixers, tons of brick and countless litres of melted asphalt, which they spread over the dirt roads. My parents gave in as well, because I had to go to school: kids couldn't grow up without school, they said, lettuce heads won't educate you.

That was when we left the white house and island of tiny crabs behind. When I found out we were leaving I climbed the apple tree's trunk as high as I could and didn't come down for several days. My mother pruned the tree to get me down and my father dug up the earth around it to extract its roots. A tree's roots are much longer than those of a human. As my parents pruned, I sat on the ground to look at my feet. I turned them over, shook off the dirt and worms. And on the bottom of my feet, all along the sole, I found them. My roots were still there, they'd got broader at the base, and shorter, but looked strong. It no longer hurt to expose them. I looked at my apple tree, submissive, allowing my parents to prune it with their four hands, sever its roots and transplant it to a pot. Without them seeing, I grabbed the pruners and sheared off, one by one, the roots growing from my feet. I bit my tongue so as to keep from screaming. My cuts raw and bleeding, I ran to the beach and got in the water. Salt from the sea, my mother used to say, cures everything. I rode with the apple tree, in the back of the van, surrounded by belongings and hugging its trunk. There were so few branches left I was sure it was going to die.

When we got to our new home in Rio de Janeiro – an apartment in a block full of other apartments – my parents placed the apple tree out in the open air. There was a balcony with no roof, so the branches could reach up, in search of sun and rain. The apple tree, the following spring, was covered in shoots. The branches filled with tiny buds that grew, forming leaf clusters that fattened and then sent out long threads that turned into white flowers.

'It's acclimatized well,' said my parents, proud.

And I adapted too. To heaving plazas full of people where I had to sit on my father's shoulders in order for us to make our way through. To traffic, to cars, to scooters, to pollution, to the smell of people. And, instead of climbing the apple tree, I took off my shoes and climbed wooden structures in public parks. The soles of my feet grew hard because I was always barefoot. I grabbed hold of creepers and vines and climbed walls and slipped into neighbours' houses, and they invited me to lunch. I played hooky from school and went to the beach, where the sand was mixed with asphalt, as though the two were part of the same beast. There I mingled with the people, who were everywhere, doing nothing, laughing at life, selling trinkets and juices and wooden whistles, sunbathing and laughing and drinking beer. There were people in every nook and on every corner, pulsating, running behind soccer balls, up in trees, on walls. There were people. Lots of people. I liked listening to them talk, seeing them move, spit, eat, sing.

And, being among all those people, I must have caught something. Right before summer my body became covered in plant shoots. My parents thought it was measles at first, so they pumped me full of antibiotics and made me stay home. Later they were told it was a tropical disease, typical of the country, nothing serious, though for me to be cured they had to get me out of there, forever. I shook myself, explained that they were shoots, told them how I'd cut the roots off my feet and that those mutilated roots were now seeking another place to emerge. They refused to listen. By then my body was covered in shoots, particularly my arms and legs, and a quite attractive one that looked like a broken tooth sprouted up on my cheek. They hurt, itched a bit, but I never complained. For weeks I couldn't leave the house, or play hooky, or go to school. I stared at the apple tree, in full bloom, which was just beginning to lose its petals.

That was when my parents decided to move us far away, so we could live with other people, in another climate. A thing like that only existed on the other side of the ocean. When they gave me the news I ran to the apple tree and climbed its trunk. It had been years since I'd done so for fear of breaking it. But that day the tree stoically withstood my weight, my yanking and shaking that made its flower petals fall even faster. Sitting up in its branches, I felt invulnerable. I wanted them to go without me. To leave us there.

But that didn't happen.

My mother pruned the apple tree until it was bare, tied its branches with packing tape and covered it in a layer of cloth to protect it from the cold in the plane's hold. Me she wrapped in a woollen coat, plus a scarf to hide my cheek-shoot, and my feet she stuffed into four pairs of socks and a stiff pair of shoes. I could hardly breathe. At the airport our suitcases were weighed and sent off on a black conveyor belt. My apple tree weighed twenty-seven kilos, dirt included. I watched it make its way off along the belt and be swallowed up by the darkness of a tunnel. I disliked flying. When I looked out of the window I couldn't see even the tiniest bit of earth, just a never-ending expanse of water, and lots of clouds.

At some point we landed. And despite the cold that hit my face when we exited the plane and despite the layers of clothing I had on, I managed to run to the luggage carousel. The apple tree was the first one out, proud, its upper crown wrenching free of the fabric, like a head popping out to breathe. I wanted to unclothe it then and there. But my parents made me go to the house, unpack the suitcases and, only then, strip off the layers of cloth. As we did, we discovered a miracle. What had been flowers before the trip were now fruit buds. Somehow, the rest, the dark and the cold of the plane's hold had accelerated the process. My parents examined my entire body, looked at my arms, my legs. They found nothing new. My shoots were still there but, it seemed, I was starting to heal.

We put the apple tree out on the terrace. It was cold, but in truth that mild sun was pleasant. It hardly rains in this country, we had to put cream on our bodies so our skin wouldn't crack. Soon my shoots dried up and disappeared, as though they'd never been with me. That didn't strike me as unusual because nothing grows in this city. The earth is brown, hard and dry, it's impossible to plant anything. I didn't want to run around the new house, or go down to the swings to freeze, or try roasted chestnuts, much less speak to people in that strange language, I didn't want to eat cured ham, or press my thumb onto a black inkpad to sign my new nationality, or play in the snow, or try lilac candies or even visit that famous park with a lake and wooden boats and lots of monstrous fish that pecked at your finger when you stuck your hand into the water. I didn't want to do any of it but I did it all.

And though I said I was happy and even learned to fake it, the truth is that at night the scars on the soles of my feet burned. I'd sit in bed and look at my feet, and I almost believed my roots were going to sprout out again at any minute. But the sea salt had done a good job.

In time my apple tree died. Trees die, too, their trunks hollow out and the roots begin to rot, though you can't tell from the outside. It never produced any apples. They don't tell you that that happens to apple trees when they get transplanted. And if it did produce apples, I wasn't around to see them. But I was there the day it died. I realized something wasn't right towards the end of winter, when it was still cold but the sun was starting to warm up. The apple tree, rather than sprouting new leaves and shoots, began to lose leaves. They dried up, shrivelled and began to fall, four by four. It became infested with aphids and ants. And one day the wind got the best of it. I was the first one to see it toppled over on the ground, tall as it was, its roots sticking out of the earth, exposed to air. But the tree was already dead, and it couldn't feel any pain.

Forests Where There Was Nothing

VALENTÍN TRUJILLO

Translated by Simon Bruni

The seminarian Rodrigo had slept badly, in his chapel in the middle of the forest. Father Félix had sent for him from the church in town: they had to mend a joist in the bell tower, damaged in the recent storm. With the bell silenced, for a few days, the priest – an octogenarian preacher born and raised in the region – had been yelling the call to Mass.

A cold mist enveloped the place. From the church tower they watched the sun climb into the sky and begin to warm the morning. The seminarian was wearing gloves with the fingers cut off and was working with a length of rope slung over the beam where the bell sat. The priest was giving him instructions. The young man was soon sweating and his hands ached. When the mist lifted and they could see the tops of the saplings, the priest contemplated the forests.

Father Félix believed that, at the beginning, in San Fernando de Maldonado there must have been wind and nothing but wind on the great, bare expanses under the celestial vault, the stars burning away above the dunes. Expanses battered by ocean gales, the airborne salt catching in shutter slats and in horses' shoes. The town had been founded at a crossroads of winds: from the pampas in the south-east, cutting across the wide, brown river, where bodies of air from the mountain range had been forming for centuries; from the Atlantic, swirling over from the Malvinas and, beyond that, the Antarctic; from Brazil, heavy with water on summer nights. A wind for each time of year but with the same effect: sand on the streets, in the houses, in kettles, in the maté, between the creases in clothes, a fine dust that found its way into shutters and hinges, making bronze forks screech and polishing teeth like a dry toothpaste. The dunes, slow and mobile like camels' backs, advanced from the coast into the city, biting into every block.

Some men drove progress: doctors, engineers, businessmen, all of them entrepreneurs. There were marshes to drain, where men sometimes fell like livestock and died in the silence of the sandbanks, in dark and oily water where vipers reproduced. The plantations marked and defined the landscape: Catalan, Sardinian and Corsican pine, Australian eucalyptus. Trees from other lands – transplanted like the men – which firmed up the soil. The sand settled, the paving stones were clean, the marshes dried up. The shadow grew.

The wind blew through a succession of leafy filters and brought health to respiratory tracts. The forests changed the landscape, and the work; they amplified the reflections of colours in the distance. The leaves fell and formed carpets that rotted with the rain and gave shelter to fungi and worms. On the outskirts of the town, saws could now be heard, poor carpenters prospered, tree trunks fell with the deep sound of a cello's notes, ovenbirds' mud nests were turned upside down, eagles traced circles in the air over the new treetops.

Faced with Father Félix's prolonged silence, the seminarian Rodrigo said, 'They saw forest where there was nothing.'

'You think there was nothing?' the priest asked.

The wind blew through the tower and whistled inside the bell.

'All this was God's work,' Félix went on. 'The empty pampas and the furious waves. Every grain of the dunes, pure, supreme creation.

Living was a test of survival and love. The struggle hardened us, and the roof of His church was the shelter to which everyone flocked.'

The seminarian fell silent and turned to look at the forests. He answered that God had given man fire and craft, cunning, as part of his intelligence. Those lush trees were a tribute to hard work and the use of reason.

'Every storm reminded us of the power of God,' Félix said to him. 'With menace and severity. The Lord's fury teaches us, don't you think?'

'The trees were transplanted and put down roots here, like we men did.'

The young man recalled Sir Henry Burnett, a subject of Her Majesty and consul in Maldonado. The anecdotes of his life, love as a foundation for the pines of the Maldonado coast: he had fallen in love with a local nurse. His son Guillermo Enrique was Uruguayan and had also planted trees. He recalled Dr Román Bergalli, who in the fight against respiratory infections had also planted eucalyptus, as well as the native Manuel Gorlero, and the poet Don Antonio Lussich who, a stubborn creature, had built his enormous house on top of the vacant hill of Punta Ballena, and as the years passed, had been surrounded by the same forest. It was not just the forces of nature that were altered by the transformation of dunes into forests. The economic forces were also transformed.

'There's more work now, Father. The woodcutters, the carpenters, the gangs driving posts into the ground and cutting boards for fences . . . The land became valuable and the owners are richer.'

The words came from his mouth in vapour form.

'There was work before, too. Any boy could earn his peanuts sweeping the sand with a palm brush. It was all we needed. The wind drove even our meagre earnings, boy. And anyone without a spoonful of hot soup to eat knew they could have lunch or dinner in the church's chapel.'

273

Father Félix paused to breathe and wipe the corner of his mouth.

'Is speculation better? Can they change our land? Can they do what they want in a world that doesn't belong to them?'

'Father, the people needed to find comfort. The need was great, remember?'

'Are our fellow men happier today? Or do they live as slaves of the forest? I saw these virgin beaches as a boy, the hard-working fishermen crossing the dunes, the cows grazing the weeds in the sand, the peach trees flowering on the estates . . . and now, I look into the distance and all I see are shades of green, and the presence of the boar.'

'Is the boar not a divine creation, too?'

The priest was silent. Rodrigo said nothing, either; Father Félix belonged to another age, he thought, maladjusted to the ungovernable present, and he turned his attention to his work on the bell. The priest preferred to remain silent. After several adjustments, the bell was fixed once again onto the plank that was perpendicular to the tower's foundations. Father Félix gripped the rope that was tied to the clapper and pulled it downwards with all his might. The noise from the bronze resounded in the air in a succession of metallic waves and penetrated the foliage until it reached the ears of the great four-metre-long hog that weighed close to a tonne and had been roaming the forests for the last few weeks. The animal's ears stood to attention. It was not a bell, but a call to his innate aggression.

How had the wild boar developed? Its leathery skin was thick and ancient, and the blanket of hair, hard like nails, had lost any distinctive colour and taken on the hues of the outdoors. His blood was a mixture resulting from three centuries of cross-breeding, of wild boars mounting domestic sows, and farm hogs mounting ownerless females, porcine generations feeding on grasses, fruit and shoots, which then mutilated the decaying flesh of flayed cattle, maggot-infested sheep, dogs and the bones of people cut down in wars and revolutions. The twisted tusks had pierced muscles and tendons, the teeth had chewed on skeletons. The wild boar had tasted human flesh and was fat and hungry. Through the thick, bushy eyelashes, the animal looked out at all that was his. In his irrational mind, he was master of the forest. He had tried to rape a girl who was menstruating. Several parties of woodcutters with dogs had attempted to hunt him down, with no success. For the priest, the boar's presence was a product of the forest, a curse of progress. Where had the great boar come from? From the persistent wind in the vacuum that was there before the trees? From the depths of the virgin fields? From the bottom of the newly created shadow?

The little wooden chapel was in the middle of the pine forest, near the coast. The seminarian Rodrigo would hack the tree branches with a machete at the tip of a bamboo cane, so that the light could enter the little house of the Lord. He lived in seclusion, with the little that he had. He kept warm with a wood burner, a couple of blankets donated by parishioners and the mushrooms that he collected from under the moist carpet of pine needles.

He believed in the forest. By living there under those treetops, consubstantiated with the new inhabitants who had relocated to Maldonado, he sensed that he was part of a new era, of a collective awakening, even if his congregation had scattered and, under the trees, a new caste was developing in which pairs mated randomly – a clan that had children outside of marriage or miscarried in holes dug with desperate hands among roots that wept resin. Woodcutters had told him about it in their stories. And women had confessed it to him every so often, when they had tried to sneak into his room to tempt him with their hot bodies, and they had left a dark cloud of doubts in his head. Each doubt was a thorn, but in this new territory, Rodrigo saw the value of a challenge, a test of his character.

The animal marked the tree trunks with his tusks and urine. The surrounding forest knew it. He sought food, females or the pleasure of scratching his back on a rock and squealing his crude happiness. His hooves left their marks in the sand and his memory retained every hectare. Rodrigo knew his fate was at the mercy of God, that the wild boar's presence was His will. The autumn sun had buried itself in the earth and the evening light had gone some time before that. He had ventured out to gather mushrooms for a stew, because the cold was biting and he needed to put some food between his chest and back. The tallow lantern moved between the black trunks like a firefly casting the faintest of lights on his bearded profile and dark cowl, like an El Greco painting. The saws had stopped sawing and the men's distant voices had faded away in the forest. He was listening to his own breathing, marked in a dense vapour in the air, and to the brush of his machete against the pine needles and the hessian bag full of mushrooms bumping against his shoulder. The blow came from behind. It lifted him off the ground and, before he landed a couple of metres ahead, he knew that the whiplash that ran from his hip to his shoulder blades was the cut from a tusk. He felt fire along that line of skin and then fell face down on the soft earth. There was no time to cross himself or feel abandoned. The lantern rolled off and went out; the machete was some distance away. The boar leaped onto the body, thrashing his head from side to side, and before long the cassock was in shreds. Rodrigo's meagre innards were less than a dinner. The hog left the bag of mushrooms untouched and disappeared.

In a low voice, Father Félix said some words in Latin, before the fresh pinewood coffin containing the seminarian's remains was lost behind the cemetery wall, now surrounded by forest. While they closed the tombstone, he reflected in silence on the naivety of the seminarian, but he also knew that his own time was up.

Early in the new year, they dealt with the wild boar. The entrepreneurs and speculators paid the police and parties of townspeople. After hours of bleeding him, eighty men with more than a hundred dogs surrounded the pig in a gully and riddled him with bullets. Only when the hog's enormous head was hanging over the stove at the country club, when the real eyes had rotted and the glass ones stared blankly into the fire, when the anecdotes about the wild boar had passed from fathers to sons and to grandsons and were distorted by time, only then did they understand that progress had arrived.

That was how the city was made. The rest came later.

Alarm

CLAUDIA ULLOA DONOSO

Translated by Lily Meyer

The best place to wait for her flight was the bathroom. She chose a stall at random, locked herself in, and sat on the water tank, entertaining herself with the sounds of the automatic toilet flushing beneath her, water coming and going, joined by streams of other people's urine and the occasional splashes of their shit. The sounds weren't unpleasant, and they were better by far than the thunder of the airport's teeming hallways and gates.

The sounds of strangers' bodies relaxed her like the sounds of nature, lifting her spirits and allowing her, in some primitive way, to feel safe. The sensation came from familiarity: She knew these sounds. They were hers, and so She knew that anyone making them was, at least for the moment, a helpless, harmless, being.

But someone knocked on her stall door, vehement, scaring her into the open. When She locked herself in the bathroom at home, He always knocked like that. He banged on the door so hard its wood cracked under his knuckles, filling the house with splinters both of them would have to breathe in. She felt them as soon as She unlocked the door, and every time He pushed it open, the air that streamed into the room stung her cheeks like a slap.

Once He was in the bathroom with her, She'd fill her lungs with that dust-laden, splinter-infested air, then go to the sink to finish the ritual. Always, She focused on the soap as it foamed between her fingers, on pretending to wash away the germs her imaginary shit or urine would have left on her skin. After that She could leave the bathroom, knowing that He'd close the door and it would be time to breathe out. Soon, his noises would begin.

She moved through the terminal, full of adrenaline, smelling the acidic sweat that rose from her armpits and her sticky hands. Her heart thudded at every step, like an unborn child kicking its mother from within.

She was thirsty. Her body was closing like a shell. Her guts were sticking together, her organs fading to an airless pink. Her hands started to shake. She went into a cafeteria, wanting only a beer, but it was morning. She'd have to go back to pretending. She pretended to be hungry. She ordered an English breakfast. When it was ready, She'd ask for a beer. Maybe two.

The Cashier rang up her bill and directed her to the dining room. With her receipt, he gave her a contraption that would let her know when her order was ready. At her table She realized that the shaking had got worse, and She took the little device and started turning it over, hoping to settle her nerves. In the middle of the exercise, She wondered what the gadget was called.

It was a disk made of two types of plastic. The base was hard and black, with a thin, translucent covering. She brought it to eye level and squinted inside it, at its pearls of glass strung together on thin metal filaments. The outside of the device looked like one of those black rubber circles they use to play hockey, and that made her think about him, about the time He told her to enrich her vocabulary. That *circle*, He said, was called a *puck*. He taught her how to pronounce it. *Puck, like fuck.* He repeated the words over and over, *puck fuck puck fuck*, moving his head back and forth.

The device lit up, shrilling and vibrating. The sound and light racing from her hands to her brain were too much for her. She started shaking again, so badly she could barely make her way through the maze of tables and diners to pick up her food. When she was a few metres from the counter, the alarm went quiet. She calmed down a little, enough to collect her breakfast, go back to the register, and order two pints of beer.

She picked at the sausages and forced down a few spoonfuls of beans before letting herself start to drink. The beer bubbled down her oesophagus and pooled in her body, and the more She drank, the less her hands shook. Every so often She took another bite, rearranged her silverware, pushed her glasses around on the tray. The device was still there, She noticed. It made her think of him. She moved it onto the table, picked up her knife and dug into the alarm until she'd broken a piece from its transparent shell.

He was English. *London Bridge is falling down* English. English like the beer She just finished, like the breakfast She abandoned in the cafeteria, like deer hunting, like cricket and rugby, like the language He taught her to speak. *Puck, fuck, suck, buck, chuck, ruck, my fair lady.* She knew all those words now. They echoed in her head, turned into a march whose drumbeat guided her towards her gate.

She passed security, keeping her eyes locked on the Departures screen. Yes, there was her flight, glowing in yellow. She stood in front of the screen, rearranging the contents of her bag. She was zipping up her jacket when a security guard pulled her aside. *Random check.*

The Guard pulled out a metal detector, and She closed her eyes. Through her lids it looked like a cricket bat, flat and long. She let him run it over the contours of her body, and when it reached her knees, an alarm sounded. She took out the little device they'd given her at the restaurant and showed it to the Guard. *What's this?*

She balanced it in her palm, a little object full of metal, its outside covered in hair and crumbs, its plastic casing shattered and ready to fall apart. Broken, completely, but the sight of it frightened her all over again. Her hands started shaking. The Guard took her arm, and She let him. *Please follow me.*

They walked through the airport together, the Guard bending towards her so they looked like a couple out for a walk, like they belonged in a park or on a beach. He was being gentle, but it didn't matter. She still burst into tears.

In the detention area, She confessed that She had been drinking on an empty stomach. She'd destroyed the restaurant's little alarm. She'd never meant to upset anybody. After the interrogation and the apologies, a familiar calm arrived: the calm that came when She was shut away, alone, in custody, when She had nowhere to go.

The Guard had offered tea, but it was too hot. She drank it anyway, burning herself. While a blister formed on the roof of her mouth, a loudspeaker she couldn't hear announced her flight number, its destination, its departure.

The Guard opened the door to return her bag. All was in order. She hoped he would lead her out of the room, but he just stood in the doorway. She wanted to move around, but not with him there, and so She sat quietly, waiting. Then He walked in.

He wrapped his arms around her and pulled her to his chest. She had just enough time to turn her head so She could breathe. Her mouth was free, her eyes, her nose, her left ear. She focused on the Guard, who was still in the room, arranging papers and collecting her empty mug while She waited, heart beating hard. Suddenly his mouth grazed the top of her head, and She thought her skull must have gone soft as a baby's. She felt her scalp giving way to his lips, his tongue, his teeth as He kissed and bit her, whispering some restraining phrase into the roots of her hair. *Don't cry.*

The words vibrated through the ridges of her brain, diffused into her chest, echoed up to her trapped ears. *Don't try. Don't cry. Try. Cry. Try.* She couldn't decipher his language enough to know what He was trying to say.

Their bodies were wrapped together like snails in their shells. When the Guard approached the couple, She managed to pull herself away, just enough to stretch her neck and exhale a few words. *Excuse me.*

The Guard paused, and He pressed his chest so close to her body that his sternum brushed against her throat. She swallowed against the pressure and managed to ask: what was the name of the thing She'd destroyed?

Pager, both men said at once.

The couple disentangled their arms. She lowered her eyes and looked at the floor, at the men's boots, four of them, black and polished like mirrors. Yes, She could see her face there, in the leather. She saw her reflection infinite times.

Castaways

DIEGO ZÚÑIGA

Translated by Megan McDowell

The water returns
What doesn't belong to it.

ALICIA GENOVESE, *AGUAS*

We learned to swim in that river.

It was a couple of summers before the Loa flooded and carried off Muñoz's cousin, and also a whole family that we never even got to know: a young couple, the wife pregnant with twins, apparently. They'd come to make a fresh start, but they were swallowed by the water instead. After the catastrophe, we had to accept that we were forbidden to go near the water. We had to find other places where we could kill time or shorten it; anything to avoid the boredom of summer, on those dirt roads, the dust that stuck to our bodies – that's how Calama was, the dust, the heat, and the sun beating down on us as if we'd done something to it.

But first we learned to swim there, in the river, with the trout and those waters that grew more intense in the February heat: the snow melted and flowed down in a torrent and made the water level rise, and we made the most of that surge, that snow, that Bolivian winter we never saw and for us meant only that: a little more water to swim in, a little more water in a river that almost all year long was a swampy piece of land, a crack in the middle of the desert.

We swam in the deepest areas, amid the rock beds that formed little wells where we could sink and disappear. It was in there, one afternoon when we were alone, that we discovered that Martínez was able to hold his breath underwater for a time that at first seemed astonishing to us, and later, supernatural.

It started as a game, who could stay underwater the longest. Then it turned into a fierce competition: take a deep breath, hold our noses, and go under until it became impossible to hold it any longer, underwater, in the dark, our eyes closed. We looked ridiculous in that scene, but we were very serious, since no one wanted the humiliation of being the first to surface.

The first time we did it, the six of us went under – Parra's little brother stayed on the surface to keep time out loud. Castro held out the longest – a minute and twenty-two seconds – followed by Molina – a minute seventeen – and then Rojo Araya – a minute eleven seconds. The rest of us couldn't hold out very long: when you're under there it's as if time stopped, the sound isolates you and you hear only the water flowing in the distance, far away, as if you're suspended in a vacuum. Only the sound of the bubbles as they rise to the surface distracts you. Stopped time was the pressure of the water in your ears, the fear of opening your eyes, and the real feeling, for the first time, of death converted into the air that filled our lungs. That was death: the awareness that it could all end, that as soon as the air ran out you'd be lost in a place you would probably never come back from.

Opening your eyes underwater was to understand that you were going to die, but none of us were capable of putting that into words. Parra was so annoyed at losing he suggested we try it again – 'I didn't take a big enough breath,' he said – and that's when we found out about Martínez.

We took deep gulps of air, held our noses, and went under at the same time, obsessed with humiliating Castro above all, never imagining that when we returned to the surface, when we all emerged almost suffocated by lack of air and the fear of being submerged forever, Martínez was going to hold out over three minutes. That's what Parra's little brother counted, 180 long seconds that seemed to us an impossible eternity for a body that by then we were seeing float, face down, with its arms completely outstretched, like a corpse the river spat out at our feet.

I think it was Rojas who couldn't stand it any more, and when the count was at 200 seconds he grabbed Martínez by the shoulders and quickly lifted him up. Martínez opened his eyes and took in a long, really long breath. He looked at us, and with fresh air now filling his lungs, he started to laugh, hard. They were peals of laughter that none of us understood, until Torres splashed water in his face and told him not to be an arsehole, that he'd scared us, we'd thought he was dead.

Martínez went on laughing for a while and then went to swim further out in the river, alone, as dusk fell. We played a couple more times, without him; he watched us from afar.

The next day, when we got to the river around three in the afternoon, Martínez had already been swimming for a couple of hours. After a while he asked us if we wanted to play the game again, the one where we held our breath underwater. None of us were very convinced, except for Castro, who wanted to compete with him. And Martínez did it again. He even held out longer: 250 seconds, and without too much effort. He lifted his head, smiled and went on swimming and going under, while the rest of us looked at each other incredulously; we couldn't understand what he had in his lungs to let him stay so long underwater. We felt like it was a supernatural power, and we wanted to use it. There was no longer any point to competing among ourselves. It was boring. We needed everyone to know about Martínez's talent.

It was probably Molina who spread the word. A couple of days later it was a Sunday, and we weren't alone at the river – several families had come from town to swim and picnic. Molina's older brother showed up with some friends, all ready to compete with Martínez.

They were a lot older than us, sixteen, seventeen years old, and they had already been to the ocean. They had swum at the beaches of Antofagasta and Iquique. It was an unequal competition, but we believed in Martínez. We'd seen him stay under for over four minutes – no one could beat him.

The first match was a tie: they stayed under for 211 seconds, and Rodríguez, who was the son of fisherman divers, came up with reddened eyes and coughed for a good while, while Martínez breathed deeply and tried to stay calm. We encouraged him with slaps on the back.

The second try was a trouncing: Rodríguez stayed underwater over four minutes, while Martínez only held out a little over two. He surfaced, in fact, coughing hard, choking, spitting, frantic. We were worried: Martínez was struggling to recover and Rodríguez was still floating face down, arms outstretched, motionless, as though on endless pause.

There was still the third attempt. If Martínez won, there would be a tie-breaker. If not, all was lost.

They were about to start when we heard the screams.

It was a neighbour of Martínez's and she was screaming hysterically, but we couldn't understand what she was saying. A man was trying to calm her down, but she kept screaming, frantic. It was a stammering jumble of words that one woman, eventually, managed to decipher: the neighbour's son was gone. A boy younger than us, and she couldn't find him on the shore, he was lost, where was he, screamed the woman as she pointed to the river.

We started searching everywhere for him. The older kids jumped into the water and the rest of us started combing the shrubs and rocks, but we couldn't find him, not anywhere, and then we saw Martínez go underwater and stay there for a long time, swimming along the river bottom, and finally he surfaced with the body. The boy was unconscious, pale, almost violet; I remember his body dark and rigid, and Martínez carrying him and laying him gently on the shore, as though apologizing for not having found him sooner.

Someone gave the boy mouth-to-mouth and hit his chest over and over, trying to reanimate the small body that we were losing. Everyone gathered around him, encouraging the adults who were trying to bring him back. The mother wasn't screaming any more: she'd started to vomit at the edge of the river, while someone else had gone to the town to look for a doctor. But the life was there and dependent on those first hands, right in front of us, that boy and death, the blows to the chest, the mouth-to-mouth, the blows to the chest and his lungs full of water, that water he spat out when we already thought all was lost, the water from the lungs and the lungs full of fresh air, alive and noisy, and a heart that seemed about to explode – we heard it with our own ears, amid the shouts and the celebration for having brought him back to life. The heart. The blows.

I think we all felt that that boy was us, that it could have been any of us lying there on the river bottom without anyone noticing we were gone. We felt it, I'm sure, even though later it would become just another summer anecdote, one of those stories that sometimes, bored, we would tell in lurid detail, a story that would grow misshapen with time, though it would always maintain intact that splendid moment when Martínez emerged from the water holding the lifeless body. Because the doctors told us later how in that precise moment, the boy in Martínez's arms was dead, clinically dead, though we didn't know it, we didn't want to believe he was dead. And that's how it was, those lungs full of water that burst out to make room for new air amid our shouts – we would remember that forever, our cries of happiness and the mother sobbing with her son in her arms. She kissed him all over his face, on the cheeks, on his eyes, mouth, she kissed him frantically, as if he were all she had in the world.

Martínez would be tasked, over the years, with snatching many bodies from the river and others from the ocean.

But he was also going to lose many times.

Life, then, was to be about that: living with those failures for the rest of his days.

About the Authors

Carlos Manuel Álvarez is a Cuban writer and journalist. He has won numerous awards for his short stories, including the Nuevas Plumas Ibero-American Fiction Prize in 2015. In 2016 he founded *El Estornudo*, an independent Cuban magazine of literary journalism. That same year, the Ochenteros programme, run by the Guadalajara International Book Fair, recognized him as one of twenty Latin American authors born in the 1980s to look out for. He has published regularly with media and publications such as the *New York Times*, the BBC, *Gatopardo*, *El Malpensante* and *Internazionale*. Sexto Piso is soon due to publish *La tribu*, a collection of essays on post-revolutionary Cuba. He lives in Cuba.

Frank Báez is a Dominican poet and writer. Born in Santo Domingo, his story collection *Págales tú a los psicoanalistas* won the Santo Domingo Book Fair First Prize for short stories in 2006, his poetry collection *Postales* won the Salomé Ureña National Poetry Prize in 2009, and another of his poetry collections, *Last Night I Dreamt I Was a DJ*, was published in a bilingual English-Spanish edition by the US publishing house Jai-Alai Books. In 2016, the Egyptian publisher Safsafa published an anthology of his poetry in Arabic. He has also published three non-fiction books in the volume *La trilogía de los festivales*, and in July 2017 he published his latest non-fiction work, *Lo que trajo el mar*. *Este es el futuro que estabas esperando* (Seix Barral, 2017) is his latest poetry collection.

Natalia Borges Polesso is a Brazilian writer and educator. Born in southern Brazil, she studied English and Brazilian literature, and holds a master's degree and a doctorate. She is the author of *Recortes para álbum de fotografia sem gente* (2013), which won the 2013 short story category of the Açorianos Literature Prize, the most important award in the state of Rio Grande do Sul. Her second book, *Coração à corda* (2015), is a selection of poems and poetic short stories. In 2016, her latest short story collection, *Amora* (2016), won the Açorianos Literature Prize and the Jabuti Prize, Brazil's most prestigious literary award. She lives in Rio Grande do Sul, Brazil.

Giuseppe Caputo was born in Barranquilla, Colombia, in 1982. He studied Creative Writing at the University of New York with teachers such as Diamela Eltit, Sergio Chejfec and Antonio Muñoz Molina; and at the University of Iowa with teachers including Horacio Castellanos Moya, Marilynne Robinson and Luis Muñoz. In Iowa he also specialized in Queer and Gender Studies. His first novel, *Un mundo huérfano*, was published in Colombia in 2016. He lives in Bogotá.

Juan Cárdenas is a Colombian writer, art curator and critic. He has written several novels: *Zumbido* (451 Editores, 2010; Periférica, 2017), *Los estratos* (Periférica, 2013), *Ornamento* (Periférica, 2015), *Tú y yo, una novelita rusa* (Cajón de sastre, 2016) and *El diablo de las provincias* (Periférica). He has also published the short-story collection *Carreras delictivas* (451 Editores, 2008). His novel *Los estratos* won the sixth Otras Voces, Otros Ámbitos Prize in 2014. He is currently one of the coordinators of the master's in Creative Writing at the Instituto Caro y Cuervo in Bogotá, where he works as an educator and researcher.

Mauro Javier Cárdenas was born and brought up in Guayaquil, Ecuador, and studied Economics at the University of Stanford. He is the author of *The Revolutionaries Try Again* (Coffee House Press, 2016; Literatura Random House, 2018). His work has appeared in *Conjunctions*, the *Antioch Review*, *Guernica*, *Witness*, *ZYZZYVA* and *BOMB*. He won the 2016 Joseph Henry Jackson Prize. He lives in San Francisco.

María José Caro was born in Lima, Peru, in 1985. She studied Social Communications at the University of Lima and has a master's degree in Communication Studies from the Universidad Complutense de Madrid. She is the author of *¿Qué tengo de malo?* (2017), which won *El Comercio* newspaper's Premio Luces, *Perro de ojos negros* (2016) and *La primaria* (2012). Her work has been published in Colombia, Chile, Mexico and Peru. She contributes to literary magazines such as *Buensalvaje*, *Vicio Absurdo* and *El Dominical* and her work features in anthologies such as *Palo y Astilla: Padre e hijos en el cuento peruano* (2010) and *Como si no bastase ya ser: 15 narradoras peruanas* (2017). She also took part in the first edition of the *Lima imaginada* literary project in 2015.

Martín Felipe Castagnet is an Argentine writer, editor and translator with a doctorate in the humanities. His novel *Los cuerpos del verano* (Factotum, 2012) was unanimous winner of the 2012 Latin American Young Writers' Award organized by the Maison des Écrivains Étrangers et des Traducteurs de Saint-Nazaire, and by La Marelle, Villa des projets d'auteurs, Marseilles, France. It has been translated into French (MEET, 2012) and into English as *Bodies of Summer* (Dalkey Archive Press, 2017). His second novel, *Los mantras modernos*, was published in 2017 by Sigilo. He has also published short stories in various publications and completed a number of writing residencies in France, Argentina and Mexico. He lives in Buenos Aires.

Liliana Colanzi is a Bolivian writer who has published the short-story collections *Vacaciones permanentes* (El Cuervo, 2010) and *Nuestro mundo muerto* (Almadía, 2016). *Nuestro mundo muerto* has been translated into English and Italian and was shortlisted for the Gabriel García Márquez short story award (2017). She is the publisher and editor at *Dum Dum editora*. She won the Mexican Aura Estrada Literary Prize in 2015 and has contributed to publications such as *Granta*, *Letras Libres*, *Gatopardo*, the *White Review* and *El Deber*. She lives in Ithaca, New York State, and lectures in Latin American Literature at Cornell University.

Juan Esteban Constaín was born in 1979 in Popayán, Colombia. In 2004 he published his first book, *Los mártires*, a collection of fictional works about writers. In 2007 he published *El naufragio del Imperio*, and in 2010 *¡Calcio!*, which won him the Espartaco Historical Novel Prize at Gijon's Semana Negra. In May 2014, *El hombre que no fue Jueves* was released, and subsequently won the Biblioteca Prize for Colombian Fiction. He writes for *El Tiempo* newspaper and has three daughters. He lives in Bogotá.

Lolita Copacabana is an Argentine writer and translator and the co-manager of the Momofuku publishing company (www.momofuku.com.ar). In 2006 she published *Buena leche – Diarios de una joven (no tan) formal* (Editorial Sudamericana), the first volume of her memoirs, which includes stories written between the ages of nineteen and twenty-three. In 2013 she edited and translated, together with Hernán Vanoli, *Alt lit – literatura norteamericana actual* (Interzona), a selection of works by young US writers. She is also the author of the novel *Aleksandr Solzhenitsyn* (Momofuku, 2015), and in 2015 she translated a book of short stories by the young US writer Paula Bomer: *Bebé y otros cuentos* (Momofuku). In 2017, she moved to Iowa to begin a master's degree in Creative Writing.

Gonzalo Eltesch is a Chilean writer and editor who holds degrees in Literature and Publishing from the Diego Portales University. Since 2008 he has been working as an editor at Penguin Random House Chile, where he currently holds the position of literary manager. His work has been recognized on various occasions, and he was shortlisted for the 2016 Municipal Literature Prize for *Colección particular* (Libros del Laurel), his first novel, published in September 2015. He lives in Santiago, Chile.

Diego Erlan is an Argentine writer. For fourteen years he wrote about art, literature and film for *Clarín*, where he also held the position of editor in the Literature and Books section of *Ñ* magazine. He has also worked as a university lecturer, television screenwriter and cultural critic for media in Argentina and further afield. In 2013 he was shortlisted for the Gabriel García Márquez Journalism Award for his report 'La larga risa de todos estos años'. His first novel *El amor nos destrozará* was published in 2012, followed in 2016 by his second novel, *La disolución* (Tusquets). That year he received a National Arts Fund fellowship to write the biography of the Argentine writer Rodolfo Enrique Fogwill, a project that he has been working on for the last five years. He lives in Buenos Aires, where he works as an editor at the independent publishing house Ampersand.

Daniel Ferreira (San Vicente de Chucurí, Colombia, 1981) is the author of the novels *Viaje al interior de una gota de sangre* (2012, 2017), *Rebelión de los oficios inútiles* (2015) and *La balada de los bandoleros baladíes* (2011). His work has been awarded the Sergio Galindo Latin American Prize for First Novels (2010), the Alba Narrative Prize (2011), and the Clarín Prize for Novels (2014). He has published features and essays in the magazines *El Malpensante*, *Letras Libres* and *Hermano Cerdo*. He is a blogger (Prize for the Best Blog Disseminating Culture in Spanish, Cervantes Institute).

Carlos Fonseca was born in San José, Costa Rica, in 1987 to a Costa Rican father and Puerto Rican mother. When he was seven, his family moved to Puerto Rico, where he went to school. He later studied Comparative Literature at Stanford University and obtained a doctorate in Latin American Literature from Princeton University. In 2015 Anagrama published his first novel, *Coronel Lágrimas*, later published in English as *Colonel Lágrimas* by Restless Books, translated by Megan McDowell. In 2017 Anagrama published his second novel, *Museo animal*, which is forthcoming in English by Farrar, Straus and Giroux. He lives in London and teaches Latin American Literature at Cambridge University.

Damián González Bertolino is a Uruguayan writer. His short story collection *El increíble Springer* won the sixteenth Narradores de la Banda Oriental Fiction Prize. He has also published the novels *El fondo* (Estuario, Montevideo, 2013) and *Los trabajos del amor* (Estuario, Montevideo, 2015). His latest novel, *Herodes*, was published in 2017. In 2016 he was included in the Guadalajara International Book Fair's Ochenteros list of twenty new voices in Latin American fiction to look out for. He lives in Punta del Este, Uruguay, where he teaches literature at secondary-school level.

Sergio Gutiérrez Negrón is a Puerto Rican novelist, columnist and translator. He is the author of the novels *Palacio* (Libros AC, San Juan) and *Dicen que los dormidos* (ICP, San Juan), which will also be published in Turkish in 2018. *Dicen que los dormidos* won the Puerto Rico Cultural Institute's National Novel Prize and was published by the institute in 2014. In 2015, he was awarded the New Voices Prize for promising Puerto Rican authors at the Festival de la Palabra. In 2016, the New York magazine *Brooklyn Rail* published a translation of one of his stories as part of a selection of contemporary Puerto Rican literature. His stories and essays have appeared in various magazines and anthologies in Puerto Rico and further afield. He lives in Ohio, USA.

Gabriela Jauregui was born in Mexico City. She is the author of the poetry collection *Controlled Decay* (Black Goat Press/Akashic Books, 2008), the short-story collection *La memoria de las cosas* (Sexto Piso, 2015), *Leash Seeks Lost Bitch* (Song Cave, 2016) in collaboration with visual artists Allison Katz and Camilla Wills, and *ManyFiestas* (Gato Negro, 2017), as well as co-author of *Taller de Taquimecanografía* (Tumbona, 2011). She has a doctorate in Comparative Literature from the University of Southern California and master's degrees from the University of California, Riverside and the University of California, Irvine. Her texts and translations have been published in anthologies, museum catalogues and magazines in Mexico, Canada, the United States, Australia and the United Kingdom. She is a co-founder of and editor at sur+ ediciones publishing collective and lives in Mexico City.

Laia Jufresa grew up in the cloud forest of Veracruz and spent her teenage years in Paris. Aged eighteen she moved to Mexico City, where she realized she did not know how to cross the street. Since then she has been writing fiction. She is the author of the short story collection *El esquinista* (Fondo Editorial Tierra Adentro, 2014) and the novel *Umami* (Literatura Random House, 2015; Oneworld, 2016). *Umami* has been translated into numerous languages, including English. It was recognized as the best novel in Spanish at the First Novel Festival in Chambery, France; it won the PEN Translates Award and was shortlisted for the 2017 Best Translated Book Award. She was selected as one of twenty outstanding Mexican authors under forty (México20 project). She lives in Edinburgh.

Mauro Libertella is an Argentine writer who has published three novels. In *Mi libro enterrado* (Mansalva, 2013), he wrote about the death of his father and their relationship. It has been published in Argentina, Mexico, Chile, Costa Rica and Peru and has been translated into Italian. *El invierno con mi generación* (Random House, 2015) is a novel about a group of friends – aged between sixteen and twenty-three – in Buenos Aires at the turn of the twenty-first century. *El estilo de los otros* (University Diego Portales, 2015) is a book of conversations featuring eighteen contemporary Latin American fiction writers. He lives in Buenos Aires.

Brenda Lozano is a writer and editor. She studied Literature in Mexico and the United States. She was been a writer in residence in the United States, Europe and South America and has been included in numerous anthologies. She edits the Chicago literary magazine *Make* and is part of the New York publishing collective Ugly Duckling Presse. Her first novel *Todo nada* (Tusquets, 2009) will be adapted for cinema. *Cuaderno ideal* is her second novel (Alfaguara, 2014). In 2015 she was selected by Conaculta, Hay Festival and the British Council as one of the most important writers under forty in her country. She currently lives in Mexico City. *Como piensan las piedras* (Alfaguara, 2017) is her first short story collection.

Valeria Luiselli was born in Mexico City in 1983. Her first novel *Los Ingrávidos* was published in English as *Faces in the Crowd* by Coffee House Press in the United States and Granta in the United Kingdom. Her novel *The Story of My Teeth* was selected by the *New York Times* as one of the 100 best books of 2015, won the *Los Angeles Times* Book Prize for Fiction in 2016, and was selected for the 2017 IMPAC Prize. Her work has been published in magazines and newspapers such as the *New York Times* and the *New Yorker,* and has been translated into fifteen languages. Her latest novel, *Lost Children Archives*, written in English, will be published in 2019 by Knopf in the United States. She lives in New York.

Alan Mills is a Guatemalan writer whose poetry has been included in numerous prestigious Spanish-language anthologies over the last ten years and has been translated into German, French, English, Portuguese, Italian and Czech. His more recent work has been creative non-fiction and fiction. His micro-novel *Síncopes* was published in Mexico and Peru, and later in France. His most recent book is a literary non-fiction work in English about the hacker culture and ancestral strategies of resistance. It is called *Hacking Coyote*, and was published first as an ebook (mikrotext, 2016) and later as a printed book in Germany (mikrotext, 2017). He has lived in Guatemala City, Paris, Madrid, São Paulo and Buenos Aires. He currently lives in Berlin, working on a doctoral thesis about *indigenista* science fiction.

Emiliano Monge is a Mexican writer and political scientist. He has published the novels *Morirse de memoria* (Sexto Piso, 2010), *El cielo árido* (Penguin Random House, 2012; winner of the twenty-eighth Jaén Novel Prize and the fifth Otras Voces, Otros Ámbitos Prize) and *Las tierras arrasadas* (Penguin Random House, 2015; winner of the ninth Elena Poniatowska Ibero-American Novel Prize); the short story collections *Arrastrar esa sombra* (Sexto Piso, 2008; shortlisted for the Antonin Artaud prize) and *La superficie más honda* (Penguin Random House, 2017), as well as the children's book *Los insectos invisibles* (Sexto Piso, 2013). His stories have also appeared in anthologies including *Lo desorden* (Alfaguara, 2013), *México20* (Pushkin Press, 2015) and *Sólo cuento VIII* (UNAM, 2016). He lives in Mexico City.

Mónica Ojeda is an Ecuadorian writer. She studied Social Communication and Literature before completing a master's degree in Literary Creation and another in Cultural Theory and Criticism. Her work has featured in the anthology *Emergencias. Doce cuentos iberoamericanos* (Candaya, 2013) and she was awarded the 2014 Alba Fiction Prize for the novel *La desfiguración Silva* (Arte y Literatura,

2015) and the third Desembarco National Poetry Prize in 2015 for *El ciclo de las piedras* (Rastro de la Iguana Ediciones, 2015). She has recently published her second novel, *Nefando* (Candaya, 2016). She teaches literature at the Universidad Católica de Santiago de Guayaquil, Ecuador, and is currently working on a doctorate focusing on Latin American pornoerotic literature.

Eduardo Plaza (born in La Serena, Chile, in 1982) is a Chilean writer and journalist. His short story collection *Hienas* was published by Librosdementira in 2016. He was shortlisted for the Paula short-story competition (2014) and the Gabriela Mistral Literary Games, organized by the Municipality of Santiago (2015).

Eduardo Rabasa is a Mexican writer. He studied Political Science at Mexico's National University (UNAM), writing his thesis on the concept of power in the works of George Orwell. He writes a weekly column for the cultural section of *Milenio* newspaper and has translated books by authors such as David Hume, George Orwell and Somerset Maugham. He has published short stories, essays, articles, literary criticism and interviews in publications such as *Nexos*, *GQ* and *Vice*. In 2015 he was selected as part of the México20 anthology project, organized by Hay Festival and Conaculta, and in 2016 he was selected for a special edition of *Esquire* magazine, which published a list of thirty young Mexicans to follow in the field of arts and culture. He lives in Mexico City.

Felipe Restrepo Pombo is a Colombian journalist, writer and editor. He began his career as a reporter for the magazine *Cambio* under Gabriel García Márquez. In 2016 he published his first novel, *Formas de evasión* (Seix Barral, 2016), which is set to be translated into English and French. He was editorial coordinator and wrote the prologue for *La ira de México* (*The Sorrows of Mexico*, MacLehose Press/Debate,

2016). He has been a guest at Hay festivals in Cartagena, Xalapa, Querétaro and Mexico City. He is currently editor of the Latin American magazine *Gatopardo* in Mexico City. Since taking up the position in 2014, the magazine has won the National Journalism Prize and has been recognized as the country's best publication three years in a row.

Juan Manuel Robles is a Peruvian writer who holds a master's degree in Creative Writing in Spanish from New York University. He has published the non-fiction work *Lima freak. Vidas insólitas en una ciudad perturbada* (Planeta, 2007) and the novel *Nuevos juguetes de la guerra fría* (Seix Barral, 2015), which was ranked by the newspaper *Perú 21* as the best novel of 2015 and was chosen by Spain's *El País* as one of 'twenty-three books for understanding the Americas'. He has published short stories in various anthologies and magazines. In 2008, he was shortlisted for the Cemex-FNPI Prize for the essay 'Cromwell, el cajero generoso'. In 2017 he published a short story collection and a piece in *Un mundo lleno de futuro*, a literary non-fiction book edited by Leila Guerriero. He lives in Lima.

Cristian Romero is a Colombian writer who studied Audiovisual and Multimedia Communication at the University of Antioquia. In 2015 he received an 'Artistic and Cultural Creation for Life' fellowship from the city of Medellin, in the short story/new-writer category. As part of the fellowship he wrote the book *Ahora solo queda la ciudad* (Hilo de plata Editores), which was published in 2016. He has also published stories in the University of Antioquia magazine.

Juan Pablo Roncone was born in Arica, Chile in 1982, and moved to Santiago at the age of nineteen. In 2007 an unpublished novel of his was awarded the Roberto Bolaño Award for Literary Creation. In 2011 he published the short story collection *Hermano ciervo* (Editorial

Los Libros Que Leo, 2011; Fiordo Editorial, 2012; Marbot Ediciones, 2013; Sudaquia Editores, 2013; and Laurel Editores, 2014 and 2016), which won the Santiago Municipal Literature Prize. Some of the stories from this book have been translated into English and have appeared in magazines such as New York's *Tweed's*, Berlin's *Sand*, and Tel Aviv's *The Short Story Project*, as well as in the *Traviesa* anthology *Childless Parents*. He lives in Santiago.

Daniel Saldaña París is a Mexican writer. He has published the poetry books *Esa pura materia* (UACM, 2008) and *La máquina auto-biográfica* (Bonobos, 2012), and the novel *En medio de extrañas víctimas* (Sexto Piso, 2013; translated into English as *Among Strange Victims*, Coffee House Press, 2016; upcoming publication in French). He has received fellowships from FONCA's Young Artists programme, the Foundation for Mexican Literature and the FONCA/Conseil des Arts et des Lettres du Québec Artistic Residencies project (Montreal, Canada). He has been writer in residence at the OMI International Center for the Arts (New York, 2014) and at the MacDowell Colony (New Hampshire, 2016). In 2017 he was the writer in residence at the Banff Centre (Canada). He currently contributes a column to the Mexican edition of *Esquire* magazine and lives in Montreal, Canada.

Samanta Schweblin was born in 1978 in Buenos Aires, Argentina, where she studied film, specializing in screenplay writing. Her short story collections *El núcleo del disturbio*, *Pájaros en la boca* and *Siete casas vacías* won the Casa de las Américas, Juan Rulfo and Ribera del Duero Short Fiction prizes. Her first novel, *Distancia de rescate* (published in English in 2017 as *Fever Dream* by Oneworld in the UK and Riverhead in the US) won the Tigre Juan and Estado Crítico prizes and was shortlisted for the 2017 Man Booker International Prize. Her story collection *A Mouthful of Birds* is forthcoming in

2019 from Oneworld/Riverhead. Her work has been translated into more than twenty languages and she has been a fellow of several institutions. She has been living in Berlin for the last four years, where she writes and gives literary workshops.

Jesús Miguel Soto is a Venezuelan writer who studied Social Communication and Arts at the Universidad Central de Venezuela. He has worked as a university lecturer, proofreader and editor. As a fiction writer he has written the short story collection *Perdidos en Frog* and the novels *La máscara de cuero* and *Boeuf (Relato a la manera de Cambridge)*. His awards include the sixty-fourth El Nacional Annual Short Story Competition (Venezuela); first prize in the seventh SACVEN National Story Competition and the twenty-third Juana Santacruz Literary Event (Mexico). Some of his stories have been published in anthologies such as *Joven narrativa venezolana II*, *De qué va el cuento (Antología del relato venezolano 2000–2012)* and *Crude Words: Contemporary writing from Venezuela*. Since 2014 he has been living in Mexico.

Luciana Sousa was born in Buenos Aires, Argentina, in 1986. She studied Literature and Journalism and has taken a number of fiction courses with writers such as Alberto Laiseca, Vicente Battista and Juan Diego Incardona. She has worked with media such as Radio Gráfica, Agencia Paco Urondo and Hecho en Buenos Aires, supporting self-managed popular-communication projects. She currently works as a press officer. *Luro*, published in December 2016 by Editorial Funesiana, is her first novel.

Mariana Torres (Brazil, 1981) is the author of the book *El cuerpo secreto* (Páginas de Espuma, 2015) and the short film *Rascacielos* (2009). She has taught creative writing at Escuela de Escritores since its founding in Madrid, in 2003. She is also part of EACWP (European

Association of Creative Writing Programmes). Mariana's work has been anthologized in *Segunda parábola de los talentos* (Gens Ediciones, 2011) and *Sólo Cuento IX* (UNAM, 2017). She was recently selected as part of CELA (Connecting Emerging Literary Artists).

Valentín Trujillo was born in Maldonado, Uruguay, in 1979. He studied Film and Journalism and is a qualified teacher of Language and Literature. In 2016 he received the Medal of Honour awarded by Uruguay's Cámara del Libro for his contributions to journalistic literary criticism. In 2007 he published the short story collection *Jaula de costillas*, which won the National Fiction Prize, and in 2013 he published *Nacional 88* together with his wife, the journalist Elena Risso. In 2016 he won the Onetti Prize in the Fiction category for his novel *¡Cómanse la ropa!* (2017). Also in 2017, Ediciones B published his biography of the Uruguayan intellectual Carlos Real de Azúa. He has two children and lives in Montevideo.

Claudia Ulloa Donoso was born in Lima in 1979. She is the author of the short story collections *El pez que aprendió a caminar*, *Séptima Madrugada* and *Pajarito*, and has won the Peruvian short story competitions *Terminemos el cuento* (1996) and *El cuento de las 1,000 palabras* (1998). In 2016 she was selected as writer in residence at Villa Sarkia, a residence for translators and writers in Finland. Her stories have appeared in various Peruvian, Colombian, Mexican and Spanish magazines and in anthologies such as *Antología de la Novísima Narrativa Breve Hispanoamericana* (Unión Latina, 2006), *Les bonnes nouvelles de l'Amérique latine* and *Anthologie de la nouvelle latinoaméricaine contemporaine* (Gallimard, 2010). She currently teaches languages in northern Norway.

Diego Zúñiga is a Chilean writer who studied Journalism at the Pontificia Universidad Católica. He has published the novels

Camanchaca (published in English by Coffee House Press, 2017) and *Racimo*, as well as a book about football, *Soy de Católica* (Lolita Editores, 2014), and the short story collection *Niños héroes* (Literatura Random House, 2016). He has won various awards for both his journalism and his fiction, including the Roberto Bolaño Prize for Young Writers; a National Council for Culture and the Arts Fellowship for Literary Writing; the Gabriela Mistral Literary Games Prize for *Camanchaca*; and a 2013 National Council for Culture and the Arts Prize for Best Literary Work, for *Racimo*. In 2016 he was the writer in residence at the Arts Faculty of the Pontificia Universidad Católica. He lives in Santiago.

About the Translators

Rahul Bery is a translator from Spanish and Portuguese to English, schoolteacher and parent. He is based in Cardiff. His translations of writers such as Álvaro Enrigue, Daniel Galera, Guadalupe Nettel and Enrique Vila-Matas have appeared in *Granta* online, the *White Review*, *Art Agenda*, *Documenta 14* and *Freeman's*, among others. His sample translation of *La Inmortal* by Ricard Ruiz Garzón was included on the 2018 shortlist of children's books recommended for translation as part of the BookTrust's In Other Words initiative.

Simon Bruni is a literary translator from Spanish, a language he acquired through 'total immersion', living in Alicante, Valencia and Santander. He studied Spanish and Linguistics at Queen Mary University of London and Literary Translation at the University of Exeter. He has received three John Dryden awards: in 2017 and 2015 for Paul Pen's short stories 'Cinnamon' and 'The Porcelain Boy', and in 2011 for Francisco Pérez Gandul's novel *Cell 211*. His translation of Paul Pen's novel *The Light of the Fireflies* has sold over 100,000 copies worldwide. Simon serves on the executive committee of the Society of Authors' Translators Association.

Peter Bush's translation of *Winds of the Night* by Joan Sales has just been published by MacLehose Press, and his translation of Prudenci Bertrana's *Josafat*, by Francis Boutle. Deep Vellum published his translation of Carmen Boullosa's *Before* and MacLehose Press, *Book*

Shops by Jorge Carrión in 2016. Archipelago will bring out his translation of Josep Pla's *Salt Water* in 2019. He recently taught at the NEH 'Gained in Translation' Summer School at Kent State University and is the Catalan mentor on the Writers' Centre Norwich mentorship programme. In 2018 Bitter Lemon will publish his translation of *The First Prehistoric Serial Killers and Other Stories* by Teresa Solana.

Nick Caistor is a British translator from Spanish and Portuguese. He has translated more than fifty works of fiction from Latin America and Spain, and has been awarded the Valle Inclán Prize for Translation from Spanish three times.

Emily Davis is a translator and software developer. When she's not busy translating fiction or writing code – which is just another form of translation – she can often be found traipsing around the foothills in her adopted hometown of Boise, Idaho. Her translations of Spanish and Latin American fiction have appeared in *Words Without Borders* and *A Thousand Forests in One Acorn: An Anthology of Spanish-Language Fiction*.

Lisa Dillman translates from Spanish and Catalan and teaches at Emory University in Atlanta. She has translated over twenty-five novels by Spanish and Latin American writers, including *Signs Preceding the End of the World* by Yuri Herrera, which won the 2016 Best Translated Book Award, and *The Transmigration of Bodies* by the same writer, nominated for the International Dublin Literary Award 2018. *The Right Intention*, her fifth translation of an Andrés Barba book, is forthcoming from Transit Books. She lives in Decatur, Georgia, USA.

Sam Gordon is a translator from French and Spanish. He has translated novels by award-winning authors Karim Miské, Pierre

Lemaitre and Sophie Hénaff, and in 2015 he co-translated Timothée de Fombelle's *The Book of Pearl* with Sarah Ardizzone. *Arab Jazz* by Karim Miské was awarded an English PEN Promotes award and was shortlisted for the CWA International Dagger. His translations have appeared in the *White Review, Palabras Errantes, Asymptote* and *Index on Censorship Magazine*. He also works as a teacher.

Lucy Greaves is a literary translator and bike mechanic who lives in Bristol, UK. She enjoys the poetry of bicycles and the mechanics of language equally.

Daniel Hahn is a writer, editor and translator with fifty-something books to his name. His translations (from Portuguese, Spanish and French) include fiction and non-fiction for children and adults, from Europe, Africa and the Americas. His work has won him the Independent Foreign Fiction Prize, the Blue Peter Book Award and the International Dublin Literary Award, among others, and has been shortlisted for the Man Booker International Prize and the *LA Times* Book Prize. He is a former chair of the Society of Authors and the Translators Association, and on the board of English PEN.

Delaina Haslam is a translator, editor and writer. She translates from French and Spanish, specializing in sociological and literary texts. She has written for and edited publications including *InMadrid* magazine and *le cool London,* and had translation blog posts published by *Glasgow Review of Books,* the Poetry Translation Centre and Yorkshire Translators and Interpreters. She's interested in collaborative translation and has been the invited translator for Poetry Translation Centre workshops, had a submission accepted for Newcastle University's Poettrio Experiment and performed collaborative translation at Sheffield's Wordlife open-mic night.

Sophie Hughes has translated novels by several contemporary Latin American and Spanish authors, including Best Translated Book Award 2017-finalist Laia Jufresa (*Umami*), PEN America Translation Prize-longlisted Rodrigo Hasbún (*Affections*), and critically acclaimed Iván Repila (*The Boy Who Stole Attila's Horse*). Her translations, reviews and essays have been published in the *Guardian*, the *White Review*, the *Times Literary Supplement* and elsewhere. In 2017 she was a recipient of a PEN/Heim Translation Fund Grant and was named as one of the 'Arts Foundation 25', twenty-five artists selected to mark each year the foundation has been supporting creative practice.

Ellen Jones has a PhD from Queen Mary University of London. Her translations from Spanish into English have appeared or are forthcoming in the *Guardian*, *Hotel*, *Palabras errantes*, and *Columbia Journal*, and in Enrique Winter's bilingual chapbook *Suns* (Cardboard House Press, 2017). In 2017 she was the recipient of an ALTA Travel Fellowship and a Writers Centre Norwich Emerging Translator Mentorship. She has been Criticism Editor at Asymptote since 2014.

Isabelle Kaufeler has been an avid reader and enthusiastic linguist from an early age. She studied Modern and Medieval Languages at Cambridge University and went on to complete a master's degree in Literary Translation at the University of East Anglia. Isabelle translates from Spanish and Italian and has a number of co- and solo translations to her name, across a range of genres. She also enjoys sharing her love of books, languages and translation with others and has taken part in the Translators in Schools programme.

Sophie Lewis has been translating from French since 2005 and from Portuguese since 2012. She has translated works by Stendhal, Verne, Marcel Aymé, Violette Leduc, Emmanuelle Pagano, Noémi Lefebvre, Sheyla Smanioto and João Gilberto Noll, among others.

Her translation of Emilie de Turckheim's novel *Héloïse is Bald* was commended by the 2016 Scott Moncrieff Prize judges, and her translation of Noémi Lefebvre's novel *Blue Self-Portrait* was shortlisted for the 2018 Republic of Consciousness Prize. In 2016 she launched Shadow Heroes, which designs and delivers workshops on translation for students at GCSE and above: www.shadowheroes.org.

Christina MacSweeney was awarded the 2016 Valle Inclán Prize for her translation of Valeria Luiselli's *The Story of My Teeth*, and her translation of Daniel Saldaña París's novel *Among Strange Victims* was a finalist in the 2017 Best Translated Book Award. She has also published translations, articles and interviews on a wide variety of platforms, including three anthologies: *México20, Lunatics, Lovers & Poets: Twelve Stories after Cervantes and Shakespeare* and *Crude Words: Contemporary Writing from Venezuela*.

Catherine Mansfield is a translator and communications professional based in London. Her translations include *China's Silent Army* by Juan Pablo Cardenal and Heriberto Araújo (Penguin Press, 2013) and *A History of the World for Rebels and Somnambulists* by Jesús del Campo (Telegram, 2008). She has translated short works of fiction and non-fiction by authors including Brenda Lozano, Rafael Pérez Gay, Juan Pablo Anaya and Felipe Restrepo Pombo for publications and anthologies including *Words Without Borders, Mexico20* (Pushkin, 2015) and *The Sorrows of Mexico* (MacLehose Press, 2016). She has been a frequent contributor of reviews and articles for Booktrust's Translated Fiction website and is co-founder of a translation agency called ZigZag Translations, which she set up while living in Bogotá, Colombia.

Annie McDermott's translations from Spanish and Portuguese have appeared in publications including *Granta, World Literature*

Today, the *Harvard Review, Two Lines, Alba* and *Asymptote.* Her co-translation of Teolinda Gersão's *City of Ulysses* (with Jethro Soutar) was published by Dalkey Archive Press in 2017, and she is currently working on novels by the Uruguayan writer Mario Levrero for And Other Stories and Coffee House Press. She has previously lived in Mexico City and São Paulo, Brazil, and is now based in London.

Megan McDowell's translations include books by Alejandro Zambra, Samanta Schweblin, Mariana Enriquez, Diego Zúñiga, Carlos Fonseca, and Lina Meruane. Stories she translated have appeared in *The New Yorker, The Paris Review, Tin House, Harper's, Vice, Freeman's* and *Granta.* Her translation of Zambra's *Ways of Going Home* won the 2013 English PEN Award for writing in translation, and her translation of Schweblin's *Fever Dream* was shortlisted for the 2017 Man Booker International Prize. She is from Kentucky and lives in Santiago, Chile.

Anne McLean studied History in London, Ontario and Literary Translation in London, England, and now lives in Toronto, where she translates Latin American and Spanish novels, short stories, travelogues, memoirs and essays by authors including Héctor Abad, Isabel Allende, Julio Cortázar, Javier Cercas, Daniel Gascón, Eduardo Halfon, Ignacio Martínez de Pisón, Evelio Rosero, Juan Gabriel Vásquez and Enrique Vila-Matas. Over the years her work has been recognized by awards such as the Independent Foreign Fiction Prize, the Premio Valle Inclán and the International IMPAC Dublin Literary Award.

Lily Meyer is a writer and translator living in Washington, DC. She holds an MA in Prose Fiction from the University of East Anglia, where she was awarded the Curtis Brown Prize for best writer, and is a recipient of a 2018 Washington, DC, Arts and Humanities Fellowship. Her work has appeared in *NPR Books*, the *LA Review of Books*, *Electric Literature*, *Elbow Room* and more.

Anna Milsom translates Spanish and Latin American fiction and is a teaching fellow in translation at the University of Leicester. In 2017, Anna co-curated the touring exhibition *TransARTation: Wandering Texts, Travelling Objects*, contributing a collaborative piece, 'Inverted (& Translated) Poem' with Mexican artist–writer Verónica Gerber Bicecci. Anna has co-translated three novels with Anne McLean: Evelio Rosero's *Good Offices* and *Feast of the Innocent*, and *The Illogic of Kassel* by Enrique Vila-Matas. Anna's translation of an extract from Luis Lomelí's *Indio borrado* was included in the 2015 *México20* anthology.

Sarah Moses is a Canadian writer and translator who lives between Buenos Aires and Toronto. Her stories, translations and interviews have appeared in chapbook form as well as in various journals, including *Asymptote* and *Brick*. Sarah's co-translation (with Carolina Orloff) of Ariana Harwicz's novel *Die, My Love* was published in September 2017.

Anwen Roys is a freelance translator living and working in Puglia, southern Italy. She completed her MA in Translation Studies at the University of Leeds in 2017. She has spent a lot of time living in Nicaragua and loves Latin American fiction.

Katherine Rucker is a New York-based translator with an MA in Literary Translation Studies from the University of Rochester, focused on contemporary Spanish-language fiction. She enjoys being in the mountains and travelling around the world to buy more books.

Julia Sanches is a translator of Portuguese, Spanish, French and Catalan. Her book-length translations are *Now and at the Hour of Our Death* by Susana Moreira Marques (And Other Stories, 2015) and *What are the Blind Men Dreaming?* by Noemi Jaffe (Deep Vellum, 2016). Her shorter translations have appeared in *Suelta*, the *Washington Review*, *Asymptote*, *Two Lines*, *Granta*, *Tin House*, *Words Without Borders*, and *Revista Machado*, among others. She is founding member of Cedilla & Co.

Samantha Schnee is the founding editor of *Words Without Borders*. From 2014 to 2017 she was a trustee of English PEN, where she chaired the Writers in Translation Committee, tasked with disbursing the PEN Translates and PEN Promotes grants. Her translation of Carmen Boullosa's *Texas: The Great Theft* (Deep Vellum, 2014) was longlisted for the International Dublin Literary Award and shortlisted for the PEN America Translation Prize. She won the 2015 *Gulf Coast* Prize for Translation for her excerpt of Carmen Boullosa's *The Conspiracy of the Romantics* and recently completed a translation of Boullosa's latest novel, *The Book of Anna*.

Serafina Vick graduated from King's College London with a first-class degree in French and Hispanic Studies in 2015. She has been working as a freelance literary translator for the last four years and specializes in contemporary Cuban literature. Her translations of Cuban poet Oscar Cruz have been featured in *Modern Poetry in Translation* and on Radio 4. She currently lives in Havana.

Born in Sligo, Ireland, **Frank Wynne** has been a literary translator for twenty years. His authors include Michel Houellebecq, Patrick Modiano and Ahmadou Kourouma. He lived for several years in Central and South America, and has translated Hispanic authors, including Tomás González, Andrés Caicedo and Javier

Cercas. In the course of his career, he has been awarded the IMPAC Prize (2002), the Independent Foreign Fiction Prize (2005), and has twice won both the Scott Moncrieff Prize and the Premio Valle Inclán. He has spent time as translator in residence at Lancaster University, the Villa Gillet, Lyons and the Santa Maddalena Foundation.

Acknowledgements

An Orphan World by Giuseppe Caputo is an extract from the novel *Un mundo huérfano (An Orphan World)*, first published in Spanish by Literatura Random House, 2016.

Villa Torlonia by Juan Esteban Constaín is an extract from the novel *El hombre que no fue jueves (The Man Who Was Not Thursday)*, first published in Spanish by Random House, 2014.

The Southward March by Carlos Fonseca is an extract from the novel *Museo animal (Animal Museum)*, first published in Spanish by Anagrama, 2017.

Come to Raise by Emiliano Monge was first published in *Welcome to Paradise* by Oswaldo Ruiz (Mexico: La caja de cerillos ediciones, 2017).

How do Stones Think? by Brenda Lozano is an extract from the short story collection *Cómo piensan las piedras (How Do Stones Think?)*, first published in Spanish by Alfaguara, 2017.

(Irrelevant) Mass Delusion in Cajas by Mauro Javier Cardenas is an extract from the novel *The Revolutionaries Try Again*, first published in 2016 by Coffee House Press. Copyright © 2016 by Mauro Javier Cardenas. Used by permission of The Wylie Agency (UK) Limited.

Umami by Laia Jufresa is an extract from the novel *Umami*, first published in 2016 by Oneworld Publications.

Teresa by Eduardo Plaza is an extract from the novel *Hienas (Hyenas)*, first published in Spanish by Librosdementira, 2016.

The Art of Vanishing by Felipe Restrepo Pombo is an extract from *Formas de evasión (The Art of Vanishing)*, first published in Spanish by Seix Barral, 2016.

Family by Cristian Romero is an extract from *Ahora solo queda la ciudad (We Only Have the City Now)*, first published in Spanish by Hilo de Plata Editores, 2016.

Niños by Juan Pablo Roncone is taken from the short story anthology *Hermano ciervo* (Spanish edition, Los Libros que Leo, 2011, re-edited by Fiordo Editorial, 2012; Marbot Ediciones, 2012; Sudaquia Editores, 2013; Laurel Editores, 2014, 2016).

An Unlucky Man by Samanta Schweblin is an extract from *Siete casa vacías (Seven Empty Houses)*, first published in Spanish by Páginas de Espuma, 2015.

Oneworld, Many Voices

Bringing you exceptional writing
from around the world

The Unit by Ninni Holmqvist (Swedish)
Translated by Marlaine Delargy

Twice Born by Margaret Mazzantini (Italian)
Translated by Ann Gagliardi

Things We Left Unsaid by Zoya Pirzad (Persian)
Translated by Franklin Lewis

The Space Between Us by Zoya Pirzad (Persian)
Translated by Amy Motlagh

The Hen Who Dreamed She Could Fly by Sun-mi Hwang
(Korean) Translated by Chi-Young Kim

The Hilltop by Assaf Gavron (Hebrew)
Translated by Steven Cohen

Morning Sea by Margaret Mazzantini (Italian)
Translated by Ann Gagliardi

A Perfect Crime by A Yi (Chinese)
Translated by Anna Holmwood

The Meursault Investigation by Kamel Daoud (French)
Translated by John Cullen

Minus Me by Ingelin Røssland (YA) (Norwegian)
Translated by Deborah Dawkin

Laurus by Eugene Vodolazkin (Russian)
Translated by Lisa C. Hayden

Masha Regina by Vadim Levental (Russian)
Translated by Lisa C. Hayden

French Concession by Xiao Bai (Chinese)
Translated by Chenxin Jiang

The Sky Over Lima by Juan Gómez Bárcena (Spanish)
Translated by Andrea Rosenberg

A Very Special Year by Thomas Montasser (German)
Translated by Jamie Bulloch

Umami by Laia Jufresa (Spanish)
Translated by Sophie Hughes

The Hermit by Thomas Rydahl (Danish)
Translated by K.E. Semmel

The Peculiar Life of a Lonely Postman by Denis Thériault
(French) Translated by Liedewy Hawke

Three Envelopes by Nir Hezroni (Hebrew)
Translated by Steven Cohen

Fever Dream by Samanta Schweblin (Spanish)
Translated by Megan McDowell

The Postman's Fiancée by Denis Thériault (French)
Translated by John Cullen

The Invisible Life of Euridice Gusmao by Martha Batalha
(Brazilian Portuguese) Translated by Eric M. B. Becker

The Temptation to Be Happy by Lorenzo Marone
(Italian) Translated by Shaun Whiteside

Sweet Bean Paste by Durian Sukegawa (Japanese)
Translated by Alison Watts

They Know Not What They Do by Jussi Valtonen (Finnish)
Translated by Kristian London

The Tiger and the Acrobat by Susanna Tamaro (Italian)
Translated by Nicoleugenia Prezzavento and Vicki Satlow

The Woman at 1,000 Degrees by Hallgrímur Helgason
(Icelandic) Translated by Brian FitzGibbon

Frankenstein in Baghdad by Ahmed Saadawi (Arabic)
Translated by Jonathan Wright

Back Up by Paul Colize (French)
Translated by Louise Rogers Lalaurie

Damnation by Peter Beck (German)
Translated by Jamie Bulloch

Oneiron by Laura Lindstedt (Finnish)
Translated by Owen Witesman

The Boy Who Belonged to the Sea by Denis Thériault
(French) Translated by Liedewy Hawke

The Baghdad Clock by Shahad Al Rawi (Arabic)
Translated by Luke Leafgren

The Aviator by Eugene Vodolazkin (Russian)
Translated by Lisa C. Hayden

Lala by Jacek Dehnel (Polish)
Translated by Antonia Lloyd-Jones

Bogotá 39: New Voices from Latin America
(Spanish and Portuguese) Short story anthology

Last Instructions by Nir Hezroni (Hebrew)
Translated by Steven Cohen

The Day I Found You by Pedro Chagas Freitas (Portuguese)
Translated by Daniel Hahn

Solovyov and Larionov by Eugene Vodolazkin (Russian)
Translated by Lisa C. Hayden

In/Half by Jasmin B. Frelih (Slovenian)
Translated by Jason Blake